THE FOUNTAIN

a&b

THE FOUNTAIN

MARY NICHOLS

First published in Great Britain in 2010 by
Allison & Busby Limited
13 Charlotte Mews
London W1T 4EJ
www.allisonandbusby.com

Copyright © 2010 by Mary Nichols

The moral right of the author has been asserted.

A CIP catalogue record for this book is available from
the British Library.

10 9 8 7 6 5 4 3 2 1

13-ISBN 978-0-7490-0840-6

Typeset in 11/16 pt Sabon by
Allison & Busby Ltd.

Paper used in this publication is from sustainably managed sources.
All of the wood used is procured from legal sources and is fully traceable.
The producing mill uses schemes such as ISO 14001
to monitor environmental impact.

Printed and bound in the UK by
CPI Mackays, Chatham ME5 8TD

MARY NICHOLS has spent much of her life in East Anglia and often sets her novels in that area. She has written numerous short stories, historical romances for Mils & Boon and family sagas, as well as a biography of her grandmother. Mary's most recent novel is the much-loved *The Summer House*.

www.marynichols.co.uk

Available from

Allison **&** Busby

The Summer House

*P*rologue

THE EARLY MORNING sun glinted on the river and sparkled in the droplets falling from the oars of the boat. The rower, a young man dressed in a dinner jacket, was showering his two passengers with water, making them squeal in pretend outrage. They had been to a college ball and now, at seven-thirty in the morning, were still enjoying themselves.

'Simon, leave off!' Penny grumbled. 'If you ruin my dress, I'll never speak to you again.' The garment was made of creamy satin and clung to an enviable figure.

'Please, Simon, do stop,' Barbara added. 'I don't fancy a swim.' She had large greeny-blue eyes beneath winged brows, a straight nose and a well-defined mouth, which was obviously more used to laughter than sorrow. Her dress was of cerise-and-cream-striped taffeta with an off-the-shoulder neckline, huge puffed sleeves and a bias-cut skirt.

'For you, sweetheart, anything.' He resumed rowing.

11

It was at Newnham Barbara had met Penny and they had hit it off straight away. Penny had unusual red-gold hair and a flawless complexion. She had been sent to college by her wealthy parents to channel her energies away from the idea of being an actress into something they considered more suitable for a young lady. Barbara didn't think it had worked. Penny only just managed to do the work required of her, being more interested in amateur dramatics and going to the theatre. This year she had taken her finals, while Barbara still had a year to go, but they had sworn to keep in touch.

It was through Penny that Barbara had met Lieutenant Simon Barcliffe. 'He needs taking out of himself,' her friend had told her. 'He's become withdrawn, not the laughing brother I waved away four years ago. You will be good for him.' His hair was slightly fairer, less red, than Penny's and his eyes were cornflower blue, but the family likeness was there in the shape of their faces, the slightly square jaw and firm mouth.

When the subject of the ball had come up, Penny had suggested Simon should partner Barbara and both had been happy with the arrangement. Everyone had been determined to enjoy themselves and try to forget the horror which most of those who had stayed behind could only half imagine. They had danced to the music of two orchestras who took it, turn and turn about, to keep it going until dawn. No one wanted the night to end, but when the electrically lit night gave way to a pink dawn, Simon had suggested taking a boat down the river to a pub he knew would be open and serving breakfast.

Simon was fun, didn't seem to be able to take anything

seriously, but Barbara guessed that was only a facade. He had come back from the hell of the trenches without a scratch, but sometimes when Barbara looked at him, she noticed a shadow pass across his face and his eyes had a faraway look, as if a ghost had nudged him. It was gone in an instant and he was his usual light-hearted self, making jokes and teasing. She had seen that haunted look on other faces, men in her hometown, who had come back from the front line, changed for ever by what they had endured. But they were the lucky ones: so many had found their last resting place in the mud of Flanders, leaving grieving wives, mothers, sweethearts.

A mile further up the river, they tied up at the landing stage of a riverside pub and sat at one of the outside tables. 'I'm going to have the lot,' Simon said, as a waiter hovered over them. 'How about you, Penny?'

'Coffee will do for me,' she answered. 'Supper at two o'clock in the morning plays havoc with my digestion. What about you, Barbara?'

'Just coffee,' she said. 'I'm going home to Melsham today. Dad's expecting me. We are going to plan a holiday in Scotland, though we can't go until the harvest is in.'

'Going on holiday with your father,' Simon mocked. 'Doesn't he have lady friends?'

'He's not like that!' Barbara said hotly. 'Dad's never looked at another woman. He wouldn't.'

'Celibate for six years, how the poor man must be suffering!'

'Simon!' his sister exclaimed. 'You're not in the army now.'

'Sorry,' he said contritely. 'Tongue ran away with me.'

13

Penny suddenly noticed the big man standing on the towpath beside his bicycle, wearing a paint-stained check shirt and corduroy trousers. She nudged Barbara. 'Who's he?' she whispered, nodding towards him. 'He's been standing there watching us for ages. Giving me the creeps.'

All three turned to look and George, who had heard all he wanted to hear, decided it was time to make himself scarce.

Chapter One

BARBARA SPENT THE day wandering about the farm with the dog at her heels, exercised her mare, Jinny, across the common near her home and came back in time to have a leisurely soak in the bath, the bathroom having been converted from a small bedroom. It was a life she loved, just as she loved the rambling old farmhouse with its mellow brick and flint exterior and the yellow climbing rose that reached her bedroom window. Her mother had planted that on the day Barbara was christened. 'I wanted to watch it grow, as you grew,' she had told her. 'My golden girl and my golden rose together.'

The whole house was full of treasured memories like that. Barbara didn't believe in ghosts, but the spirit of her mother was everywhere. It was in the bricks themselves, in the decorations and furnishings, in the garden. It was beside her when she cooked. It stood over her when she painted, a silent but accurate critic. Until her mother died she had not known a minute's anxiety, beyond having to confess to her teacher she had skimped her homework or when the cat's unwanted kittens had to be disposed of. She always cried buckets over those. Safe and loved, she never expected the blow, and when it fell, she had no one to lean on, no shoulder to cry on but her father's, and he had been grieving himself. Together they had weathered it, made a life without the loved one, and now she could look back with a smile at the pleasant memories and reminisce with her father. 'Do you remember when...'

Leaving him to go to college had caused her some soul-searching. As the daughter of a well-to-do farmer she could stay at home and paint pictures to her heart's content and wait for the plaudits if they came, but she wanted to be independent, and though her father never grumbled, she knew the farm was nothing like as prosperous as it had been in her grandfather's time and she did not want to be an added burden. She planned to teach art at a local school, where she could live at home, painting in her spare time. When she explained this, he had smiled and said if she wanted to go to college, then of course he would find the wherewithal to send her.

She pulled the plug on the cooling bathwater, wrapped herself in a towel and went to her room. Her dress was the same one she had worn at the college ball but that did not matter since there would be no one at tonight's affair who had been there. Sweeping her blonde hair into a chignon and fastening it with combs and pins, she took a last look in the wardrobe mirror and went down to join her father.

He was waiting for her in the drawing room, standing by the hearth with one foot on the fender. At forty-four, he was a good-looking man whose thick, dark hair had the merest suggestion of grey at the temples and whose figure was supple enough to belong to a much younger man. He moved forward and took her hands to hold her at arm's length. 'I suppose it was worth the wait. I shall be the envy of every young blood there.'

Before the war the Harvest Supper, which was grander than a supper, more a dinner followed by a ball, had been held in Melsham each year at the end of the first week in September, but this was the first since the war. Barbara recalled, as a child, watching enviously as her parents went off without her, her mother looking radiant in a flowing ball gown, her father in evening dress, so much in love it hurt her to remember. Now she was going with him, but Simon's remarks preyed on her mind. 'Are you sure you want to partner me?' she asked.

'What's brought this on?' he asked with a smile. 'Are you having doubts about my staying power?'

'No, of course not.' She couldn't tell him what was in her mind, couldn't bring herself to say it aloud, as if voicing the notion that he might prefer to take a lady friend would put the idea into his head. 'I thought you might be bored.'

'Let me tell you, my girl, I can dance the night away as well as anyone, and just because I have a grown-up daughter, doesn't make me decrepit.'

Relieved, she slipped her arm through his, smiling up at him. 'Let's go, then.'

Dinner was over and the dancing had begun when he made his way over to Barbara's table and stood before her. He was a few years older than she was, a very tall man with broad shoulders. He had dark-brown hair cut short and parted in the middle, matching dark eyes and a serious expression. Everything about him seemed serious, almost sombre, even down to his tailcoat, black cummerbund and his shining patent shoes, though they were really no different from what all the men were wearing. But there was something about him that made him different and she didn't think it was only his size.

'Miss Bosgrove, would you care to dance?'

She glanced at her father, sitting beside her. 'Go on, my dear, don't mind me.'

She rose to face him. A hand, a very big hand, went about her waist and the other took hers in a firm, dry grip. She laid her other hand on his shoulder and they whirled away in a Viennese waltz.

'How did you know my name?' She tilted her head to look up at him, wondering where she had seen him before.

'It wasn't difficult to find out. Your father is well known in Melsham, isn't he?'

'I suppose he is. The family has been farming in the area for generations. Do you always find out the names of people before you ask them to dance?'

'Only if I intend to ask them out.'

She laughed. 'That's a new angle, I must say.'

'It's the truth.' The sombre look had disappeared and he was smiling, making her realise he was handsome in a rugged kind of way. 'I would like to see you again.'

'But I don't know you from Adam!'

'It's not Adam, but George. George Kennett.'

18

'I'm Barbara.'

'I know.'

'What else do you know?'

'That you live with your father at Beechcroft Farm, that you are studying at Cambridge and you have friends called Penny and Simon.'

Cambridge! The man with the bicycle, the man in the checked shirt and the paint-stained trousers, who had stared so long and so hard. 'What were you doing in Cambridge?'

'You noticed me?' He had certainly noticed her. The redhead was the more glamorous of the two girls, but it was Barbara who had caught his eye. Somewhere, sometime, he had known he had seen her before and that had been borne out when she mentioned Melsham, his own home town.

'That's what you intended, wasn't it?'

'Not at all. I was hardly dressed to impress, was I?'

'Everyone has to work,' she said, though her mind went back to Simon. He seemed to get along quite happily without it but, according to Penny, their father was putting pressure on him to join the family stockbroking firm. 'What do you do?'

'I'm a builder. I was in Cambridge converting an old house into student accommodation. It was easier and cheaper to live in lodgings and cycle back and forth than travel forty miles home every day.' An influx of undergraduates coming back to complete their studies after serving in the armed forces needed accommodation. George had won the contract for the painting because he had put in a bid that was ridiculously low. He was single, lived

19

at home with his mother and had no overheads. Until he had bought a van he had pushed his paint, brushes, tools and dustsheets from job to job in a handcart. He could not afford to stable and feed a horse, and besides, he was convinced the horse had had its day.

But painting and decorating were only the beginning: he had plans. One day, he would have a thriving business, a grand house and a motor car, and not a second-hand van which had cost him thirty hard-earned pounds only the month before. Half the time he could not afford to put petrol in the tank, which was why he carried his bicycle in the back of it.

'The work in Cambridge is finished now and I've just won a contract to convert a couple of old houses in Melsham town centre into flats,' he told her. He would need help for those but he could take on casual labour and there was plenty of that about: soldiers who had survived the bloodshed had come home to find jobs hard to come by and were grateful for whatever work came their way. Lloyd George had promised homes for heroes and the government was encouraging builders by giving them grants to build them. George meant to have a slice of that, but to do that, he had to have a viable business. A strong pair of shoulders, a few brushes and a handcart hardly qualified, which was one of the reasons he had invested in the van and found a yard which he could call business premises. You couldn't run a business from a small terrace house with no front garden and only a narrow back entry.

'Do you live locally?' she asked.

'Yes, Melsham born and bred. Doesn't my accent give me away?'

'I didn't notice your accent particularly.'

He was pleased to hear that: he had made a great effort to eradicate the Norfolk accent he had grown up with; it didn't help when trying to impress the people he had to do business with.

The music ended and he took her arm to escort her back to her table. There was no sign of her father. 'I meant it, you know,' he said, sitting beside her.

'Meant what?'

'That I want to see you again.'

She laughed, unnerved by his intense gaze. 'You've got a nerve...'

'If you don't ask, you don't get,' he said. 'I've nothing to lose.' He paused and looked closely at her again. 'Have you? Anything to lose, I mean.'

'No, I suppose not.'

'Would you like me to fetch you a glass of wine?'

'Yes please.'

She watched him go. It was difficult to tell his age but she surmised he must be in his late twenties. He had lost the slimness of youth, if he had ever had it, and was well developed and self-assured. A big man in every sense. He paid for the wine and came back, carefully carrying two glasses through the throng of people who crowded at the edge of the floor, waiting for the band to begin playing the next dance.

She thanked him and began to sip the bubbly wine. 'Don't you have a partner?' she asked as he resumed his seat.

He smiled. 'Now, would I have brought a girl with me when I intended to ask another out?'

21

'You came with that intention?'

'Of course. I thought I'd made that clear.'

She laughed in an embarrassed way. 'I don't know what to make of you.'

'I saw you in Cambridge and heard you talking about Melsham and decided I'd like to get to know you. It was no good mooning about because I hadn't the gumption to do anything about it, was it? I go for what I want. Always. Do you blame me for that?'

He didn't seem the sort of person to moon anywhere. He was a pushy, overconfident young man who fancied his chances. 'No, I suppose not.'

'Then have dinner with me on Saturday evening.'

'I don't know…'

'Dinner, nothing more, just a meal. At The Crown. I'll book a table, shall I?'

'So long as you understand I'm not making any kind of commitment.'

'Of course not. I wouldn't expect you to.' He rose to go. 'I'll pick you up at seven.'

She didn't tell him her address: he was bound to know it.

The Crown, once a coaching inn, now a busy hotel, occupied a prominent position on Melsham marketplace. The town had once been the agricultural centre of the region and had a larger-than-average market, more triangular than square. At the apex stood St Andrew's church. On one long side there was a row of shops in differing styles of architecture, none of which was outstanding. On the other stood the town hall and beside that a terrace of handsome Georgian houses, one of which was a doctor's surgery, another a solicitor's, and the remaining two George was going to convert into flats. The base of the triangle consisted of the railings and gates of a small park, in front of which stood a stone cross on a plinth to commemorate those who had fallen in the war, and nearby was a pool where the old village pump had once dispensed water to the inhabitants. Barbara hardly spared it a glance as George ushered her into the hotel.

That first dinner was spent learning more about each other. She told him about her mother and how miserable she had been when she died. 'It was her heart,' she said. 'I never guessed...'

'I am sorry,' he said, putting his huge hand over hers.

'It was six years ago and Dad and I have come to terms with it now.'

He told her he lived with his widowed mother in a terraced house in Victoria Street in the old centre of Melsham and leased a builder's yard from which he ran his business. But he had plans, had mapped out his progress through life as if planning the route for a long trek, step by step, including, it seemed, when he should marry. Thirty or thereabouts was the right time, he told her, when he'd had time to make something of himself, a little money behind him to offer a wife, to know what he wanted.

'And what do you want?'

'A thriving business, a motor car, a nice house, and a wife and family.'

She laughed. 'In that order?'

'It is the most sensible order.' He seemed relaxed, but

he was twirling the stem of his empty wine glass in his fingers and she realised he was nervous. It made him suddenly more human.

'Are you always sensible?'

'I try to be. It's the way I've been brought up, I suppose. Having no father, I've been the man in the house since I was knee-high to a grasshopper. My mother made great sacrifices to give me a good start in life and I can't let her down.'

'I'm sure you won't,' she murmured, wondering how long it would be before the stem of the glass broke in his hands.

'I served my apprenticeship with Gosport's before the war. Even then old Gosport was a doddery old fellow, too slow by half.'

'You didn't go into the army yourself?'

'Yes, I served nearly two years.' He had been twenty-three when war broke out, fit and healthy, just the sort of man the army were looking for, but his mother had persuaded him she needed him more than his country did: he was her only support and without him she could never manage and so he had resisted the blandishments of the posters telling him his country needed him. That did not mean he was a coward, but as his mother pointed out, not everyone was a fighter and someone had to keep the country running. He could also see advantages: with so many men away, the war might provide opportunities for advancement if he kept his wits about him. In 1916, short on volunteers and with more and more casualties decimating the numbers of men in uniform, the government had introduced conscription and he had been called up.

To his mother's enormous relief, he had not been drafted overseas immediately but set to work with a paintbrush on some barracks being built for the new intake, and later for the Americans who came over in their thousands. He had kept his head down and got on with his work but the time had come when he was put on a draft to go to France. The week before he was due to go, the war ended.

'You didn't go back to Mr Gosport afterwards?' she asked.

'No. I decided the time had come to set up on my own account.'

'And stole his customers.' She didn't know why she made such a bald statement, except perhaps to pull him out of his complacency, but if that was the case it didn't work.

'It's a competitive world out there, Barbara. Gosport understands that. I only took the small stuff he didn't want. I'm not big enough to compete for anything else. But one day I will be. The profit I make from the flats will be ploughed back into the business, into getting more and bigger contracts. Then I'll take on more men; I'm going to be somebody in this town, Barbara.'

'Do you always get what you want?'

'Not always right away, but I persevere until I do.'

He was insufferably confident and she didn't know why she agreed to see him again but she did, and over the long vacation, except for the fortnight she and her father were walking in Scotland, they spent almost every evening and Sunday afternoon together. He treated her with courtesy, bought her chocolates and flowers and made her aware

25

of her own sexuality, though he had done no more than kiss her. And that he did well, making her want more, but afraid of where it might lead. He must have known how she felt, because he always drew back from the edge, leaving her aching and breathless, but at the same time relieved. She didn't think she would have the courage to say no if it came to the crunch. Was she falling in love with him?

When the new term started they would not be able to see each other so often. If she learnt to forget him while she was away, involved herself with student activities, she might find the chemistry was not as strong as he supposed. The trouble was that he had no intention of allowing her to cool off. There was an enormous bouquet waiting for her in her room when she returned to college. 'I miss you already,' it said on the card.

And then there were letters, a barrage of them. He didn't seem to mind that her answers were brief and impersonal. He loved her, he said, and one day she would acknowledge that she loved him. She was young and he wasn't asking her to name the day or anything like that. He needed a few more contracts before he was in a position to ask her to become his wife. She wondered if he had confided in his mother or whether she was being left to guess, just as her own father was.

He knew she had been seeing George during the holiday and had called him 'that brooding Byron' but he didn't know the extent of their relationship. She didn't really know it herself. Dad might have been able to advise her, but she couldn't talk to him about it, couldn't help feeling disloyal, as if she planned to desert him. They had not talked about what would happen if and when she married. She was only nineteen; there was plenty of time to cross that bridge when they came to it. Then the bridge loomed up long before she expected it, and it was not her doing, but her father's.

She came home for the Christmas holidays a day early, intending to surprise him, buying the ingredients for dinner on the way. She loved to cook for him, and they would sit over the fire and talk about college and farming and what had been happening in her absence, and make plans for Christmas, just the two of them.

She took a cab from the station and let herself in the front door. The house was quiet, but then she heard the sound of running water in the bathroom. She put the food on the kitchen table and carried her case upstairs, meaning to call out to him, but as she reached it the bathroom door opened and a young woman came out wearing nothing but a towel. She had a superb figure, with long, shapely legs, and though Barbara could not see her hair which was also wrapped in a towel, her face, even without make-up, was stunningly beautiful. Barbara, glued to the spot, was aware that her mouth had fallen open, but she couldn't find anything to say.

It seemed an eternity before the girl laughed. 'You must be Barbara.'

'Yes.' Her voice was a croak. 'Who are you?'

'Virginia Conway.'

'What are you doing here?'

'Oh dear, I can see by the scowl on your face this is going to be difficult.'

'I'm not scowling, simply asking a perfectly

straightforward question.' She turned her head as her father came out of his bedroom in a dressing gown. A dressing gown in the middle of the afternoon! She couldn't believe it of him. Tears sprang to her eyes and she blinked hard.

'Barbara, we weren't expecting you.'

'That much is obvious. How could you, Dad? How could you? And in Mum's bed too.' That was what shocked and hurt most, the fact that he could forget his dead wife so far as to take another woman into the bed he had shared with her all the years of their marriage, the bed in which Barbara had been born. Unable to face them, she ran into her room and slammed the door.

'Barbara!' her father called. 'Come out, love, and let me explain...'

Leaning her back against the closed door, she heard Virginia's voice. 'I told you to tell her, didn't I? You should have done so ages ago. Now, we've got off on the wrong foot.'

Barbara couldn't believe her ears, didn't want to believe them. Her father and... Who was she? How and when had they met? She stood leaning on the door, staring at the portrait of her mother hanging on the opposite wall. She had painted it from a snapshot, the year after her mother died. Painting was her escape, her release for emotions she didn't know how to handle. She had shut herself away for hours, concentrating on colour and form, forgetting everything, even the time, and some very weird creations resulted, things she destroyed almost immediately, their therapeutic work done. But the portrait, painted a little later when her emotions had calmed, was kept. Everyone who saw it said she had managed to catch the essence of her subject, the laughing eyes, the smiling mouth, the person Margaret Bosgrove had been.

The memory of her dying mother sent the tears rolling down her cheeks. She and her father had sat by her bed for hours, while the clock ticked her life away, and afterwards, numb with grief, they had clung to each other. Had he forgotten that? Had he forgotten how sweet and wonderful his wife had been, how she had soothed him when he had had a bad day, laughed with him, cried with him, scolded him sometimes. How could he take another woman into that same bed and not be reminded?

'Barbara!' The sudden knock on the door made her jump. 'Come out, please. We must talk about this. I know you're upset...'

'Has she gone?'

'She's going.' She heard him speak to Virginia and the woman's angry response and then a door banging. 'She's gone to get dressed, then she'll leave.'

Barbara waited until she heard footsteps going down the stairs and the front door slam, then slowly eased open the door. Her father was sitting on the top step of the stairs. He stood up slowly and came to her, putting his arm about her shoulders. 'My poor pet. What a way to find out. I meant to tell you, I really did.'

'When?' She allowed him to lead her downstairs and into the kitchen, where she sat at the table and watched while he put the kettle on. It was a big room, the hub of the farm, with a black-leaded cooking range, a large dresser on which plates were arranged and cups hung on hooks. There were cupboards on the other walls and shelves for pans and above their heads a washing line that could be lowered and raised by a pulley. It was the domain of Mrs Endersby, who came in each morning to cook and clean, but she had gone home and the kitchen was empty.

'When what?'

'When were you going to tell me? When did it start? How long...?'

'In the summer, while you were at college.' He spooned tea into the pot, keeping his back to her. 'She called, said she'd heard I had some stabling I wasn't using, wanted to know if she could keep her horse here. I said yes. After that she came every day and somehow we seemed always to be bumping into each other.'

Barbara had seen the horse in the stables when she had been home in the summer, but her father often let people keep their mounts there and she had thought nothing of it. 'But you didn't have to bring her into the house. You didn't have to take her upstairs, did you? Oh, Dad, how could you? Whatever would Mum say?'

He turned to face her. 'I think, my love, she would be pleased that I had found someone who made me happy.' He sat down opposite her and reached for her hands. 'Virginia does make me happy, you know. I want to marry her...'

'Marry her!' She pulled herself out of his grasp. 'But she's—'.

'Young. Yes, I know. She's thirty. But that's no barrier to falling in love.' He rose as the kettle whistled shrilly and poured boiling water on the tea leaves.

'But you loved Mum.'

'Of course I did. There will never be anyone like her, but, darling, I am still young enough to want the love of a woman. One day you will want to marry yourself and then—'

She gave a cracked laugh. 'And I felt guilty, as if I were betraying you, just because George wants to marry me.'

'He does?' He sounded surprised.

'Yes. I told him I couldn't leave you.'

'Leaving me is not the point. I accept that it will happen one day, but you are young and still at college. There is no hurry.'

'But you are in a hurry, aren't you? You couldn't even wait to put the ring on her finger.'

He chuckled. 'Did I raise a prude? You are the young one, Barbara, part of the modern generation. I thought you would take it in your stride.'

'Would you take it in your stride if you found me...you know...?'

'That's different.' He paused and pushed a cup of tea towards her. 'Oh, this is so difficult and I didn't want it to be. I want you and Virginia to be friends. This is your home, it always will be, but I want it to be hers too.'

She looked up, startled. 'It's all been arranged, hasn't it? Cut and dried. That's why she was angry when you asked her to leave.'

'I'll go and talk to her later. I'm sure she'll understand.'

'Understand what?'

'That you were taken by surprise and once you get used to the idea...' His voice tailed off. What could he say? That she would welcome a new mother, that they might become friends? That whatever she said, he would

31

not change his mind? He had found love a second time and that was not something granted to every man and he was not going to let it slip through his fingers, not even for his outraged daughter, whom he loved too.

It was all too much to absorb in one go. She scraped back her chair, grabbed her coat and left the house, churning everything over in her head, but the shock was too raw to think rationally. She told herself it was the secrecy she hated, not the fact that he had fallen in love. If Virginia had been his own age, if she had not been so beautiful, most of all, if they hadn't used her mother's bed, she might have understood. How she got to the middle of Melsham, she could not afterwards remember. She must have walked, though it was three miles.

George was driving home along the road beside the market when he spotted her sitting on the low wall surrounding the fountain, staring into the far-from-clean water. He stopped the van and walked over to her. 'Barbara, what are you doing here?'

She turned a tear-streaked face towards him. 'Oh, George.'

He sat down beside her and put his arm about her shoulders. 'What's the matter?'

She didn't answer but put her head on his chest and, try as she might, she could not stop the tears from spilling. 'Don't cry, love. Tell me what's wrong and I'll see if I can put it right...'

'You can't.'

He took a large handkerchief from his pocket and gave it to her. 'Try me.'

She sniffed and mopped up her tears. 'It's Dad. He's got another woman.'

'Good for him!'

'How can you say that? You haven't seen her. She's been in my mother's bed with him.'

He hugged her to him, smiling over the top of her head. 'I can understand how you feel. I'd feel the same if my mother...' He paused, thinking of his mother; he would hate it if she married again, but pigs would fly before that happened, she had told him more than once. 'But, darling, your father is still a young man, still in his prime, it's only natural he'd want some company. You were at college and he was lonely.' He waited for her to argue, but she didn't. 'How has it hurt you? He doesn't love you any the less...'

'He loved my mother. What they had was special...'

'I'm sure he doesn't love her any the less either.' He put his finger under her chin and lifted it so that she was forced to look at him. 'I bet she's not a bit like your mother, is she?'

'She's young and pretty, not that Mum wasn't, but... Oh, I don't know. You think I'm being unreasonable, don't you?'

'No, I think you've had a shock, that's all. Now, cheer up, sweetheart. Think of it as a stroke of good fortune for your father. One day you will marry me and then he'll need someone.'

She smiled suddenly. 'You never miss a trick, do you?'

'But it's true.' He raised her to her feet. 'Come on, you'll freeze to death sitting here. I'll take you home.'

She walked with him back to his van. 'He says he's

going to marry her. She's going to come and live at the farm. I don't know how I'm going to cope with watching her handle Mum's things, seeing the way he looks at her...'

'Then we will have to do something about it, won't we? Marry me now, instead of waiting. It means a slight change of plan, but nothing I can't handle.'

'Do you always try to turn everything to your advantage?'

'I was thinking of you. If something has made you unhappy, then I want to put it right. I love you, Barbara, you know that, it's no secret...'

'And you always get what you want.' She spoke flatly, but it was comforting to know he cared.

He opened the passenger door of the van, wishing it were a car. But he needed a van for his work and at the moment he couldn't afford both. He brushed the seat with his gloved hand and waited for her to settle herself, then shut the door and walked round to the driver's seat and started the engine. It was decidedly noisy and not conducive to conversation. He waited until they stopped outside her house before he spoke again. 'I've got tickets for the New Year's Eve Ball at the town hall. You will come with me, won't you?'

'I don't know...'

'Oh, come on, Barbara, the world hasn't come to an end, you know.'

'I know it hasn't. I'm not a fool.'

'Then you will?'

'Yes, I'd love to. And thank you for being so understanding.'

34

'That's what love is all about, isn't it? Mine, yours, your father's.'

'Yes. I'm being very naive, aren't I?'

'It's one of the things I like most about you.' He leant over and kissed her cheek before getting out and opening the door for her. She was so confused she didn't question that naivety was a strange attribute to find endearing.

She let herself in the house, determined to talk to her father, to try and understand how he felt, to put herself in his shoes and tell him she was happy for him. She would be bright and cheerful and ask him about the wedding, be grown-up and sensible. But he was not at home; he must have dashed off after Virginia the minute she left.

She wandered round the house, looking at everything, the comfortable old furniture, the pictures and photographs, the porcelain ornaments her mother had collected over many years. She picked up a little shepherdess, standing with a crook in one hand and a lamb cradled in the other arm. She stood admiring its delicacy, the pale colours of the girl's features contrasting with the blue of the dress and the green of the grass on which she was standing, remembering the day the tiny tip of the crook had broken when her mother was dusting it. All three of them had dropped on hands and knees to search for it in the pile of the carpet. Barbara's sharp young eyes had spotted it first and picked it up with a cry of triumph. Dad had glued it back in place, commenting that the repair would take pounds off its value. 'It doesn't matter,' her mother had said. 'It's like its owner, a little worn.' Barbara had laughed and so had Dad, and she had not realised the significance of the remark.

She replaced it carefully, then cooked the dinner she had planned to surprise him with, but he did not come for it. When it was past keeping warm any longer she scraped it into the bin and went to bed, where she lay sleepless for hours. Surely he knew they needed to talk? She wanted reassurance, to explain how she had felt on seeing Virginia in the house, to tell him she was sorry for her outburst, that all she wanted was for him to be happy. Instead he had stayed with his new love and shut her out. She dozed off at last, only to wake when she heard him come in and creep up the stairs and past her room. She looked at the clock on her bedside table. It was five o'clock and the light was strengthening. She turned over and buried her head in the pillow. She was no longer his little girl to be cuddled and pampered: she was a grown woman. But she felt so alone.

'Mother, this is Barbara.'

Elizabeth Kennett was very tiny, with birdlike features and small, dark eyes. Her hair, once fair, was faded. She was, Barbara guessed, in her fifties. She wore a high-necked white blouse and a long black skirt.

'How do you do, Mrs Kennett,' she said, offering her hand. 'It is very kind of you to invite me.'

'Not at all. I've been looking forward to meeting you. Come into the parlour, there's a nice fire in there.'

To Barbara, used to the large rooms of the farmhouse, George's home seemed tiny. The stairs went up almost at the front door and a hallway went alongside with three doors leading into the downstairs rooms: first the parlour, then the dining room and at the far end a tiny kitchen.

The parlour had a square of carpet on the polished wooden floor and was furnished with a sofa and two armchairs, a bookcase, and a display cabinet with a cupboard under it. On a chenille-covered table in the centre of the room stood a tray containing three glasses and a bottle of wine. There was an ornate mirror over the mantel on which stood a chiming clock and some ornaments. Several photographs of George at various ages adorned the papered walls. Christmas chains in red and green and silver were strung across the room and holly decorated the pictures.

'Would you like some champagne?' George asked.

'You've got champagne?'

'Yes. It's a celebration, not just Christmas.' He picked up the bottle and pulled the cork with a satisfying pop, then poured the wine. 'A toast,' he said, handing round the glasses. Barbara waited expectantly, wondering what was coming. 'To Kennett's!' He laughed at her puzzled expression. 'It's the name of my new company. I am no longer George Kennett who does a bit of building work, I am Kennett's, the Builders. It's all set up and I've got my first sizeable contract.'

'Congratulations.' She raised her glass. 'To Kennett's, the Builders.'

'To you,' his mother said. 'I'm proud of you, son.'

He hugged her. 'I know you are, Mum, and I couldn't have done it without you.'

She wiped a tear from her eye. 'I'll go and see how dinner is getting along.'

'Can I help?' Barbara asked.

'No, you stay and talk to George.'

Elizabeth had been taken aback when George suddenly

announced he had every intention of marrying Barbara Bosgrove. She had had him to herself for so long, had brought him up, made huge sacrifices to send him to grammar school, bought his uniform and all the sports kit he needed, had watched him grow more and more like his dead father. At twenty-nine, it was time he married, but it was going to hurt. On the other hand she knew John Bosgrove was well-to-do and owned acres of land. His daughter was a catch for her son. She would raise his status and that was something Elizabeth desired above everything. Her son was going to be a somebody in Melsham, erasing the recollections of its older inhabitants, who had long memories and liked to gossip. It would be the culmination of her life's work.

'I know she's a cut above me,' George had told her. 'But that's good, isn't it? Not that I am ashamed of my roots, because I'm not. I'm proud of you and what you've done for me. Nothing can change the love I have for you, but what I feel for Barbara is different.'

Of course it was different! He didn't need to tell her that. But this feeling of inferiority, of having to strive harder than anyone else and his fear of failure, was a chip on his shoulder he could never quite eradicate and to cover it he had cultivated a confident, brash attitude which was sometimes a little too abrasive. She supposed that was her fault. It was she who had nurtured his competitive instinct, told him that if he put his mind to it, he could be as good as any man who had two parents instead of one. She had been determined he would never suffer from the lack of a father and he had repaid her with singular devotion. Those ties were too strong to be broken by a slip of a girl.

* * *

38

'Tell me about your new business,' Barbara said after his mother had gone. She wanted to talk, to hear him talk, to stop herself thinking of her father enjoying his Christmas with Virginia. He hadn't asked her to make herself scarce, quite the contrary, but she knew their cosy little twosome was over and life at the farm would never be the same again, so when George asked her to meet his mother and spend Christmas Day with them, she had agreed. She was going back to college in the new year and would come back at Easter to attend her father's wedding and settle down into a completely different regime and she didn't know how she was going to cope with that. Virginia was always moving things about, delighting in telling her what changes she would make when she became Mrs Bosgrove. We're going to do this and that, she would say, putting her arms round her father's neck, shutting Barbara out.

George drew her down beside him on the settee. 'I knew there was a council contract going and I wanted it, but without a viable business behind me, I didn't stand a chance. To get that contract I had to take on a proper labour force and buy tools and machinery. It also meant a bigger yard, a proper office. It was a gamble, but I undercut the opposition and got the contract. It's taken all Mum's savings, but she'll get them back with interest.'

'You are very close to your mother, aren't you?'

'Yes, of course. My father died when I was a baby. Mum brought me up alone. I owe everything to her.'

She smiled. 'Including your tenacity?'

He laughed. 'That too.'

'What does she think about me?' He had been so understanding and comforting over the business with

Virginia, helping her to put it into perspective. And he had been honest with her about his ambitions, his personal aspirations. Beside him, Simon seemed a stripling, which was unfair, considering he had spent the best part of four years in the trenches and that would surely age a man. Why had she suddenly thought of Simon? Since Penny had left college, she had not seen him. She had liked him, had liked his quicksilver mind, his ability to make her laugh, but he belonged to a different life, one far away from Melsham and her father and the problems that beset her here. She had kept in touch with Penny so she supposed that one day she might meet Simon again, but they would be like strangers, the easy familiarity they had enjoyed would be gone.

'She wants me to be happy. Just as your father wants you to be happy.'

She turned startled eyes on him. 'You've spoken to him?'

'Naturally I have. I wanted his approval.'

She began to laugh. Nearly twenty years after the old queen had died, he behaved like a Victorian. Was that his mother's influence? Whatever had her father made of him? 'And does he approve?'

'Yes, so long as it's what you want.'

'I don't know what I want.'

'You will,' he said confidently. 'When the time comes to ask you properly, you will know.'

His mother came into the room at that point and announced that Christmas dinner was on the table and they followed her into the dining room. Barbara wondered what he meant when he said 'when the time comes'.

It came at the New Year's Eve Ball, as the clock chimed midnight and everyone turned to their neighbour with kisses and cries of 'Happy New Year! May 1920 be all you hope for it.' Caught up in the euphoria of the moment, she accepted.

Chapter Two

THE DRESS WAS made in heavy white silk, the bodice curved over her breasts and down over her slim hips to the floor. There was a huge bow at the back of the waist that fanned out into a train. Penny set the orange blossom circlet on Barbara's blonde hair and carefully arranged the lace veil over her shoulders. 'There! Now you can look.' Barbara moved carefully over to the mirror. The veil softened her features, gave her a dreamy quality which was not altogether false. She was living in a dream. Nothing was quite real.

'Nervous?' Penny was wearing a pale lime-green dress in the same style as Barbara's but without the train. But unlike Barbara's, which had a boat-shaped neck filled in with lace, and long narrow sleeves, Penny's was off the shoulder and had short puffed sleeves. Both had matching velvet capes lined with white fur to keep them warm. February was hardly the month for a wedding.

'Terrified.'

'You aren't having doubts, are you?'

She wasn't, was she? George loved her and she loved him and she meant to be a good wife to him, to have his children, to help him in his business, to be there supporting him. Always. It was how her mother had been with her father and theirs had been a particularly happy marriage, which was why she could not understand his obsession with Virginia. Virginia was nothing like her mother. She stopped her thoughts from spiralling away and turned to Penny. 'No, of course not.'

'Good. I'm off.' She rose and went to the door. 'See you in church.'

Barbara stood looking round the room. It looked bare. The picture of her mother, the bookcase containing her books, her tennis racket which had been propped in the corner, sundry photographs and ornaments, had already been taken to her new home. Dad had offered her the furniture too, but even the small amount she had taken had crammed their bedroom to bursting point and there was no room for more. George had laughed and said there wouldn't be space to swing a cat. Her battered old teddy bear sat on a cushion on a basket-weave chair, looking at her balefully with his one beady eye. She had picked it up to take with her, but then George, helping her carry everything down to his van, had seen it and laughed. 'You're never bringing that old thing with you, are you?'

'Why not?'

'It's a child's toy and you're not a child. Leave it. We're looking to the future, not dwelling on the past.'

She walked over and stroked its nose, then turned her back on it and hurried from the room and went downstairs to join her father before her overflowing emotions got the better of her.

He looked distinguished in his tail suit. His face had very few lines and the little grey in his hair served to make him look distinguished. Just lately he seemed a lot younger, though she would not admit it might have anything to do with Virginia. He had done his best to persuade her to finish her studies. 'Why the rush?' he'd wanted to know the morning after the new year ball, when she told him she wanted to marry George straight away. 'I've nothing against George Kennett, he's a likeable enough young man, but he is only just starting in business, it's not going to be easy and you are so young. Why not wait a year or two?'

'I don't want to. Please, Dad, give us your blessing, it's important to me.'

He loved her and had always spoilt her a little, more than her mother had. He had sighed and reached out to take her hand. 'If you're sure...'

Now she smiled at him, eyes sparkling with unshed tears. Everyone said getting married was an emotional experience and she was certainly finding it so. He offered her his arm. 'It's not too late to change your mind, you know.' He wished he had tried harder to dissuade her but, to his eternal shame, had realised that this marriage would be a way to avoid conflict between his daughter and Virginia. If they were not living under the same roof, sharing their lives, then he would not be torn apart by their antipathy towards each other. But was he being fair to Barbara, catapulting her into something she might regret?

'I'm not going to change my mind. Are you?'

He looked startled, as if she were confirming his fears. 'No, but I sincerely hope that's not the reason for this...'

'Of course it isn't,' she said quickly, picking up her posy of lily of the valley from the table. 'I only meant that if you can fall in love and want to get married, so can I.' She meant it, she really did.

Dora Symonds, who had never been married, loved weddings, and she could never pass a church if she saw white-ribboned carriages at the gate. Brides were lovely and grooms were handsome and, like the chimney sweep with his brushes, she liked to wish them well.

'Blimey!' she said, as Barbara emerged from the large hired car and took her father's arm to be escorted into the church. 'If it i'n't John Bosgrove and his daughter, old enough to be married. Don't time fly?'

'Who's John Bosgrove, when 'e's at 'ome?' Rita demanded. In her late twenties, she was a younger version of her mother, though her hair was a natural carrot colour and her mother's owed more to a bottle. Both were plump and freckle-faced. Dora had a black shawl pulled tightly over her deep-puce dress and a battered straw hat with red ribbons. Rita wore a three-quarter coat but no hat. Between them was a young girl in a faded blue coat several sizes too small for her. She was bored and looking mulish. The women ignored her.

'He owns Beechcroft Farm, that big house on the Lynn road. The family's been there for donkey's years.'

'How d'you come to know him?'

'There i'n't many people I can't name in this town, me girl, you ought to know that.'

'True,' her daughter said and laughed.

'It weren't like that,' Dora said, huffily. 'Not with 'im it weren't. I knew his wife more'n him. She was always good to me, never judged me. I met her at the church...'

'Church? You?' Rita laughed again. 'I don't believe it!'

'They were giving away second-hand clothes. Mrs Bosgrove arranged it for the poor and needy and I was needy all right, leastways you were growin' that fast I couldn't keep you in clothes. She helped me choose dresses and shoes for you. Give me a guinea too to keep us outa the workhouse. She died a few years back. I often see him in town and he always speaks.' She grinned at John and called 'Good luck' to the bride as she made her way down the church path on her father's arm. 'Let's wait and see them come out, see who it is she's marrying.'

'Whatever for?' Rita demanded. Her feet ached, the potatoes and onions and the bit of scrag-end in her shopping bag was heavy and Zita was tugging on her arm. 'They'll be ages yet and I haven't got time to stand about doin' nothin'.'

Reluctantly Dora moved away and did not see George Kennett, or his mother in her beige silk suit and matching hat, which was just as well. It would have spoilt her day.

The service seemed to be over before it began and most of the time Barbara was shivering, though whether from cold or nerves she couldn't tell. Then she was walking down the aisle on her husband's arm, Mrs George Kennett, and out into the weak sunshine, smiling at well-wishers who

47

stood along the church path. There were photographs and showers of confetti and then everyone climbed into motor cars, carriages and pony traps, or took Shank's pony, back to the farmhouse for the reception.

'Happy?' George asked her, as they mingled with their guests.

'Yes, very.'

'Happy?' asked her father, standing beside Virginia, who wore a navy silk dress, matching three-quarter coat and a large navy hat with a pink rose on the brim.

'Happy?' queried Penny, dragging Simon behind her. He was the same as ever, blonde hair falling on his forehead, his smile very much in evidence. It was strange how the sight of him brought a great lump to her throat. She told herself that it was because he reminded her of a carefree time which could never come again.

She shook the mood away and smiled. 'Yes, very.'

'Good,' he said. 'And you can tell your husband from me, if he doesn't treat you right, he'll have me to answer to.' He was looking at her in a strange crooked way, his eyes boring into hers, sending her messages she could not, would not interpret.

'I heard that,' George said. And though he was laughing, making a joke of it, Barbara sensed undercurrents. Could he be just a little jealous? Had he understood more than she had?

She looked up at him. Beside the slim-hipped Simon he appeared very large, a man beside a boy. His grey tail suit seemed to be stretched across his broad chest, as if he had grown an inch or so since it was fitted. She stood on tiptoe and kissed his cheek. He grinned with pleasure.

Penny and Simon melted away. It left her feeling strangely down: she would like to have talked to them, asked what they had been doing with themselves since she saw them last, shared a few memories of college with Penny, which seemed such a long while ago.

'How long before we can escape?' George whispered in her ear.

'We have to cut the cake and you have to make a speech. Then I'll go and change.'

George couldn't leave his business to have a proper honeymoon and so they were going to have a weekend in London, which was all the time he could spare. 'We'll have a proper holiday when the business is on its feet,' he had told her.

They arrived at their hotel in time for dinner and afterwards went to the Haymarket to see a music hall. Barbara would rather have seen a play, but she had left the choice to George and in a way she was glad: the bright antics of the performers made her laugh, made her forget for a little while, the night to come. She was not ignorant of what to expect but she was apprehensive.

'Drink?' he queried, when they arrived back in their room about eleven o'clock. A maid had been in and drawn the curtains, so they were enclosed in their own little world. There was a huge flower arrangement on a round table and an ice bucket containing a bottle of champagne with two glasses beside it.

She had already had more than she was used to. She laughed nervously. 'Are you trying to make me tipsy?'

'Not at all. I want you to remember tonight for being all you had hoped it would be.'

She went over to him and reached up to link her hands behind his neck. 'I am sure it will be, but...'

'You're not afraid, are you?'

'No, a little nervous, though.'

He kissed her. 'So am I.'

'Good heavens, you're not...' She paused. 'Are you?'

He grinned, kissing her again. 'No, but I'm afraid to spoil it by being clumsy. It's important, you see.'

He was sweet, saying the right things, doing the right things to allay her fears. She had kissed other boys in an experimental way, had been kissed herself, but no man had invaded her body. She giggled suddenly. 'I'm awfully green...'

He kissed her again, moving his lips from her mouth, down her throat and into the neckline of her tubular dress. He undid the buttons and slipped it off her shoulders, then fiddled with the straps of her underslip until her breasts were exposed. He cupped one in his hand and ran his thumb gently over the nipple. She felt every inch of her responding in a shivering, excited way. She kicked her dress from around her feet and pushed herself closer to him. Her petticoat, suspender belt, stockings and knickers went the way of the chemise. There was a tingling in her groin, a damp, soft surrender to sensation, and then as his hands and lips worked their way over her, a need to participate, to help this tumult along, to make it blossom. He lifted her and stepped backwards and they fell together onto the bed. He lowered his head to kiss her belly, his lips roving down into her pubic hair. She moaned softly. He stopped and took off his own clothes, not watching what he was doing but looking into her face, studying her features, the fine brows, lovely eyes, flecked now with passion, the mouth, partly open, waiting.

He smiled and lowered himself gently onto her, his mouth covered hers and she could hardly hold back the flower waiting to burst into glorious bloom. The tiny shock when he penetrated she hardly noticed. She opened to him, taking him into her, deep inside her, so that his limbs and hers, his mouth and hers became a single writhing body. He made it last, so that in the end she was crying out, digging her hands into his back, pushing herself against him, forcing him to quicken. And then suddenly his whole weight was lying on top of her and he was gasping for breath.

A moment later, he rolled off her. 'My, you learn quick.'

'Put it down to love.' She did not ask him how he had come to be so skilled, how it was he knew exactly what to do to rouse her; she had a feeling she would not like the answer. A minute later he was asleep and she lay awake. With him sleeping soundly beside her, she began to realise the enormity of the change in her life. She was no longer the spoilt daughter, she was a wife, George's wife, so long as they both should live.

The next morning, they set out for a walk. Post-war London was a shock. All the old buildings were there, Buckingham Palace, the Tower, London Bridge, the shops, but the people looked weary: four years of war had sapped their energy. And there were so many beggars about, men missing limbs, with placards round their necks proclaiming their poverty, others apparently healthy except for the haunted look in their eyes. That look reminded her of Simon, though he was not reduced to begging. How much worse it must be for these poor men. And there were children, ragged and barefoot, their eyes large in pinched little faces. Her heart went out to them and she emptied her purse of small change into their eager hands.

'There are too many, Barbara,' George said. 'You cannot give to them all.'

'I know.' It was said with a sad little sigh.

They returned to their hotel for lunch and in the late afternoon they caught the train home.

Barbara intended to find herself a job; she wasn't particular what sort of job, she told George, she simply wanted to be useful. After all, he was still feeling his way and any money she could bring into the house would help, leave him with more to plough back into the business. She was unprepared for his veto.

'No,' he said, with a stubborn set to his mouth. 'If I couldn't support a wife, I had no business getting married.' He had grown up with pre-war ideas of a woman's place, when the relative roles of husbands and wives were clearly defined: the man was the provider, the wife stayed at home and did not question him.

'But I can't sit around doing nothing.' It wasn't as if she was being selfish: her desire for a job was for both their sakes.

'Then help Mum.'

'I would if she'd let me, but most of the time she doesn't want me to. I feel like a guest.'

'That's nonsense. This is your home.' His voice took on a placatory tone. 'Darling, I need you right here.'

'In your bed, you mean?'

'Don't be vulgar, Barbara, it doesn't suit you.' It was funny how he could be so wonderfully sexy at night and never mention it during the day. And even at night, it was not the same as it had been in London. She thought it was because his mother slept in the next room and the walls were very thin. She imagined every creak of the bed springs, every soft moan was heard; it inhibited her and she suspected George was aware of it too.

For the sake of peace she gave in, and putting her sketch pad and water colours into her bicycle basket, pedalled out to the fens and painted the landscape, splashing the page with great streaks of pink and purple and grey, dotting the foreground with pollarded willows and water birds, empty rowing boats and broken reeds. Sometimes she put herself into her pictures, sitting on the riverbank, staring out over the flat fields or lying in a drifting rowing boat. That was how she felt, a drifter. Surely she shouldn't feel that so soon after the wedding? Shouldn't she be feeling fulfilled and happy, just being a wife? Elizabeth seemed to think so.

'I never had the opportunity to stay at home,' she told Barbara one day, when they were washing up after the Sunday roast, always eaten in the middle of the day, though the rest of the week they had their main meal in the evening. 'George's father was in the navy, a handsome man, big too, like George. I fell for George right after we married and then he went off to sea again...'

'And he didn't come back?'

'Yes, of course he did, when his ship was in port. Then on one voyage he left his ship when it docked in Canada, had some fool idea he could find a gold mine and come back rich. He never did. Died out there.' She spoke flatly, without emotion. It had happened a long time ago and the cruel edge to her memories had faded. Most people thought she had spent a lifetime mourning a beloved husband, that she had been overwhelmed by grief, but the truth was that it had been a relief: heaven knows what would have happened if the bastard had come back. 'After that it was just George and me. I had to go out to work, I had no choice. I went cleaning during the day, took in washing at night.'

'Yes, but times have changed. Lots of women go out to work now, married or not. It's nothing to be ashamed of.'

'For George it is. He knows how I struggled, how I was always tired, having to cook the dinner and do the housework and other people's washing, having to ask neighbours and friends to fetch him from school, worried to death in case he was ill and I lost a day's work. He doesn't want that for you.'

'I know that, but I haven't any children and I don't have any housework to do because you do it all.'

'I need to keep busy and I know how I like things done.' To which there was no answer.

The washing-up done, they joined George in the sitting room. He was sprawled in an armchair reading the Sunday paper.

'Let's go for a walk,' Barbara suggested.

'No, I'd rather stay here. Sunday is the only day I can have five minutes peace and quiet to read the paper. Besides, I have to do the books before tomorrow.'

'Can I help with them?'

'No, it would take too long to explain.' He smiled to mitigate his refusal. 'But thank you for offering, darling.'

She sat down and picked up some knitting. Elizabeth did likewise and for perhaps half an hour no one spoke, until Barbara could stand it no more. 'I'll make a pot of tea.'

'I'll do it,' Elizabeth said. 'You stay with George.'

Barbara sank back into her chair. Useless again, not wanted. She could hear her mother-in-law in the kitchen, running water into the kettle, lighting the gas cooker that George had recently bought for her, setting out cups and saucers, and she longed for a home of their own. 'George,' she said tentatively. 'This council contract you've got. Is it a big one?'

'Middling. Why?'

'You said we could buy a house when you were paid for it. You did mean that, didn't you?'

'I did, but the trouble is it's not been all plain sailing. I have to make sure of getting the next contract and the one after that and that means oiling wheels...'

'Oiling wheels?'

'Yes, keeping people sweet, you know.'

'Bribery?' She was shocked.

'Not exactly, but you can't expect to get contracts, especially if you're a small, untried firm, without greasing a few palms.'

'Is that how you got the contract you're working on now, or shouldn't I ask?'

'Ask all you like. I found out which of the council officers had an Achilles heel – this chap's wife was ill, needed an op. I paid for her to have it done.'

'But surely that's illegal?'

'Everyone does it. You don't get a look in if you don't.' He smiled at her. 'Don't look so shocked. It's how it works.'

'And this man persuaded the council to accept your tender?'

'No, he couldn't do that. He simply told me what all the other quotes were and I made sure I undercut. I've had to cut corners and I'll have to pay suppliers late to make it work, so you see, the house I promised is a little way off yet. Be patient, my darling, you shall have your house, I promise. The next contract will be a big one. It seems Lloyd George meant it when he said we would build homes for heroes, and the town council have been given a grant to build a hundred and fifty houses to rent. And with Donald Browning opening all the tenders when they arrive, I reckon I'll get it.'

'It needn't be very large,' she said, afraid that his ambitions in that direction might match his other aspirations and she would have to wait until he could afford the perfect home. She didn't want a perfect home; she simply wanted somewhere of her own. And it seemed that to get it, she must condone what she knew must be dishonest and risky practices. 'If I got a job, we could do it quicker, couldn't we?'

'No. You know my views on that, Barbara.' He stood up, just as his mother came in with the tea tray. 'I'm going into the dining room to do those books. I'll have my tea there.'

'I'll bring it to you,' Elizabeth said, setting the tray on the table.

He disappeared. Barbara watched her mother-in-law for a few seconds, then stood up. 'I don't really feel like tea, after all. I think I'll go for a ride.'

Most weekdays she went up to the farm to exercise Jinny, going when she knew Virginia, who was personal secretary to the local estate agent, would be at work, but today she felt so restless she was prepared to risk bumping into her. What she most wanted was to talk to her father, to ask him if he thought she was being unreasonable to want a job and to question him about the ethics of bribing a council employee, but she couldn't. For one thing, she had seen very little of him since her wedding, and for another, it would be disloyal to George. This was something she had to sort out for herself.

She didn't go up to the house but made straight for the stables, propping her bicycle against the fence. There were five horses in the stalls, contentedly munching hay. Her own mare, Jinny; Virginia's chestnut, Amber; the sturdy pony her father used to pull the trap and two big farm horses. She was just taking her saddle down from a hook on the wall when she was startled by a sound behind her and spun round to see Virginia standing in the doorway, dressed for riding in jodhpurs and hacking jacket. She had her hat in her hand and her long blonde hair was tied back with a narrow ribbon. 'Hallo, Barbara,' she said. 'You are quite a stranger these days. How's married life?'

'Very good. How are you?'

'Very well.'

'And Dad?'

'He's finding the farm hard going. He's a little tired.'

'I'll pop in and see him when I come back from my ride.' She could not imagine her father giving up his farm. It had been his whole life and his father's before him. What would he find to do if he could not be out tramping the fields, looking after the stock, talking to his neighbours about yields and harvests? He would be lost.

'He will like that, he's always saying he does not see enough of you.' She paused. 'I love your father, Barbara, and his happiness is important to me. We have that in common, don't we?'

'I very much hope so.'

'Then let's try and be friends. For John's sake.'

'All right.' Solemnly, they shook hands. And then, as they were obviously both going riding, they spent the next hour on horseback, cantering over the meadow and down the bridleway to the common, where they enjoyed a gallop before returning home.

'Barbara, I want to ask you something,' Virginia said, as they dismounted.

'Oh.'

'Will you be my bridesmaid?'

'Me? But bridesmaids aren't usually married, are they?'

'I'd have said matron of honour, but it sounded so old.' She laughed. 'So what do you say?'

Marriage must have made her more tolerant. She found herself saying, 'Of course. I'd like it very much.'

'Good. Let's get the horses settled and go indoors. You can talk to John while I make some tea. Then I'll show you my dress; it might give us some ideas for yours.'

* * *

58

George looked up as his mother came in to take away his empty cup. 'How's it going?' she asked.

'OK. Where's Barbara?'

'Gone riding. She's bored, George.'

'I know, but what can I do about it? You know how it is with the business. It needs all my attention at the moment.'

'Why don't you give her something to keep her occupied?' She smiled at his questioning look. 'I'd love a grandchild.'

'I'd love to give you one, but we decided no children until we have a home of our own. There's no room here...'

'Yes, there is. That little front bedroom is big enough for a cot. There's plenty of couples have families in houses this size, big families too.'

'I don't know,' he said doubtfully. 'Barbara's very young...'

'Not that young. And she doesn't have to agree. Just do it.'

He laughed. 'Oh, Mum, you devil!'

They were still laughing when Barbara came back into the house and it did nothing to make her feel less isolated.

'I saw Virginia this afternoon,' she told George, that evening as they settled by the fire. 'She asked me to be her matron of honour.'

'And you agreed?'

'Yes.'

'That's a step in the right direction, anyway.' He tried not to smile, but she caught the look he exchanged with his mother. 'Virginia Conway is a nice girl, not the wicked stepmother of your imagination.'

'I didn't know you knew her.'

'She was in my class at school.'

She supposed it must have registered that her husband and her father's bride were roughly the same age, but until now she had not thought about it. 'Anyway, we went riding together and had coffee and talked about the wedding. It's to be the second Saturday in April. You will be able to manage it, won't you?'

'Of course.'

'I saw Dad too. He's lost a lot of weight. We had a long chat.'

'I am glad to hear that,' Elizabeth put in. 'It's sad when parents and children quarrel. You hear so much of it, these days. Families breaking up, children defying their parents and going their own way. Thank God, George and I never had that problem.'

'Neither did Dad and I.' She almost snapped it, but swiftly moderated her voice and accompanied it with a smile. 'It was nothing.'

'Nothing,' Elizabeth repeated. 'It was enough to make you fling yourself at the first man who'd have you.'

In the silence that followed, George looked across at Barbara and saw the bleak look in her eyes. He reached out and took her hand. 'Mum, that's not fair. You know I always meant to marry Barbara, and we simply brought it forward, that's all.' He smiled at his wife. 'Isn't that so, darling?'

'Yes,' she whispered, shaken to the core; she had not realised before just how much Elizabeth resented her presence. Her mother-in-law had always been cool towards her, but she had not been openly hostile. The unease she had felt before she went riding returned tenfold and she longed to get away. If only they could afford a home of their own.

She decided to have a day in London to buy her outfit for her father's wedding and use it as an excuse to see Penny, and it would take her out from under her mother-in-law's feet for a few hours.

Penny met her at Liverpool Street station. She was looking very glamorous in a double-breasted coat fastened with a single enormous button. It had a fur collar and fur cuffs to the sleeves. 'Let me have a look at you,' she said, holding Barbara at arm's length and surveying the belted overcoat she had had for some time; new clothes, Barbara had recently discovered, were a luxury they could not afford. 'You're looking a little peaky.'

'I'm fine. I didn't sleep too well last night, that's all.' She gave a shaky laugh. 'It must be the excitement of coming up to town and seeing you again. You look stunning.' She surveyed her friend. 'And you've had your hair cut.'

'It's all the rage.' Penny twirled round. 'Do you like it? It is so easy to manage. You should try it.'

'I don't know what George would say if I went home shorn.'

Penny laughed, leading the way out of the station, throwing a few coins to the beggar who was sitting against the wall out of the keen wind. 'We'll have lunch first and then we'll go shopping. I've got lots to tell you and I want to hear all your news.'

Barbara expected to go to the cab rank, but instead Penny made for a cream-coloured car, parked at the kerb. 'Yours?' she asked.

'No, it's Simon's, but when he heard you were coming he offered to lend it to me. It's a beauty, isn't it?' It was too. It had gleaming chrome headlights and door handles and a spare wheel strapped on the luggage compartment at the back. The upholstery was brown leather. 'He would have been here himself, but he had to go to the office. Dad finally persuaded him to buckle down to work. He sends his love.'

'Oh.' She didn't know what to make of that. 'And can you drive it?'

'Of course. It's easy. You should get George to buy one.'

'He needs his van and we can't afford both, but when the business is on its feet, he says we'll have one.'

Penny drove them to a little restaurant in a back street which, she assured Barbara, was managing to defy the shortages and produce edible meals and was a place where they could talk uninterrupted. 'Now spill the beans,' she said, when they had ordered.

'What about?'

'Married life. Is it all it's cracked up to be?'

'Why, thinking of venturing yourself?'

'No fear! I'm intent on a career. A husband would only get in the way.'

'And how is the career?' She didn't want to talk about marriage.

'I had a walk-on part in a play and I was the victim in a murder film, killed off within five minutes of the start, neither of which will put my name up in lights, but you have to start somewhere. One of these days someone will notice me.'

'I don't see how they can fail to. You'll always stand out in a crowd.'

'Thank you. Enough about me. What about you?'

'Nothing to tell.'

'Oh, I don't like the sound of that. You are not having regrets, are you?'

'No, of course not.' It was said a little too quickly and Penny looked hard at her, but she was saved from comment by the arrival of the waiter with their order. They sat back while he set everything on the table and left them to serve themselves. 'What's it like, making films?'

'It's not like being on the stage. It's all done in short scenes. The title is put up on a screen and the actors actually speak the words to get the timing and the actions right. One of these days, we'll have talking pictures. They've been experimenting with recorded sound but they haven't been able to synchronise the action with the sound yet, but it will come and it will have a tremendous impact. Some of the actors we've got now have terrible accents. It will be a dreadful shock to their devoted followers to hear their voices. They'll have to learn to speak properly or they won't last.'

'You have a lovely voice.'

'Thank you. You need a good voice for stage work. And wireless. That's the coming thing. There'll be wireless sets in every home before long, you see. Simon thinks I should stick to films. I can't make up my mind. What do you think?'

'Don't ask me. I'm the last person to advise you. I can't even make up my own mind about getting a job. I've never had one.'

Penny grinned. 'Child bride, straight from college to domestic bliss.'

'Something like that. But I don't have enough to do at home, Elizabeth does everything. The thing is, what could I do? I'm not qualified for anything.' She smiled. 'And don't you dare say it's my own fault for not finishing my course. I had enough of that from Dad.'

'I won't. No good crying over spilt milk. So, what have you got going for you?'

She paused to butter a roll. 'You're presentable, you're articulate and your smile is a knockout. You can read and write and add up.'

'Office work, you mean?'

'Or shop work. Something high class. A dress shop perhaps. Or an antique shop. I know! An art gallery, then they'd show some of your pictures and you'd be famous. We'd become famous together.'

Barbara laughed. Penny was good for her, she cheered her up, made her get things in proportion, even if she had no intention of following her advice. 'I don't think George would like that somehow. He is against working wives.'

Penny laughed. 'Oh, how very Victorian! Barbara, this is 1920. Women have become emancipated. Put your foot down.'

'I can't. Whenever I mention it, we almost quarrel.'

'Only almost?' Penny laughed. 'Do it. Have a good row and get it over with. If you don't, you'll regret it, I promise you. You'll always be the one to back down.'

Barbara had no answer to that. They ate in silence for a few minutes and when they finished Penny insisted on paying the bill. 'I can afford it,' she said, when Barbara protested. 'Dad gives me an allowance, but as it happens I'm not paying for this, Simon is. He told me to treat you.'

'That was kind of him, though I can't think why he should.'

'Because he wanted to, I expect. He's very fond of you. I think it was quite a blow to him when you married George.' She did not wait for Barbara to comment, which was just as well because she did not know what to say. 'Bond Street, here we come.'

They went from shop to shop, trying things on, and in the end Barbara chose a pale-blue chiffon tubular dress over a silk slip, a pair of tan kid sandals and a small cloche hat in tan, with a ribbon bow at the side in a blue to match the dress. 'I mustn't outdo the bride,' she said, twirling round to look at her rear view in the fitting-room mirror.

Penny laughed. 'No, but you're not exactly enamoured of the idea of your father marrying again, are you?'

'I just wasn't sure Virginia was right for him. She's so young, the same age as George.'

'Surely that's for your father to decide?'

'Yes.' She managed a smile. 'If Dad wants her, then who am I to object?'

'What changed your mind?'

'You could say I've matured and learnt about marriage and what it means.'

'And what does it mean?'

'Being less self-centred. Thinking of your husband first, making him happy.' She paused, realising Penny was about to quiz her about it and had to be forestalled. Although she confided most things to Penny, she didn't think she could tell her about Elizabeth's cutting remark: it was too near the bone, something to push into the recesses of her mind and try to forget. She wanted to believe she had misunderstood, that her mother-in-law had been joking. Some people had a funny sense of humour.

'It works both ways, you know.'

'Of course I know. George is loving and generous. There isn't anything he wouldn't do for me.'

'Except allow you to go to work.'

'He's just a little old-fashioned, that's all. He likes to pamper me.'

The wedding ceremony was over, attended by half the town, or so it seemed to Barbara, all wanting to wish John Bosgrove and his new wife well. The bride had looked a picture in her white lace gown and John was a handsome and distinguished man. There were many more guests than had been at her own wedding, Barbara realised with a pang, though that had been her own fault for marrying so hastily.

'I don't intend to be your typical farmer's wife,' Virginia told Barbara. 'I'm keeping my job. At least, for the time being.' They were standing in the drawing room at the farm, crushed among the other guests, all holding glasses of champagne and trying to balance plates of wedding cake at the same time. Her father was being jovial to a group of fellow farmers.

'But there's a lot to do on a farm, you know. Mum was always busy, she never went out to work.'

'I am not your mother, Barbara.'

'Sorry, I shouldn't have said that. What does Dad say about you working?'

'He tells me to do whatever makes me happy.'

'He would.'

Virginia gave her a rather startled glance, as if she were reading more into the comment than the two words she had spoken, but at that moment one of the other guests intervened to speak to the bride and they became separated. Barbara mingled with the company, chatting inconsequentially, though her thoughts kept coming back to the fact that George hadn't said, 'Do whatever makes you happy.' George had put his foot down. She looked over at him, talking to her father. Was he expounding his views on a woman's place in society? She moved to join them. They were talking politics.

The next day she saw the advertisement for an assistant stuck in the window of a craft shop which specialised in picture framing. It also sold prints and original paintings on a commission basis. It seemed to be tailor-made for her, and because she was still feeling peeved with George she pushed open the door and went in. She was given an interview there and then, at the end of which she was offered a job. The pay was minimal, only ten shillings a week, but that didn't matter. It was something to get her out of the house, a way of bringing money into it, if only a little. She went home treading on air.

Her euphoria lasted until the evening. Why she thought

George might be pleased for her when faced with a fait accompli, she had no idea. Even in the midst of his lecture on the subject of working wives, she could hear Penny's words: 'Have a good row and get it over with.' The trouble was that it wasn't a row. He refused to get angry. 'You know how I feel about it,' he said without raising his voice. 'And I'm more than disappointed that you went and did it behind my back.'

'You wouldn't have agreed.'

'Knowing that, why do it?'

'I've got to do something, George. I'll go crazy, if I don't.' She intercepted the look which passed between her husband and his mother; it was as if they were enjoying a secret joke. 'Anyway, I've said I'll take it.'

He sighed. He hated rows, always had. He supposed it had something to do with having to stand on his own feet very early on. He remembered his first day at school. Being an only child, he had never had to relate to other children, had never learnt to share anything. He reacted with tears and anger and sheer bloody-mindedness but, by the time he went to grammar school, he had learnt how to win friends, mostly by buying them – a bag of sweets, a currant bun and, later, cigarettes and beer. He had discovered he had a facility for manipulating people and that was something his mother had never taught him. It might have come from his father, but as he had never known that gentleman he couldn't be sure. All he did know was that quarrels were to be avoided, tempers controlled, if he was ever going to get what he wanted from life and make his mother proud of him. But his mother was not his only consideration now: he had a wife and there had to be some give and take. In any case it would not be for long.

'Well, as you seem so determined,' he said. 'You'd better give it a try.'

She had won, but it didn't feel like a victory. Elizabeth, without actually saying so, made it plain Barbara had transgressed, and George himself was only pretending to agree. She didn't know if the win was worth the price in nervous tension. Only while she was at the shop, and involved in serving customers and familiarising herself with the stock, did she feel the strain seeping away. She enjoyed it and would have loved to share her enthusiasm with George when she went home each evening, but she dare not. They spoke about everything else: Elizabeth's day; local gossip; a car crash which had happened just outside the town; the division of Ireland which didn't seem to have solved its problems; the growing unemployment and what George would do about it if he were in charge; and the latest film to reach Melsham's tiny picture house. Anything except how Barbara had spent her day. It was almost as if they had to pretend her job did not exist.

It didn't exist for long. One morning, in the middle of July, she woke up feeling nauseous and had to rush to the bathroom to be sick and she couldn't face her breakfast.

'You know what's wrong with you, don't you?' Elizabeth said, standing over her, teapot in hand. 'When did you last have the curse?'

She stared at her mother-in-law. There was a gleam in her eye which looked suspiciously like triumph. 'I can't be. George is taking precautions. We agreed...'

'That doesn't answer my question.'

She began counting back. What with starting a new job and everything to learn, and the atmosphere at home, she had been too preoccupied to notice she was late. 'It's only a week or so over.'

'Have you been late before?'

'No, I'm usually as regular as clockwork.'

'There you are, then. Mistakes can happen in the best regulated families. So-called precautions are far from foolproof.'

She was sick again before she left for work, but she struggled in, though she felt dreadful and must have looked deathly because they sent her home again. But by the time George came in at six o'clock that evening, she was feeling better and decided Elizabeth must be wrong.

As soon as the meal was cleared away, George spread some plans out on the table and began working on them. Barbara went to help Elizabeth wash up.

'Have you told him about the baby?' Elizabeth asked.

'I don't know there is a baby. It's much too soon to tell. Just because I was sick...'

'Go and tell him now. I'll finish off here.'

It was easier to do as she was told than argue. She put the tea cloth down and went back into the dining room. George was drawing on a large sheet of tracing paper over what appeared to be a street plan. He didn't look up and she stood at his elbow watching him making slight changes to the lines which appeared through the transparent paper.

'George, your mother thinks I might be pregnant. I've only missed by a week, but I was very sick this morning.'

He put his pencil down and looked up at her, grinning. 'Wonderful.'

'But I can't have a baby here. There's isn't room and...' She couldn't add that she was sure his mother would take over the child; it would never be entirely hers and George's while they had to share a home. 'You said not until we had a home of our own.'

'And we will.' He smiled and tapped the papers on the table with his pencil. 'By the time the baby is born, or very soon afterwards, this will become reality. We will have our own house.'

'Really?' She flung her arms round him from behind and put her cheek against his. 'Then, of course, I'm pleased as punch. That's if I'm really pregnant.'

'Go and see the doc. He'll tell you.'

'It's too soon. I'll go in a week or two.' She paused. 'But that's not a house plan, is it?'

'No, it's the ground plan of the new council estate. One hundred and fifty houses and I've got the contract to build the lot.'

'And did you have to...' She was going to say 'cheat' but changed her mind. '...oil wheels, to get it?'

'Of course.' He didn't know how it had happened, but Donald Browning's part in the affair of the flats had become known and he had been asked to leave, which was why he was now on Kennett's payroll. He would never amount to much but he did know how the wheels of local government turned and he got on well with both suppliers and customers for his apparent ponderous honesty. It was that which had convinced his employers that his lapse from his usual integrity had been due to his wife's illness.

He was not prosecuted and nothing was made public.

'And the profits will be enough to buy our house?'

'It won't cost us a penny.' He laughed and pulled the plan from under the tracing paper. 'This is a plan for one hundred and fifty houses and where they are to go on the available land.' He tapped the tracing paper. 'This is a plan for one hundred and fifty-one houses on the same land.'

'I don't understand. You're going to build one more than they've asked for?'

'Yes. They'll never know the difference.'

'But you can't do that. They know how many bricks and things you need. They aren't going to pay out for more.'

'They won't have to. It won't cost them a penny either, that's the beauty of it.' He was so obviously pleased with himself, he couldn't keep his scheme to himself. 'I'm not the only one who oils wheels, you know. Suppliers of bricks and tiles and timbers are all prepared to put their hands in their pockets to get orders. I give them the order for bricks for one hundred and fifty houses and they supply sufficient for one hundred and fifty-one. No paperwork, just enough to build an extra house. The same goes for tiles and roof timbers and windows and floorboards, plaster and paint, the lot.'

Barbara was horrified. Oiling wheels was bad enough, but this. 'But it's dishonest.'

'No, simply clever business practice.'

She was appalled. 'But the council are bound to find out in the end.'

72

'I haven't cheated them, except out of a tiny piece of land. They'll hardly notice that and they won't want to make a fuss about it, if they do. How d'you think it will make them look? They won't want the publicity.'

'Oh, George,' she said, thoroughly worried. 'Why do you have to do it?'

'I'm doing it for you. You want a home of your own and this is the only way of getting it without having to wait years and years.'

'Are you saying it is my fault? Because if you are...'

'No, of course not. I want it too.'

She was about to remonstrate again, but he silenced her with a kiss.

How easily she was bought, she thought, as she lay awake that night. George was sleeping the sleep of the innocent beside her while she lay sleepless, full of guilt, conjuring up all sorts of punishment, both for him and herself. Something dreadful might happen to the baby, if there was a baby; she wasn't even sure of that. The man, Donald, might spill the beans, someone from the council might find out. George would be arrested. Why was he so confident he wouldn't be? Did all business really run on such shamelessly oiled wheels? Even if it did, it was wrong. And she was condoning it. She was betraying her principles for a quiet life, for a home of her own. But what else could she do?

Chapter Three

GEORGE WENT AROUND with a permanent smile on his face, full of bonhomie towards everyone. In spite of talk of depression and unemployment, his business was doing well. True, his suppliers didn't like his delaying tactics when it came to settling bills, but they knew he was going places and a little patience now would be rewarded with bigger orders in the future. And the future looked promising. As he told Barbara, one contract didn't make a successful business; he had to go after others and that meant wooing people out of working hours, and to do that with some aplomb he bought his first motor car, a brown Morris Cowley. He went to council meetings because it was vital to know what was happening in the town as soon as it happened, before it happened, if possible. He joined the golf club, maintaining more business was transacted at the nineteenth hole than ever was done in the boardroom. He frequently wined and dined prospective decision makers and members of the council. It was imperative to keep them sweet. Barbara never knew where he was. And their house was a long way from being finished.

'No point in trying to find him,' Elizabeth said, the day Barbara's labour pains began. 'You'll be hours yet.'

The two women had been washing up the coffee cups after their mid-morning break. It was the only chore Barbara was allowed to do. She knew some young women of her acquaintance envied her idleness, but they weren't living with their in-laws. Elizabeth liked doing things her way, and she resented any suggestions Barbara made for change. But it wasn't that so much as the fact that she was there, doing everything for her son, just as she always had, cooking, mending, making sure he had clean socks and a newly starched collar every day, packing his sandwiches. But today Barbara was glad of her mother-in-law's presence. She was unsure at what point to ring the midwife and the doctor on the telephone George had recently had installed. She didn't want to appear to be panicking, but the thought of the baby arriving before the midwife filled her with apprehension.

They finished the washing-up and went to sit in the front room. Barbara picked up some knitting, but she was too aware of the strange things that were happening to her body to concentrate on it. By the middle of the afternoon, the pains were much stronger and more frequent, and Elizabeth agreed that it was time to make a move. 'Go up and get on to the bed,' she said. 'I'll fetch Mrs Milton.'

Barbara nodded, unable to speak as another contraction seized her in its grip. She held her breath, waiting for it to pass and then toiled up the stairs, made the bed up with the rubber sheet under some old flannelette sheets, undressed and put on her nightie. She was sitting on the edge of the bed with her head down and her hands between her knees when Elizabeth joined her. 'She's on her way, said not to disturb the doctor yet, she'll send for him when the time comes.'

'Did you ring George?'

'Whatever for? This is women's business, nothing to do with men, not until it's all over. Now, come along and get into bed.'

Her waters broke a few minutes later, and by the time the midwife arrived, her contractions were only a minute or two apart. 'You're only just in time,' Barbara said through gritted teeth, as another spasm attacked her.

'Nonsense, you've got hours yet.' She was a big capable woman who was not prepared to stand any nonsense from her mothers, but she changed her mind when she examined her patient. 'Seems like this one's in a bit of a hurry.' Barbara hardly heard her: she was concentrating on trying not to disgrace herself and scream. Between the spasms she heard the midwife instruct Elizabeth to ring the doctor.

The pains were thick and fast now, but neither Mrs Milton nor the doctor, who had arrived with commendable speed, seemed sympathetic. They were intent on making her suffer, urging her to push, telling her it wouldn't be long now. They had been saying that for hours. Now she had to push, had to rid herself of the lump that was giving her so much agony. And then something huge and wet slithered between her thighs and the pain subsided. She heard the baby cry and opened her eyes to see Mrs Milton lifting it onto the scales. 'A girl, six pounds five ounces,' she said, then looked at her watch. 'Half past eight, tenth of March 1921.'

The afterbirth was quickly disposed of and the new little life was cleaned and wrapped and put into Barbara's arms. She had a daughter, a perfect, rosy-limbed baby, with tiny fingers which had a surprisingly strong grip, a red nose and a lot of dark hair. Barbara lay looking at the bundle in her arms and was moved to tears by the wonder of it.

Elizabeth came in, bearing a cup of tea, and stood looking down at the baby. 'She's beautiful,' she said and there was a catch in her voice. 'And she's just like George.'

'Is she?' Barbara looked at her daughter, searching for the likeness, but she couldn't see any resemblance to her rugged-featured husband, except the dark hair. 'Have you rung him?'

'He's on his way. He'd been to a meeting, and was just about to come home, so you timed it nicely.'

George was over the moon with his daughter and it didn't occur to him that being close at hand when she was born was any part of his fatherhood. They called her Alison Margaret Elizabeth.

Her father came in to see her the following day, bearing a huge bunch of daffodils. 'From the garden,' he said, stooping to kiss her. 'How are you, sweetheart?'

'Fine, just fine.' She buried her nose in the flowers, visualising the garden at the farm, the borders round the lawn crowded with the yellow blooms. Impatiently she brushed the tears from her eyes and smiled up at him. 'Do you want to see your granddaughter?'

'Of course.' He turned to the cot and stood looking down at the sleeping baby. 'Except for the dark hair, she's just like you. I remember the day you were born. I was bursting with pride.' He turned to sit on the side of her bed, his own eyes moist. 'I'm still very proud of you.'

She reached for his hand. 'Oh, Dad, I'm so sorry.'

'Goodness, what for?'

'Being so bitchy about Virginia. I didn't understand...'

'But you do now?'

'Yes, I think so.'

She wished their new house had been finished in time, but it was still some weeks to completion. George said it couldn't be helped, he had to concentrate on the hundred and fifty he was supposed to be building because there was a time clause in the contract and he couldn't afford the penalties for being late. So, like it or not, she had to continue living with her mother-in-law. But at least she now had something to occupy her.

Feeding, bathing and dressing Alison and taking her out in her pram filled her days. Sometimes they went shopping, sometimes to the park and sometimes she wheeled the pram up to the Newtown estate past the new council houses, to the one on the corner which adjoined a street of private houses. She would stand looking up at the house, wanting it finished, wanting to move in, but full of apprehension. Nothing George said could make her feel any easier in her mind about how it had been obtained. She had sleepless nights about it, and that made George laugh. 'I can see it was a mistake to tell you anything,' he said. 'You don't have the stomach for business. Forget it, will you? Let me do the worrying.'

'So you are worried.'

'Not at all. You will have your house and I will make lots of money.'

The last time she had been there, the roof was on and plasterers and carpenters were working inside. Retribution could not be long coming, she was convinced of it.

And then George came home one evening carrying a bottle of champagne. 'The house is ours,' he said, washing his hands at the kitchen sink, before rooting around in a drawer for a corkscrew. 'The council numbered the houses today.'

'And they found one too many. Oh, George!'

He laughed. 'You should have seen their faces. They counted them twice and stood scratching their heads, wondering how it had happened.'

'What did you say? What did they do?' Her heart was pounding in her throat, in spite of the fact that he seemed to be treating it as a joke.

'Oh, I enlightened them, told them the last one was mine, paid for outside the contract. They went away to ask the chief officer what to do about it.' The cork left the bottle with a satisfactory pop and he began pouring the wine into the glasses his mother had fetched. 'He sent for me.'

'Then what?' Elizabeth asked, because Barbara had been struck dumb.

'I told him straight out what I'd done. He was a bit miffed at first, but I pointed out the publicity wouldn't do him or the council a ha'porth of good, the *Melsham Gazette* would have a field day and he'd be a laughing stock. No one would blame me, they'd probably say if I could pull one over on the authorities, then good luck to me. He saw my point. I'll send him a case of Scotch for being such a good sport.'

'You mean you got away with it?' Barbara couldn't believe her ears.

'I told you I would, didn't I? I swore to keep mum, so you two must promise not to tell any of your friends.'

'It's not something I want to boast about,' Barbara said tartly.

Nor did she, not even to Penny when she came down for Alison's christening at the beginning of May. She looked at her god-daughter, cradled in Barbara's arms, wearing the long christening robe Barbara herself had worn, but did not take up the invitation to hold her. She was uncomfortable around infants: they had a disconcerting habit of discharging the contents of their stomachs from one end or the other and the cream linen suit she was wearing had cost her all of twenty guineas. She admired from a safe distance and allowed Virginia, the baby's other godmother, to do the honours.

Barbara envied her friend her smart clothes. She had bought a new dress for the ceremony, but most of the time she wore a cotton blouse and skirt which was more practical while she was breastfeeding. They held a small party which overflowed into the back garden, though that was no more than a long strip of lawn with a gate at the end. George had set out hired tables and chairs and brought in a caterer. He went round pouring champagne, accepting the congratulations of his friends as if he alone had accomplished the miracle that was their daughter.

'I bet he doesn't get up when she cries in the night,' Penny said to Barbara. She didn't know why she did not like the man. It wasn't only that he had taken Barbara from Simon – who had never complained of his loss, but she knew her brother through and through and beneath that smiling exterior was a man who felt deeply disappointed – but that she simply didn't trust George Kennett, and she hoped for Barbara's sake it would not all end in tears.

'No, but he works long hours and needs his rest and I really don't mind.' They had come indoors to the front room so that they could sit and chat comfortably. 'Enough of me. What have you been up to?'

Penny looked at her friend over the rim of her glass and decided not to say what was in her mind, that in her opinion George was a selfish dominating brute and before long Barbara would become a drudge with no life of her own. 'I've got a lead in a West End play.'

'Congratulations!' Barbara's eyes lit with pleasure.

'I'm going to have a party after the first night when we know what the critics say. It will either be a celebration or a solace. You'll come, won't you?'

'Oh, Penny, I wish I could, but I can't leave Alison.'

'Of course you can. It'll only be one night and Mrs Kennett will look after the baby. It's not for a couple of months, she'll be weaned by then, won't she?'

'Yes, but it's not just that. I'm not sure when we're moving...'

'You're just making excuses. You're vegetating, you know that, don't you?'

'No, I'm not. It's simply that I know I'll be busy.'

'Busy doing nothing,' Penny said firmly. 'When did you last pick up a paintbrush?'

'I'll do plenty of that soon.' She laughed. 'We're decorating the new house ourselves. It will save George having to pay his painters to do it.'

'I didn't mean that and you know it.' Penny could see that the newness of marriage was already wearing off and her friend was not as blissfully happy as she pretended.

'I'm sorry, Penny. You must be very disappointed in me.'

'Yes, I am. I thought you had more spirit.'

'I'm tired, that's all. It will be better when Alison sleeps through the night.'

'Then you'll find other excuses. If you neglect a talent, you lose it. Think about that.' She looked up as Elizabeth came into the room and wondered how much she had heard. 'Hallo, Mrs Kennett.'

'It's Miss Barcliffe, isn't it?' Elizabeth said, as if she didn't remember her.

'Yes. I'm sorry I can't stop, I'm rehearsing this afternoon.' She picked up her crocodile handbag and turned back to Barbara. 'I'll send you an invitation. Be sure and come.'

'What invitation?' Elizabeth asked, plumping up the cushion on the chair Penny had used, as if she couldn't wait to erase the evidence of her presence.

'A party she's giving to celebrate a new play she's acting in. I told her I couldn't go.'

They moved into the new house on a scorching day at the end of June. Numbered 1a Cambridge Crescent, and not, as Barbara had expected, 150a Newtown Estate, it had one large living room and a kitchen with a gas cooker, two bedrooms and, unlike the neighbouring council houses whose baths were in the kitchen, it had an upstairs bathroom whose water was heated with a gas geyser. The bathroom was Barbara's delight. The one at Victoria Street had been added to the back of the kitchen by George just after the war, but having a bath meant you had to stoke up the kitchen range hours beforehand to get hot water.

She spent days going round the shops choosing carpets, curtains and furniture, sometimes taking Alison in her pram, sometimes leaving her with Elizabeth. She took an immense amount of trouble, using her flair for colour to make it special. It had to be to eradicate the feelings of guilt which still beset her. But the distempered walls in a pale coffee colour were a little too bare.

'We need a few pictures,' George said, hanging their framed wedding photograph up in the lounge and rooting in a box for another of his mother. He had no picture of his father, which Barbara thought rather strange. But photographs were not what was needed, she decided, and after he had gone to work, she set about covering one of the bare walls in the sitting room with a mural.

It was great to have a brush in her hand again, to look down at the different coloured pots of paint she had set out on a small table, and know that she could create something lasting, something that was unique to her. Alison was asleep and in no time at all she was totally absorbed. She painted a rural scene, a meadow with daisies and buttercups, running down to a ribbon of river, where a small dinghy sailed. The sky was cobalt blue and the sun a golden orb. A young man on a bicycle rode along the towpath. A girl sat in the shade of a tree, fondling a dog. She stopped to give Alison her lunch and ate a sandwich herself, and then went straight back to it, propping Alison up in the corner of the sofa so that she could talk to her about it, just as if her daughter could understand. And then George came home and spoilt it all.

Dinner wasn't ready, something he could have forgiven if she had been busy unpacking the tea chests of small possessions which they had accumulated while living in Victoria Street, but the chests hadn't been touched and she had wasted the whole day, daubing that monstrosity on the wall. 'When I said pictures, I meant real pictures,' he said. 'In frames.'

'Then I'll give it a frame,' she said angrily and, picking up a brush, dipped it in brown paint and drew a thick line round it. 'There! Now it's got a frame.'

'It's too big. It dominates the room. Whatever made you do it, Barbara?'

'I felt like it.'

'Felt like it! I wish I could neglect my work to do something useless simply because I felt like doing it.'

'Perhaps you should. Perhaps if you gave yourself

a little time off now and again, you wouldn't be so grouchy.'

'I'm not grouchy. I'm simply pointing out that it's not—'

'What you employ me for?' She couldn't help saying it; it simply burst out of her. She felt guilty about his dinner, but not about the picture. And she was disappointed he didn't see any merit in it at all. Was he right? Didn't she have any talent after all? She looked at it critically and saw all its faults: its perspective wasn't quite right and the man was too big compared with his bicycle, and she wanted to weep. Instead she became angry. 'I am not one of your employees, George. I am your wife.'

'Quite,' he said.

And then she burst into tears.

He looked perplexed, raised his hands and then dropped them to his sides, at a loss to know what to do in the face of this torrent of grief. 'Oh, do stop it, Barbara, it's nothing to cry about,' he said. 'I hate weepy women.' He took the handkerchief from his top pocket and handed it to her. 'I suppose you have taken quite a lot of trouble over it. You never said you might do it or I might have been prepared...' He stopped and looked more closely at the painting, showing a belated interest in it. 'I see now. It's the Cam and that's supposed to be me on the bicycle, the day we met. But you should be in a rowing boat, not under the tree.'

'It's not you and it's not me,' she retorted, gulping back her tears. 'It's just a picture, that's all, a bloody stupid picture. I'll go and get you something to eat.' And she disappeared into the kitchen and fetched cold meat and

86

salad out of the larder. She knew he didn't consider salad a proper meal, but it was the middle of summer after all. And she didn't feel like cooking.

When she returned to the sitting room with the tray, he was sitting in the armchair, jogging Alison up and down on his knee. 'Who's got a new tooth, then?' he was asking her. 'You'll soon be eating proper dinners and then going to school and, before you know it, you'll be all grown up and the image of your beautiful mother.'

Barbara stood and watched them and her heart contracted. He really was a doting father and she had wasted a whole day because the picture wasn't all that good. And George was right: it was far too big. 'I'm sorry,' she said, setting down the tray. 'I got carried way. I'll get rid of it. You're right, it's awful.'

'I didn't say that.' He paused. 'Look, I don't want to stop you painting if you enjoy it. But not on walls. Do pictures, something small and delicate, flowers or animals. Submit something for the art competition at the summer fete. You never know, you might win.'

She hated his condescending attitude but it wasn't worth another argument, so she smiled and took Alison from him. 'I'll think about it. Now, come and have your dinner.'

The next day she went out and bought several rolls of wallpaper, and by the time George came home in the evening, the mural was hidden beneath full-blown cabbage roses. She didn't like them, but she knew George would.

* * *

The watercolour she submitted for the art competition at the summer fete was a picture of a field mouse, with bright eyes and long whiskers, sitting among barley stalks, surrounded by red poppy petals. She was genuinely surprised when it won first prize and went up to collect a postal order for two shillings and sixpence to enthusiastic applause. She didn't feel she deserved it: the picture was competently painted but, in her opinion, it was twee and had nothing new to say about the countryside. She'd only done it to please George.

But there was someone who valued it. Seven-year-old Zita Younger stood in the marquee where the entries were exhibited and looked at it with her head on one side. Her dark hair fell across her face and she pushed it out of her eyes with a gesture which had become second nature. She was a serious-looking child, with stick-like arms and coltish legs. She wore a torn flower-printed frock and scuffed sandals without socks. She thought the watercolour was lovely and she envied the talent of someone who could bring the little animal to life on paper.

'There you are, you little bugger! What are you doin' hidin' in 'ere?'

She turned to see her mother marching towards her, determination etched on a face whose freckles no amount of powder could disguise. 'I wasn't 'idin'. I was looking at the pictures. I like this one.'

'Very nice,' her mother said, without even glancing at it. 'Now, come on or Gran will be home before we are.' She grabbed Zita's arm and marched her out of the tent, across the grass and through the park gates onto the market square. 'I don't know why we came, 'ti'n't as if there's anything new to see. It's the same old thing year after year and all costing an arm and a leg.'

'That's silly,' Zita said, running to keep up. 'Nobody pays for things with arms and legs.'

'And we'll have less of your cheek.' Rita was wearing dangerously high heels, but she could move when she wanted to. With Zita in tow, she skirted the market, dived down a side street and eventually came out onto a road of dilapidated houses, whose front doors opened straight on to the pavement. They were due to be pulled down under a slum clearance scheme, but until the houses on the new estate had been allocated, most were still occupied. The council had promised to house everyone who had been given notice to quit, but Rita didn't think she'd get one of the new ones. For a start, they were being allocated to men who had served in the armed forces and Rita didn't have a man, not now she didn't. Her husband had disappeared seven years before, and besides, the rent was bound to be more than she could afford.

She opened the front door of a house in the middle of the terrace and pushed Zita into the front room. A man Zita had never seen before got up from the battered horsehair sofa. Another of Mum's boyfriends, she thought, and then changed her mind when she heard her mother's gasp of surprise. 'Christ! What the hell are you doing here?'

He smiled. He had very white teeth, Zita noticed, and clear blue eyes. 'Is that the way to greet your loving husband after such a long absence?'

'Seven years!' she said. 'Seven bloody years. What makes you think you can just walk back into my life and turn everything upside down again?'

Zita stood looking from one to the other in puzzlement. He smiled at her. 'You must be Zita.'

'Yes, and a lot you care,' her mother said.

'Now don't be like that,' he wheedled. 'I've had a long journey and I'm tired. Make us some tea, there's a good girl, and I'll tell you all about it.' He turned to Zita. 'You'd like your old dad to stay, wouldn't you? We can get to know each other...'

Zita remained dumb. She supposed she must have known that some time, somewhere, she had had a father, but she had never thought of him as being alive, nor as handsome as this man was. He had dark crinkly hair, brown eyes and a military-style moustache. He smiled at her while he dug in his pocket and extracted a half-crown and held it out to her. Her eyes lit up at the sight of it, but before she could take the money her mother had snatched it.

'Bribery won't work, so you can forget it. If you've got money to spare, I'll have it. This'll pay for your tea if nothing else.' And with that, she flounced into the kitchen, leaving man and child staring at each other, the one in friendliness, the other in bewilderment.

'You'll give me a welcome, won't you?' he said, subsiding back onto the sofa and pulling her down onto his knee. 'Your dad's been having a bad time and he needs somewhere to lay his head.'

'You could go to bed,' she said, seriously considering his problem. 'Though I don't know where. There's only two bedrooms, one for me and one for Mum.'

He leant back and laughed. 'There's a good girl to be so concerned for her dad. But never mind, before the day is done, your ma and I will come to an understanding.'

'Not bloody likely!' This from her mother who stood in the doorway, hands on hips. 'You're not treating this place like a doss house, 'ere today and gone tomorrer. What do you think I am, a ruddy doormat?'

'No, never that,' he said with a smile which made his eyes twinkle and revealed his white teeth. 'You're too good at getting up and hitting where it hurts.'

She laughed, remembering the last of the many rows they had had, just before he left home seven years before. She had kicked him where it hurt; she doubted if he had been able to use that particular bit of his equipment for several days, which must have been a great disappointment to the tart he had been exercising it on. 'And I'll do it again, if I have to.'

'You'd be the loser,' he said, grinning. 'No one else.'

'Is that so? And what makes you think you're God's gift to women, Colin Younger?'.

'There was a time,' he began and then turned to Zita, who was looking from one to the other. 'Clear out, little'n. Go and have your tea. Your mum and I want to have a little talk.'

Reluctantly Zita went into the adjoining kitchen and spread a slice of bread with margarine and plum jam and sat down to eat it, pondering on this new development. She remembered once telling one of the boys in her class at school that she didn't have a dad, only to be

91

told everyone had to have a dad, it couldn't be done otherwise.

'What can't be done?' she had asked.

'Havin' kids. Don't you know nothin'?'

'An' you do, I suppose?'

'Yeah.' He had told her in great detail, disgusting her to the point of disbelief.

'You're a liar, Bobbie Smith, that's what you are.' But there was a seed of doubt in her mind. Other titbits she had overheard in the school playground seemed to confirm what he said.

'Cross my heart,' he'd said, doing just that. 'Tha's how you were con...con...' The word escaped him. 'Tha's how you got inside your mum's belly and grew into a baby. You knew that much, didn't you?'

'Yes,' she said. 'Sylvie's mum told her just afore her little sister were born. She didn't say how she got there, though.'

'Well, now you know.'

But where had that man been all her life? She wondered if he had come to stay and what her Gran would have to say about it when she arrived.

Gran had quite a lot to say. Rheumatism prevented Dora Symonds getting about as agilely as she would have liked but it had done nothing to still her tongue. She took one look at the prodigal, mopping up the last of a plate of bacon and eggs with a piece of bread, and let rip. 'What the 'ell are you doin' 'ere? You idle good-for-nothin' scumbag.'

He looked up and grinned. 'Why, Ma, it's nice to be so 'ighly thought of. I'm eatin' me dinner.'

'Well you can clear off. If you think you can come back 'ere and upset everyone, you got another think comin'. We don't want you 'ere, livin' off the backs of other people, mostly poor Rita. Useless you are, always were, always will be. God knows what she ever saw in you.'

He did not seem in the least put out. 'I reckon it was my manly body, Ma.'

'Oh, we know all about that. It's all you're good for.'

'At least I married her,' he retorted.

'And a fat lot of good that did her.'

'Listen who's talkin'. What did you ever do for 'er, except teach her how to be a tart? Now clear out, you're giving me a pain in the belly.'

For once in her life Dora was silenced. She stared at him with her mouth open. He had penetrated the layers of brashness and carelessness with which she cloaked herself and made her squirm inside. It was a cloak she had worn so long, it had become real; so real and so thick that the old Dora had all but shrivelled and died. No one of their acquaintance would ever have said Dora Symonds was anything but a cantankerous old bat with a tongue like a razor. She didn't love anyone, didn't know the meaning of the word, and if Rita had grown up to be like her, it was hardly surprising.

She looked away from him to Rita who stood with a plate of bread and margarine in her hand, looking from one to the other. The exchange between mother and husband was nothing new: she had heard it many times before, but not for the last seven years, and in that time memory had dulled the rancour. She had come to rely on her mother to look after Zita while she worked and, whatever she was or had been, she was far more reliable than an absent husband. She put the plate on the table. 'I'll not have you talking like that to Ma,' she told him. 'If you can't be civil, then clear out.'

'Oh, so it's a choice you're making, is it? I'm your husband, or had you forgot that?'

'Yes, I had,' she said. 'Leastways, I did my best to. Ma was here, which was more than you were. How d'you think I managed? D'you think money grows on trees? You must do, for you never provided me with any.'

He fumbled in his pocket, withdrew a handful of crumpled five-pound notes and threw them on the table. Then he picked up another piece of bread and continued to mop up the ketchup on his plate. 'That's all I've got.'

Rita picked up the notes and began smoothing them out, counting them as she did so. 'Seven,' she said, laughing. 'Five pounds a year. When do I get the next instalment, in another seven years?'

'I'll get work.'

'Work!' shrieked Dora. 'Work, he says! My God, do you mean to say you're expectin' to settle down 'ere as if nothin' 'ad 'appened? Rita, for Chris' sake, send him packin'.'

'It i'n't nothin' to do with you,' he told her. 'It's for Rita to say.'

Dora looked at Rita and knew she had lost. Rita had always been as soft as butter where Colin Younger was concerned. God knows what she saw in him, apart from a handsome face, and even that had deteriorated over the

94

years. There was grey in his hair and he had a pot belly that strained over the belt of his trousers.

Rita shrugged. 'Ma, I gotta give it a try. For the sake of the kid.' Which was a statement so palpably dishonest that it reduced Dora to helpless laughter and puzzled Zita who had been listening to the exchange with a great deal of curiosity and no understanding.

Dora shrugged. 'OK. Have it your own way. I'll be off home, then...' Dora lived in a tiny hovel in Farrier's Court, a cobbled yard just off the market, squashed between the blacksmith and a cobbler. It had no running water and no main drains. It was where Rita had been born and brought up in direst poverty and from which she had escaped to marry Colin.

'Ma, you know I need you.'

'No, you don't. Let that 'usband of yourn look after his daughter.'

'What does she mean by that?' Colin queried, looking up at Rita, still standing by his chair, but doing nothing but gaze at her mother in helplessness.

'Ma looks after Zita while I work evenings,' she said.

'Doing what?'

'Barmaid at The Crown.'

He smiled. 'No need to change your arrangements. I'll come with you. See if the old place has changed.' He got up and reached for his jacket which he had draped over the back of his chair.

Rita picked up her handbag and followed him. She didn't know why she did. Her ma was right: he had brought her nothing but grief and yet there was something about him that could still tug at her insides. It was all very well to say she was better off without him, that she never wanted to set eyes on him again when he wasn't around, but when he was in the same room, grinning at her, she seemed to lose her ability to say no. And there was the added incentive that they might get one of the new houses if Colin could say he was an ex-serviceman. Was he?

He turned to look at her as they strolled towards the marketplace where The Crown had stood since the days when it was a coaching inn. She was wearing a tight black skirt which was short enough to show her calves and a bright red blouse which clashed with her ginger hair. And she was fatter than he remembered, but he didn't mind that. It was good to be home. It was the only home he could remember.

He had been brought up in an orphanage. He could vaguely remember his mother taking him there and handing him over to the matron, telling him to be a good boy and one day she would come back for him. It hadn't occurred to him he would never see her again. It had taken him a few weeks to realise that grown-ups didn't always keep promises, even important ones.

Only several years later was he told that she had died, and by then he had been fostered by a woman called Edna Day. Mr Day was in the merchant navy and Colin had only seen him when he was on shore leave. He hadn't liked Keith Day because he monopolised Mrs Day on these occasions and he hadn't had a look in, which had been, he decided afterwards, better than the abuse he subsequently received when that gentleman returned home for good. When Mrs Day had given birth to a son of her own, Colin had become surplus to requirements. He hated the new arrival and his behaviour became naughtier and naughtier until one day he had tipped the baby out of his pram. No harm was done but it was the last straw as far as the Days were concerned. He was labelled 'out of control' and put in a children's home for wayward children.

Five years later, at thirteen, considered by then old enough to fend for himself, he had been found lodgings and a job in a grocer's shop and left to get on with his life. The shop had proved too much of a temptation, and before long he was in court for taking cigarettes and booze, both of which he needed to give to his mates. You couldn't expect people to be friends with you if you didn't give them things, but they had proved as fickle as everyone else. They turned their backs on him at the first sniff of the law. He took the rap alone. It became the pattern of his life until he met Rita.

Always afraid of close relationships, he had never taken any girl seriously, never opened his heart, never shown the tiniest amount of sentiment. Girls had to take him as they found him, brash, boastful, cruel, or they didn't take him at all. Why Rita should affect him differently he did not know. Maybe it was because she didn't ask him to give her things, maybe because her own background had been equally deprived. Dora Symonds was a tart, everyone knew it, and many's the time Rita was left to fend for herself as a child while Dora went to the pub. But she had spirit and a zest for life he found appealing. She laughed a lot and she could give as good as she got in a slanging match, which she seemed to enjoy as much as he did. He had married her in 1912 when she told him she was pregnant. God knows why he had done that: he couldn't cope with marriage and he especially couldn't cope with fatherhood, but the child had been stillborn and, unable to understand Rita's misery over it, he had left. A year later he had drifted back, simply because he had nowhere else to go. The arrival of Zita in the spring of 1914 had sent him off again. 'Footloose and fancy-free,' he was fond of saying, except that most of the time he wasn't free but serving time for one thing or another.

'Where've you bin all this time?' she asked him.

'Here and there.'

'Not in the war, I'll wager, cos I'd have had an allowance, wouldn't I?'

'We were all in the war.'

'I meant serving as a soldier. Or a sailor.'

'No. Didn't fancy it.' He paused. 'It's over now, and I meant it about getting a job.'

She didn't ask him how he had avoided conscription. 'You always do.'

'This time I really mean it. I'm done with wandering. I want to settle down.'

She suppressed her desire to laugh: perhaps he was sincere, or at least as sincere as it was possible for him to be. Honesty had never been one of his virtues. 'What sort of job?'

'Anything. Labouring in the building trade, I've done a bit of that.'

'Then you'd better try Kennett's. George Kennett has done very well for himself and I heard he's expanding.'

'OK. I might just do that.' He smiled to himself. It meant he could stay, that she was taking him back. She didn't say it in so many words and he was not such a fool as to express gratitude.

Chapter Four

BARBARA WOKE ON the morning of the tenth of August knowing the day was a milestone in her life, but she was given no time to dwell on it. Five-month-old babies make no allowances for their mother's twenty-first birthday and Alison was awake at five and demanding attention. Barbara crept wearily from her bed, put on a dressing gown and went into the next room to see to her. She changed her nappy and fed her, sitting in a chair by the window and looking out onto a summer day which promised to be a scorcher. She was reminded of childhood birthdays which, coming as they did in the middle of the school holidays, were always memorable and happily anticipated for days beforehand. Sometimes her parents took her on a picnic to a local beauty spot, or to watch the seabirds on the marshes. Sometimes they went to Cromer or Hunstanton, where she would paddle in the sea and make sandcastles and then eat fish and chips out of the paper. At dusk they would return home, red as lobsters from sun and wind, with sand in their shoes and a bucketful of cockles to boil. The shells were afterwards distributed along the garden path and scrunched underfoot for weeks until they became as fine as dust. She was suddenly filled with longing for her father and the comfortable old farmhouse.

She would go and suggest a day at the seaside. 'We'll paddle in the sea and build you a sandcastle and eat a picnic. You'll like that, won't you, my lovely?' she said, kissing the top of her daughter's head. 'It will be like old times.'

'What will?'

She swung round at the sound of George's voice. He was standing in the doorway in his pyjamas, watching them. 'A trip to the sea. I'm going to ask Dad to take us in his car.' Even her father had succumbed to the advantages of a motor instead of the pony and trap. 'Would you like to join us?'

'I can't. After the meeting with Donald, there's a site visit and I have to see my accountant and the bank manager this afternoon.' He wandered off towards the bathroom, while she went downstairs to make his breakfast. The postman knocked while she was filling the teapot. He handed her several envelopes and two small parcels, one of which was from Penny and the other from her father. Penny's parcel contained an expensive perfume and a note. 'Wear this when you come to my party.' She smiled as she sprayed a little on her wrists and sniffed appreciatively; it was typical of Penny not to take no for an answer.

The other package contained an antique silver brooch

with a large amethyst in its centre which had belonged to her mother. 'Your mother always intended you should have this on your twenty-first,' her father had written on the enclosed card. She held the brooch on the palm of her hand and her mother's warm presence seemed suddenly very real. Her eyes filled with tears and spilt down her cheeks. 'Oh, Dad,' she murmured. 'You do know how to hurt, don't you?' But she knew it was never intended to hurt but to heal, and that made her tears flow faster than ever.

George came in and put a gift-wrapped package on the table in front of her. 'I bought this for you.'

Her genuine cry of pleasure as she opened it was brushed aside. 'I'm sorry we can't go out somewhere to celebrate tonight, I've got a meeting. I'll make it up to you another time. I might be late, so don't wait up for me.'

She sighed but said nothing. George was always going to meetings of one kind or another.

As soon as he had gone, she packed a picnic and filled a couple of flasks, one with coffee and the other with Alison's midday feed, and set off for the farm. She found her father drinking coffee in the kitchen in stockinged feet, wearing corduroy trousers and an old check shirt. The wellington boots he wore when working on the farm stood on the doorstep. He looked up with a smile of pleasure as she brought the pram into the kitchen.

'Barbara, what brings you here so early in the morning?'

She laughed. 'What a greeting! I wanted to see you, that's all, and to thank you for the brooch. It's the best present ever.' She put her arms round his neck and kissed his cheek.

'I always liked it on Mum.' She fetched a mug and sat opposite him to pour herself a coffee from the percolator on the table. 'How are you?'

'I'm fine. How's that granddaughter of mine?'

He rose stiffly to go over to the pram and it was then that she realised how painfully thin he had become. His cheeks seemed to have sunk, darkening his eyes, and his clothes hung on him as if they had been made for a much larger man, which indeed they had. She was shocked. He was ill and had been for some time, judging by his appearance. Why had no one told her? She tried to remember when she had last seen him and realised it had been over a month.

'You've lost weight,' she said.

'I was getting too fat anyway.' He was bending over the pram and she could not see his expression. 'She's a beauty, isn't she? May I pick her up?'

'Of course.'

He lifted the child and took her back to his chair to sit with her on his knee. 'Babies grow so fast, it seems only five minutes since you were this size. Now look at you, twenty-one and a wife and mother. No longer my little girl.'

She caught the note of wistfulness in his voice. 'I'll always be that, Dad.'

'Yes.' He tickled Alison under the chin and was rewarded with a broad smile. 'Who's a good girl, then? Who's going to grow up just like her mother?' He turned to Alison. 'I don't see nearly enough of her. Or of you.'

'I'm sorry, Dad, I'll make it up to you, I promise. I've packed a picnic. I thought perhaps you would take us to

104

the sea for the day. If you can spare the time, that is.'

His eyes lit with pleasure. 'Capital idea. I'll leave a note for Virginia, just in case we're late back.'

The alacrity with which he agreed pleased her. She would have him all to herself for a few hours and maybe she could find out what was wrong with him.

It took a great deal of gentle prodding, while they sat on the beach building a sandcastle for Alison's benefit, though she was much too young to appreciate it. He had a heart condition, he told her, nothing to worry about so long as he took things easy, which was why he had rid himself of his herd of Jersey cows and the two big horses and bought a tractor. 'It's an uphill job making a decent living out of farming these days,' he told her. 'I've rented out the far fields and just look after the fifty acres near the house. It's enough.'

'And Virginia?'

'Oh, she's a tower of strength. I don't know what I'd have done without her.' He paused before going on. 'Enough of me, what about you?'

She told him what he wanted to hear, the little details of her day, that George was busy and successful, that she loved her little house; she could not tell him that her husband's business methods worried her to death, that the house was a standing accusation of malpractice, that she was bored to tears. And her father's obvious happiness in his marriage made her realise there were flaws in her own. She brushed a strand of hair from her face, angry at herself for even entertaining such negative thoughts.

'Penny has a part in a new play,' she said, to change the subject. 'She's asked me to a party to celebrate.'

'Will you go?'

'I don't know. There's Alison, you see, and I know George won't want to go. I don't blame him,' she added quickly in case he thought she was complaining. 'He has nothing in common with Penny.'

'Perhaps not, but there's nothing to stop you going, is there? You mustn't cut yourself off from all your old friends. Friends are too precious to cast aside, you never know when you may need them.'

She looked up at him. Had he read between the words she had actually spoken and perceived her unease? Did he understand her longing to break out of the rut and find something to talk about other than babies and household matters, and the guilt for entertaining such rebellious thoughts at all? 'I'll think about it. Perhaps George's mother will have Alison.'

'If she doesn't, we will. You deserve a break.'

'You have references?' George said, leaning back in his office chair, twisting a pencil in his fingers, and surveying the man who sat opposite him. On the desk between them was a pile of papers on which he had been working, a glass containing whisky, a telephone and a photograph of Barbara with Alison on her lap. The baby was a delight, with dark hair and blue eyes which would probably become darker as she grew older. She had chubby cheeks and a winning smile and he loved her beyond reason. He wished he could have gone to the coast with them today, but business had to come first. For the past year there had been something of a housing boom. George couldn't build houses fast enough and he needed good men, which was why he had agreed to see Younger.

'No. I've been out of the country,' Colin told him. 'But you know how it is, home and family draw you back in the end, so here I am. I'm an experienced brickie but I can turn my hand to most things, carpentry, painting, plumbing.' Colin smiled easily, taking the measure of the man before him. He'd lay odds he wouldn't be averse to bending a few rules if it served his purpose. 'I do what I'm asked to do,' he said meaningfully. 'So long as I'm paid for it.'

They understood each other and George needed men who didn't stand about arguing, but got on with what they had been told to do, especially if what they had been told to do was a bit shady. 'Right,' he said. 'I'll give you a month's trial. Report to Mr Browning on Monday, he'll fill you in on the details.'

Colin stood up. 'Thanks, Mr Kennett.'

He left the office with a broad grin on his face and George returned to the plans which lay on his desk and which he had hastily covered when his secretary showed Younger into the room.

Before he left the council, Donald had told him of a scheme to develop the old airfield site just outside the town, which had not been used since the war. 'The idea is to build an industrial park,' Donald had said. 'Large and small units, to be let out and bring employment to the area. Once the units are filled, there'll be a need for houses for the workers. Expansion is the name of the game.' It was a policy that suited George down to the ground. 'Of course, the new bypass will have to come before any building starts.'

George knew that. Melsham's narrow streets and marketplace, good enough in the days of horses pulling carts and carriages, were becoming more and more clogged by cars and vans, and the bypass would have to come first, because the road onto the park must go off that and not pass through the town, which would only exacerbate the traffic problem.

He had secretly acquired a sizeable chunk of the airfield with borrowed money and was simply biding his time. But times were difficult, inflation and unemployment had risen to unprecedented levels and Melsham, being a rural community, was affected by a strike of agricultural workers. They had been earning as much as two pounds ten shillings a week during the war and immediately afterwards, but when the guaranteed prices for corn were abolished their pay had been halved. In Norfolk the farmers had tried to bring it down to a pound a week, resulting in the strike of ten thousand men. And that was affecting everyone including George and the council plans.

There was controversy over the bypass and the use of the derelict airfield, which was reported in the *Melsham Gazette* and debated hotly in the letters' page. Those who were for it said it would wake the town up and drag it into the new Industrial Age. Those against it maintained that the felling of a belt of trees in a countryside with fewer trees than anywhere else in the country was a desecration, to which their opponents argued that the old airfield was an eyesore and a properly landscaped industrial site with carefully planted trees and shrubs would enhance rather than detract from the area. The nature lovers countered with the statement that they were not against an industrial site, simply against the felling of mature trees to build a road to it.

Without the bypass there would be no industrial site. George was beginning to feel a sense of panic. The interest on the money he had borrowed was horrendous and he had to push the project through before he bankrupted himself. Tonight he had arranged to meet Ron Harrison, the leader of the town council, to try and enlist his support.

Penny's drawing room was packed and buzzing with conversation and laughter and the sound of music played very loudly on the gramophone. Barbara paused on the threshold, wondering why she had come. A couple of years before she would have been joining in the chat about parties and who was going out with whom; who had done well in exams and who had flopped; holidays abroad and career prospects; drinking too much, laughing too loudly; having fun. Now she felt out of it and so much older than her contemporaries. Wife and mother. What could she possibly have in common with these beautiful young people? She had no exams or job prospects to worry about, no youthful love, requited or unrequited, intruding into every waking thought, no plans which could be abandoned the moment a better offer came along. No plans at all, in fact.

Why had she come? George hadn't wanted her to, telling her it was a daft idea to go all that way just for a party. It wasn't as if she would know anyone except Penny, and those theatre and film people were all a bit weird...

'I know some of them. They are my friends.' Evening after evening spent alone reading and knitting had made her want to scream and she didn't seem to be able to paint. The prospect of a night in town had suddenly become irresistible. She had tried to explain she hadn't had a night out since Alison had been born and she wasn't going to run off with an actor, she simply wanted a break. Grudgingly he had given in, but he couldn't go himself, even if he wanted to: he had a meeting to attend.

Now, surrounded by glamorous women in sack-like dresses which, for all their shapelessness had cost their wearers the earth, and handsome, self-assured men, her confidence ebbed away and she felt like turning tail.

'Darling, you're here, at last!' Penny, in a dress of lime-green silk which had more material in the sleeves than in the skirt, hurried over to hug her. 'I'd almost given you up.'

'The crowd was so thick outside the theatre I couldn't get a cab.'

'Yes, I had no idea there would be so many. What did you think of it?'

'Very good. I am sure you will get lots more offers after this.'

'Come and meet everyone.' She took her arm and pulled her forward.

Bemused, Barbara found herself being hauled in front of actors and actresses, producers, stagehands and newspaper reporters, together with a sprinkling of students and ex-students, one or two of whom she already knew. Penny left her with a young man called Justin. 'He's a producer,' she said. 'So be nice to him.'

Barbara stood sipping champagne, trying to think of something bright and intelligent to say but all she could think of was, 'Do you produce plays?'

'Films. I'm hoping to recruit Penny. *Home Close* could be the making of her.'

'What's it about?'

He smiled and sipped his drink. 'You must wait and see. Let's just say it's a comedy with a serious side to it, something for the actors to get their teeth into.'

'I shall look forward to seeing it.'

'Are you an actress, Barbara?'

She laughed. 'Good heavens, no!'

'Barbara is an artist,' said a familiar voice at her elbow. She turned to see Simon at her side, casually dressed in slacks and open-necked shirt. He was smiling in that odd way he had, which made her want to smile back. 'But sadly she has forsworn her talent to be a wife and mother.' He sighed melodramatically. 'Such a terrible waste!'

'Simon, don't exaggerate,' she said, unaccountably pleased to see him. 'I only dabble.'

'But you wanted to be a famous artist.'

'Dreams,' she said. 'Childish dreams.'

'And now you have put aside childish things in favour of motherhood.'

'Yes.'

'Too soon,' he said. 'Much too soon. A flower bud cut off before it had time to blossom.'

'You are being silly. I'm not cut off. Just because I'm married, doesn't mean I don't live life to the full.'

Justin, realising the conversation was becoming

111

personal, drifted away. Simon took her arm and guided her to a sofa which had been pushed into the corner of the spacious apartment, now so crammed with people it seemed box-like. 'Come and sit down and tell me all about it.'

'About what?'

'About this full life of yours. Do you realise we haven't seen each other for...how long is it?'

'You came to my wedding.'

'So I did, but only to take a look at the man who had the power to make you abandon everything you had set your heart on. I'm afraid I took an instant dislike to him.'

'Why?' she asked in surprise.

'He had you. The little green god got the better of me.' He laughed but she detected a hollowness in it which startled her. 'And now you are here, looking stunning. That colour suits you.'

She looked down at the hyacinth-blue dress. 'Why, thank you, kind sir.'

'Your glass is empty. Shall I fetch you another?'

'Yes, please.'

While he was gone, she sat looking about her, seeing the bright clothes of the young people about her, the flash of their legs and upraised arms as they twinkled to a waltz tune on the little patch of clear floor, hearing their raised voices as they struggled to be heard over the sound of the music. She tried to imagine what George would have made of them and gave up when the vision she created was one of disharmony. He didn't fit. But did she? It was gratifying to be paid compliments, to be lightly flirted with, to feel glamorous for once, but half of her was wondering if Elizabeth had managed to get Alison to sleep and if George had found the dinner she had left for him to heat through.

Simon returned with brimming glasses. He handed her one and sat down beside her, casually putting his free arm along the back of the sofa behind her. 'Now, tell me all about your life in the country.'

'It's very little different from life in the city, these days,' she said, sipping her drink, conscious of his arm behind her. 'We do have the motor car, you know, and electricity and some of us even have a telephone.'

'My, that was a little sharp, wasn't it? Why so defensive?'

'I'm sorry. Perhaps I don't like being taken for a country bumpkin.'

'Is that how you feel?'

'No, of course not,' she lied. 'You made it sound like that.'

'Did I? Then I am sorry. You're every bit as gorgeous as anyone else here. More, in fact.' He paused and his arm left the back of the sofa and found its way across her shoulders. She knew she ought to remove it, but she didn't like to make a scene. Besides, it was a long time since she had enjoyed a little harmless flirting. 'Let's start again, shall we?'

She turned towards him, wondering for a moment exactly what he meant. They could not start again, not from when they first met, she a student and he a soldier; they were both different people, had moved on, grown more mature, and in so doing had moved apart. He was smiling at her, almost as if he understood her thoughts and she felt herself colouring. 'My life in the country is uneventful...'

'But you have recently had a daughter. Surely that was not uneventful.'

'No, of course not. She is beautiful and good and fills my days.'

'I bet you haven't picked up a paintbrush since she was born.'

She laughed. 'And there you would be wrong.'

'I'm very glad to hear it. What have you done?'

'Lots of things. A few watercolours...'

'Have you exhibited them?'

'Of course not. I'm not that good...'

'Whose fault is that?' he asked softly. 'You could have been. You cut yourself off from all your old friends, deserted us for another way of life altogether.' He paused, while she remained silent and contemplated the bubbles in her glass. 'I do hope it was worth it.'

She ignored his last comment. 'I didn't desert anyone. Penny is still my friend.'

'And me? What about me?'

'What about you?' she asked.

'Do you need to ask?' His voice was soft. 'You shook me, you know, getting married like that. I thought we had something going, something special...'

She stared at him in surprise. Why had he not said anything to her at the time? Would it have made any difference? 'I didn't know. I thought we were just good friends.'

'That wasn't how I saw it. I was looking forward to something more. One minute we were going along nicely and I was trying, ever so gently, to prise you away from Daddy, then out of the blue, there's this great wrestler with hands like dinner plates...'

'Oh, Simon, he isn't like that.'

'No? What is he like, then?'

'He's generous and kind and... You don't really want to hear about him, do you?'

'No, you're right, I don't.' He stood up, pulling on her hand. 'Come on, let's dance.'

They found a small space on the floor, not big enough to do more than shuffle on the spot. It was simply a way to stand very close to each other, he with both hands round her waist, she with her arms about his neck. He was very little taller than she was and their cheeks touched. His was cool and smelt of cologne and she was aware of a little shiver of anticipation, of daring and, to her own astonishment, of desire. Her limbs were quivering with it. He turned his head and brushed her lips lightly with his own. Bemused, she heard him whisper, 'Shall we get out of here?'

Without waiting for a reply, he took her hand and led her from the room into the hall, where it was cooler. 'That's better,' he murmured, pulling her into his arms and holding her so close she could feel his heart pumping against her own. He lowered his lips to hers, setting up such a tumult inside her, she was lost to all reasonable thought. She lifted her arms and put them round his neck, so that he was able to pull her body even closer to his own. She felt the curve of his thigh against hers... Suddenly she pulled herself away. 'God, what am I doing?'

He smiled, reluctant to let her go. 'Enjoying yourself, I

hope. Let's find somewhere more comfortable.' He started down the hall, pulling her with him.

'No! Oh, no! I'm sorry, Simon, I must go.' She ran from him, grabbed her coat from the hallstand, picked up her overnight case from where she had left it just inside the door and fled into the night.

She could hear him calling her to wait, but she ignored him. At the end of the street she found a cab to take her to Liverpool Street station. Only then did she realise the last train had gone and she had the rest of the night to spend on the platform, a prospect which filled her with alarm: there were some very unsavoury characters dossing down in odd corners. What a fool she'd been, first to allow the encounter to get out of hand and secondly not being able to cope with it when it did. But most of all, it was her own libidinous reaction which shocked and mortified her. She was a married woman and a mother; she had no right to lust after other men.

She arrived home next morning, bleary-eyed, just as George was leaving for work. The remains of his breakfast lay on the kitchen table, some uneaten toast, a marmalade-daubed plate, a coffee cup with the dregs still in it, several opened envelopes and a copy of the *Daily Sketch*.

'You're early,' he said. 'I didn't expect to see you until I knocked off tonight.'

'I decided to come home early.'

'Good.' He appeared not to notice her exhaustion. 'I'm off.' And with that he kissed her cheek, picked up his briefcase and left the house without a word about the party, not a single enquiry whether she had enjoyed it or how she had managed to arrive home at breakfast time.

She went to bed to catch up on lost sleep.

She was so tired she thought she would fall asleep as soon as her head hit the pillow, but it was not to be. The sounds of the morning penetrated the bedroom: traffic, people's voices, a wireless playing next door, a child crying. But most of all, her own confused thoughts buzzed louder than any external sound and kept her awake. *I thought we had something going, something worthwhile...* Had he really meant that? Was there something there, a spark which only needed one small incident to create a fire? It nearly had, oh, it so nearly had!

She should never have gone to that party, should never have allowed him to kiss her. It only served to highlight how far removed she was from the heart-free ambitious student she had once been, how much her life had changed. And however much she tossed and turned and insisted that she regretted nothing, that she loved George and was devoted to Alison, there remained a small part of her which refused to knuckle down. It was as if the person who had been Barbara Bosgrove had been snuffed out with her wedding vows and a new, alien being called Barbara Kennett had taken her place. And she rebelled against it. She lay there thinking of all the ways she could assert her independence, but every one of them she dismissed as hurtful to those she loved: her husband, her daughter, her father.

Sighing, she got up and went to fetch her daughter from her mother-in-law.

She spent her evenings painting, but the horse she was working on wouldn't go right: the head was lopsided and the jawline was wrong. It wasn't only the failure of the painting that made her angry – given time she could work at it and maybe get it right – it was everything. It was boredom and frustration and loneliness.

She sighed, washed out her brush, checked that Alison was asleep and had not thrown off her covers, then went downstairs just as George came home. She reached up to kiss his cheek. 'You look tired.'

'I am a bit.' He sank into one of the armchairs and picked up the newspaper.

'Have you eaten?'

'Yes. I had a bite at the Conservative Club before the meeting. Good God!' He sat up suddenly and pointed to a photograph in the local paper. 'That's Colin Younger.'

'Who's he?'

'One of my workers, picketing with farmhands. He's supposed to be off sick. I'll have his guts for garters.' He got up to pour himself a whisky from a bottle he took from the cupboard in the fireplace recess. 'I'll have to get rid of him.'

'Why? Has he done anything you could sack him for? Ethically, I mean.'

'You think doing that is ethical? He isn't a farm worker. If he brings his Commie ways back to my yard, he'll ruin everything. I can't afford unrest among my workers.'

Although the trees had long gone and the bypass was nearing completion, the contract for the industrial site had yet to be awarded and the delay was making George tetchy. He could not persuade those who held the purse strings that now was the time to move, and waiting for the economy to improve would not help it to do so. Time after time the project had come up on the council agenda, time after time the meeting had been adjourned with nothing resolved. But today, after intensive lobbying, the council had agreed to buy the land from him, pinning him down to a figure that was less than he had hoped, but enough to pay off the bank and finance building the first unit. The profit from that would pay for the second. The logistics were ticklish, but once the cash started to flow, he'd manage the lot. He had to find a way of neutralising Younger. He couldn't simply sack him, because the man would be sure to cause a public furore and he couldn't afford adverse publicity. The contract was not that secure. Old Gosport was bidding for it and he was a popular figure in the town.

Colin swaggered into the yard the following Monday morning, prepared to brazen it out if anyone mentioned seeing his picture in the papers. He hadn't known the cameras had been pointing at him until he had seen the newspaper. Rita had been furious that he had put his job at risk, had gone on and on, yak, yak, yak, until, in exasperation, he had given her a clip. It wasn't a hard blow but she had gone for him like a witch, slapping, clawing, kicking. He'd had to hit her again to stop her. This morning she was a mess; he couldn't bear to look at her. He didn't care if he did get the sack. He'd clear off again, find something else.

The foreman met him as he crossed the yard. 'Colin, Mr Kennett wants you in his office.'

Shrugging, he set off for the outside stairs of the building which housed the stores on the ground floor and the office above. Kennett was at his desk, reading his post. 'Shut the door, Mr Younger.'

Colin obeyed and approached the desk. 'You wanted to see me?'

'Yes.' George put down the letter he was reading and looked up at the man facing him. He was a big man and towered over the desk. 'Sit down.'

Colin sat and George got up and went to the window, where he stood looking down into the yard. The men were busy loading two vans, copper pipes, cans of paint, tools, ready to go out on site. No unrest there. Yet. He turned back but he did not sit down again. 'I know you are the union rep, Mr Younger, and I have to accept that, but I won't have the work on my yard disrupted. I want your assurance that you have no plans in that direction.'

'That depends. If the farm workers persuade the other unions out, then I would have to consider my duty—'

'Your duty is to those who pay your wages, wouldn't you say?'

'Only so far. I owe the men—'

'Your responsibility to the men is to do nothing to put their jobs at risk. They won't thank you if you do.' He paused, wondering how to go on, though he felt fairly sure of his ground. 'It would be easy for me to find your work unsatisfactory. Your timekeeping is not good—'

'Are you trying to sack me, Mr Kennett?'

'No, I don't think sacking you is the answer, do you?' He was smiling now and Colin wondered what was coming next. 'You do understand my problem?'

Colin grinned. 'Course I do. What do you want from me?'

'I think perhaps a little secondary picketing, but not with the agricultural labourers. Closer to home. I am told the workforce at Gosport's is unsettled: they've not had the bonus they were promised. Do you follow me?'

'Yes, but I'd have to promise them something.'

'A job at Kennett's and bigger bonuses if we get the contract for the industrial site. But don't be too open about it. It's your promise, not mine, I only hinted. Otherwise do whatever is necessary to bring them out. You understand?'

'I understand you need that bloody contract. What's in it for me?'

'Two hundred, if I get the contract.'

'Make it four and promotion to foreman and it's a deal.' He stood up and held out his hand.

Reluctantly George took it and then went back to the window to watch him clattering down the stairs and crossing the yard. He could hear his tuneless whistle fading as he went.

The story of the fire made front-page news in the *Melsham Gazette*, alongside the report that the government had stepped in and made the farmers back down. George registered relief, before moving on to look at a picture of a warehouse burning fiercely, with fire fighters silhouetted against the flames. It wasn't until he turned to the text he realised that it was Gosport's business premises. A man had been seen running away and was being sought in connection with it. There was a description of him, but not a very good one; the witness had been more concerned with calling the fire brigade. Mr Gosport Senior had been taken to hospital with severe shock; his son was busy assessing the damage. First signs indicated that it would run into thousands: flammable building materials, timber, paints, oils had all been totally destroyed; even the stacks of bricks had been scorched and cracked by the heat and were unusable. Only the twisted metal of the building itself remained.

George, at home for once, read the report with a sickening sense of shock. He had sent Colin Younger to sabotage Gosport's ability to take the contract, not destroy him. It had been Younger, hadn't it? Or was it a terrible, but fortuitous coincidence? Even in shock, George could appreciate the consequences. The old man would have been insured, but the assessors would take a long time settling the claim, especially if the fire chief confirmed it was arson. Even if they paid up promptly, it would take ages to replace the ruined stock. Gosport had been pre-empting the contract, getting into a position to make an early start, just as George himself had been doing.

He felt a sudden surge of elation. As long as no one suspected he had any involvement, he was home and dry. And he hadn't been involved, had he? He hadn't asked that crazy fool to set fire to the place; if Colin Younger had done it, it had been his own idea. All the same he must tread carefully, react appropriately. He would speak to Gosport, tell him how shocked he was, offer assistance, though not actually give any. And a word in the right ear would ensure Younger was put out of circulation for some time.

'Look at this,' he said to Barbara, handing her the folded paper. 'Poor old Gosport.'

She was in the middle of reading it when the doorbell rang. He went to answer it and came back with a tall man in a scruffy tweed suit. 'Barbara, Mr Younger and I have some union business to discuss. Do you mind?'

She put the paper down and stood up. 'No, of course not. Would you like a cup of tea, Mr Younger?'

'No,' George put in before Colin could answer. 'He's not stopping. Just give us a couple of minutes, would you?'

She left the room and closed the door softly behind her, but not before she heard George say, 'What the devil do you mean by coming here? I don't want to be involved.'

She stood still, listening. The house was no more solidly built than its council neighbours and the door was nothing more than two layers of thin board over a frame.

'You are involved. Do what you have to, that's what you said.'

'Yes, but I didn't mean you to...'

The man chuckled. 'It did the trick, though, didn't it? Worth a miserly five hundred.'

'Five hundred? Are you mad?'

'The price has gone up.'

'If you think I'll answer to blackmail...'

'Dear, dear, who said anything about blackmail? That's a nasty word. But I've been thinking of moving on, pastures new and all that, and a little going-away present wouldn't come amiss. Best thing all round, don't you think?'

'You're a fool if you think I keep that much in the house. Come to the office tomorrow at midday, give me time to go to the bank.'

Barbara moved away and went into the kitchen where she sat at the table and stared with unseeing eyes at the kitchen clock which hung on the wall. Her heart was thumping and her hands were shaking. George had been oiling wheels again, that was obvious, and this time it seemed he'd laid himself wide open. What had he done? And why bring in a man like Younger? Even she could see he was a dodgy character and George himself had said he was a troublemaker.

She heard the man leave and a few moments later George came into the kitchen. 'Any chance of a cup of coffee?'

She put the kettle on the gas stove. 'What did he want?'

'Nothing. A bit of union business.'

'Is he causing trouble?'

'Nothing I can't handle.'

What to do? What to say? Should she admit she had been listening outside the door, ask him what was going on? It would provoke the most awful row. No, it wouldn't, because he refused to row. He'd tell her it was nothing for her to worry about, he knew what he was doing. They were unable to communicate on anything but a very superficial level and Barbara began to think Penny had been right: she was in danger of vegetating, becoming a cabbage, staying home alone night after night.

'I'll go and dish up dinner,' she said. 'By the way, I saw your mother while I was out and asked her to come to lunch tomorrow.' There was still tension between the two women, but it had eased a little since Alison's birth. 'You will be home early, won't you?' George usually left off at half past twelve on Saturdays, but just lately there had been any number of reasons why he had been kept late at the office.

'I'll do my best.'

The woman standing on the step had frizzy carroty hair, a freckled nose and green eyes. Her black skirt was too tight considering she was somewhat plump. It was topped by a shabby jacket. 'I've come to see Mr Kennett,' she said. 'They told me at the yard I'd find him here.'

'He doesn't usually deal with business matters at home,' Barbara told her. 'Couldn't you wait and see him at the office on Monday?'

'This i'n't business, it's personal and it's urgent.'

'Come in. I'll go and fetch him.' She stepped aside to let the caller in, then turned to go back to the sitting room, unaware that Rita had followed her. 'George, there's someone to see you.'

George looked past her to the woman behind her. 'Who are you?'

'My name's Rita Younger, Mr Kennett.'

'God in heaven!' The exclamation came from Elizabeth who was sitting with Alison on her lap. 'What are you doing here? What do you want with my son?' She had turned very pale but there was such venom in her blue eyes it frightened Barbara.

'I'm sorry to butt in,' Rita said, glancing briefly at Elizabeth but addressing George. 'My husband's disappeared, packed his bags and cleared off. I thought you might know where he's gone.'

'Me?' George queried. 'Why should I know where he is?'

'He told me he'd been doing a special job for you, said it was hush-hush and he was going to be promoted.'

'Nonsense. No doubt he's got himself in a scrape and is making himself scarce. Nothing to do with me. Now, I must ask you to leave.'

Barbara, appalled at her husband's brusqueness, showed Rita to the front door. 'I'm very sorry we couldn't help, Mrs Younger,' she said. 'I hope your husband contacts you soon.'

'And pigs might fly,' Rita said with a laugh. 'Oh, well, back to the grindstone.' And she was off, tottering down the short path to the road on her high heels.

Barbara returned to the sitting room. Elizabeth was still hostile. 'That woman spells trouble, George. Keep out of her clutches.'

He laughed. 'For heaven's sake, Mum, she's only the wife of one of my employees. Ex-employee, as it happens. What are you getting so worked up about?'

'I'm not getting worked up. It's just...' She paused, realising she had to go on or be quizzed. 'Her mother was – probably still is – the town whore. And judging by the look of the daughter, she's following in her footsteps.'

'I don't think we should jump to conclusions,' Barbara said quietly. 'She seemed genuinely worried about her husband.'

The man's disappearance was down to George, Barbara was sure of it, but did her mother-in-law know something she did not? Ought she to tackle them about it or go and see Mrs Younger and talk to her about it? But what would that achieve? If her own confused feelings were anything to go by, Mrs Younger would be better off left in ignorance.

Rita was more angry than worried. For over a year Colin had been settled, going to work like a lamb every day, giving her housekeeping money every Friday. True, he kept a large chunk to spend at the pub and he went out with his mates on a regular basis, but he took her out sometimes too. And he had been excited about this special job Kennett had given him, saying it would be the making of them. And then he had disappeared. She should have known it was all pie in the sky. God knows why she'd believed him: he always had been a lying bastard. But then, so was George Kennett, she'd bet her last shilling on it.

'It's that wife of his I feel sorry for,' her mother said when Rita relayed the encounter. 'You remember, we were outside the church when they got married? I didn't realise it was Kennett's boy she was marrying until I read it in the Gazette afterwards. Mr Bosgrove got married again hisself soon after. I met him in the grocer's the other day buying cheese...'

Dora had a tendency to ramble and Rita cut her short. 'Do you know Mrs Kennett? George's mother I mean. I've never spoken to her in my life that I know of and yet she seemed to hate me on sight.'

'Stuck up bitch!' Dora said. 'She always did think she was a cut above everybody else. Even at school. Her father kept a grocery store. It weren't no more than the front room of their house, but she always had plenty of food and sweets and we didn't have much of anything in our family. She'd bring sweets to school and hand them to her special favourites.'

'And you didn't get any.' Rita laughed. 'Oh, Mum,

how can you bear a grudge for so long?'

'I don't bear her a grudge, my lovely. She's the one with an axe to grind, not me.'

'Are you going to tell me about it?'

'No. Best let sleeping dogs lie.'

Two days later they learnt that Colin had been arrested for arson. Rita knew perfectly well that George Kennett was at the bottom of it but she could prove nothing and Colin, when she was allowed to see him, refused to confirm it. He wasn't a grass, he said, but as his fingerprints had been found on an empty petrol can and that, together with the description of the man seen running away, was enough to convict him, he was going to plead guilty and rely on his brief to offer mitigating circumstances. 'I'll serve my time,' he said, leaning towards the grille that divided them. 'Then I'll get even with Kennett. I gave his name as an alibi, said I was working late at the yard, but the bugger refused to confirm it. He's not going to get away with it.'

Because of his guilty plea the trial was a short one. Rita sat in the gallery and heard him sentenced to five years in prison. She caught his eye as he was escorted from the dock. He grinned at her and stuck his thumb up, a gesture which was reported by the *Melsham Gazette* as 'defiant and unrepentant to the last'.

Long after it had been to all the big cities, *Home Close* came to the tiny picture house in Melsham. George said he had no time to go and see it, but Barbara asked Elizabeth to sit with Alison so that she could go. Sitting in the stuffy, darkened cinema, she watched Penny bringing the character of Irene Littlechild to life. It was a comedy and the plot was convoluted, but among the laugh-out-loud antics of the characters, there was some real pathos.

Irene's husband, Ronald, was having an affair and Irene had, in the end, found out about it. She drove to work, trying to think of ways of getting her husband back. Even though there was no sound except that of the in-house pianist, tears could be seen streaming down her face. She was driving all over the road. The scene changed to a lorry coming in the opposite direction and Barbara sat forward in her seat, holding her breath. She could easily imagine the loud blasting of the lorry's horn, the screeching brakes and the huge crash. The next scene was in the hospital and Ronald was rushing down the corridor to be with Irene. Their reconciliation left Barbara in tears. She stood up for the National anthem and then shuffled out with everyone else, sniffing and blowing her nose, glad George was not with her because he would have laughed at her.

As soon as she arrived home, she checked with Elizabeth that Alison had been good, then went to the telephone and asked the operator for Penny's number.

'Pen, I've just been to see *Home Close*. You were wonderful.'

Penny laughed. 'Bit over played, wasn't it?'

'Not at all. You had the audience in tears.'

'Thank you for those kind words, darling. On the strength of that performance I have been offered a really meaty part in a new film. I'm thrilled to bits. But enough about me. How are you? How's Alison? I'm sorry I couldn't get down for her birthday. Did she like the teddy bear?'

'She loved it, takes it to bed every night.'

'And how are you?'

'Expecting again.'

'Congratulations. When's it due?'

'Next April. George is pleased.'

'Of course he is. Who wouldn't be?' There was a slight pause, then she said, 'Did you know Simon is getting married?'

Simon. For a moment it seemed as if her heart had stopped and time had gone into reverse. She was back in a crowded room, squeezed on a sofa and he was saying *I thought we had something going, something special.* Why could she never forget that? Why could she never forget how it felt to be in his arms? She hated herself for it. If she had married him, would he have left her alone night after night, as George did? And those thoughts led to guilt. George was out so much because he cared for her, wanted the very best for his family. And though he rarely talked about the business, he did talk about his plans for them: the dream house he would build, with a large garden and a paddock for Jinny and a pony for Alison, a little bungalow for his mother so she didn't have to climb stairs, a new car – two new cars. He would do it too, he was nothing if not determined. That was how he had won her in the first place. She should remember that more often.

'Barbara, are you still there?'

'Yes. I thought I heard Alison. You were telling me about Simon. Who's the lucky girl?'

'Dodo Marston. She played my sister in *Home Close.* You met her at my party.'

'Did I?' She didn't remember anyone at that party, except Simon; she hadn't been there long enough. But she remembered the character in *Home Close*. She was beautiful and could turn on the charm and the tears with equal ease. Was she like that in real life?

'Yes. It was where Simon met her. You should have stuck around.'

Barbara resisted the temptation to ask why. Penny knew she would not have left the party without a reason, and though she had never asked what it was, Barbara had a feeling she had guessed. She managed a light laugh. 'Is her name really Dodo?'

'No, it's Dorothy, which doesn't exactly convey glamour.'

'Give him my congratulations, won't you?'

'Of course. Look after yourself and kiss Alison for me.'

George came in as she was replacing the receiver. He put his briefcase down beside the hall table and dropped a kiss on her cheek. 'Who was that?'

'Penny.' She followed him into the sitting room where he poured himself a whisky and slumped into an armchair to drink it. 'Had a bad day?' she asked.

'Bloody awful,' he said irritably. 'No one seems to know the meaning of a good day's work for a good day's pay anymore. A delivery of timber hasn't arrived and it's holding me up. Inflation has gone sky-high and I'm paying through the nose for all my supplies because the bank has put up interest rates again. Don't you read the papers? No, of course you don't, you'd rather sit in the dark and watch trash.'

She did not respond, afraid that if she did wind him up

131

into losing his temper, it would be an explosion so mighty that their whole world would fly to pieces. Alison, who adored her father, would suffer and so would her unborn child. Right on cue, he gave her a sharp kick. She smiled and put her hand on her belly, feeling him move. She didn't know why, but she was sure she was going to have a son.

Chapter Five

NICHOLAS GEORGE WAS born at three o'clock on the morning of third of April 1923 at Melsham hospital. He was a lusty seven and a half pounds and George was delighted. He had a daughter he loved, but a son was special, a son could join him in business and make it 'Kennett & Son'.

On the day of the christening, George decided to photograph them all, grouped around Barbara and the baby, whom he positioned on the settee. Alison knelt beside Barbara, obeying her father's instructions to hold the baby's hand and smile at him. 'Mum, you sit the other side of Barbara, I want the whole family in.' He set the delay and raced round behind the settee and bent towards Barbara, smiling down at his son. The flash coincided with the ringing of the doorbell.

'That'll be Dad and Virginia,' Barbara said, handing Nicholas to her mother-in-law so that she could let them in.

She was shocked by her father's appearance. The strapping man who loved to be out of doors working on the farm, who liked to ride and shoot and fish, could hardly walk from one chair to another without becoming breathless. He was patently ill, but he smiled and sat with his grandson on his lap, sipping a glass of champagne, assuring everyone he felt fine. Virginia took him home at seven and helped him to bed, then she crept downstairs to eat a lonely supper. When she went up to bed herself, he was already dead. He was smiling, as if he had been enjoying a private joke when he drifted off.

Even though she had known her father was ill, Barbara could hardly take in the news when Virginia rang at seven the following morning. Her father had always been so strong and healthy, her bulwark. She didn't want to believe it. George fetched his mother to baby sit and then drove her over to the farm, but there was nothing she could do except sit with Virginia in the kitchen drinking endless cups of tea. She had idolised her father. It was to her father she had gone to solve her childhood problems, and to some extent, those of her adulthood, those she felt able to confide. He had never failed to give her good advice. The only time their relationship had been strained was over his marriage to Virginia, but he had convinced her that it was right for him, and she had come round to accepting it. She was still not one hundred per cent sure of Virginia, but there was no doubt the widow was genuinely grief-stricken.

'He loved you,' Virginia said, after a long silence, when the only sound was the ticking of the old clock on the dresser. 'He was always talking about the things you had done as a child, riding, playing the piano, school reports, your painting, that sort of thing. He was proud of you.'

'I know. I wish I had been with him more at the end. I feel so guilty...'

'Guilt is all part of grief, or so they tell me,' Virginia said. 'It must be, because I am riddled with it.'

Barbara turned to her in surprise. 'What have you to feel guilty about?'

'I wasn't with him at the end, I was down here, eating my supper.'

'Oh, come now,' George said, putting a hand on her shoulder. 'You stayed with him until he went to sleep. He didn't wake up, so his life ended then, you mustn't feel guilty about that.'

She looked up at him. 'No, I suppose not. You are such a comfort, George.'

'Do you want me to help with the funeral arrangements?' he asked. 'You shouldn't have to cope alone.'

'Oh George, would you? I've been dreading it, though he left instructions. He wanted to talk to me about them, but I wouldn't listen. I stuck my head in the sand and told myself he would live for years and years. He wrote them down instead. They're in his desk with his will. I haven't opened it.'

'Leave everything to me.'

John Bosgrove's funeral service was as dignified as his end. Besides the immediate family, aunts, uncles and cousins came from wherever they happened to be living, sombrely

135

clad but not in deep mourning: he had not wanted that. From the town came representatives of the NFU, the golf club, the Rotarians and the church where he had worshipped all his life.

Barbara, following the coffin down the aisle with George and Virginia beside her, was uplifted to see so many. Her father had been loved. Penny was there, elegant in a slate-grey jersey suit and black hat; and beside her Simon looking incredibly prosperous, with a glamorous Dodo at his side. Barbara's step faltered at the sight of him, then she looked ahead towards the coffin and continued on her way with a firm tread. Tucked away in a back pew almost hidden by a column, she caught sight of Rita Younger and someone who could only have been her mother. She gave them a wry smile, glad that her mother-in-law had stayed behind to look after Alison and the baby.

Afterwards the mourners returned to the farmhouse for tea and sandwiches, standing about chatting to each other, sometimes even laughing, though not unkindly. They all had memories, nostalgic, bittersweet, happy, sad. Barbara endured as long as she could, then crept away to the stables and put her arms round Jinny's neck and cried, hot, scalding, grief-laden tears she could not shed in company.

'I saw you leave, thought I'd find you here.'

Startled, she looked up to see Simon in the doorway. 'I thought you might need a shoulder to cry on.'

She turned and flung herself into his arms. He held her silently, feeling her misery through her shaking shoulders, sharing it. His was the best comfort she had known since her father's passing: no words, no platitudes, no prattle about practicalities. With no one else there to see her, it was unadulterated, selfish grief. And after it came calm. The sobs eased and she looked up at him through a blur, smiling a little, her voice still watery. 'I've ruined your jacket.'

'It'll clean.' He pulled a handkerchief from his pocket and gently mopped up her tears, almost making them flow again. 'Do you feel better now?'

'Yes, thank you. I'm sorry I'm such a drip. I can't believe he's gone. He meant so much to me.'

He grinned ruefully over her head: it was her love for her father which had triggered her marriage to George and he knew, though she had never said a word to him, that it was a disaster, just as his own marriage was. There was no point in saying anything to her, it was all water under the bridge and water didn't flow backwards. 'I know.' He paused. 'Do you think you can you cope now?'

'Yes.'

'Let's go in, then. I'm afraid I'll have to leave soon. Dodo wants to get back to town. Work, you know.' It wasn't work; he did not want to stay and be tormented by the sight of Barbara whom he loved and might have had, but whom he had lost. He had been a mess when he came out of the army, unable to settle, not knowing what he wanted, trying to pretend that limbless bodies and sightless eyes were the price you paid for war and, if you had survived intact, then you should be glad, not eaten up by guilt. By the time he had come to some sort of shaky truce within himself, and decided it was useless blaming himself for the mistakes made by politicians and generals, it was too late, Barbara was married.

He should never have tried to seduce her at Pen's party. He had never apologised for that, simply because he had not seen her again until today and putting it in writing was too risky: he did not know if George read her letters. If she had forgotten it or put it out of her mind, it was best not to remind her, but he wished he could forgive himself.

They turned and walked back to the house side by side. Once there, Dodo claimed him. Barbara went and stood beside George and took his hand, giving him a watery smile.

George began building the units on the industrial site amid gloomy forecasts from almost everyone that it would be a financial disaster. Gosport openly said he was grateful for the fire: it had stopped him ruining himself as Kennett's was doing. That George was not ruined was down to his foresight and, to Barbara's continuing shame, a total lack of business ethics. He spent more time than ever oiling wheels and cultivating anyone who could help him: bribed, threatened, diversified. It was no good protesting, he simply told her he was not doing anything more than hundreds of others were doing to survive. If she didn't like it, she could always sell the farm.

To Barbara's surprise and delight her father had left her the farm with the proviso that Virginia, to whom he had left a small annuity, was to live there as long as she wanted to or until she married again. 'It's a white elephant, Barbara,' George had told her, two months after the funeral. 'It's too big for one person.' He had come home for lunch and they were facing each other across the kitchen table with bowls of soup in front of them. Alison had finished hers and scrambled down to play under the table with some wooden bricks. Nick was asleep in his pram, but would wake soon demanding to be fed.

Barbara kept one ear open for him as she spoke. 'I can't sell it, you know that. It's Virginia's home.'

'You can if she agrees. I could find her something smaller, easier to run.'

'But it was my childhood home, where I was born and grew up. My parents loved that old house and so do I. Dad knew that. It's why he left it to me.'

'That's sentimental claptrap. You can't let sentiment interfere with business and Kennett's could do with a cash injection right now. There's the industrial site to finish...'

'With businesses going to the wall almost daily, it would be madness to sell the farm to finance that. Go to the bank if you need money.'

'I've reached my limit there.' He was trying to be calm, but she was making it very difficult. Juggling money, handling employees, placating suppliers were the breath of life to him and held no terrors, but Barbara in one of her obdurate moods was a different thing altogether.

'The farm is the only thing I've got of my own. Everything else is yours.'

'And what's wrong with that? You know I'll always look after you. Have I ever begrudged you anything?'

She wanted to say, 'Nothing but your time and affection,' but knew it would spark another, more wounding, argument and she shied away from that. 'No, but if Dad wanted the farm sold he'd have sold it himself, wouldn't he? Or left it to Virginia outright.'

'All I'm asking is for you to think about it.'

Nick woke and his pathetic wails for food diverted her. She picked him up and settled down to feed him. George watched them in silence for a few minutes, then went back to work, leaving her lonely and vulnerable. She needed a friend, someone she could confide in, but there was no one. She couldn't say anything to Elizabeth who would undoubtedly take her son's part. She might have been able to talk to Penny but Penny was filming in Spain and, in any case, she knew what her friend would say: 'Hang onto your assets.'

Somehow George kept going. He expected his workers to accept lower wages, and though they grumbled, it was better than no work at all. Bonar Law had died and been succeeded as prime minister by Stanley Baldwin but he was soon in trouble and a general election was called. George campaigned as hard as anyone, knocked on doors, spoke at public meetings, harangued and argued. Although Melsham was a safe Conservative seat, the result over the whole country was a victory for the Labour Party and Ramsay MacDonald was invited to head the first ever Labour government, albeit with Liberal support. 'It won't last,' George said and was proved right when another election was held in October.

The Conservatives swept back into office, helped by a fraudulent letter published in the newspapers purporting to be from the President of the Communist International, calling on British workers to prepare for armed revolution. As far as George was concerned, it meant he could start lobbying for new contracts, but with his capital tied up in the industrial site and Barbara being bloody-minded over selling the farm, all he could do was play a waiting game and hope something would turn up.

Lady Isobel Quarenton, returning from her weekly visit to Melsham market, discovered a leak in the manor roof. What made her look up as she got out of the car, she didn't know. Perhaps it was the sun winking on the upper windows or a biplane flying overhead; whatever it was, it was fortuitous because she noticed several slates missing.

James, her last surviving servant, who was butler, footman, gardener and chauffeur rolled into one, was shutting the passenger door of the Bentley, before driving it round to the coach house. 'James,' she said. 'Had you noticed those tiles were missing?'

He looked in the direction of her pointing finger. 'No, My Lady. Had I done so, I would have drawn your attention to them.'

'I'd better go and see what the damage is.' Maintenance of the once lovely old house was horrendously expensive and getting worse and she simply did not have the money; her only income was a tiny annuity her father, the Earl of Cotterham, had left her and the rents from a couple of cottages which had once been part of the estate. Inflation had reduced the former to next to nothing in value and the cottages also needed repairs.

Her mother had died when she was a child and her father of influenza in 1918, which was probably a blessing: he would have found the changes in their fortunes impossible to live with. But Melsham Manor was her home; she had never known another. Cosseted and protected all her life, and having no brothers, which might have made a difference, she had had little opportunity to meet young men, certainly none her father approved of. Consequently she had never married and now she lived alone, except for James, whose whole working life had been spent in the service of the family. Given the opportunity to leave, he had refused to budge on the grounds that she needed him. He did everything about the house and garden except the cooking, which she managed herself. One man couldn't be expected to do so much and so it didn't get done. But leaking roofs were important.

The attics, which had once housed kitchen maids, parlour maids, chambermaids and footmen, were now filled with lumber: old furniture; lampshades; toys; an old cradle on rockers; suitcases full of school books which her mother would never throw away; umbrella stands; a stag's head; a stuffed owl whose glass cover was broken; tennis rackets; board games; a blackboard and a desk put up there when the schoolroom became redundant, all of it thick with dust and festooned with cobwebs. She hadn't been up there for years and was appalled by the clutter. But she couldn't ask James to clear it out and she couldn't face doing it herself. She picked her way carefully through it to the spot beneath the missing tiles. It wasn't difficult to find because the ceiling had collapsed and the floorboards beneath the hole were wet. If it rained again, it would seep down to the room below. Something had to be done. She went downstairs and rang Kennett's.

It was the first time George had been inside the gates of the manor. There was a weed-encrusted gravel drive leading to the front door of a substantial mansion which was mostly Georgian, though one wing, at right angles to the main facade, was older and there was an extension at the back which had been added more recently, but everywhere spoke of neglect. His professional eye roamed over it as he got out of his car and rang the bell.

He was admitted by the butler and conducted to the drawing room where her ladyship was waiting for him. It was a well-proportioned room with a high ceiling and long windows which looked out onto a paved terrace. There was an Adams fireplace on which stood an ormolu clock and two small figurines. A display cabinet beside it contained a few pieces of porcelain. Lady Isobel was sitting in a winged chair by the empty hearth. There was a small table beside her on which stood a small vase of flowers and a family photograph.

'Mr Kennett, My Lady,' the butler said. George noticed that the sleeves of the man's jacket were slightly frayed, though the creases in his trousers were knife-sharp.

It was difficult to tell how old her ladyship was, probably in her forties, he decided. She was dressed in a shapeless purple frock and her hair was dragged up into a bun on top of her head which she held very upright.

'Mr Kennett,' she said, in her precise, well-modulated way. 'I am afraid I have lost a few tiles from the roof and the rain has penetrated the attics. I need a quote for repairs.'

'That's no problem, My Lady. If I might take a look.'

She instructed James to show him the way and sat down to wait for him to come back.

* * *

Following the servant, George climbed an impressive flight of oak stairs which curved up from the marble-tiled entrance hall, then walked the length of a gallery to more stairs at the back of the house. These were narrow and carpeted in cord, which was threadbare. At the top he found himself in a long corridor lined with doors. James opened one of them. 'In here, sir.'

George looked round the damaged room, picked up some fragments of plaster and rubbed them between thumb and finger, stamped on the wet floorboards, then asked James for a pair of steps and climbed up through the hole in the plaster to take a closer look at the tiles. Then he went downstairs, out of the front door and down the drive far enough to peer up at the roof, then he wandered round to the back, taking in the old stable block and returning to the front door, where James was waiting to escort him back to the drawing room. In spite of the neglect, the building seemed basically sound and would repay a few thousand spent on it. The trouble was that he didn't think Lady Isobel had a few thousand and he wondered why she continued to live there in such decaying splendour.

'Well?' she queried. 'How much?'

'It needs doing urgently if the first-floor bedroom ceilings are to be saved,' he said. 'There are a lot more loose tiles besides those that have already come off and more will come down with the next wind. I can't be sure how many until we get some scaffolding up and look closer, but it will be almost impossible to match them. If you want the job to look anything at all, you really ought to have the whole roof done. Some of the timbers are saturated and I noticed a bit of woodworm. The wet floorboards need replacing; one or two are downright dangerous. As for the ceilings—'

'I didn't ask for a catalogue of disasters, Mr Kennett, I asked how much to patch it up.'

He pretended to consult the notes he had made but the figure he had in mind had very little to do with what he had written. 'A few thousand, My Lady.'

'How many thousand?'

'Three, at least, maybe more.'

'That's ridiculous.' She was shocked. 'I can't afford to throw money away.'

'It would be throwing it away not to have a proper job done,' he said. 'This is a lovely old house, it deserves to be looked after.'

'You don't need to tell me that, Mr Kennett, but I think your estimate is too steep. Mr Gosport would not have been so expensive.'

'No, My Lady, which is perhaps why he is no longer in business. Times have changed. Inflation is higher than it's ever been.' He paused, watching her face carefully. 'I could use some of the tiles from the old wing, which will give you a good match at the front, and then re-roof the back with cheaper tiles. That would bring it down to two and a half thousand...'

'Still too much.'

He waited, allowing the full horror of what he had said to sink in, before adding, 'There is another way...'

'What might that be?' She spoke warily.

'I noticed that there is a triangular piece of land in the corner of your grounds close to Mill Road, which is separated from the main grounds by a copse of trees. I would guess it's just over an acre. If you let me have that plot free gratis, I'll do the work for half price.'

'If you want it to build one of those dreadful estates with matchboxes for houses, the answer is no, Mr Kennett.'

'Not an estate, my lady, one house for myself and family. I'll fence it and access it from Mill Road. You won't even know we're there. So what do you say?'

'That land has been in our family for hundreds of years. My father would turn in his grave.'

'Better to part with a tiny piece of land which is useless for anything else, than lose the whole house, don't you think? You will, if the roof isn't looked after.'

She knew perfectly well he was trying to bamboozle her, she could see the gleam of avarice in his eye, but she really didn't have the money for the repairs and they had to be done. This was a way out, and what was an acre, after all? 'I'll think about it,' she said.

'Don't think too long, My Lady. If it rains again or the wind gets up...' He left the rest of the sentence in the air.

'I believe the forecast for the next twenty-four hours is fair,' she said with some asperity. 'I will telephone you with a decision tomorrow.'

'Very well, My Lady. I look forward to hearing from you.'

She didn't take the hand he offered but turned and rang for James to show him out.

She would come back to him, he knew. All he had to do, he told himself as he walked to his car, was to make sure that the bill for the repairs was double a fair price for the land and that wouldn't be difficult to fiddle. If the tiles were taken off the Victorian wing very carefully, their second-hand value would cover the cost of the new tiles, even allowing for those he put on the front and a few breakages. It would cost a few man-hours, but that would help to keep his men in employment when he might otherwise have to lay them off. The damage to the roof timbers was minimal, the woodworm was not extensive and could be treated. And a few new floorboards and a bit of plaster wouldn't break the bank. With luck, the land would cost him nothing at all. He would have the bigger house he had been promising himself on a prime site. But he wouldn't tell Barbara, not yet. He was still miffed with her over the farm and wasn't going to let her off the hook that easily.

They were growing more and more distant with each other and Barbara didn't think it was only because of her attitude over the farm. He was never at home but it was a long time before she admitted, even to herself, that he might have found someone else. The signs were there: the late nights, the vague excuses, the faint smell of perfume that clung to him. Their sex life, once so satisfying, had dwindled to a quick thump every couple of weeks, which left her miserable and unsatisfied. And when she tried to initiate something herself, he was always too tired, or he had a work problem on his mind. He was always polite, never angry, which did nothing to help her accept it.

She was stagnating, sinking into a mire of household routine which was unshakeable. Get up, take Alison to school, put Nick in his pushchair to go shopping, do the washing, ironing and housework, grab a snack at lunchtime and be at the school gates at four o'clock. Then home, give both children their tea and cook dinner, that was if George was coming home to eat, most of the time he didn't and then she would sit with a tray on her lap, a mass of nerves and worry. Was her marriage falling apart? If she pretended nothing was wrong, would the problem go away of its own accord?

She didn't want the trauma of a broken marriage and the hurt it would cause the whole family. She would have to start again on her own and that wouldn't be easy: she had no qualifications, no experience, no money and she would be blamed for the breakdown. Besides, she thought, she still loved her husband and she adored her children; they were the most important people in her life, more important than her own happiness. And perhaps she was being a dog in a manger over the farm. If she did something about that it might put things right between them.

'George, am I free to sell the land Dad left me, even if I keep the house?'

They had just finished Sunday lunch and he was sitting in an armchair reading the *Sunday Times*. Alison was drawing and Nicholas was thumping a drum Elizabeth had given him and making an awful din. Both were attractive children, but he had the sunniest smile and was, even at his naughtiest, adorable. Alison was much quieter, very intelligent, and less prone to tantrums. Given a book or a piece of paper and some coloured crayons, she could amuse herself for hours.

'Yes, but I don't see how that helps,' he said, carefully laying aside the paper.

'I was thinking. If you're strapped for cash, why not abandon the idea of building another house? We could move into the farmhouse ourselves and convert the stable block into a self-contained home for Virginia. The structure is perfectly sound.'

'That's the daftest idea I've heard yet,' he said. 'Do you think I'm the sort of man who'd live in a house owned by his wife? People will think I'm on my uppers. I want a modern house with every convenience, and doing repairs and modernising would swallow up all the money the land made, wouldn't it?'

'Not necessarily. You are a builder, after all and—'

He cut her short. 'I have already negotiated the land for our new house. I intend to start building as soon as I can spare the cash and the men.'

'You have? Where is it? Why didn't you say?'

'It was meant to be a surprise. I've bought an acre from Lady Quarenton, on the corner by Mill Road.'

'Does that mean you don't want the farmhouse after all?'

'I never said I didn't want it, simply that I didn't want to live in it. But if you're determined not to sell, why not let it? The rent would come in useful.'

'But what about Virginia?'

'There's this house,' he said. 'Shall we give it to her when we move out, hand the deeds over? Make it a final settlement. It will leave you to do what you like with the farmhouse.'

'Do you think she'd agree?'

'Leave her to me. I'll go up and see her after work tomorrow. I think I can persuade her it's a good idea.'

She took the drum away from Nicholas. 'Then do it, please, and put the sale of the extra land in hand. Use the money any way you like.'

He left his chair to bend over and kiss her. 'Thank you, darling. It couldn't have come at a better time.'

Virginia was in the stable grooming her horse when George arrived. She was wearing jodhpurs and a pullover that looked as though it might have been one of John's. It's sloppiness enhanced, rather than detracted, from her slim figure. He took her in his arms and kissed her, then stepped back to hold her at arm's length. 'God, you're beautiful.'

She laughed. 'In this old thing?'

'We can soon remedy that.' He pulled the jumper over her head and threw it over the side of the stall before pulling the strap of her brassiere down so that he could kiss her breasts, one by one, licking his tongue round the nipple and nipping them with his teeth when they rose in response. She pulled his shirt out of his trousers, undid the fly and pushed her hand inside. Oh, he was so hard, so big, so exciting, everything she could wish for and she wanted him. How she wanted him!

It had begun as a simple interest in her welfare after John died, then a mutual sharing of problems, and after that it had escalated into something far more important. He was dynamic, purposeful, successful, handsome in a rugged way, and very sexy. Did Barbara know that? Virginia doubted it.

'God, George, I need you. I need you right now.'

'Me too.' He took her hand and pulled her towards the

stairs to the hayloft, where they undressed each other in a frenzy of impatience. Nude she was like a goddess; he couldn't see enough of her lithe body, still youthful and untouched by ugly stretch marks. Two or three times a week for the last six months, he had feasted his eyes on it, stroked it, kissed it, entered it. And she loved it. Loved him, she told him time after time, crying out when she climaxed, gripping him with her thighs, holding onto him, as if she were drowning. She revelled in it, in everything they did, the strange places they found to indulge in sexual fantasies, the risks they took.

'George, how long can we keep this up?' she asked, some time later, when they were lying side by side, with their bodies glowing and the smell of straw and sex in their nostrils.

'For ever, I hope.'

'You're simply sticking your head in the sand. Barbara will find out sooner or later.'

'Why should she? I make no secret of the fact that I take an interest in your affairs. Which is why I'm supposed to be here. She wants to sell the land and let the farmhouse. I'm supposed to find out how you feel about moving into something smaller.'

'You know how I feel about it, George.' She rolled over and propped herself on her elbow to look at him. 'I want to get out of here. It's haunted by John and his first wife. Everywhere I look I see them, every time I move even the smallest ornament, I imagine them standing over me, disapproving. To me it represents a year or two of happiness and endless months of horror watching him die.'

151

'I'm going to build us a bigger house, so how do you like the idea of moving into the one we're in now? You would own it outright which is more than you do the farm.'

'It's OK by me, so long as we can still be together.'

'Then, I'll put it in hand.' He reached for his clothes, picked the straw out of them and dressed. 'I'd better be going.' He bent over to kiss her. 'See you soon. There'll be lots of legitimate reasons for me to come now.' He laughed. 'Business reasons.'

She stayed where she was for several minutes after he had gone, then slowly dressed herself and went down to finish grooming her horse.

Things didn't improve on the business front: the economy lurched from one crisis to another. Bankruptcies were at an all-time high, leading to massive unemployment. Barbara's sympathies were all with the men who were out of work and she felt guilty that she had so much, that her children were plump and well clothed, that George seemed to be able to maintain his lifestyle with barely a hiccough. 'I work damned hard for it,' he told her, more than once. She forbore to remind him of the money that had come from the sale of the land belonging to the farm. He was touchy about that, even though it had been his salvation.

They moved into their new home in the spring of 1926. George christened it *The Chestnuts* because a couple of the old trees were included in the garden. The house was large and modern with every possible labour-saving device built into the kitchen, including a refrigerator. There were four bedrooms and a luxurious bathroom. Barbara had enjoyed furnishing it, though George had haggled over every single item, bullying the poor shopkeepers, who were struggling as much as he was, into huge discounts. And though she was glad to leave their first house, which had always been associated in her mind with sharp practice, if not downright dishonesty, she wished he hadn't used so much of the proceeds from the sale of the land to build it; the plot alone must have cost a fortune. She had intended the money to help with the business, not for her own comfort.

He had an answer to that, as he had for everything. 'It proves George Kennett is not only a survivor but a winner,' he told her when she mentioned it one morning at breakfast, the only time of day they had more than two minutes together. 'If he can build a house like this in the middle of a recession, then there must be something special about his business acumen. Besides, it kept the workforce busy when I might have had to lay some of them off. What sort of message would that have sent out, do you suppose?'

'Lay them off? Things aren't that bad, surely?'

'They will be if the miners have their way. The country relies on coal for almost everything. If my customers suffer, then I suffer.'

Barbara hardly blamed the miners. They had a dreadful job to do, tunnelling away in semi-darkness under the ground, many in seams so poor, they had to dig the coal out lying on their bellies, getting ill with lung troubles and failing eyesight. The trigger that caused the unrest was the lifting of subsidies, which left the mine owners struggling and they demanded wage cuts from their employees.

'Four pounds a week, I ask you!' George said, tapping the newspaper report he had been reading. 'That's more than I pay my skilled workers. Holding the country to ransom, that's what they're doing. In the old days—'

'They sent women and children down the mines,' she said, spooning boiled egg into Nick's mouth. 'It took a lot of hard work to put an end to that.'

'Don't be silly, there's no comparison.'

It was always the same: whenever she tried to voice an opinion counter to his own, he dismissed it, as if she had no brain to think for herself. She must be the little woman, the homemaker, a shadow of her husband. Almost in defiance, she started painting again, setting up her easel and paints in the spare bedroom and working away in the lonely evenings after the children had been put to bed. It was a large canvas of a girl sitting on a rock gazing out to sea. She didn't know why she chose that theme, but it seemed to suit her mood.

In the event, remembering how they had let the miners down the last time, the Trades Union Congress called out the dockers and the transport, iron and steel, gas and electricity workers and a general strike began on the third of May. Uncollected rubbish began to pile up in the streets, commuters couldn't get to work, raw materials weren't getting through to factories and the threat of food shortages sent some people scurrying to the shops to buy up things like sugar, tea and coffee in spite of government warnings not to do so. And there were long queues at all the petrol stations. The army and navy were called in to move goods, and volunteers suddenly appeared prepared to drive trucks, trains and trams, and man the telephone exchanges. People in the rural communities fetched out long disused pony traps and roamed the woods for fuel.

'It's almost impossible to get about,' Penny told Barbara in one of her periodic telephone calls. 'What with amateurs driving trams and buses and car owners volunteering to take people to work, London is one big traffic jam. And picketing strikers are throwing stones and slashing tyres. Simon got a gash on his face from a half brick. He was only doing his bit, driving a tram. He came through the war without a scratch and now he'll have a scar on his face.'

Barbara pictured Simon's unblemished handsome face and her heart gave a sickening lurch to think of it being disfigured. 'Is it very bad?'

'You know Simon. He's making a joke of it, as usual: says it will make him even more attractive to the ladies and they won't look sideways at him anymore because he has no war wounds to show he did his bit.'

'Tell him I'm sorry.' She meant more than just sorry he had been injured, but sorry for everything else, for the unnecessary guilt he seemed to carry around with him, for the fact that she had used him for comfort when her father died and had none to offer in return, for the feelings she still had for him, feelings which seemed to have survived her marriage and which she could never speak of.

'I will. How is it with you?'

'Apart from the fact we can't travel on public transport and have to be careful about using coal, not much is different.'

'How's the new house?'

'It's fine. I'm just about straight. You'll have to come and visit. I haven't seen you for ages.'

'I will as soon as I've got a day to spare. I'm busy filming at Cricklewood, or I would be if everything had not ground to a halt over this strike.'

'Perhaps it won't last long.'

She was right. The general strike collapsed after only nine days, though the miners stayed out until August when hunger forced them back to work. Some of the smaller mine owners had gone out of business and there were no jobs to go back to. They left their homes and drifted south looking for work.

Charities were set up to help not only the miners, but others hit by unemployment, and Barbara volunteered her services to an organisation set up in Melsham to help unemployed men and their families. Alison was at school and Elizabeth was happy to look after Nick.

Mrs Gregory, who was its driving force, was a woman of enormous proportions, very efficient but with a heart of gold, who put Barbara to work making soup in a kitchen set up in an empty shop. By the time the soup was ready, there was a long queue of ragged, half-starved applicants. Barbara had known there were poor people, struggling to get by, but she was appalled to think that in a comparatively affluent place like Melsham, there were men in rags and children without shoes.

Later she took her turn manning a clothes store, sorting and ironing donated garments, sewing on buttons, ranging shoes in pairs, and putting clothing too worn and dirty to be passed on into bags for the rag-and-bone man. From not having enough to do, she now didn't have a moment to spare. She found herself with a new circle of friends: colleagues in the charity including Lady Quarenton who worked as tirelessly as anyone. She ceased to worry what George was up to every minute of the day, and because there was always something going on, some humorous or sad tale to tell, she became a more interesting person in herself. It didn't happen overnight: she had her difficult days when nothing seemed to go right, days when she wished she had time to have her hair done, when it was an awful rush to get to the school by four. But on the whole she began to enjoy life again.

George viewed this new Barbara with tolerant amusement. It kept her off his back and let him get on with his work without having her forever peering over his shoulder, trying to catch him out oiling wheels, not to mention being able to see Virginia whenever he liked. Virginia had moved into their old house and the farmhouse was let to an American colonel who had come over during the war and liked England so much he had married an English girl and stayed. Things were on the up and George intended to stand for Melsham Town Council in the forthcoming local elections. It was easier to control what was happening in the town from the inside, instead of having to lobby for everything he wanted.

Barbara was busy on the picture she was calling *Girl on a Rock* the evening he was elected with a majority of a hundred and fifty. It was Virginia who was photographed standing behind him on the rostrum, though in his acceptance speech, he was at pains to say his wife had supported him throughout and would have been with them that night but their small daughter had a tummy bug and needed her mummy, which left Barbara fielding solicitous enquiries for several days afterwards.

It meant he had another excuse for not being at home in the evenings. Council meetings were notorious for going on and on and he was duty-bound to stay to the end. 'Most of it's waffle,' he told Barbara. 'Some of them have no idea how to come to the point, but I have to listen. In the middle of the dross, there might be something worth listening to. And of course, I have a contribution to make. Quite an important one, as it happens.'

'I'm sure, you have,' she murmured, folding the ironing which had been airing on the clothes horse. He had been a great deal more cheerful of late, possibly because he had got his own way – or most of it – over the sale of the land and his election, but was he being unfaithful? The signs were still there, though she tried not to think of it, tried not to wonder who it might be. His secretary? Someone he had met at work? When these soul-destroying thoughts invaded her mind, she deliberately pushed them from her, refused to listen to herself, kept herself busy painting in the long, lonely evenings when the children slept soundly and the house was quiet.

Because of the children she couldn't go with George when he went on a business visit to Paris with a combined delegation from county council and Melsham Town Council, though she knew some wives were going, paid for by their husbands. She helped him pack in a flurry of last-minute instructions, watched as he kissed the children goodbye and stood on the step with them, waving as the car went off down the drive to the station. Then she turned back indoors with a sigh that was almost one of relief.

Chapter Six

GEORGE SMILED AT Virginia across the hotel lounge and nodded imperceptibly towards the lifts. She smiled back and mouthed, 'Don't be long,' and then drifted off to the reception desk to pick up her room key.

The discussions officially broke up at six, though some of the delegates planned to continue informally after dinner, and though George would have infinitely preferred to spend the evening with Virginia, he had elected to remain. There were still two sizeable sections of the Melsham Industrial Park not yet developed and he was determined to tie at least one French engineering company down to investing in Britain, and Melsham in particular. He was representing Melsham Town Council, of course, not Kennett's, but if there was anything in it for him personally, he meant to be in a position to take advantage of that too.

He sat back in his chair and lit a cigar, watching

Virginia's sinuous figure in its black jersey dress as she stepped into the lift and was carried upwards. He had used his influence to get her a job in the office of the county council's chief executive the year before and it had turned out very well. She had quickly learnt council procedure, how to set up meetings and agendas, write notes and minutes, to liaise with other departments and keep everyone sweet. Arnold Bulliman, a crusty old relic nearing retirement, was already finding her indispensable and he hadn't stopped to consider that others, more senior, might feel put out that she had been given a place with the delegation so soon after taking up her post. She was young and beautiful and she always seemed to have a special smile for him which made him go weak at the knees. It amused George. 'I just hope you can keep him out of your bed,' he had said, just before they left England.

She may have been able to keep the chief executive out of her bed, but not George. He was in it every night. They had to be very careful, of course, very discreet, pretending to have no more than family connections. During the day they kept their distance and all communication was on a strictly business footing. There was the odd passed note and the veiled message left with the desk clerk, all very dangerous, very exciting, heightening the rapture of their lovemaking, which was thoroughly abandoned.

On their last night he sat on the edge of the bed, to smoke a cigarette and telephone Barbara, while behind him, Virginia, nude and shining, her blonde

hair spread about her shoulders, was marching her
fingers down his back to his buttocks and stirring
him up again. 'What's that? No, of course there's
no one here. I'm in my room. The line's bad, lots
of interference.' He jerked his elbow into Virginia
to silence her giggling. 'I'll be home tomorrow, but
it might be late, so don't wait up for me. Kiss the
children for me. Bye now.'

'Oh, God, George, I wish we weren't going home
tomorrow, ' Virginia said when he rang off. 'I want to
keep you for ever.'

'You don't wish it any more than I do, sweetheart.'

'Then why don't we stop all this hole-and-corner stuff
and come out into the open, be together?'

He smiled, though what she suggested was out of the
question. He could not jeopardise all he had worked
for, his standing in the community, his affluence, his
reputation, for the sake of an affair, however pleasurable.
'Darling, one day perhaps we will, but you know how
things are...'

'Yes, I know how things are. I am condemned to the
role of the other woman, the secret love...'

'But that's what's so good about it, my sweet. You are
my secret love. Always.'

'Always secret?'

He smiled and bent to kiss the tip of her nose. 'No,
always my love.'

'Don't patronise me, George. I am not Barbara, I won't
be put off by lies and excuses.'

'What's brought this on?' he asked, stroking her arm
with the back of his hand. 'End-of-holiday blues?'

163

'It's not a holiday, we're supposed to be working.'

'I know and we have done very well too. And a lot of that is down to your charm and efficiency. It has been noted in high places.'

'Funnily enough, I enjoy it.'

'Then let's enjoy this, shall we?' He bent and kissed her mouth, opening it with his tongue, exploring, while his hands began caressing her body, still damp and sticky from the last time. He lifted his head and looked into her eyes. 'You do enjoy it, don't you?'

'Oh, George, you know I do.' She put her arms round his back and pulled him down on top of her. 'You are so...so...'

He grinned. 'Sexy?'

'Yes, but lovely with it.'

'That's because I love you and I love doing this to you. I think about it all the time, even when we're apart.'

She had to be content with that. It was all she was going to get. The alternative was to give him up and that was too much to ask.

Barbara sat in a deckchair in the garden, watching Nick splashing in an old tin bath she had brought out and filled with water. Completely naked except for a white cotton sun hat, he was slapping the water and laughing. The drops of water glistened on his chubby body and brought a lump to her throat. 'We'll have to go and fetch Alison soon,' she said and laughed as he scooped water in a seaside bucket and threw it over her. 'You little terror!'

It was the first time she and George had been apart since their marriage and it had turned out to be a tranquil time. George was such a busy person, rushing here and there, talking to people, arranging things, bolting meals, that life with him was a desperate attempt to keep pace. He was as liable to dash in and demand a quick meal or a clean shirt as he was to telephone to say he wouldn't be home until late. She hadn't realised how on edge she had been until he went. Knowing he was miles away on the other side of the channel had given her a breathing space, a period of calm. She had enjoyed being lazy, lying in the garden, playing with her children. She hauled Nick out of the water and carried him indoors where she patted him dry, dressed him in a pair of shorts, a little shirt and sandals, then fetched his pushchair.

Alison loved school and was always one of the last to emerge, but she didn't like Barbara going in to find her. She appeared ten minutes after everyone else, dragging her satchel along the ground. Barbara could never afterwards explain why she suddenly decided to make the small detour which would take her past their old house, except that Virginia was always saying she did not see enough of the children and, with George away, there was no great hurry to go home.

There was no one there and every window was tightly closed. She went round the back and then returned to the front gate, looking up at the house, with a puzzled expression.

'You looking for Mrs Bosgrove?' The voice came from the other side of the dividing hedge. It was followed by the head of a young woman appearing above the foliage.

'Yes.'

'She's out of the country on business. Paris, I think she said.'

Standing there on a pavement which was hot enough to fry an egg, Barbara suddenly felt icy cold, frozen to the spot.

'It's Mrs Kennett, isn't it?'

The voice, coming from behind her, startled Barbara out of her immobility and she turned to stare at frizzy red hair, bright lipstick and a freckled face. Her gaze travelled down to a pink blouse and a skimpy brown skirt. 'I'm sorry?'

'Are you all right?' the new arrival asked. 'You look as though you've had a shock.'

Barbara pulled herself together. 'I expect it's the heat. You're Mrs Younger, aren't you?'

'That's me. Look, I only live round the corner. Why not come home with me and have a cuppa? You look as though you could do with a sit-down.'

'That's very kind of you, but I'm all right, honestly.'

'Oh, come on, tea'd go down a treat, wouldn't it? And I bet the kids would like a glass of lemonade.'

Barbara, who didn't want to go home, didn't want to confront her fear, to acknowledge that there really had been someone in the room with George when he telephoned, allowed herself to be led away. Virginia's neighbour, who had listened to the exchange with her mouth open, watched them go with a look of disbelief.

George Kennett's hoity-toity wife and Rita Younger, what a combination!

Rita lived in one of the early council houses George had built and already they were looking neglected. Some of the tenants, who took a pride in their home, had taken the trouble to paint them themselves, but many had not, arguing that it was the council's duty. Barbara noted that Rita had done nothing to hers and inside the furniture was decidedly shabby and there was dust everywhere.

'Did you find your husband?' she asked. Any subject of conversation was better than being quizzed on why she had been standing outside Virginia's gate looking as if someone had dealt her a blow to the body and winded her.

Rita pushed a steaming mug of tea across the kitchen table towards her and turned to mix the children's lemonade with crystals from a packet. Alison, slightly bemused by this strange departure from their normal routine, took hers and politely said, 'Thank you.'

'You're welcome,' Rita told her, handing the other to Nick, who grabbed it quickly and put it to his mouth. Barbara made him say thank you and turned to sip her tea.

'No, you couldn't say I found him, exactly,' Rita said, when Barbara began to think she had forgotten the question. 'He did a bunk.' She had become adept at lying about what had happened to Colin, pretending she didn't care that her husband had deserted her yet again. It was better than telling everyone he was in prison. 'As soon as anything happens he doesn't like, he just clears off.'

'Had something happened he didn't like?'

Rita looked at her over the rim of her cup. She didn't think Mrs Kennett knew the truth; she was simply making small talk to get over the fact that she'd had an almighty shock. Rita didn't expect to be told what it was, though she could guess. She didn't live far from Mrs Bosgrove and she had seen Kennett's new Humber outside the gate on more than one occasion. 'Don't know. Not at 'ome, it didn't. At work, p'rhaps.'

'Oh.' Barbara remembered the conversation she had overheard between George and Mr Younger and wished she hadn't asked the question. 'I'm sorry, Mrs Younger.'

'Don't often get called Mrs Younger. I'm Rita to everyone.' She chuckled suddenly and her eyes lit with defiant humour. 'That's when I'm not being called something worse. But you don't need to be sorry. It wasn't your fault.'

'Do you know where your husband is now?'

'Oh, the bugger came back two days ago. Right at this minute, I reckon he's in the betting shop.' Time off for good behaviour he had told her when she said he was out sooner than she expected.

'Oh dear, I'm truly sorry. He's not working?'

'He says he's going back to Kennett's, said he went round the yard yesterday but Mr Kennett was away and he had to speak to him in person.'

'My husband is abroad, but he's coming back tonight; I expect he'll be in the office tomorrow.'

'I'll tell Colin, though whether the lazy sod will do anything about it, I don't know.'

Barbara looked swiftly at Alison. Language like that was not something the child had ever heard, but she was looking out of the window at a cat stalking something in the long grass and appeared oblivious.

'Do you have a job, Mrs...Rita?' Barbara asked.

'I'm a barmaid at The Crown in the evenings and I'm an office cleaner in the mornings.' She grinned. 'Greedy of me, I suppose, when there's so much unemployment, but I need both jobs. I enjoy them, specially the bar work. Lots of people to talk to, a free drink now and then and meals on duty. It don't leave me too much time to meself, but what good would that do me? I'd only sit at 'ome and feel sorry for meself. Feeling sorry for yerself is just about the worst thing you can do. Another cuppa?'

'No, thank you, I really must be going. It was very kind of you to ask me.'

Alison had managed to finish her drink without getting it down her front but Nick had not only smeared it round his face and into his hair, he had let it drip down his shirt which had a large ochre stain. Barbara picked him up and put him in the pushchair.

Rita looked up as a girl came into the kitchen. 'Here's my Zita,' she said.

The girl was about thirteen, dressed in a grubby gymslip. She had dark glossy hair braided into a pigtail. She bore no resemblance to Colin Younger and very little to Rita. But she reminded Barbara of someone, though she could not place whoever it was.

169

Rita laughed, sensing Barbara's puzzlement but not the reason for it. 'Good-looking gel, i'n't she?'

'Mum, for goodness' sake,' Zita protested.

'Ma says she's the spittin' image of my dad.'

'Your father?'

Rita laughed. 'Yes, I promise you I had one, even if Ma never let on who he was.'

'Don't you know?'

'No. Are you all right now? Not still feeling faint?'

'No, I'm fine. It was silly of me. Too long in the sun. Thank you for the tea.'

'You're welcome. Come again. Any time you're passing.'

In the early hours of the morning George crept up the stairs, undressed in the dark and got into bed beside Barbara. Laying tense and still, pretending to be asleep, she could smell Virginia's perfume clinging to his skin. Now she knew who her rival was, the scent was easy to identify. She wanted to turn on him, to scream and batter him with her fists, to kick him out of bed, anything to release the burning torment inside her, the bitterness of being betrayed, the humiliation of being cast aside, the sheer unadulterated jealousy.

Lying with her back to him, she felt him fidgeting carefully so as not to wake her and a few moments later he was gently snoring. How could he sleep? How could he do this to her? Why, if he had to have an affair, did it have to be with Virginia? The memory of her first meeting with her stepmother came back, sharp as if it had happened the day before, Virginia in a bath robe, sleek

170

and beautiful, totally at home in her father's house. The hurt then had been so bad she couldn't bear to live in the same house. She remembered her mother-in-law's caustic comment: *It was enough to make you fling yourself at the first man who'd have you.* That wasn't true, was it? She loved her husband or she wouldn't now be in such torment.

She watched the dawn come up, the gradual lightening of the room until she could pick out the shape of each piece of furniture, then George's case, standing by the wardrobe, and his clothes flung on a chair. The light became pink and golden and then she could see the top of one of the chestnut trees which gave the house its name. She rose and went to stand by the window, looking out. The sun was coming over the trees which separated The Chestnuts from Melsham Manor, huge and orange, suffusing the sky in vermilion and pink. There wasn't a cloud to be seen. Behind her George still snored. She wanted to get dressed and run down the drive, along the lane by the common, across the fields, back to her childhood home, back to the nest. Only Colonel Macready would wonder what on earth had got into her. Perhaps she should pack her things and take the children away, somewhere where George would never find them. Poor kids!

She turned as George stirred and, unable to face any sort of conversation with him, grabbed her clothes and ran for the bathroom.

She was cooking breakfast when he came down to the kitchen. He smiled and bent over to kiss her cheek. 'You were up early,' he said, in a perfectly normal voice.

171

'I couldn't sleep.'

'No? You were dead to the world when I came in.'

'And when was that?' She hadn't meant to sound so sharp; it just came out that way.

'Oh, around midnight. The boat train was late getting into London and we stopped off for a bite before catching the last train to Melsham. Is there something wrong? You're looking pale.'

What to do? What to say? How did one go about surviving when your whole world was falling to pieces? 'I'm perfectly well.'

'Well, you don't look it. What have you been up to while I've been away?'

'What have I been up to? You have the gall to ask me what *I've* been up to?' Her voice was rising and she quickly moderated it. 'Shouldn't I be asking *you* that question?'

He took a deep breath to steady himself. She couldn't have found out. 'You know perfectly well what I've been doing. It was a highly successful visit. We managed to tie up a deal with a French engineering company. It means new jobs in Melsham. Everyone is pleased as punch.'

'Congratulations.' She was about to ask him if Virginia had been pleased too, when Alison wandered into the kitchen in her nightdress, her dark hair about her shoulders and her eyes still heavy from sleep.

'Daddy!' She flung herself into her father's arms to be hugged and kissed.

'Have you been a good girl while I've been away?'

'Yes. Did you bring me something? You promised you would.'

'Of course. You don't think I'd break a promise to you, do you?' He looked up at Barbara, standing in the middle of the room, and smiled. She turned away to get Alison's breakfast and when she turned back, father and daughter were leaving the room hand in hand. 'I made you a drawing at school,' Alison was saying. 'It's the seaside.'

Barbara found her eyes filling with tears. How could she shatter that trust? There was nothing she could do but soldier on and hope he would come to his senses without her having to say anything.

George was still musing on the altercation he had had with Barbara when he arrived at the yard and was in no mood to be civil to Colin Younger when he found him waiting on the stairs to the office. 'What the hell are you doing here?'

'Time served, Mr Kennett,' Colin grinned easily and followed George into the room. 'I've come home and you can't blame a man for that, can you?'

'We made a deal...'

'That was years ago and I honoured it, but a man can't be expected to stay away from his wife and family and all the comforts of home for ever, can he? And you've done pretty well for yourself, I hear. Councillor Kennett, no less, a bigwig with a big house and a smart car and no competition to speak of. And who have you got to thank for that? I was the one that kept his mouth shut and did his time.'

George sighed. He'd got enough problems with Barbara and Virginia without blackmail added to them. 'I didn't ask you to start a fire, that was your idea, so don't try blackmailing me.'

'Go to the cops and complain then. I dare you to.'

'I have nothing to tell them.'

'Too right, you haven't.' Colin grinned and, without waiting for an invitation, sat in the chair opposite the desk behind which George had taken refuge. 'If I were to mention five hundred pounds, they'd be more interested in that, wouldn't they? It had to come from somewhere and there'd be an investigation, bank accounts, things like that. I've got nothing to lose, I've served my time, you haven't.'

'You could have told the police about it when you were arrested,' George said, sitting back in his chair and making a steeple of his fingers, just to prove how relaxed he was. 'Why didn't you?'

'I'm no grass.' He grinned. 'Besides, there are other ways of skinning a cat. Rumour, hints, gossip, you really can't afford that, can you, Councillor Kennett? And suppose the *Melsham Gazette* got hold of the story?'

George picked up a pen and fumbled in a drawer for his chequebook. 'How much?'

'I'm not asking for money, Mr Kennett, you can put that away.'

George looked up in surprise. 'What do you want, then?'

'A job. A good job, mind – foreman, that's what you promised me, wasn't it? Something well paid, with some status to it, so I can go home with my head up. All legit and above board.'

George stared at him for a full minute, wondering what the man would do if he sent him off with a flea in

174

his ear, and decided not to risk it. He scribbled a note to Donald. 'Take this to Mr Browning, he's in the yard somewhere. But any hint of trouble and you're out, do you understand?'

Colin took the note and left. George heard him clatter down the stairs, making the iron ring, then turned back to the paperwork on his desk. At noon he was interrupted by the arrival of his mother.

It was so unlike her to visit him at work, he looked up in alarm. 'Mum, is something wrong?'

'Yes, there is. I want a word with you.'

'Can't it wait? I'm very busy, as you can see.' He indicated the papers strewn on his desk. 'You'd think they'd manage to carry on for five days without getting in a mess, wouldn't you?'

'Shut up, George, and listen for once in your life, will you?'

'I'm listening.'

'I'm telling you this because no one else will and because I don't want to see everything you've worked for – your business, your position in the town, your marriage, your reputation, everything – go down the pan for a few moments of dubious pleasure.'

Somewhere in the pit of his stomach he felt a frisson of apprehension. 'For God's sake, Mum, what are you talking about?'

'Don't blaspheme. I mean you and Virginia Bosgrove.'

The fear grew and resolved itself into a tight knot, thick and dark and menacing, making him feel physically sick. If his mother knew, who else? He stared at her, wondering whether he could get away with denying it, which was what he would have done had Barbara accused him, but seeing the steely determination in her eye, he knew he could not.

He forced himself to sound reasonable. 'Virginia is Barbara's stepmother, and since her husband died, I have been looking after her affairs, you know that.'

'Affairs is the right word.'

'You've no call to use that tone.'

'I'll use any tone I like if it's going to make you see sense.'

'Who's been telling you this? Was it Barbara?'

'Does Barbara know?' Her surprise told him it hadn't been his wife 'Oh, George, you fool! You crass, reckless fool.'

'Who did tell you, then?'

'Half of Melsham. If Barbara hasn't heard about it, she soon will, unless you put a stop to it.'

He forced himself to sound calm. 'You shouldn't listen to gossip.'

'When the gossip involves my son and the welfare of my grandchildren, then I listen. I do not comment, but I listen. I'm listening now. And what I'm hearing is a man in a hole he's dug for himself, and it's getting deeper with every word he utters.'

'If that's what you think, why are we even talking about it?'

'We're talking about damage limitation, George. We're talking about putting a stop to it before it ruins you. Melsham won't forgive you, you know; it's an old-fashioned kind of place, it likes its prominent citizens to be pillars of respectability. What do you think your chances are of being re-elected if this affair goes on? You'll be the shortest serving councillor of all time. The Gazette will have it all over the front page. Is that what you want?'

'No, of course not. It won't come to that. Why are you getting so worked up?'

'I thought I'd brought you up to be decent and honest. You never knew your father, and I hoped—'

'Oh, Mother, don't be ridiculous. I can't help it if I don't live up to his ideals.'

She gave a short, humourless laugh, but decided not to disillusion him. 'Never mind his ideals, what about yours? George, whatever possessed you?'

'I don't know. It was just one of those things...'

'Things don't just happen with you, George, you make them happen, always have. How long has it been going on?'

'Since John Bosgrove died or at any rate just after.'

'What's wrong with the life you had, son?' she went on, speaking softly. 'Barbara has been a good wife to you and a good mother to your children.'

If he was surprised at his mother taking Barbara's side, he did not voice it. 'I didn't say she hadn't. It's just... Oh, I can't expect you to understand.'

'Oh, I understand all right. The grass is greener on the other side of the fence, that's all it is.'

'No, it's not! It's not a bit like that.'

'Do you want a divorce?'

'No, of course not. Anyway I've got no grounds.'

'Barbara has, and now the law has been changed, she can use it. What's sauce for the gander...'

'She wouldn't do it.'

'Can you be sure? Think about it. Everything we do has a consequence, George, and the consequences of this could be horrendous. A broken marriage and desperately unhappy children. Don't they mean anything to you anymore?'

'Of course they do. I love my children. And they love me. They don't judge me.'

'They might in years to come. They love their mother too, don't forget. And what about Barbara? She's the one who has to carry on looking after the home and family, who has to bear the strange looks and whispers, the gossip that there must have been something wrong with her or you'd never have gone off the rails. You make her feel worthless, George, of no importance. I can tell you it's not a nice feeling at all. She deserves better.'

Why was she lecturing him, defending Barbara? It was so out of character he was astonished. She'd only been married a couple of years before his father had gone abroad and after his death she remained a widow, keeping his memory, trying to mould her son in his image. Well, he wasn't his father, he was his own man and he needed relief from the pressures of his life. She didn't understand that. Neither did his wife, who was only interested in her house and children; he needed more than that. 'Have you been talking to her about it?'

'No, I most certainly have not. That doesn't mean I don't know how she must feel. Finish it, George, before it finishes you. It isn't worth the grief.' She stood up. 'Now, I must go. I'll leave you to think it over.'

He sat on after she had gone, staring into space, his

work forgotten. His mother had made him feel more of a heel than ever Barbara could. He found himself looking at a future in which all the bright goals he had set himself receded from his grasp. It wasn't that he hadn't been aware of the risks, but whenever he thought of them he told himself he thrived on risks. Half the success of his business had been down to calculating the risks and then defying them. It had been a mixture of good judgement and luck. Was the balance of luck tipping away from him now? He picked up the phone and rang Virginia.

'There's going to be a reception at the town hall on Friday,' George told Barbara that evening. 'It's to celebrate the success of the trip to Paris.'

'So? You don't expect me to go, do you?' She didn't want to go, to be the subject of whispers, derision. They all knew, they must do; the wife was always the last to find out. Why couldn't he see that all she wanted to do was find a dark corner somewhere and hide?

'Of course. What will everyone think if I turn up without my wife?'

'Nothing, seeing as you nearly always do.'

Her eyes were bleak as winter, full of misery. He felt a stab of remorse. He had loved her once, had found her beautiful and funny and charming. Where had all that gone? 'Don't be silly. I've asked Mother to come at lunchtime and look after the children so that you can have your hair done and pamper yourself a bit. Buy a new dress.' He bent to kiss her cheek. 'Now, I'm off. I'll be home about six.'

She watched him pick up his briefcase and leave the

house, heard his car go, and had absolutely no intention of going to that reception.

It was Elizabeth who persuaded her to go. It was the last day of term and the children were being let out of school at midday. Alison had been loaded with pictures she had drawn which had been unpinned from the wall where they had been displayed for weeks; a red balloon on a string; a shoe bag stuffed with plimsolls and a cardigan which turned out not to be hers. Elizabeth arrived as she was piling everything on the kitchen table. While Barbara put the kettle on the gas stove, Elizabeth pulled Nick onto her lap and hugged him. He scrambled off again and ran into the garden.

'I swear he grows every time I see him,' she said, looking covertly at Barbara, busy setting out cups and saucers, taking milk from the refrigerator, fetching the tea caddy from the cupboard. There were great hollows under her eyes, and her lips, devoid of make-up, looked dry and pale. She moved with a kind of listlessness. Elizabeth's thoughts went tumbling back through the years, back to that other misery, to the last time she had seen Fred, the misery and anger and the struggle that followed as she tried to bring George up alone. 'You look as though you haven't been sleeping,' she said carefully.

'No, I haven't. It's the heat, I expect.' Her smile was a wry twist of the lips, no more. She put a cup of tea in front of her mother-in-law. 'I don't think I'll go tonight.'

'Why not?'

She couldn't tell her the real reason, couldn't be that disloyal, and besides, Elizabeth adored her son; she would see no wrong in him, would blame her daughter-in-law.

Perhaps it was her fault, some inherent failure to give her husband what he wanted. She wasn't beautiful enough, talented enough, socially outgoing enough, was probably a dreadful failure in bed; she had no way of knowing. 'They are so false, these receptions,' she said. 'No one seems genuine, all trying to cultivate whoever will do them most good, finding fault with their opponents, talking about people behind their backs...'

'If you're there, they can't talk about you behind your back, can they? They can't begin to wonder why George Kennett is there without his wife.'

Barbara looked at her sharply. 'Are they talking about me behind my back?'

'I don't know. Is there any reason why they should?'

'This is silly...'

'You go, Barbara. Get yourself up in your glad rags and go. You're a beautiful woman, you know, an asset to George. He knows that.' She paused. 'I tell you what. I'll take the children home with me for the night, and tomorrow I'll take them on the train to the sea. You and George can have some time to yourselves. What do you say?'

Barbara looked across at her mother-in-law and wondered what had prompted her to make the suggestion. 'It's very kind of you,' she said. 'But—'

'No buts.' Elizabeth reached out to cover Barbara's hand with her own. 'My dear, you have one advantage that no one else has and it's a very big one. You are George's wife. Use it. Use it for all you're worth.'

Barbara couldn't understand Elizabeth. She was a most unlikely ally and yet she was certainly behaving like one.

Why wasn't she siding with George, blaming her daughter-in-law for the breakdown of her son's marriage? Perhaps she didn't know. Then what was all that doublespeak about?

After Elizabeth had taken the excited children away, Barbara went into town and splashed out on a new dress, a green silk sheath with a pouched bodice gathered into a low waistline, from where floating panels of chiffon fell below the hemline. The sleeves were long and full and the neckline boat-shaped. She had lost weight recently, the plumpness of motherhood had sloughed off her, leaving her with an enviable figure. She had her hair washed and cut into a gentle bob and returned home. In the flurry of packing the children's overnight things, waving them goodbye and shopping, she had no time to think about the evening, and it was only when she returned to the empty house, her slight return of confidence ebbed away.

By the time George came home, she was a quivering mass of nerves and had to force herself to get ready. 'You look wonderful,' he said, when she finally joined him in the sitting room where he was waiting, handsome in white tie and tails, his dark hair carefully slicked back, his big hands cradling a whisky tumbler. 'We should dress up and go out more often.' To which there was no answer.

To Barbara's surprise, everyone seemed genuinely glad to see her. They came and shook her hand, or kissed her briefly, told her she was looking stunning and what a lucky devil George was. Slowly, helped by several glasses of wine, she began to thaw, to stop shaking. Then, across the room, she saw the object of her fear and her heart rushed into her throat and she began to tremble again. Virginia was dressed in a long midnight-blue dress which shimmered with sequins; it was split up one side and revealed shapely calves and feet in high-heeled strap shoes which made her taller than anyone around her. Her blonde hair was swept up into a chignon, emphasising a long neck. She was surrounded by a crowd of men and women and seemed to be holding them in thrall with a story she was telling. Their laughter carried across the room.

Barbara risked a look at George. He was standing motionless, watching Virginia, his expression inscrutable, though a nervous tic worked in his jaw. Had they quarrelled? Had she tired of him? Was that the reason for Barbara's own return to favour? The shaking stopped and she had an inexplicable desire to laugh. Careful, she told herself, don't throw away the advantage you've got.

'Shall we see if we can get something to eat?' he said. 'I didn't have time to eat today and I'm hungry.' He put his hand under her elbow and guided her towards the buffet table set out down one side of the room.

Later she saw Virginia and Donald Browning in earnest conversation. He was chewing the end of his moustache. 'I didn't think Donald would be invited,' she said, picking at the sausage roll on her plate.

'Why not?'

'Because this is a council reception and he left under a cloud.'

'Water under the bridge, my dear. Besides, I believe Virginia invited him. She didn't have a partner and they're both single. And both lonely, I shouldn't wonder.'

She nearly choked on her pastry and had to take a

gulp of wine to wash it down. 'Of course,' she said. 'How nice for them both.' That was what the evening was about, to tell her, so obliquely she might have missed it, that the affair was over, that she needn't worry anymore. There was to be no craven admission, no expression of regret, no gentle reconciliation. Without a word being said she was supposed to put it out of her mind, to forget all about it, and it was done somewhere so public, he knew she wouldn't make a scene. Cunning bastard! 'The lady mayoress is looking a trifle neglected, George. Do you think we should go over and talk to her?'

After speaking to the mayoress, they moved on to chat to Arnold Bulliman, and after that, with Mr Gosport, who had aged dreadfully since she had last seen him. George greeted him as if he were an old friend, pumping his hand and asking him how he was enjoying his retirement. 'You're well out of it,' he said.

'Yes,' he said, smiling gently. 'I'm sure I am.'

'Silly old fool,' George said, as they moved away. 'He'd never have survived another year.'

'Don't you feel just the tiniest bit sorry for him?'

'Of course I do. A whole lot, as a matter of fact. That fire was the last straw. I wouldn't wish that on anyone.'

The crowds were beginning to thin out, goodbyes were being said, coats collected. Barbara left George to go to the cloakroom to pick up her stole. Virginia was there, putting on lipstick. Barbara almost turned and went out again, but then she remembered Elizabeth's words: *You have one advantage that no one else has. You are his wife.* She went forward smiling. 'Virginia, how nice to see you. We saw you across the room but couldn't get near in the crush. It's been a pleasant evening, don't you think?'

'Yes.' The smile was so firmly fixed there wasn't a hint of a wobble. 'How are you, Barbara?'

'I'm very well.' She handed her cloakroom ticket to the attendant. 'I hear you did very well in Paris. George was singing your praises.'

'That was kind of him.'

'Well, that's George all over. Kindness itself. I tell him it will be his undoing one day. People take advantage, you know. Well, must be off, he's waiting in the car.' Picking up her stole, she turned on her heel and walked steadily out of the room, down the corridor and out into the night.

'You took your time,' George said as she got into the car.

'I stopped to talk to Virginia.'

'Virginia?' His voice was carefully controlled. 'What did she have to say?'

'Nothing actually.' And then she spoilt whatever tiny victory she had gained by adding, 'I did all the talking.'

Instead of driving away, he turned towards her. 'What have you been saying to her?'

'Nothing much. Take me home.'

'When you tell me what you said to Virginia. If you've upset her—'

'Me? Upset her?' she shrieked. 'I notice you don't ask if I've been upset.'

'You said she didn't say anything.'

'George, I am sick to death of this cat-and-mouse game. Do you take me for a fool? Do you think I don't know what's been going on?'

'Nothing's going on.'

'You're a liar, George. She was in your room, in your bed in Paris, and it wasn't the first time, was it? How do you think that makes me feel?'

'You're being ridiculous.'

She supposed it was the sort of conversation that had taken place between husbands and betrayed wives throughout history, full of resentment and bitterness and hurt. She had wanted to be different, to be dignified for the sake of her children. And her pride. That she was like every other wife in a similar situation did nothing for her self-esteem. She stared through the windscreen, watched the car park emptying, saw nothing, dare not look at him.

'What are you going to do about it, George?'

'Do about what?'

'Oh, for God's sake, are you going to sit there pretending injured innocence or are you going to behave like a man and face up to what you've done?'

'I am certainly not going to sit here listening to this.' He put the car in gear and roared off, turning out of the car park onto the road much too fast.

'You'll get us both killed if you drive like that,' she said dully.

He slowed down and they drove on in silence, the air between them heavy with accusation, guilt and resentment, and the kind of bleak misery that admits no hope, no end to a situation which is past endurance but which has to be endured.

As soon as he stopped the car at the door, she got out, went into the house and up to their bedroom and slammed the door behind her. She kicked off her shoes, peeled off the lovely dress and flung herself face down on the bed. She knew he would not follow her. She half expected him to go out again, back to his mistress, to tell her the attempt at reconciliation had been a total failure and he was all hers. But he didn't. She heard his heavy step coming up the stairs very slowly and then pass her door and go into the guest room. The door clicked behind him.

She was in the kitchen, sitting over a cup of coffee at six the next morning, when he appeared in his dressing gown. She looked up but did not speak. He poured himself a cup of coffee and sat down opposite her. 'You're up early.'

'There didn't seem any point in staying in bed. Do you want something to eat?'

'I'm not hungry. That buffet last night is still sitting on my stomach. It wasn't that good, was it?'

'No.'

He put his cup down on the saucer with a crash. 'This is getting us nowhere.'

'No, it isn't.'

'What do you want me to say?'

What she wanted was for it never to have happened, to be loved by him as she once was, to go back to a time when the thought of either of them cheating on the other was inconceivable. 'Say what you like, anything that comes into your head. Just talk, can't you? I want to know why, what I've done...'

'You haven't done anything. But then I haven't done anything, either. Not what you think.'

187

She stared at him. 'So, you do at least know what I think?'

'You think I've been having an affair with Virginia.'

'And haven't you?'

'No.' He smiled, sure of his ground again. 'I've been a fool, no doubt of that, but for you to think I've been to bed with her is very hurtful. She is your stepmother. I wanted to help her and help myself as well.'

'Oh, I don't doubt that.'

'Don't be sarcastic, it doesn't suit you. I meant getting her a job as secretary to the chief executive. I have been seeing rather a lot of her, not to make love to her but to get information out of her. I suppose we must have been seen. That's how rumours start. All so silly, really.'

'But you're already a councillor, privy to council business. Why do you want a spy?'

'Oh, Barbara, you can be so priggish sometimes. It's not spying.'

'No, then what do you call it? And why do you need it?'

'I'm a town councillor, not a county councillor, and there's still a lot goes on behind the scenes that never gets made public, wheels within wheels, mutterings behind closed doors, that sort of thing. Old Bulliman confides in Virginia a lot, things that never come out in public meetings, things that are not always passed down to town level...'

Once she might have believed him, but not anymore. 'And she tells you. Not very loyal of her, is it?'

'Depends where your loyalty lies, doesn't it?'

'Do you pay her?'

'No, of course not.'

'I wonder why not?'

The sarcasm was lost on him, or if it wasn't, he chose to take her remark at face value. 'She is simply grateful for what I have been able to do for her, giving her the house, finding her a job, that sort of thing.'

'Grateful enough to climb into bed with you.'

'Barbara, haven't you heard a word I've been saying? That's your trouble, you never listen. What's the good of talking to you...?' He got up and stood looking out of the window onto the parched garden.

'OK, go on. I'm listening.'

'There's nothing more to it.'

'What about Paris?'

He turned back to her. 'Virginia did come to my room one night. She came to discuss something about the negotiations, something that had happened after I left the meeting. I left early to buy the children's presents. And yours too. You did like the perfume, didn't you? You didn't say.'

'I had other things on my mind.'

'Honestly, Barbara, she was only bringing me up to date. I never dreamt...'

She wanted to believe him, wanted it so desperately that she was halfway there, but it was difficult, especially when he mentioned perfume.

'George, you came home reeking of Virginia's perfume. You didn't need to get that close to exchange information, did you?'

He made a valiant effort to look mystified. 'Did I? I don't know how... Oh, yes I do. We were sitting together

189

on the train and she fell asleep with her head on my shoulder.'

'And why couldn't you tell me all this before? Why did you deny there was anyone in your room if it was all so innocent?'

'I don't know. I suppose I didn't want an argument with you, didn't like the idea that you didn't trust me. I didn't see why I should have to explain. It was simpler to deny it.'

He had had all night to marshal his excuses and arguments and he had done it very well. She wondered if he would have been so plausible if she had forced him to talk when they arrived home the night before when they had both been so angry. She poured herself another cup of coffee.

'Well?' he said. 'Do you believe me?'

'I believe you.' She spoke flatly, without conviction, but he accepted it, probably in the same spirit she had accepted what he said, to save tearing each other apart.

'Thank God for that.' He slumped down in the chair opposite her and put his arms on the table. 'I've been a fool, I freely admit it. We'll start again, shall we? Like it used to be. We'll have a holiday, take the children to the seaside. I'll clear up the problems on my desk and we'll go. What do you think?'

'OK, but there's to be nothing like it, ever again. Not ever, George. From now on, there's to be no more underhand dealings, business or otherwise, then there can't be any room for misunderstanding, can there? I won't be able to jump to the wrong conclusions.'

'I promise.' He got up and kissed her cheek. 'I'd better go and get dressed.'

She watched him go, feeling shattered, as if she had been buffeted in a storm at sea, pitched this way and that, fighting waves which threatened to engulf her. She hadn't believed his explanation, but she wanted to believe he was trying to make amends. He knew what he stood to lose and so did she. Believing it could be made right was not weakness, it was strength.

Chapter Seven

'M RS KENNETT? IT'S Mrs Gregory. Are you very busy?'
Barbara had been sitting at the kitchen table,
looking at the remains of breakfast, reluctant to move and
face the day, when the telephone rang. 'Not especially. Why?'

'I've been asked to escort a young lad to Liverpool
Street station and hand him over to another escort. He's
being sent to an approved school in Surrey. I'm afraid I
can't go and I thought of you. You will be paid expenses.'

'When?'

'Tomorrow. I know it's impossibly short notice, but
say you will.' There was a slight pause before she added,
'His name's Tommy White. He needs someone strong but
sympathetic. The poor lad's had a terrible life.'

'Yes, of course I will.' She did not hesitate, did not
even say, 'I'll have to ask my husband,' as she would have
done a few days earlier. A day away from Melsham, away
from George and thoughts of George was just what she
needed.

'Good. I'll meet you at the station.'

Elizabeth was happy to look after the children and George made no objection when she told him that evening. She wondered if he might seize the opportunity to go and see Virginia. 'Stop it,' she told herself. 'Think of something else.'

Tommy was thirteen years old and already an experienced delinquent, Mrs Gregory told her when she brought the boy to the station. He had been put into a children's home because his single mother could not cope with him, and had been in and out of several since then. Usually he ran away, taking the petty cash with him, and was only brought back when he had spent the money and been caught breaking into a house or a shop to replenish his funds. Where he slept when he was out, he never said, shrugging his shoulders and muttering, 'Nowhere,' as if nowhere was a place on a map. His latest escapade had involved setting fire to a house where he had been squatting and nearly killing a tramp who was fast asleep against the boiler in the basement. 'I'm sure you can cope on a one-to-one basis,' she told Barbara, as she handed him over.

Barbara's initial trepidation disappeared as she chatted to him, trying to keep him occupied. He wasn't the tearaway she had expected but a little boy as unhappy and confused as she was herself and her heart went out to him. Feeling sorry for him kept her from feeling sorry for herself. At Liverpool Street, she handed him over to his next escort and, not wanting to go home, took the tube to Chelsea, where Penny had moved into a new flat.

'Do try and come up for my house-warming, she

had told Barbara during a telephone conversation when she moved in. She hadn't gone, of course, half afraid of meeting Simon. He might still be able to make her forget she was a happily married woman. Happily! So much had happened since that last time, she was not sure what happily married actually meant.

Halfway up the steps to the front door she looked up and saw him standing at the top and it stopped her in her tracks. 'Hello,' he said.

She pulled herself together. 'Simon. How nice to see you.' He looked very affluent in a charcoal pinstripe suit of impeccable cut, a white shirt and an expensive-looking silk tie. As she joined him, she noticed the small scar on his left brow, but it certainly wasn't disfiguring.

'You too. Penny's not in. Was she expecting you?'

'No, I was in town and came on the off chance. I haven't seen her for ages and it seemed an ideal opportunity to catch up...' She knew she was speaking too quickly and took a deep breath to slow herself down. 'You don't know how long she'll be?'

'Not long, she knew I was coming.' He paused. 'Look, why don't we go for a cup of tea and come back later. You're not in a hurry, are you?'

She hesitated. Elizabeth would look after the children until George came home, and how often did she have a chance to see Penny? And Simon. There was no harm in it and it would be nice to know that she could still carry on a conversation with someone like him, still grab his attention, feel flattered by it. 'No, I'm not in a hurry.'

'Good.' He put his hand under her elbow in such a natural way, she did not even think about it.

He took her to a small discreet café, with net curtains, white tablecloths, real silver cutlery and muted live music. She looked round as they followed a neatly uniformed waitress to a table.

'Will you be mum?' he said, when the waitress returned with their order and set it on the table: a beautiful china teapot, matching cups and saucers, milk jug, sugar bowl and a plate of cakes. 'You seem to be dressed for the part.'

She looked down at the brown tweed suit, mannish shirt and tie, and comfortable brogues she had decided were appropriate to her role, and laughed. 'It's not very glamorous, is it? But suitable for the job I was doing.' While she poured the tea, she went on to tell him about the escort job, still nervous, still speaking too quickly.

'Very commendable,' he said when she suddenly stopped. 'And I am grateful to the young beggar for bringing you to me, but it's such a fearful waste...'

'Waste, how can you say that? He is a child, who's lost his way—'

'I didn't mean the boy, I meant you, because you're young and beautiful and far too talented to be doing jobs best left to old biddies with nothing better to do.'

'Talented?'

'Yes, of course. I saw that picture you did for Penny, the one of the sea pounding on rocks and the girl sitting on the edge in that diaphanous dress and her hair damp with the spray, watching the waves. She looked sad, as if she was thinking of jumping in. Is that how you felt when you painted it, kind of sad?'

'I can't remember,' she said. But she did remember. She had been feeling miserable because she and George were drifting apart and she had been sure he was seeing someone else, though she had not known it was Virginia. Alone with the children she had tried to keep cheerful for their sakes, and hadn't realised her misery had translated itself to the canvas.

'It's good,' he said offering her the plate of cakes. 'What else have you done?'

She took a jam tart. 'Not much. I don't have the time.'

'You would rather be out doing good deeds.'

'I enjoy it. I meet so many interesting people.'

'Tell me about them.'

Her nervousness gradually evaporated as she told him about the charity, peppering the tale with amusing stories, and from there it was a short step to explaining why she had needed the stimulus of something useful to do. It was easy to talk to him: he was a good listener and his questions, though innocuous in themselves, led her to say far more than she intended, though she shied away from anything more than a superficial mention of George.

Simon noticed it, noticed the emptiness in her eyes, the dark shadows beneath them, the slight hesitancy, and knew she was not happy. Beneath the light-hearted chatter, there was a sense that if she did not keep talking, if she came to a sudden stop, she would be overwhelmed, would become the girl on the rock. He reached across and laid his hand on hers. She did not pull it away.

'You know,' he said, slowly. 'You should come up to town more often, get away just to be yourself for a few hours. You're trying to be all things to all people and the real Barbara has got lost. You have to find yourself again...'

'Oh, Simon, that's silly...' But it wasn't silly, it was exactly how she felt. She laughed. 'Where do you suggest I go to look for myself?'

He grinned, making a game of it. 'Where were you last seen?'

'I don't know. Was it this morning when I left home?'

'No, further back than that. I think it was before you were married, when you were at college. Of course, there may have been sightings of you occasionally since then, times when the young Barbara broke through and showed herself.'

'Like when?'

'At Penny's party.'

'Why then? Because I was stupid enough to let you kiss me? I thought you'd have forgotten that.'

'I haven't forgotten it. Nor do I regret it, except it made you run away. I think you were more frightened of being yourself than of me. I wouldn't have done anything you didn't want to, you know.' His voice was sensuously soft and her heart began to thump in her chest. She gulped her tea. 'The real Barbara would have known that. The real Barbara would have laughed and passed it off; the artificial one ran away.'

'You're talking nonsense. I'm beginning to wish we hadn't started this conversation.'

'That's the pretend Barbara talking. Do you want to know what other sightings there have been?'

She was glad he had moved off that disastrous party. 'Tell me.'

'At your dad's funeral; you came back then. You were the girl I had known, the loving daughter, a little lost, but real, all the same. I could feel your grief.'

'You were very kind. I appreciated it.'

'Glad to be of help.' His words were flippant but his eyes were not. They were studying her closely, asking unspoken questions, questions she did not want to answer, dare not.

'That was the last time you saw me, there can have been no 'sightings', as you call them, since then.'

'There's one. The picture you painted for Penny. That girl is you. Oh, she does not have your colouring, but it's you just the same, yearning for something across the ocean, in the sky, something out of reach...'

'You can't see all that in a picture. And it isn't me.'

'Come back to Penny's flat and I'll prove it to you. She might be back by now.' He beckoned the waitress for the bill. It was exorbitant, but he didn't turn a hair as he paid it.

'We've done nothing but talk about me,' she said, as they strolled along, picking their way through the crowds. 'What have you been up to since we last met? Any children yet?'

'No, that's not on the agenda at the moment. Dodo is pursuing her career.'

'Do you mind?'

'Mind? Why should I? I knew about it before we married. Besides, I have to establish myself too, you know.' Barbara caught the sharp defensiveness in his tone, as if it were a sore point he was tired of explaining. She knew exactly how that felt.

'You look very prosperous.'

'Thank you. I don't do too badly.'

They went up to the flat in the lift and Simon used his own key to let them in, calling as he did so, 'Penny, are you home?'

But there was no one there. He wandered round while Barbara stood hesitantly in the doorway. The apartment was spacious with large high-ceilinged rooms, decorated in muted brown and beige, with additions of dusky pink and the odd touch of lime. Except for one or two pictures, including Barbara's *Girl on a Rock*, the walls were plain. It was quiet and restful.

'She left a note,' he said, returning from the kitchen with a sheet of notepaper. He had taken off his jacket and tie. 'She says she's sorry she missed me, but she's had to go out again.'

'Oh, then I'd better be going.'

'Nonsense. We haven't looked at the picture yet. I really do want to know what you were thinking and feeling when you painted it.'

She had hoped he'd forgotten it. 'But this is Penny's home. Should we...?'

'She won't mind. In fact she'd be annoyed if I didn't entertain you.' He disappeared into the kitchen again and came back with an opened bottle of white wine and two glasses. 'I found this in the refrigerator, it should be all right.' He poured two glasses and left them on mats on a coffee table before coming to stand in front of her. 'Come on, let's have that headgear off, and that jacket. We can't study the picture and make comparisons with you dressed like that.' He pulled off her cloche hat and flung it on a chair, then slipped her jacket off and hung it over the back of another chair. 'This too.' He turned her to face him and gently removed the tie. His fingers, coming into contact with her throat, sent a frisson of something that was half pleasure, half fear, and she wondered what was coming next. If he made another attempt to seduce her what would she do? He smiled, as if reading her thoughts. 'That's better. Now you look human again.'

'Shouldn't you be going home? Won't Dodo be wondering where you are?'

'No, she's filming up in Yorkshire. I was supposed to be spending the evening with Penny, but as you see, she's stood me up. Not that I mind when I have such a marvellous substitute.'

An uncomfortable feeling of disquiet, which had begun when she realised Penny was not at home, grew almost to panic. 'Simon, I really think I should go...'

He grinned ruefully. 'Oh, dear, the real Barbara has disappeared again, just when I thought we might get another sighting.'

'Oh, that silly game...'

'It's not a game, Barbara,' he said, drawing her towards the picture on the wall opposite the Adam fireplace. 'Look at that.'

'What about it? It's nothing very special.'

'Oh, yes it is. Very special. Look at that girl's face. Can't you see it?'

'Me? No. It's your imagination.'

He turned her about so that she was looking in the mirror over the mantelpiece, seeing her own reflection beside that of the picture. 'Now tell me those are not your eyes, that's not your chin and mouth. It's a self-portrait.'

She turned away to pick up her wine and took a mouthful. It was very cold and refreshingly dry. 'It wasn't intentional.'

'No, perhaps not. But it's what those eyes are saying that I find so fascinating. How did you manage to convey so much bleakness, so much emptiness without them looking lifeless and blank? They don't, you know. There is life there. It is crying out to be recognised.'

She gave a cracked laugh. 'Simon, that's fanciful. Eyes are eyes. It's the structure around them, the brows and skin tones, that make the expression. And the mouth.'

'The mouth. Well, I could go on about the mouth too. Smiling and yet not smiling. Oh, it is turned up at the corners; it even shows the teeth a little, but it is a sad mouth. It makes me want to do something about it.'

'Do?' she asked in alarm.

He lifted his hand and gently traced the outline of her mouth with the side of his forefinger. 'I want to see this happy again.'

'I am happy.'

'Are you? Then come and sit down and tell me how you are happy.'

'How?' she asked, allowing him to draw her to the sofa to sit beside him. She was in a kind of daze, aware there was some truth in what he said, wondering how he could be so perceptive. It wasn't the picture – or she didn't think it was – he was using that as a way of illustrating what he meant.

'Yes. Tell me exactly what makes you happy.'

'My children, my home, my friends, my husband...'

'I notice your husband wasn't first on the list.'

'I didn't put them in any particular order. Simon, why are you interrogating me?'

'I want to find the real Barbara underneath that...' He indicated her brown skirt and plain blouse. 'disguise.'

She laughed shakily. 'It isn't a disguise, unless wanting to look practical and efficient, when I'm nothing of the sort, is a disguise.'

'Why did you put them on in the first place?'

'I told you, I was on duty.'

'I didn't mean today.' He poured more wine. 'I meant why did you start doing this so-called duty?'

'I told you that too. To be helpful. There are so many poor and suffering people in the world and I find it fulfilling. It keeps me busy and stops me from feeling sorry for myself.'

'So you do sometimes feel sorry for yourself?'

She hadn't meant to admit that and began to squirm uncomfortably. He was determined to delve deeply, more deeply than she had ever done herself. 'Who doesn't?' she said lightly.

'Tell me about those times too. Tell me about the times when you're bored out of your mind, when you'd like to scream because everyone expects too much of you, when no one seems to understand how you feel.'

She looked at him sharply, surprised that he could have put it so succinctly. 'Why?'

'Because, my dearest love, you need to get it off your chest, and I will never tell a soul.'

The endearment slipped so naturally from his tongue she hardly noticed it, or if she did, it was with a kind of gratitude. 'Are you inviting me to find fault with my life, with George?'

'If it makes you feel better. It might, you know. You'll go home a new woman.'

She laughed suddenly. 'Simon, this is the strangest conversation I've ever had.'

'OK, let's forget that, let's take it as read. I love you, always have.' He lifted her hand and kissed the back of it, passing his tongue over her knuckles and making her shiver. The desire was there, she felt it in every quivering fibre of her. 'I need you as much as you need me. I want to scream sometimes too. I want to roll back the years, to remember when you were a student and I was... Well, let's forget what I was.'

'Why?'

'Because I was a mess. I didn't know what I wanted. I was afraid to be serious, afraid to love, afraid my good fortune would run out on me. And in a way it did, because I lost you.'

He reached over and kissed her on the mouth, a feather-light touch, almost tentative, waiting for her reaction. She did nothing because she could not. Her body was stirring in such a warm, pleasurable way she was savouring it, concentrating on the trickles of sensation which were running through her belly and down her thighs, knowing he had loved her then, still loved her. And she? She was too confused to know what she felt, didn't want to analyse it.

'I could show you what you missed,' he went on. 'What we have both missed.' He took her face in his hands and kissed her properly. She lost her head, her body was doing her thinking, making her let go of her last vestige of self-control.

She clung to him while he undressed her, kissed him as furiously as he kissed her, murmuring endearments between each kiss, each flick of his tongue. He stripped himself off and pulled her down onto the rug, beginning the kissing all over again. She watched the top of his head as his lips roamed down her naked body to her pubic hair and felt a huge, undeniable desire which made her open her thighs and arch her back. She cried out and pulled savagely at his golden hair, demanding he enter her. Now. At once.

'Patience, my love,' he said, settling himself over her, making no move to get inside her, though she could feel him, hard and erect, on her groin. 'We must make it last.'

'I can't.'

He slipped into her and kissed her on the mouth. 'Darling, Barbara,' he said, thrusting into her, making her cry out, gripping him, wanting him. 'How I love you.' And then he stopped talking, until the very end when he cried out once just before he collapsed onto her.

'Oh, my God,' he said when his breath returned. 'I unleashed a whirlwind, didn't I?'

She smiled dreamily. She felt as if she had hurled herself into that tempestuous sea, not knowing whether she would live or die and by some miracle had been washed up on the shore, exhausted but alive. Alive. 'Wasn't that what you intended all along, with this talk of finding the real me?'

'Something like that.' He rolled off her and lay on his back, looking up at the ceiling. 'But not entirely. I was sad knowing you weren't happy. You weren't, were you?'

205

'Not exactly.'

'And now? Do you feel better?'

'Yes, I think I do.' She sat up, her naked body glistening with sweat. 'Do you think I could have a bath?'

'Of course. We'll have one together. Our last act of silliness, and then I think I had better take you to the station, before I disgrace myself all over again.'

'No regrets?' he asked, as he handed her into the train. He was once more the suave businessman and she was the practical Barbara Kennett, wife and mother ready to settle down again, to go on doing the things she had been doing for years, to smother her dreams.

'Have you?'

'Most decidedly not. Whatever you do, my love, don't feel guilty.' He took her hands as she stood at the carriage door, leaning over the open window. 'No one has been hurt, no one at all. The truth is, you needed it. Do you know, that look has gone from your eyes?'

'What look?'

'Like the painting, sad and wistful. Your eyes are as bright as stars. I did that for you. Remember that. And if you ever need me, you know how to find me. You have only to shout and I'll hear you from the other end of the world.'

'Oh, Simon.' She was torn between a reluctance to leave him and the urgent need to see her children. She felt strange, as if what she had just done might change them, might make them love her the less even though they could know nothing about it.

'Goodbye, my love,' he called, as the train drew away.

'One day...' His last words were lost as the train took her from him.

She went into the carriage and found herself a seat. Now she had to go back, wanted to go back, wanted to cuddle her children and be reconciled with her husband. Simon was right, no one had been hurt by what they had done; it did no good to feel guilty. If anything, she felt better able to cope, knowing that she was still attractive, still able to generate passion in someone like Simon, who could have the pick of goodness knows how many glamorous girls, and who had a lovely wife.

What about his wife, she wondered? Were they happy together? She hadn't asked and he hadn't volunteered the information, though she didn't think he was keen on her being away so much, just as she didn't like George never being at home. Two people with a niggling grievance, that's what they'd been, two people looking for solace.

She arrived home in a cheerful frame of mind, explained that she was late because she had stayed in London to see Penny. And life went on.

Honest George, he called himself, when electioneering to be returned to the town council, but all that meant was that he was extra careful, so careful he hadn't seen Virginia for months, except in the distance, flitting down the corridor of the county council offices or going into the café on the market for a cup of coffee, or, worst of all, working in her garden when he went past on his way to or from the golf club on a Saturday.

There had been days, early on, when he had been tempted to call, especially as she telephoned him at work and left messages for him to get in touch, messages that became more and more urgent, more pleading, as the days and weeks passed. But to give in would be fatal. He would never be strong enough to put her from him a second time, to harden his heart to her tears all over again. He had told her it was only until the gossip died down and he had got in with Bulliman, then they could get together again. It was cowardly, he knew, but he hoped she might realise for herself that it couldn't, mustn't, happen. He and Barbara had established a kind of equilibrium, a contentment which had nothing of the passion and abandonment of a love affair, but was easy to live with. Let Barbara do her good works: it all helped with the image he wanted to create. He was even prepared to put himself out, to get the children's tea or baby sit so that she could go to one of her charity committee meetings. He decided to give her a car for her birthday, it might make up for the fact that he had an evening engagement and would not be able to take her out.

Barbara celebrated her twenty-seventh birthday quietly at home with the children while the second-hand Austin Seven sat in the garage. The gift pleased her because it meant she could take the children out when George was too busy to accompany them. The new George was very little different from the old one: he was still out nearly every evening and, she suspected, still oiling wheels, but thank goodness he was not still seeing Virginia and for that she was grateful. Had he, like her, needed something to ease the tension? The memory of her meeting with Simon filled her with a mixture of pleasure and guilt, which she tried not to dwell on. 'Don't feel guilty,' he had said. 'No one's been hurt.'

After she had put the children to bed, she went to work on a new painting. It was a beach scene with two children in the foreground building a sandcastle – her children – Alison with her smooth, dark hair tied in a ponytail, Nick with his corn-blonde curls. She put all her love into those two and it showed in the brightness of their faces, the roundness of their golden limbs, the way they laughed. There was a Punch and Judy nearby and lots of smiling faces and people sitting on deckchairs. The sea was blue and calm, just rippling towards the shore, and the sky was almost cloudless. Cloudless skies were boring, she decided, putting in a few soft puffs of white and a small biplane trailing a message. She hadn't decided what that message should be before she discovered she was pregnant and the euphoria vanished.

How was she going to tell George? They had not planned another child and he had always used a sheath. Now she had to convince him that there must have been something wrong with one of them. It was not a decision she reached without a great deal of heart-searching, but the alternative was too terrible to contemplate. George might expect to be forgiven for being unfaithful but she knew, as surely as she knew her husband's many moods, that she would never be granted the same leniency.

She told him one morning while he was eating his breakfast toast. It was early and the children were still in bed. It had to be then because she had to run from the table to be sick and he asked her what was wrong.

'Pregnant?' he echoed. 'But you can't be.'

'There must have been a flaw in one of the sheaths. They aren't guaranteed one hundred per cent, are they? That's what you said when I fell for Alison.'

He didn't comment on how that had come about. 'Are you sure? You're not just late?'

'I'm sure.' She poured herself a cup of tea and sat looking at it, knowing she would be sick again if she drank it.

He studied her for a long time, watching her face, reading her apprehension in her expression. For one heart-stopping moment she wondered if he would deny it had anything to do with him, accuse her of going with someone else, but it never entered his head. And now the guilt she was supposed not to feel weighed her down. It could still be George's child: the sheath could have been faulty, but that argument didn't make her feel any better. She had no business feeling hard done by over George and Virginia when her sin was just as great. She had forfeited her right to feel aggrieved.

'When's it due?'

'End of February.' She was doing her best to keep her voice light but her heart was hammering. How was she going to bear it? But telling him, without knowing for sure the child was not his, would be flinging away their very last chance of happiness. And it wasn't as if it had been a proper affair, something strong enough for her to want to destroy a marriage and split up a family. She stood up and went behind his chair to put her arms round his neck and kiss his cheek, smooth and smelling of aftershave. 'George, I do love you, you know.'

'I know, my dear. And I love you too. And the new little one will round off our family nicely. I wonder what the other two will think of it.'

It was the first time for ages that he had said he loved her. Why now? Why say it now, when she had this horrible cloud of guilt hanging over her? Was that how he felt about Virginia, overwhelmed by guilt and unable to speak of it? What a pair they were! 'They'll love it,' she said.

He stood up and picked up his jacket from the back of his chair. 'I must be off. There's a finance committee meeting tonight, so I'll grab a bite in The Crown after work.'

He pecked her cheek and left by the front door, picking up his briefcase on the way. She watched him go, then went back to the kitchen to sit with her elbows on the table and her chin in her hands, staring into space. The boot was well and truly on the other foot now.

Ought she to tell Simon? What good would it do if she did? Would he even want to know? Would it make her feel any less guilty? Would it make George a different kind of person? But if he found out... Supposing the baby looked like Simon? Supposing some time in the future it all came out? But supposing it was George's, after all? It could be. She must keep her secret.

Rita carried the tray over to where George sat in a corner of the bar and set the plate of mixed grill in front of him. 'Anything else, Mr Kennett?'

'No, thank you. I'll have another beer, though.'

She picked up his empty glass and went to pull him another pint. When she took it over to him, he was no longer alone. Virginia Bosgrove was sitting beside him. She was picking chips from his plate and eating them while he talked, his head lowered towards her. Oh, there was no doubt about what was going on. Did Mrs Kennett know her husband was such a bastard? She suddenly remembered the day she had met Barbara standing outside Virginia Bosgrove's house, transfixed with shock by something the woman next door had said. Poor Mrs Kennett!

After he came out of prison, Colin had told her about the arson, hinted at other things George Kennett would not like made public, but she had thought he was exaggerating or making things up to make himself look big. Big he certainly was, but he wasn't a philanderer. He might give her a thump now and again, but he hadn't gone with another woman, not in Melsham, not on his own doorstep. She put the beer on the table in front of George but he barely glanced at her.

'You shouldn't have come here,' George said. After all the trouble he had taken to avoid her, not answering her letters and phone calls, trying to put her from his mind, she had to track him down, today of all days. 'Don't you care that we'll be seen together?'

'Not anymore. You said give it a few months, time for

Barbara to get used to the idea, give you time to get in with Bulliman, then we could be together. It's been over four months.'

'Do you think I haven't noticed?' he hissed at her. 'Do you think I don't count the days since I last saw you? To speak to and hold, I mean, not in the distance going about your work: that doesn't count.'

'Then why is it taking so long? Surely Barbara can't still want you...?'

'Funnily enough she does.'

'You did tell her?' She stopped picking at his food and leant towards him so that her long hair fell over her face. She scooped it out of the way with her hand. Idly he wondered why she had started wearing it loose. He didn't like it like that. He preferred it in a chignon which made her look cool and sophisticated, highlighting the contrast between the public Virginia and the unfettered Virginia in bed, which was a Virginia he liked to keep to himself. 'George, you did tell her?'

'Of course I did. I told you I would, didn't I?'

'Then why won't she release you?'

'It's difficult, especially now.' He paused. 'She's pregnant.'

'Oh, my God! And you said... How could you, George?'

'I couldn't live with her and not...'

'Why not? If she knows about us, knows you would rather be with me, then she's perverted to go on wanting you.' She paused to look him in the eye, but he avoided it. 'You didn't tell her, did you? You haven't said a word to her.'

213

'Yes, I have.'

'Not plainly enough, evidently. Look here, George, either you want to be with me and nothing else matters, or you want to stay married to Barbara and be bored to death for the rest of your life. Which is it?'

'Do you need to ask?'

'Yes, or I wouldn't have. Oh, George, if only you knew what a hell the last four months have been for me, pretending nothing is wrong, being friendly to Barbara, not going to town council meetings in case I bump into you...'

'I shan't be on the council long, if there's a whiff of scandal.'

'Is that more important than loving me?'

'No, of course not.'

'I need to know, George, I need to be sure.' She paused. 'There's someone... Well, he likes me and he's free and... Oh, George, I'm hellishly tempted.'

The thought of someone else making love to her, taking possession of that beautiful body, brought him up short. His heart was pounding and his hands began to sweat. He couldn't let her go. 'But I've told you, over and over again,' he said. 'Look, let me pay the bill and we'll go somewhere... I've got an hour or so to spare.'

It was when they got up and left together Rita knew she had been right. She turned back to serve another customer and noticed that Colin was propping up the bar a little further along and he had seen them too. She was hardly surprised when he came home from work a couple of days later and told her he had been promoted and given a pay rise. In fact, he had been put on the salaried staff: he was one of the managers, paid once a month, with two weeks' holiday and an annual bonus.

Chapter Eight

BARBARA RANG FOR a cab in the early afternoon of 21st February 1928. It had been a dreary, raw week, when the sky was grey and overcast and even the fields and gardens seemed colourless, a waiting time between winter and spring, not freezing as it had been a few weeks earlier, but full of cold dampness, the sort of week which made you feel as if summer would never come again. But earlier that day, the sun had broken briefly through the mist and it was during that short spell of sunshine she felt her first contraction and knew that she was about to bring a new life into the world.

Because Alison and Nick were getting old enough to ask awkward questions, they had decided the baby should be born in the cottage hospital. She called a cab and asked the driver to take her round by Victoria Terrace to alert Elizabeth who was going to look after the children for her. Then she went on to the hospital alone. She didn't ring George's office. She wanted to see the baby first, to hold it and look at it and have it all to herself for a brief time before he came claiming them both. She had counted back the weeks carefully and knew the day it had been conceived, almost knew the hour. It was bang on time; she had known that morning when she woke that today was the day. She told the nurses that her husband was out of town and could not be reached until the evening.

Jeremy John was born a few minutes after nine o'clock and two minutes later was put into her arms. He had very little hair but what there was of it was nearly white, and when he opened his eyes, they were as blue as cornflowers. There was a huge lump in her throat. She touched his hand, ran her fingers round his tiny fingers, felt his chubby thighs and perfect toes, gazed at his little pink face and smiled stupidly. 'He's lovely,' she said, almost in surprise, as if she couldn't believe she could be so blessed. 'Perfect.'

She had almost managed to convince herself that George was her baby's father, but looking at the infant lying contentedly in her arms, she knew he was not. There was not a single feature to remind her of her husband but any number to make her think of Simon: the fair hair, the clear blue eyes, the shape of his jaw. She wanted him beside her to share in the wonder of what they had brought into life, but that she could not do. Not ever.

The sister came into the room. 'Your mother-in-law rang a few minutes ago,' she told Barbara. 'She's going to try and get in touch with your husband.'

He arrived an hour later almost hidden behind a huge bouquet of hothouse flowers. He laid them on the bed and stooped to kiss her cheek. 'How are you?'

'Fine. How are you? And the children?'

'Fine. They were almost too excited to go to bed when I told them they had a baby brother.'

'What do you think of Jeremy John? I've decided he's going to be Jay-Jay. It suits him, don't you think?'

He moved over to the cot at the foot of her bed to look down at the infant. 'He's a grand little chap.' He reached out and stroked a finger round the baby's face and she wanted to scream out, don't touch him, he's mine, not yours. 'My goodness, what blue eyes he's got. Like a summer sky.'

He reached into the cot and picked Jay-Jay up, bringing him to her bed, sitting on the side of it, cradling the infant in his arms, looking down at him with a delighted smile. She felt the tears coming again and could not stop them. They rained silently down on the coverlet, tears of regret, of guilt, of sorrow that something which had once been so good, so precious, had turned so sour.

'Barbara, why are you crying? Is something wrong?'

'I'm being silly,' she said, attempting a smile. 'Don't worry about it.'

He stood up and put the baby into her arms. 'I'd better get back.' He bent to kiss her. 'Cheer up, old thing. You'll be all right, once you get home.'

As soon as he had gone she began to breastfeed her baby, holding him almost too tightly, sobbing her heart out. She wanted Simon. She wanted him to share this moment, but she had shut him out too.

Breakfast was always a busy time in the Kennett household. George rose early to be in his office before eight; Alison and Nick had to be bullied out of bed, made

219

to dress and eat some breakfast and Jay-Jay cried pitifully for his first feed of the day. George mislaid folders he had been studying the night before, the children lost socks and spelling lists; milk was spilt, toast burnt, and dirty nappies had to be changed and the baby bathed. It was a miracle when it all sorted itself out: George left for work, Alison and Nick were dressed in their outdoor clothes and Jay-Jay, fed and wrapped up, was put in his pram for the short walk to the school. And then, blessed, blessed peace, she was alone with only the baby for company and he was good as gold, sleeping or kicking his feet in his pram while she got on with the household chores.

She loved her children, loved hearing stories of school and their special friends, listening to their grievances, monstrous in their eyes, watching them eat, indulging them more often than she ought; but her own personality was being overwhelmed, her own needs ignored. It wasn't as if she and George had a life together in the evenings when they could talk to each other of the day's happenings, have a little grumble, commiserate with each other, laugh together. He didn't belong to her, he belonged to his workers, to the voters, to the council, to Virginia; Barbara came way down on the list.

She didn't think he had given Virginia up, though she conceded he had tried in the beginning. She had tried too, been especially loving, but something had happened to make him backslide and she had no idea whose fault it was. She took trouble with her appearance, didn't slop around in a dressing gown, made him appetising meals, though half the time they were ruined when they had to be kept hot for hours, and she tried to make interesting conversation when he came home. That was the hardest of all because there was nothing she could say which didn't sound like a complaint or an accusation. And how could she complain when her own guilt hung over her like a cloud? This was what their marriage had come to: it was as if they were standing on either side of a chasm so wide that even when they stretched out their arms towards each other, their fingers didn't touch.

George came home unexpectedly one day during the Easter holidays and found her trying to cope with three fractious children with colds, a mountain of washing and ironing and nothing done towards a meal. Alison had been sick on the sofa, Nick was at his naughtiest because he didn't feel well and Jay-Jay was crying to be picked up. She had cleaned up the sofa but it was damp and the smell still clung to it. She half expected him to rail at her for her incompetence, to tell her that other mothers coped with a house and three children. Instead he said, 'We'll get you some help.'

And so Kate Watkins arrived. She was in her fifties and a widow who had brought up four children, all of whom were off her hands. Her presence gave Barbara a new lease of life. She renewed her charitable work because it was needed as much as ever, and finished painting *Children on a Beach*, adding a tubby Jay-Jay to the scene, propped in a pushchair, his blue eyes intent on the Punch and Judy show.

George decided it did his image as a self-made man, the entrepreneur who provided Melsham with several hundred jobs, no harm at all to be seen to have a luxurious lifestyle. Employing a housekeeper, which was the title he used when referring to Mrs Watkins, was just the beginning. His affair with Virginia, though still a compelling force in his life, had been muted and kept very much under wraps. Virginia didn't like it, but she acquiesced, knowing she would lose him if she complained. He was like a juggler with half a dozen balls in the air at once and that gave him a great buzz; he couldn't imagine a time when he might drop one of them.

He bought the premises next door to the yard. 'I'm going into retailing,' he told Barbara. 'If people can't afford to have work done by the professionals, then we'll sell them the materials to do it themselves and when they botch it, we'll be there to put the mistakes right. Everyone knows it costs more to undo someone else's bad workmanship than start from scratch. Profit margins will be tight, but if I keep a firm hold on expenses, it'll work. After all, there's only Doughty's tin-pot hardware store in Melsham, so we'll be filling a gap in the market and providing a service.'

Barbara's reaction was to think 'Poor Mr Doughty', but she knew better than to voice it. The work went ahead and Kennett's became one of the largest employers in Melsham, a fact which was not lost on his fellow councillors or the workers themselves. He was swimming against the economic tide and seemed to be making headway. He was popular with the man in the street, who saw only his carefully nurtured public image. 'My door is always open,' he was very fond of saying, but in trying to live up to that and keep his business flourishing, he had little time for his wife and family.

The problems of the nation, characterised by high unemployment and workers' discontent, were discussed in the pubs and clubs and on football fields. The need for something to be done was the chief subject of conversation when a general election was called early in 1929. George was in the thick of campaigning on behalf of the Conservatives and Barbara found herself pushing leaflets through letter boxes while Jay-Jay laughed at her from his pram.

'You may laugh,' she said to him one day when she was busy working the Newtown Estate. 'It's not your feet dropping off. I don't know why I do it. I don't even believe what's in them.' She bent over to tickle him, smiling when he chuckled. 'Don't you tell a soul I said that.'

'Dear, dear, talking to yourself, that's a bad sign.'

She whipped round to find Rita grinning at her. She was wearing a three-quarter-length red coat and a black skirt which was only a little longer and revealed quite a lot of black-stockinged calf. A deep cloche hat with a turned-down brim was pulled down over her red hair but it was only partially successful in hiding a black eye and a bruised cheek. 'Rita, what happened to you?'

'I walked into a door. Trust me not to look where I'm going. What are you doing out this way?'

'Delivering these leaflets for George. The trouble is I wonder how many of them are actually read and whether I'm wasting my time.' She laughed suddenly. 'I shouldn't be saying that, should I?'

'Don't worry, I won't tell. Why don't you dump the rest and come and have a coffee?'

'Oh, I couldn't do that, dump them I mean.'

'Who's to know? 'Ere, give 'em to me. I'll deliver them, then you can come with a clear conscience.'

They transferred the box of envelopes from the pram to Rita's bag and set off for the café on the marketplace. Barbara had no idea where the leaflets would end up; she felt sure they would not be posted through letter boxes. She pushed the pram into the café and found a table in a corner where it would not be in the way, while Rita beckoned to the waitress.

'You've got a bruise there too,' Barbara said, nodding towards a purple mark on Rita's arm just above the wrist. 'Was it the same door?'

If it had been anyone else making that remark, Rita would have told her to mind her own business, but she couldn't say that to Barbara, who hadn't a spiteful bone in her body and had troubles enough of her own. In spite of their different backgrounds, they had become friends, not in any close sort of way, but they met now and again when they were out shopping. They always chatted easily, drawn together by some hidden empathy neither had tried to put into words. Nor had they told their respective husbands, knowing it would cause friction. 'Yeah, well, this door had hands.' She laughed and put her hand to her lip when she found it hurt.

'Oh, Rita, I'm so sorry. Why do you stay with this door with hands?'

'I don't know. It's like a habit you can't break.' She shrugged. 'What else would I do? Where would I go? And you know how it is, a sort of habit you can't break out of.'

Barbara knew exactly what she meant. 'There must be something you could do.'

'There isn't, you know. I've thought of going to the police, but that'd mean going to court and that's not what I want. I just want 'im to stop using me for a punch bag, but that's askin' for the moon because he doesn't know any better. He had a rough life as a kid. Lost his parents and was brought up by foster parents. They turned 'im out when he began to grow up and cause a bit of trouble.'

'But that's no excuse...'

'No, but I weren't no angel, I tricked him into marrying me...'

'How?'

'I seduced him and got myself pregnant, so he had to marry me...'

'Is that what you wanted? Marriage, I mean.'

'Yes. I wanted to get out of the life I was in. My mother, well...' People like Barbara had no idea how the other half lived. 'Don't get me wrong, she was, and is, a good mother in her way, but she never had a penny from the bastard who fathered me. I never knew him and she'd never tell me his name. But you don't want to know all this.'

'If it helps to tell me, then I'm interested. It won't go any further, I promise.'

'It's ancient history anyway. Ma got pregnant but the feller was married and he didn't want to know, so she was stuck. With a kid hanging onto her apron strings, she had no chance of finding work or a husband, not one of her own anyway, so is it any wonder she did what she did?

She had to keep me fed and clothed. I never went hungry but I had a helluva lot of uncles.' She smiled crookedly, almost defiantly. 'It didn't bother me. It wasn't until one of the uncles started touching me up when I was alone, I realised what was what...'

'How old were you?'

'Twelve or thirteen, don't remember exactly. I kicked him in the balls and he let go. Ma came in then and threw him out and then she came down on me, said I'd tempted him, that if I weren't careful I'd end up like her. I didn't understand. It was then she told me the truth. I'd often heard people say "like mother like daughter", but I'd taken it as a compliment. Mum was pretty, you see, with lovely dark hair, not ginger like mine, and she was nearly always laughin'. But you had to – laugh, I mean – if you were going to give someone a good time. That's what she called it. When I look back I don't know how I managed to stay so ignorant, but once I did know, I made up my mind I wasn't going to end up like her and the only way I could think of preventin' it was to get married. I met Colin when I was seventeen. I was pretty in those days and sexy with it and...' She gave another grin. 'I deliberately set out to get pregnant.'

'What happened?'

'Oh, he married me, but the baby died. Colin couldn't cope. We were both too young. He lost his job and the one after that and then he began drinking and taking his frustration out on me. He'd get disgusted with hisself and leave me to go looking for jobs in other places, but he always came home when he lost 'em and, daft bugger that I am, I always took him back. That's when I fell for Zita. Born in 1914, she was. I don't know where he went after that, then seven years later he turned up again. Seven years, I ask you! When he first got a job at Kennett's, he promised to turn over a new leaf and for more'n a year he didn't lay a finger on me, then off 'e went again. There was some sort of trouble...' She stopped, realising that Barbara probably didn't know the truth and it was not her place to let the cat out of the bag. 'He's not been too bad since he came back. Your husband gave him another job, so he's stuck around.'

'So, what happened this time?'

'Oh, it was something and nothing. He said he needed a drink and started groping in my bag for the money. There was only a pound and a bit of loose change and I needed it, so I grabbed it back. That did it. He gave me a good going over and took the money anyway, I might just as well have given it to him in the first place.'

'Have you tried talking to him about it, explaining how you feel?'

'Course I 'ave. It's like talking to a brick wall.' She laughed and drained her cup. 'Or a door.'

'I'm sorry. I wish I could help.'

'Oh, don't mind me, love, I'll get the better of the bugger yet.' She spoke so cheerfully it was difficult to take her seriously, which was, Barbara supposed, Rita's way of coping. 'Now, tell me what you've been up to. Apart from shoving bits of paper through letter boxes, I mean.'

Barbara found a few amusing anecdotes about the children and by the time she arrived at the school gates at a quarter to four, having drunk two cups of coffee and gorged herself on cream cake, she was feeling more cheerful.

Her truancy, which is what it felt like, or her vote, couldn't have made any difference to the outcome of the election. Although for the first time Labour under Ramsay MacDonald had the greatest number of MPs, they could not govern without the support of the Liberals and Melsham remained staunchly Conservative. George and Barbara were invited to the reception to thank those who had helped the successful candidate.

Barbara didn't want to go. She had done nothing to help, had in fact sabotaged the effort by handing her leaflets over to Rita. And she certainly hadn't voted for the man. He was too much like George, full of bluster and his insincere smile sickened her. But as she could not give these reasons to George, she dressed in a gown of blue chiffon with a hemline of handkerchief points and accompanied her husband to the Conservative Club, where an orchestra played background music and everyone talked too loudly, mostly about the idiocy of the electorate and the impossibility of getting anywhere with a Labour government.

'What can a woman know about Labour relations?' George said derisively referring to the appointment of the first woman to sit in the cabinet with the job of Minister of Labour.

'I should think as much as a man,' Barbara said.

'Women should stay at home and mind the house,' he said, reminding her of her own abortive attempt to go out to work, out of the question now. What with her children, her charitable work and the social demands of her husband, she had no time for anything else, no time to go to the theatre or see a film, no time to wander round

228

art galleries and museums, once a favourite pastime. She had even missed Penny's last film. Most films were talkies nowadays and she could hear as well as see her friend.

It was strange that they had remained such good friends when their lifestyles were so different. They did not see each other often but they wrote and talked on the telephone. Of all the people she knew, Barbara felt she could confide most to Penny, though she wondered if it would have made any difference if Penny had known what happened in her flat the last time she had seen Simon.

'Mrs Kennett, is no one taking care of you?'

George had gone and it was Donald Browning who stood beside her. He was no taller than she was in her heels, and his face was homely rather than handsome, especially with that straggly moustache. George's hints that he was interested in Virginia seemed not to have any basis in truth, unless, of course, he had realised where his competition was coming from and had dropped out of the running. He indicated the empty glass in her hand. 'Can I get you another drink? Something to eat perhaps?'

She handed him the glass. 'Thank you.'

He disappeared through the noisy throng but was soon back, carrying two full glasses. 'There, not a drop spilt.'

'Thank you, Donald. Now, tell me all your news. I don't see much of you these days.'

'We've been very busy, Mrs Kennett, what with the building work and the new shop, and of course, George is often on council business, so I'm more or less in charge.'

'But you must have a private life, a little time to call your own.' She was blatantly prying and wondered if he knew it.

'Not a lot.' He smiled. She was one of those really nice people, who made you feel as if whatever you had to say was important. She was interested and interesting. The dress she was wearing tonight emphasised a figure just on the full side of perfect and though she wore a little make-up it was not obvious. George Kennett might be the bee's knees when it came to running a business, but he was a bastard where women were concerned. How did he get away with it? 'But that's how I've wanted it, ever since my wife died,' he told her. 'George was good to me over that. I owe him a lot.'

'I'm sure he doesn't think of it like that.'

He knew that was exactly how George *did* think of it. 'It's all right for me, I have no one waiting at home for me, but it must be hard for you, seeing so little of your husband.'

'But if my husband is a public figure, then that's one of the things I must accept, isn't it?'

'You are very tolerant, if I may say so, Mrs Kennett. George is a very lucky man.'

'Oh, enough of the flattery. How did we get on to talking about me anyway? I asked you about yourself.'

'There's nothing to tell. I did start seeing someone, a year or two ago, but nothing came of it. She turned to me when the man she was seeing packed her in. I said I could live with that, but she never really gave him up and it all started up again.'

She had asked and she shouldn't complain when the answer was not the one she wanted to hear. But every fibre of her was crying out in despair. Had he mentioned it on purpose to warn her? He was standing beside her, chewing on his moustache, and though his face was carefully expressionless, the knuckles on the hand that clutched his glass were white. She couldn't continue to stand there, on the edge of a mass of rejoicing, half-drunk people; she had to get away before the smile she had fixed on her face slipped. She put her glass down on a table behind her. 'I had better go and look for George. His mother is looking after the children and I don't like to keep her up after midnight.'

She could not see her husband in the room and went out into the corridor. There was a gleam of light under a door further along. She walked towards it and opened it. She wasn't being deliberately stealthy, but that was how it must have seemed. They sprang apart, but not quickly enough. She had seen the tousled hair, the flushed faces, the unbuttoned clothing. Virginia was backed against a desk, her breasts were half exposed and her skirt was up round her thighs.

'Barbara!' George hurriedly began buttoning his flies but it was too late. She turned and left them. There were no words for what she wanted to say, nothing she wanted to hear.

He went to follow her, but Virginia pulled on his arm. 'Let her go.'

'I can't.' He pulled himself from her grasp and went after his wife.

'If you go after her, George, don't think of coming back,' she called after him. 'I've had enough of this cloak and dagger stuff.' But he was already striding down the corridor away from her.

* * *

231

Barbara went home in a taxi, asking the driver to wait and take Elizabeth home. By the time George arrived, she was alone and sitting on the sofa in the drawing room with a large tot of whisky in her hand. She couldn't seem to gather her thoughts at all. It was as if someone had punched her in the stomach and followed it up with a blow to the head. While nothing had been said aloud, she had managed to live with her suspicions, to pretend the affair was long over, but to have the confirmation of her own eyes was tearing her apart.

He stood in the doorway, watching her, expecting a tirade, preparing himself to deal with it, though the explanations which had fallen so convincingly from his tongue before would not come to his rescue this time. He stepped into the room and stood in front of her. 'What can I say? I'm sorry.'

'Sorry?' She looked up at him. 'You mean sorry that you were caught?'

'No. That I've hurt you.'

'Hurt me?' There was venom in her voice. 'You've destroyed me.'

'Oh, for God's sake, don't be so melodramatic. You're hurt I know, but to say I've destroyed you is rubbish.'

'You have. You've made me into a boring, uninteresting housewife, a mindless mother, with nothing to say for herself, no words but what you put into her mouth. In order to please you, I've become the woman you wanted me to be, but instead of being satisfied with your creation, you've turned away, looked elsewhere for your pleasure. It's not fair, George. I hate you for it.' And suddenly she meant it.

'It wasn't like that. I didn't mean it to happen.'

'Then you had better tell me what it was like. Why on earth did you marry me?'

Why had he married her? He tried to bring it back, the first time he had seen her in Cambridge, the frisson of excitement when he had learnt she came from Melsham and that her father was a somebody, respected in the community and wealthy to boot. She represented a challenge. And he could never resist a challenge, it was part of his nature. And she had loved him; the glow of pride that had given him seemed small in comparison with the soaring ecstasy he had experienced with Virginia. The trouble was he only knew that in hindsight. At the time... Oh, what was the use, he'd messed it all up. 'I loved you,' he said. 'I still love you.'

'What?' She looked up into his face for the first time and wished she hadn't. 'You're surely not going to tell me Virginia means nothing to you? It's been going on too long for that to be true.'

'No, I'd be lying if I said that. But it's different.'

'Yes, she's not your wife. She's your mistress. Do you lie in bed and laugh at the way you pulled the wool over my eyes?'

'No, of course not.' He went to the cabinet, poured himself a drink and refilled her glass when she held it up to him.

'I don't believe you. I don't believe a word you say anymore.'

'I hated deceiving you. I tried to end it several times, but she kept on at me, writing, ringing me up, waylaying me. I just gave in. I was weak.'

'Weak?' She laughed harshly. 'You're the strongest man in Melsham. You can manipulate anyone and everyone, including Virginia, including me. Well, not anymore.'

'What are you going to do?'

'I don't know. I can't think straight tonight. I've had too much to drink. Tomorrow I'll decide. But I tell you this, I'm not going to stand by and do nothing like I did before.'

'No, I suppose not. I've been a fool. Will it help if I say it's over between Virginia and me and it won't happen again?'

'You mean you'll be more careful. God, George, how could you? Anyone might have come into that room, not just me.'

He knew that, had known it at the time, but Virginia had been all over him, even in the crowd at the party, hissing at him that she didn't care who saw them. He'd taken her into the office to calm her down. She wanted their affair made public, believing it was the only way she would get him to leave his wife. It made him so furious he had grabbed her by both arms, wanting to shake some sense into her. Instead he had kissed her, brutally, without tenderness. But that only served to rouse him, giving him a monumental erection. He forgot where he was, forgot everything outside their two entwined bodies and his need to get inside her. If Barbara hadn't come in, would he have gone the whole hog, made love on that dusty desk, or even the floor? He felt weak at the knees over the risk he'd taken.

Everything he had worked and schemed for, his business, his work on the council, his ambition, his family had all been put at risk. And for what? It was a question he couldn't answer. Animal magnetism? Chemistry? Lust?

Or was it true love? But he loved his wife too. And he adored his children. He sat down beside her, but refrained from touching her. 'Barbara, I am utterly ashamed. It will not happen again. I'll never go near her again. You have my word on it.'

'Your word?' She gave a cracked laugh. 'That means nothing to me.'

'Then how can I prove I mean it?'

'You can't.' She put her glass down and got unsteadily to her feet. She was drunker than she realised: her knees were wobbly and she felt sick. 'I'm going to bed.'

She clung onto the banister rail as she stumbled up the stairs, then wove an erratic course to her bedroom, leaning on walls and grabbing hold of furniture on the way. She slammed the bedroom door behind her and collapsed, fully dressed, across the bed.

She woke in the early hours of the morning with a monumental headache and her evening dress all rucked up round her. She took it off and flopped back onto the bed, lying sleepless for hours. But she couldn't stay there, much as she wanted to. Another day was dawning and the children needed her. She washed, dressed and went downstairs, her limbs obeying her mechanically but she felt numb.

George had gone. The remains of his breakfast were still on the table, an empty coffee mug, a plate with toast crumbs on it. There was also a note for her propped against the marmalade pot. 'We'll talk tonight. Don't go away. I love you.'

She smiled grimly. Don't go away. Where the hell did he think she could go?

Penny's telephone call later that morning seemed like an answer to a prayer. She had taken the children to school, chatted with the other mums, listened to them gossiping and then come home with Jay-Jay to find Kate busily at work in the kitchen. Kate wanted to talk, to ask if she had had a nice time at the party, wondered aloud if she ought to try and press the evening frock she had found thrown on a chair or whether it would be better sent to the cleaners. The sound of the telephone came to Barbara's rescue and she hurried into the hall to answer it.

'Oh, Penny, thank heaven it's you.'

'Why? What's wrong?'

'Everything. Nothing. Oh, I'm just fed up, don't take any notice. How are you?'

'I'm fine. There is something wrong, isn't there?'

'I can't talk about it. Not now. Not yet.'

'Then come up and see me. That's why I rang. I thought you might like to come to the premiere of *Dragon Castle* on Saturday and stay for the party afterwards. I can give you a bed for the night.'

Barbara hadn't realised the film was near completion, let alone ready for release; it only seemed five minutes since Penny had told her she had landed the part. 'I don't think I'll be very good company.'

'Course you will. If you need to get away a bit, what better opportunity?'

'What makes you think I need to get away?'

'Sixth sense. So how about it?'

'There's the children...'

'Let George look after them for once. I won't take no for an answer. Come early, give yourself time to relax and get yourself up in your glad rags. I want you on top form.'

'Oh, Penny, you're a tonic.'

'Good. See you Saturday. Bye for now.'

Barbara put the phone down and returned to the kitchen. 'Kate, if George is busy on Saturday can you look after the children and stay overnight? I've been invited to Penny Barcliffe's new film premiere.' She managed a smile. 'I'd really like to go but I'm not sure what my husband has booked.'

'Don't worry, Mrs Kennett, I'll look after the children. They're no trouble at all.'

'Thank you. Can you keep an eye on Jay-Jay now? I want to take that dress to the cleaners and book a hair appointment.'

She gathered up the dress, stuffed it into a shopping bag and left Kate happily washing the kitchen floor, watched by Jay-Jay from his playpen where he stood rattling the bars. George may not like her plans but to hell with George! Why should she go on putting him first, when he so obviously didn't care a toss about her? If she was going to be more assertive, now was a good time to start. She might even stay longer than one night. It would serve him right if she stayed away altogether. But she couldn't do that; she couldn't leave her children. And George would never let her take them. She was trapped.

'Going to Penny's?' He couldn't believe it. 'I thought we were going to sort this thing out, talk it over.'

'What is there to talk about?'

237

'Us.'

'Oh, us.' It was very difficult putting on an air of indifference when every nerve and sinew wanted to howl and beat his chest with her fists. 'There is no us.'

'Barbara, for God's sake, don't be like that. It's not like you.'

'How do you know what I'm like? You've never bothered to find out.'

'I know it's not like you to be bitter and vengeful. And it won't help. I need a little understanding, forgiveness...'

'And what about my needs, have you ever considered those?'

'I've tried. But part of that has been working hard, to give you a comfortable life, to make a home for us all...'

'Then why destroy it?'

'I don't want to destroy it. It needn't happen. I want us to stay together. Don't you want it too?'

'Not at any price.'

'Then help me change. Stay with me, we'll spend the weekend together.'

'What about all the other weekends. The days and weeks, the rest of our lives?'

'Those too.'

'Then this weekend is mine, for me to get away and make up my mind. If you mean what you say, you won't go anywhere near your mistress while I'm gone.'

He winced at the word mistress. It had been spoken with such venom. He didn't know she could hate; for once in his life he knew the meaning of fear. How could he face his work force, his council colleagues, his constituents, if she left him? Who would look after the children? Would she take them with her? He might not see them again. 'But you will come back?' There was a measure of pleading in his voice.

'Oh, yes,' she said. 'I'll come back. My children are here.'

Chapter Nine

FLASHBULBS WERE POPPING all over the place and the crowd jostled each other on the pavement as the celebrities left their limousines and made their way into the theatre. Penny looked stunning in a white crêpe halter neck dress which clung to her slim figure from breast to knees, where it was slit to give her room to walk. There was a colourful dragon embroidered all down the front, its fiery breath blazing up onto one shoulder, its tail looping round over her neat bottom. The back of the dress was scooped out as far as the waistline. It was a seductive dress which drew whistles from the men in the crowd.

She was accompanied by her leading man in a plum-coloured velvet evening jacket and matching bow tie. He was tall, dark and handsome and very aware of the admiration and sighs of those who had come to watch. At the door, they turned to allow the photographers to take pictures, then they disappeared inside.

Barbara, who arrived in the following car with Simon,

felt self-conscious, knowing that everyone was busy putting names to the celebrities; they would be puzzled over her, asking each other, 'Who on earth is she?' She was thankful that the hairdresser had made a good job of piling up her fair hair, which emphasised the slenderness of her neck and narrow shoulders. Her make-up had been done by Penny's own maid, and she had managed to make the dark eyes and hollow cheeks, caused by sleepless nights spent weeping, look interesting, even a bit glamorous. But that wasn't how she felt. She felt hollow. There was nothing inside but emptiness.

'Smile,' Simon whispered, as a flashbulb went off only inches from her face. 'Pretend you're a star.' In evening dress, as all the men were, he was thinner than she remembered him and his clear blue eyes held a hint of self-mockery. Those eyes, which she saw every day of her life in Jay-Jay's chubby face, unnerved her more than a little.

'A fat chance of that.' It didn't take a genius to guess that Penny's invitation had been a spur-of-the-moment thing when she realised Barbara was feeling low, but it didn't stop her feeling like a fish out of water. She hadn't bargained on being paired with Simon either. She had expected him to come with Dodo. It was a surprise to learn they had decided to divorce.

'It wasn't working out,' he had told her just before they set out from Penny's flat. 'My work keeps me in London and hers is all over the place and she likes to date other men. And I wanted children, she didn't.'

'I'm sorry.' What else could she say? Tempted as she was to tell him he was already a father, she couldn't, knowing the consequences would be catastrophic. But the secret was like a lead weight in her breast.

'It can't be helped and it has its compensations.' He smiled as he spoke. 'I might otherwise have missed a new sighting of a very rare bird indeed.'

She had laughed, genuinely laughed, for the first time in a week. 'Simon, you can be so silly, sometimes.'

'I know, but why not? If we can't laugh at our problems, what is the point of it all? Now come on, we're going to enjoy ourselves tonight.'

The film was a spooky one, but it suited Barbara's mood, which was black as night. Not that Simon intended it to stay that way. At the party afterwards he was attentive and smiling and apparently oblivious of the glitz all around him, with eyes only for Barbara. She drank too much, laughed too loudly and danced a lot. But exhaustion claimed her in the end and she sank onto a sofa in Penny's overheated lounge, leant back and shut her eyes.

'You're done for, aren't you?' His voice in her ear was gently concerned and it wasn't tonight's tiredness he meant. He had always been able to read her moods and he knew, without being told, that she was at the end of her tether.

'Mmm. I think I might be drunk.'

'It won't do you any harm. It's hot in here. Let's go out on the balcony and gaze at the moon.'

The balcony was tiny and it looked out over the street, with its regularly spaced lamps shedding pools of yellow light onto a row of parked cars; all Penny's friends drove cars. Above the rooftops the sky was clear and studded with stars. He put his arm about her waist and she leant her head on his shoulder and they stood side by side, silent and unmoving. A car door slammed; someone or something knocked over a dustbin and behind them the sound of conversation and laughter came to them over the music of a gramophone. None of it impinged: they were cocooned in their own little world of quiet contemplation.

'We are a couple of idiots, aren't we?' he murmured.

'Are we?'

'Yes. We've let ourselves be led by the nose, both of us. I had no right to lecture you about losing the real you, I did it too.'

'What are you going to do about it?'

'I don't know. It depends. But we don't need to worry about that tonight, do we? Tonight is for us.'

She turned her head to look up at him, wondering if he meant what she thought he did. He smiled and kissed the end of her nose. 'More therapy?' she murmured.

'Only if that's what you want.' She wasn't happy. He could sense it, just as he could sense everything about her, every nuance of emotion, every quirk of her character. He wanted to tell her that he could make her happy, that he loved her, that they belonged together, but he held back, afraid of her reaction, of spoiling the little they had.

'Oh, Simon, I don't know what I want. I only know that it's so comforting standing here with you. And I do need comfort just now.'

He turned her in his arms and gently kissed her on the mouth. There was no pressure, no urgency; he was simply asking the question, waiting for her to give him an answer.

She reached up and took his head in her hands and kissed him back. He took her hand and led her back indoors, past the noisy drawing room, to her bedroom.

'What's that?' Simon was sitting up in bed smoking a cigarette, waiting for Barbara to wake up. Seeing her again, being with her, making love to her, had been balm to his injured soul. She was wonderful in bed, caring and receptive, tender and passionate, in tune with everything he did. It was like coming into safe water after a storm. He'd wanted to tell her so, to explain about Dodo, but it would have spoilt their time together and he did not want to think about his wife, let alone talk about her. And so he had tried to keep it light, a bit of fun.

His eyes had roamed round the room. His own clothes and Barbara's were scattered about, a pair of stockings lay tangled with his shirt, a brassiere was draped over a stool. One high-heeled shoe lay on its side under the dressing table; where the other was he could not see. A make-up bag and a perfume spray stood on the dressing table. But it was the parcel that caught his eye. It was flat, done up with brown paper and string and was propped on a chair.

'What's what?' She had slept well but it was hardly surprising after the night they had had. It had been wonderful, easy and relaxing at first, as they slowly explored each other's naked bodies, then gradually the tempo had increased as she became more and more roused. She had a vague memory of really wild behaviour, of hands and arms and legs thrashing about, of mouths and tongues everywhere, of a sensation of soaring, of brilliance far beyond the bedside lamp they had left on.

They had come together so perfectly, so beautifully, she had simply collapsed in sheer delight and not moved again.

'That.' He pointed. 'It looks like a picture.'

'It is. I brought it for Penny. But it didn't seem appropriate to give it to her yesterday.'

He got out of bed, naked, and walked across to pick it up. Drowsily, she watched him, admiring the long legs and slim hips, the absence of any sign of a pot belly. He was unselfconscious about his nakedness. Noticing where her eyes were travelling, he looked down at himself and grinned. 'Oh, what the hell!' Putting the parcel down he returned to the bed and stood looking down at her.

'No, Simon,' she said. 'We can't. It's late and I need a bath.'

He reached out and took both her hands in his, pulling her from the bed. 'Come on, then.'

She resisted, laughing, but he propelled her into the adjoining bathroom and turned on the bath taps. As the warm water filled it, he lifted her into it and got in behind her. He soaped her all over, letting his hands slip over her, kissing her wet skin, licking his tongue round her neck and behind her ears, making her shiver. He grasped her buttocks in his hands and lifted her onto him. Steam enveloped them. She felt she was drowning not in liquid, but in a kind of ecstasy that lifted her out of the shell of her body onto some higher plane. She had never experienced anything remotely like it before. Different from the first time, different from the previous night of uninhibited passion. This was more heartfelt, more ecstatic. It was perfect.

Afterwards he padded off in search of towels. She stepped out, taking a towel from him and rubbing her hair. They did not speak, each knowing that the night which he had said belonged to them was over. He dressed in casual trousers and a shirt and, while she found a dress and clean underwear in her case, carefully unwrapped the picture. It was only when it was exposed and she looked at it from across the room, she realised how much like Simon Jay-Jay was, more than she'd ever noticed before. Already his baby blonde hair was darkening into something approaching red-gold, almost exactly the same shade as Penny's. She held her breath.

'*Children on a Beach*,' he murmured. 'It's very different from *Girl on a Rock*, isn't it?'

'You told me that was too sad,' she said, wondering if it had been such a good idea to bring it. 'This is meant to be a happy picture, a companion piece, if you like. Do you think Penny will like it?'

'No doubt of it. Are these your children?'

'Yes.'

'You've caught them beautifully, especially the baby. He is so full of life, the bright eyes, the chubby cheeks. I think I'd put up with almost anything to have a family like that.' He paused to look at her and his wistful smile turned to concern. 'Why are you crying?' He put the picture down and came to stand in front of her, taking her shoulders in his hands. 'Oh, my darling, I've upset you. I'm sorry.'

'You haven't upset me.' She sniffed and fumbled for a handkerchief. 'I've been a bit low lately, that's all.'

'Do you want to talk about it?'

'I can't. I'm sorry.'

He waited, but when she didn't speak again, he said, 'Fair enough. Let's go and find Penny.'

'Do you think she knows you were here all night?'

'Probably. But she'll understand.'

'If she does, it's more than I do.'

'Come on, now, no regrets. It was great, wasn't it? The best ever.' He picked up the painting to cover the need to hide the fact that he was as near to tears as he had ever been in his life. If only... He refused to let himself go down that road.

They found his sister in the kitchen. She was dressed in a red silk dressing gown and was sitting at the kitchen table with a cup of coffee in front of her. Beside it stood an aspirin bottle. 'Hi, you two,' she said. 'What a night! Help yourselves to coffee. Make some toast or something. I've got to go out. I must have been mad to agree to a newspaper interview after a first-night party. I look like death.'

'You look gorgeous, as always,' Barbara said.

'Barbara's brought you a present,' Simon said, resting the bottom of the painting on the kitchen table facing her. 'What do you think of it?'

'It's lovely! Oh, Barbara, are you sure you want me to have it?'

'Of course I do. Simon said *Girl on a Rock* was sad, so I thought I'd paint a cheerful picture to balance it.'

'If you haven't got room to hang it, I'll take it off your hands,' Simon said.

'Why would you want it?' Barbara asked him, her voice unnaturally sharp. Surely he hadn't guessed?

'Because you painted it.' His answer was meant to disguise the true reason. 'If you go on like this, you'll be famous one day and it'll be worth thousands.'

'Well, you can't have it,' Penny said. 'It can hang next to the other one. You can put it up while I'm out. Barbara, you'll be here when I come back, won't you? We've hardly had a minute to talk.'

'I really ought to be thinking about going home.'

'Wait until after lunch. A few hours won't make that much difference, will it?'

'I suppose not.' She didn't know why she agreed. As soon as Simon had unwrapped that picture and she had looked at that painting with fresh eyes, heard him say he would give anything for a family like that, she wanted to rush straight back to her children and hug them to death. But then she thought of the other side of the coin: her life with George and the prospect of years and years more of that daunted her. And there was her own guilt. It weighed heavily on her. Somehow she had to come to terms with that before she faced her husband again. 'While you're gone, I'll go for a walk, get a breath of fresh air.'

She knew Simon would go with her, but that was better than staying in the flat with him. She knew what would happen if she did and she didn't trust herself. Her life seemed filled with regrets and now there was another to add to all the others. And yet, Simon was her solace, and she knew she loved him, had always loved him. But where did that leave George and her life with him?

Quite apart from personal traumas, it was a dreadful year. Unemployment was still the main worry at home.

There was unrest in India, and in Germany the Nazi party was gaining ground. In America there was a kind of boom, when everyone seemed to be speculating on the stock exchange until some of the more prudent investors realised the madness of it and began selling. The bottom fell out of the market in October, recovered briefly only to crash again in November, and naturally there were repercussions all over the world.

George had to juggle his finances harder than ever. Honest George, he called himself, but Barbara knew that was a sham. He continued to bribe, cajole and deceive. Whether he had kept his promise not to see Virginia again, she wasn't sure, mainly because they led almost separate lives, he with his business and his politics, she with her voluntary work and her painting. And her children. They were her life.

She had been tempted to confess her affair to George but decided it would serve no useful purpose, except to ease her own conscience. She had to live with that, just as she had to live with the fact that she was not the only woman in her husband's life, that she had to share him. God give her strength to bear it because there must be no more trips to London. Simon, dearest Simon, must be forgotten. She must look after her family, paint pictures and go about her charity work, trying to do some good where it was most needed, and if there was any justice in the world, it would all come right in the end.

In 1931, when rumours were rife that Britain was on the verge of bankruptcy, Ramsay MacDonald agreed to lead a coalition government to deal with the financial crisis.

The measures they took, draconian in many people's eyes, included an increase in income tax, higher duties on beer, tobacco and petrol and cuts in civil service salaries. Worst of all, unemployment allowances were cut and a means test imposed. The pound lost a fifth of its value.

A general election was called in October and George campaigned as hard as anyone. He was at the town hall on the night of the count, buttering up the Conservative candidate who, if elected, could be very useful to him. Barbara stayed at home listening to the news on the wireless while she painted. It was the last item which grabbed her attention. There had been a traffic accident on the Great North Road in pouring rain. Incredibly no one had been killed, but Simon Barcliffe, the brother of the well-known actress, Penny Barcliffe, had been injured. Barbara didn't wait for more, but rushed out to the hall to ring Penny. Her friend was out, but she left a message with her maid to ring back and returned to the sitting room to wait for her call. At midnight she gave up and went to bed.

It was at breakfast next morning she learnt that there had been a huge Conservative landslide. 'There'll be the usual celebration,' George told her, buttering toast. 'I'll let you know the date.'

After he had gone, she got the children off to school, then cleared up the breakfast things, listening for the telephone. It rang in the middle of the morning.

She snatched it up. 'Penny, I heard the news. How is he?'

'He's got cracked ribs, a broken leg and a lot of bruises.'

'Where is he?'

'Peterborough General. I'm ringing from there.'

Peterborough was not far; she could do it in little over an hour and Kate would look after Jay-Jay. 'I'll come, shall I?'

'He'd like that.'

She found her friend in a small waiting room, nursing a mug of coffee. She was grey with fatigue, wore wide trousers and a sweater and, without make-up, certainly looked nothing like the glamorous Penny Barcliffe her fans knew. Barbara sat down beside her. 'How is he?'

'Better than yesterday. He'll be pleased to see you. He was mumbling about you when they brought him in.'

'Me?' she queried in surprise.

'Yes, don't sound so surprised. I knew there was something going on between you when you came up for the premiere of *Dragon Castle*, and I'm pretty sure it wasn't the first time...'

Barbara didn't attempt to deny it. 'Oh, Pen, I don't know what to say. We were both feeling low and it was no more than two close friends comforting each other. I've never ceased to regret it, except...' She stopped suddenly.

'You were going to say except for Jay-Jay, weren't you?'

Barbara's breath caught in her throat. 'Jay-Jay?'

'Oh, Barbara, I wasn't born yesterday and I'm not judging you, but Jay-Jay is Simon's son, isn't he?'

'Don't ask me that, Penny, please.'

'I don't need to ask. I have the picture of the children on the beach. It's plain enough to me. Does George know?'

'No. No one does...'

'Not even Simon?'

'There was nothing to be gained by telling him. After all, it was not a real affair, and getting pregnant was simply an accident. I've tried to put it behind me...'

'I don't think you have. And I know Simon hasn't.'

'What do you mean?'

'Oh, come on, Barbara. Two people couldn't be more in love...'

'You wouldn't tell Simon about Jay-Jay?' she asked, breathless with alarm.

'No, but I think you should.'

'What would be the point? Jay-Jay is part of our family and that means George is his father in all but the seed that made him. I can't risk losing all my children, because that's what it would mean if George ever found out. I can't do it, I just can't.'

A nurse came into the room before Penny could add to her argument. 'Miss Barcliffe, Mr Barcliffe is awake and asking for you.'

Penny took Barbara to the private ward, then crept away, shutting the door behind her. Barbara, aware that she had gone, walked to the bed. Simon was lying on his back with drips attached to each of his arms and one plaster-encased leg supported in a hoist. His eyes were dull, but when he saw her, they lit with pleasure.

'Barbara.' His voice was husky. 'You're a sight for sore eyes.'

She sat on the chair beside the bed, forcing a bright smile. 'How are you?'

He attempted to grin. 'OK. They say I'll mend. Good of you to come.'

'I wanted to. What happened?'

'It's all a bit hazy.' He remembered the rain and the road stretching boringly ahead, leaving him with nothing to think about but Dodo and the divorce. It had been a messy business, acrimonious and expensive. He'd offered her the matrimonial home, but that hadn't been enough, she wanted alimony, lots of it. The trouble was that he and his father were still trying to fight their way out of the stock market crash and he could not afford it. He had gone to see her in Scotland where she was working to try and sort it out.

Life with Dodo hadn't always been bad. Attracted by her looks, her figure, her zest for life, he hadn't been unwilling when she made it clear she fancied him. He had even been amused when she flirted with every good-looking male who crossed her path, telling himself that the very fact that she did it openly meant there was nothing to hide and the acting profession was like that. But playfulness soon palled when it was unaccompanied by any sense of responsibility, when her ambition meant she was prepared to do anything to pursue it, even sleeping with producers, casting directors and leading men. Penny didn't need to do that to be a success, but then Penny had more real talent.

Why had he clung to the remnants of his marriage for so long? It was apathy, he supposed, the feeling that it didn't matter one way or the other. It would have been different if there had been someone else in his life, but there was no one. Except Barbara. And she had gone back to her husband and children, to the life she knew.

'Simon?' Barbara's worried voice came to him through his reverie.

He reached out and took her hand. 'It's all right. I was thinking.'

'About what happened?'

'Yes,' he agreed. It was easier than telling the truth. 'I remember it was raining so hard the windscreen wipers couldn't clear the screen and all I could see ahead of me were the blurred tail lights of the vehicle in front. It was sort of mesmerising and I suddenly realised the red light was much closer and the rear of a lorry loomed up almost on my bonnet. I slammed on the brakes. The car skidded sideways and clipped the corner of the lorry before running into the ditch beside the road.'

'Thank God you weren't killed.'

'Amen to that. Enough of me. Tell me about yourself. How are you? And the children?'

'They're fine. Growing up now, of course. Alison is ten, taking her entrance exam next year for Melsham Grammar School. Nick is sports mad.'

'And the youngest? Jay-Jay, isn't it?'

She swallowed hard. 'Yes. He's toddling about now and full of mischief.' She prayed he would not notice how unnatural her voice sounded and covered it by prattling about her charity work. She stopped when she noticed he was smiling. 'What's the matter? Have I got a smudge on my nose?'

He smiled. 'No, I was thinking of how you looked the last time we met. In the bath, your beautiful body shiny with lather, your wet hair plastered to your face. And laughing. It's a picture that haunts me.' It was that picture he had in front of him when he crashed, a shadowy, insubstantial form behind the metronomic windscreen wipers. 'We were good together, you and I. I should never have let you go.'

'I had to, you know that. There was no future for us...'

'No future then, no future now,' he murmured.

'I'm sorry, Simon.'

'No need to be. Penny said you'd never leave your children. Can't say I blame you. Of course, you could bring them with you. I'd be happy to take them on.'

It was terrible. She should not have come. It was as if she could not let go, as if she had to cling to a past which could have no relevance in the present, fleeting moments of happiness to be kept and savoured in darker moments, nothing more. Except Jay-Jay. Had Simon guessed the truth? She was convinced she was right not to tell: it would not help anyone. She forced herself to sound calm. 'You know I would never take them from their father...'

'No, of course not. I respect you for that.' He reached for her hand. 'Will you come and see me again?'

'I don't know. It's difficult...'

He sighed heavily. 'Another rare sighting of Barbara Bosgrove come and gone. How many years before the next, I wonder?'

She managed a smile. 'I think that particular bird has become extinct.'

'Pity.'

She bent to kiss him on the forehead but he put his hand behind her head and drew her down to kiss her properly. 'Goodbye, my love,' he murmured. 'Try not to forget me altogether.'

She crept from the room before he could see how

wobbly her smile was. Once in the corridor, she fled, so blinded by tears she did not see Penny sitting outside the door.

Somehow she got home without crashing the car. She left it in the drive and raced up to her studio where she knew she wouldn't be disturbed. She needed to be alone, to think. Flinging herself into the armchair she curled herself in a tight ball, hugging herself, afraid to cry in case she wouldn't be able to stem the flood when it came.

It wasn't just Simon, it was the way the past had all come flooding back. Every rebellious thought, every ill-considered deed she had done since she married, had its roots way back, to a time when she was single, to how she felt and acted when she found her father with Virginia. Simon's words echoed in her head: *One minute we were going along nicely and I was trying, ever so gently, to prise you away from Daddy, then out of the blue, there's this great wrestler with hands like dinner plates...* How could she have been so blind? Not only then, but later, when she and Simon had gone to bed together, pretending it was just therapy. It had been the real thing. Penny had seen it. *Two people couldn't be more in love...*

The tears flowed at last, running down her face unchecked, tears of regret, of guilt, of despair. And finally they dried up on a note of determination. Feeling sorry for herself wouldn't help. She took a deep breath, got up, washed her face in cold water, repaired her make-up, and went downstairs to get on with her life. There wasn't anything else she could do.

When George came home he was far from pleased when Barbara told him where she'd been. 'Penny Barcliffe only has to crook her little finger and you go running,' he said, standing in the kitchen watching her make a pot of tea.

'Oh, George, for goodness' sake. Simon's been in a serious accident. Penny was worried about him and Kate was happy to look after Jay-Jay for an hour or two.'

'You know how I feel about the Barcliffes.'

It was all so silly, so acrimonious, so exhausting, and yet it was symptomatic of their relationship. 'I'm sorry you don't like them, George, but they are my friends.'

'They? Now we're getting down to it. It's not just Penny, it's that brother of hers...'

Did he know? Was he guessing? Or was he simply saying the first thing that came into his head? 'You're talking rubbish,' she said, taking her tea into the drawing room and leaving him to follow. He stood over her for several silent seconds, then turned on his heel and slammed out of the house.

George walked; he didn't care where he went, anything to get away. He'd made the mistake of his life marrying Barbara Bosgrove. She had been too immature, looking for a father figure. His mother had been right, she had latched onto him to get away from a situation she couldn't handle. Now if he had married Virginia...

He had known her before she met John Bosgrove, they had even gone on one or two dates in their teens. She was passionate and understanding, uninhibited in bed, did things Barbara would never have dreamt of doing, made him feel good about himself. She didn't keep on at him about his business methods either. You had to have your wits about you, take advantage of other people's cupidity, bend the rules now and then, and Virginia understood there was nothing wrong in that. To listen to Barbara, you'd think he'd committed murder. Well, he had the answer to that: don't tell her anything. If he wanted to brag about a deal he'd done, the way he'd pulled the wool over someone's eyes, made a rival squirm, then Virginia was the one to tell. She had always praised him, called him her 'clever old thing' and then she would stroke his forehead and massage his shoulders, and all the tension would drain away from him.

He stopped suddenly, realising he was outside her house. He went up the path and banged on the door. When it was not immediately answered, he banged again.

'For Chris' sake, George, what are you playing at?'

She stood in the circle of light from the hall behind her, which made the flimsy wrap she was wearing transparent. He could see her breasts and rounded hips, the dark mound of her pubic hair, her thighs. 'I want to come in.'

'Well, you can't. You got me out of bed.'

He grinned, wanting her so badly it was a physical pain. 'We could go back there.'

'No. You totally ignore me for years and then you come banging on my door in the middle of the night and think I'm going to welcome you with open arms…'

'You are, aren't you? Going to welcome me, I mean. Oh, come on, sweetheart, let me in. You can't stand there all night looking like that, you'll have every man in Melsham coming to see the show.'

She looked down at herself and drew the robe closer about her body, then made to shut the door. He pushed against it. 'I'll kick up a row until you do let me in.'

She sighed and stood aside to allow him to pass her, before closing the door and leading him into the kitchen. 'I think you need some strong black coffee.'

'I need you.'

'What's brought this on all of a sudden?'

'I should never have married Barbara.'

'So, what's new? We both know that. I suspect she knows it too. According to you, there's nothing you can do about it. You're too careful of your public image, too worried the scandal will ruin you. You want your cosy little home – big house, actually – your malleable little wife, your children, your position in the community. But not content with that you want your little bit on the side, your hidden mistress, also malleable. You're a greedy man, George Kennett.' She turned to face him, handing him a cup of scalding coffee. 'You want to have your cake and eat it.'

'Oh, Ginny, not you too. I thought you understood...'

'I understand you've had a row with your wife.' She picked up her own coffee and stood sipping it, watching him. 'So, what was it about?'

'She's seeing someone else.'

Virginia laughed. 'So? Isn't that what you wanted? Grounds for divorce which would leave you the innocent party, image untarnished.'

'What grounds? I can't imagine Barbara being unfaithful, she's not the type. She's too strait-laced.' He had been telling himself that ever since he left the house, but the more he thought about it, the more doubts he had. There were all those times she had gone to London to see

Penny. How could he be sure it was only Penny she had seen? And there was that premiere she had attended. She'd stayed the night too. He racked his brains to remember how often her charity had taken her away all day, times when she had been evasive about her movements. How could he be sure?

'What's sauce for the goose is sauce for the gander,' she said.

He didn't want to think about that. He set his coffee cup down on the table and reached out to take hers from her. He put it down beside his own and took her in his arms, kissing her hungrily, letting his lips roam over her face and down her neck, pulling the flimsy robe off her shoulders to reveal her breasts. He bent his head to kiss them, using his tongue and making the nipples stand up dark and tantalising. 'I have only to do this and I'm as hard as a poker. And you want it too, I can tell.'

She pulled out his shirt, ran her hands down his body and inside his trousers and laughed. 'OK, so let's go upstairs.'

Later, she said, 'I must have been mad giving in to you.'

'You love me,' he said, lying naked beside her and nibbling her ear lobe. 'And I love you.'

'Always, or only when Barbara gets you down?'

'Always.'

'So you think we should take up where we left off, do you?'

He lifted his head to look at her, alerted by the tone of her voice. 'Better than that.'

'You mean you'll ask Barbara for a divorce?'

In the euphoria of being with her, making love to her again, he was ready to promise anything. 'Yes. I'll find out more about her and Simon Barcliffe...'

She gave a bark of a laugh. 'Still worried about your image, I see.'

'No, but she'll take me to the cleaners if I leave without grounds. I was just thinking of ways and means...'

'You'd better find them because if you don't, there'll be no more tumbles on this bed or any other.'

'You don't mean that.'

'Yes, I do. How many years have I been hanging about waiting for you? Ever since John died. That was nearly ten years ago. I'm not waiting any longer. You'll tell Barbara the truth and move in with me or you can stay away for good.'

'OK. I get the message. I can't lose you, Ginny, I really can't.' But he had to find a way to save face, and blaming Barbara was worth considering. Could he prove her infidelity? He could tell one or two people confidentially, let the story go the rounds; would that ensure that public opinion was on his side? Reluctantly he tore himself away and went home.

To stop herself brooding, Barbara began a frenzied attack on all the drawers and cupboards in the house, turning everything out but not having the heart to throw anything away, putting it all back again: toys; half-finished knitting; dresses she would never wear again; ornaments; old photographs; pictures she had forgotten she had painted.

There was one she had done from a photograph taken at Jay-Jay's christening, with Elizabeth nursing the baby and Alison and Nick grouped about her. That had been a funny sort of day, watching George acting the proud father and feeling happy and guilty and loving all at the same time. It wasn't a bad painting but she could never look at it without those searing emotions returning and plaguing her, so she had put it out of sight. But perhaps Elizabeth would like it.

She hadn't seen her mother-in-law for two or three weeks, what with the election and Simon's accident and George behaving strangely, up one minute, cracking jokes and teasing the children, down the next, scowling or silently immersed in thoughts he would not, or could not, share. After a snack at lunchtime, she wrapped the picture in brown paper and set off for Victoria Street, taking Jay-Jay in his pushchair.

She was surprised when she arrived at the house to find the newspaper stuck in the letter box and the milk still on the doorstep. Full of misgiving, she pulled the newspaper from the letter box and bent down to peer through it. She could just make out Elizabeth lying at the foot of the stairs. Bumping Jay-Jay in his chair, she ran along the alley which divided the two sets of terrace houses to the rear gate and up the garden path to the back door. Mercifully it wasn't locked. Her mother-in-law was lying in the hall with one leg on the stairs, the other doubled under her. She had a lump on the side of her head, just above her eye. Barbara dare not try to move her but when she gently touched her wrist she could feel a fluttering pulse. She went to the telephone and rang for an ambulance, and while she waited rang the yard, but George was out; Susan, his secretary, said she didn't know where he was. Fifteen minutes later the clang of a bell told her the ambulance had arrived.

How long Elizabeth had been lying there, no one could tell – several hours according to the ambulance men. Barbara rushed home and left Jay-Jay with Kate, asking her to stay and see to Alison and Nick when they came home from school, and then drove to the hospital.

Elizabeth had been taken up to a ward. Barbara was told she had concussion and a broken femur and the doctors were going to pin the hip with a sliver of bone from her shin. Barbara tried again to contact George. It was nearly six o'clock but she just caught Susan before she left the office, only to be told George had not returned and had probably gone straight home. She rang the house. Alison answered the phone.

'He's not here, Mummy,' she said. 'Is Granny very bad?' The catch in Alison's voice reminded her how much the children loved their grandmother.

'Not too bad, darling, don't worry. If your father comes in, tell him to come to the hospital, will you?'

'OK. Do you want to speak to Aunty Kate?'

'Yes. Oh, no, my pennies have run out. Tell her I'll be home as soon as I can.' She put the receiver down and returned to the ward.

Elizabeth was awake but obviously in pain. 'Was it you who found me?' she asked.

'Yes. I went round with a painting I thought you might like. Can you remember what happened?'

'It was after breakfast, about nine, I think. I'd gone up to make the bed. I tripped and fell downstairs from top to bottom. The carpet is beginning to fray. I've been meaning to ask George to do something about it, but he's always so busy and then I forgot. I blacked out, then I came round a bit. I tried to move and found I couldn't. I shouted for help but no one heard me and then I must have drifted off. Next thing I knew I was in the ambulance.' There was no self-pity in her voice, no grievance that she had been lying there undiscovered for something like six hours, no moaning about the agonising pain which had made her drift in and out of consciousness all day. No blaming George over the frayed carpet.

'I've been trying to get hold of George,' Barbara said. 'I think he might be at a council meeting. I'll go to the town hall and see if I can find him. It's no good ringing, there'll be no one on the switchboard.' She stood up. 'I'll be back soon.'

The town hall was in darkness. If there had been a meeting, it was over. She went home but George had not returned, and after reassuring Alison and Nick and tucking them into bed, she set off, once more, for the hospital. She pulled up outside The Crown, wondering if George might have called in on his way home. She left the car and went inside.

It was closing time and Rita was busy clearing the glasses from the tables. Colin was leaning on the bar with a glass of beer at his elbow. There was no sign of George.

'Hallo,' Rita said. 'Don't usually see you in here, do we?'

'I'm looking for George. His mother's had an accident. She fell down the stairs and broke her femur. They're going to operate. Trouble is I've forgotten where George said he'd be tonight. You haven't seen him, have you?'

'Sorry, he's not been in tonight.' She turned to her husband. 'Have you seen him?'

'No, not since this morning.'

'Oh, well, it was a long shot. I'll go back to the hospital.'

'If there's anything I can do, let me know,' Rita called after her.

Her husband grinned and took a swig from his glass. 'You could have told her to try Virginia Bosgrove. I saw him pick her up in his car at lunchtime.'

'Is that still going on? Poor Barbara. Do you think she knows?'

He shrugged. 'How should I know? And I'm not going to tell her. What the eye don't see, the heart don't grieve over. That man will get his just deserts one day, you mark my words.' It sounded like a threat and she gave a little shudder of apprehension.

Chapter Ten

Iᴛ ᴡᴀꜱ ɴᴇᴀʀʟʏ midnight before Elizabeth went up to theatre and there was nothing more Barbara could do for her, so she set off for home again. As she rounded a bend, her headlights picked up a car parked in a part of the old road left behind when the bypass was built. It wasn't until she drew level that she realised the car was George's and there were two people in it. George and a woman. She braked, intending to confront them, but changed her mind and drove on. In any clash with George she needed to be able to think clearly and right now she was too tired for that.

The two people in the car were silently staring ahead at the dark outline of the trees which had escaped destruction when the new road was built. A full moon hung over the branches and lit the scene in a silvery glow that was almost good enough to see by. At any other time, they would have called it romantic. Tonight there was bitterness and disappointment, anger and recrimination.

They had been to Hunstanton for the day and it wasn't until they were approaching Melsham she had brought up the subject uppermost in her mind. 'Have you talked to Barbara about the divorce, like we agreed?'

'I'm still gathering evidence. It's tricky. They've covered their tracks too well.'

'Excuses, that's all it ever is with you.' Her voice was harsh with bitterness. 'I told you what would happen if you let me down again, didn't I? Now you can take me home.'

'Virginia, you're being silly,' he had said, pulling into the lay-by.

'Yes, silly to think you could ever change, silly to think you would give up your comfortable life for me. Well, I've come to my senses...' Her anger gave way to tears. She made no attempt to wipe them away, was hardly aware of them, as she tried to see into a future without him. Always holding herself in readiness for him, knowing half Melsham knew what was going on and the other half must be kept in the dark at all costs, had cut her off from any social life worthy of the name. She had been every kind of a fool, still was if she didn't manage to harden her heart and resist the overwhelming desire which threatened to crumble her resolve to dust. 'Leave me and go home, George, you've made your choice.' She went to open the car door, but he grabbed her arm.

'For God's sake, Virginia, don't be so melodramatic, it's only a slight delay. Have a little patience.'

He was startled when she screamed with hysterical laughter, making so much noise she could not hear a word he was saying, and when he tried to touch her, she shrugged him off. He started the engine and drove her home. She had quietened by the time he stopped at her gate, but she flung herself out of the car and slammed the door without speaking. He drove home, so angry and frustrated he could not think coherently.

Barbara, still fully dressed, met him in the hall. He put his briefcase down on the polished wood floor, endeavouring to switch off his anger and become the long-suffering, hard-working husband. 'You needn't have waited up.'

'I had to. I've been trying to contact you all evening. I tried everywhere, council offices, Donald Browning, The Crown.'

'Why? I thought I told you I had a Rotary dinner. I couldn't get away.'

She resisted the temptation to call him a liar. 'Your mother's had a fall. She's in Melsham General—'

'Why the hell didn't you say so before, instead of rabbiting on about where I'd been?'

He was seething with anger, but she was sure it had nothing to do with her; the mood had been on him before he came into the house, but if she were not careful she would bear the brunt of it. She answered him calmly. 'She fell down the stairs. When I left the hospital an hour ago, she was being taken up to theatre to have a broken hip pinned.'

Without another word, he turned on his heel and went out again. Barbara heard him roar off down the drive, then went to bed. Although she was exhausted, she didn't sleep, her mind was too full of what she had seen in that lay-by and what she intended to do about it. The woman had been Virginia, she was sure of it. George had not changed and she supposed he could not change; she had been wrong to hope. She felt empty, as if her life had been drained from her; there was no emotion, no passion, she was too numb for that. She lay there, staring out of the window at the night sky, until the stars faded and the sun rose. It was not a time for confrontation or for making irrevocable decisions which she might later regret. Her punishment, so long dreaded, was here and now, and there was nothing she could do but take it on the chin and not let anyone see how much she was hurting. Automaton-like she rose and dressed and went downstairs to cook the children's breakfast and see them off to school.

George sat at his mother's bedside all night, watching and brooding. Full of his own importance, things he had to do, the election campaign, pleasures he could never share with her, he hadn't been to see her for weeks. Yesterday, he had been out with Virginia, while his mother lay unconscious at the foot of the stairs, tripped by a frayed carpet he should have replaced long before. Without her, he would have amounted to nothing, just another working-class lad living for pay day every week, with no ambition, no drive. He owed his success to her. It was dawn when he saw her eyelids flutter and leant forward to take her hand. 'Mum.'

She opened her eyes and murmured, 'Ah, George, you came, then...'

Even that sounded like an accusation. 'Of course I came. The minute I heard. How are you feeling? The doctor says you're going to be as good as new...' He stopped because she had gone back to sleep.

The door opened behind him and a nurse came in. 'Mr Kennett, I think you should go home and rest. Come back this afternoon. Mrs Kennett will be awake by then and you'll be able to talk to her.'

In the ten days she was in hospital, he visited her every day, was more often at home in the evenings, took more interest in the children, making Barbara wonder if his mother's accident had made him see the error of his ways, and he had at last given Virginia up. She could only take each day as it came, and hope it would last.

Two months later everyone but George was astonished to read the announcement of Virginia's engagement to Donald Browning in the Melsham Gazette. Barbara didn't know what to make of it, but hoped that she had been right and Elizabeth's accident had brought George to his senses.

Elizabeth was relieved. 'About time too,' she said when George went to visit her. He had stopped all his other work to put his men onto building her a bungalow in the garden of The Chestnuts, but until it was ready he called in to see her every evening before he went home. She had been knitting a jumper for Jay-Jay while listening to the wireless, but when he came in she switched it off and put her knitting to one side. 'You must offer to give her away.'

He was appalled. 'I can't do that.'

He had been hurt and angry with Virginia when she told him. 'You won't be happy,' he had prophesied. 'You can't be happy with anyone but me and I need you...'

271

'We've been through it all before, George, and enough is enough. Donald's been wanting to marry me for years. You and I are finished.'

'You can't mean that.'

But it appeared she did. A fortnight later the wedding invitation had arrived, addressed to Mr and Mrs George Kennett. He was forced to congratulate Donald and accept. But going to the wedding was one thing, acting in an official capacity quite another.

'Why not?' Elizabeth demanded. 'It will silence the gossips. You've been given a chance to put things right, which is more than some men get...'

'You don't know what you're talking about.'

'I do, you know. I'm not blind and I'm not deaf. It's not fair on Barbara or your children.'

He gave a cracked laugh. 'Had it never occurred to you that Barbara is not the innocent she seems? The truth is, she's got someone else, has had for years.'

Elizabeth was shocked. 'I don't believe it. I'm sure I'd know...'

'Why should you? He doesn't live round here and she's very clever.'

'Then you'd better do something about it. Either prove it or forget it.'

'That's easy for you to say. You and my father loved each other...'

'He was taken from me,' she snapped.

'I know, but I was simply pointing out that you were lucky not to be stuck in a loveless marriage. It's more than simply apportioning blame and putting an end to it. If Barbara counter-sued she'd get custody of the children and that would break my heart. Besides, there's no point now, with Virginia getting married.'

'Exactly,' she said.

The day of the wedding, the week before Easter 1932, was fine and sunny, though not yet warm. Virginia, dressed in pale-blue crêpe, with a large picture hat of pale-blue straw trimmed with silk flowers and blue velvet ribbon, hung on George's arm as she went down the aisle. Besides the whole Kennett family, there was a handful of guests filling the first two or three pews of St Andrew's church. Donald's son and his family, over from Canada, and his brother from Yorkshire, were on his side of the aisle, together with a representative sprinkling of working colleagues, including Colin and Rita. Colin had been yard manager at Kennett's ever since Donald took over the hardware shop. His steady climb up through Kennett's had surprised everyone, though apart from Barbara and Rita, the Kennett and Younger families did not meet socially.

Barbara, in a straight lime-green silk dress with a tiered overskirt of matching lace, and a navy domed hat with a turned-down brim which she hoped would hide her eyes, hadn't wanted to come, but it would have looked odd to refuse, especially as George had been inveigled into giving the bride away. She guessed he was using the occasion to get the message across that rumours there was anything between him and Virginia were unfounded. She became sure of it when she heard his speech at the reception held in the function room of The Crown.

'I've known Virginia many years,' he said, smiling. 'Though I hesitate to tell you how many. Looking at her today, you wouldn't believe me anyway.' He paused for the laughter, which rippled for a moment and faded. 'But that is not why I agreed to give her away.' His choice of words was particularly apt, Barbara decided, as he continued. 'As most of you know, she became a member of our family when she married my wife's father, and as a member of the family, she is loved and cherished by us all.' He paused again. 'I would not give her away to anyone, but Donald is also a very special person, friend and colleague and, after today, also part of the family. I give you a toast: the bride and groom, Virginia and Donald.' He raised his glass and looked towards the newly-weds. 'To you both. May you have long life and happiness.' He took a sip as others rose and echoed the toast, but only Barbara noticed the twitch in his jaw, which told her he was under severe strain.

She supposed she ought to be pleased if the marriage meant the end of George's affair, but she couldn't quite bring herself to believe it and felt desperately sorry for Donald. He appeared to be happy, replying to the toast and chatting to everyone. Virginia was laughing a lot, accepting kisses and good wishes as if she really was a bride in love with her husband.

'Funny match, don't you think?' said a voice at her elbow.

Barbara turned to find Rita beside her in a pink and fawn check dress which made her plump figure look even plumper. She had a huge black straw hat on her red curls. 'How so?'

'He's a bit old-fashioned, not even good-looking, and she's...well, she's younger and taller than he is, and glamorous too. I can't help feeling he's bitten off more than he can chew.'

'Let's hope not. He deserves some happiness.'

'Don't we all.'

Barbara found herself wondering if there had been more problems in the Younger household. 'That's true. How are things with you?'

'Oh, so-so. Zita's left home, so we don't have her wages coming in anymore and things are tight.' Zita had been working at a horticultural nursery ever since she left school. It paid a pittance but it was better than no job at all. She had always been artistic and wanted to be a sculptress, to be famous and paid for her work, but nobody else believed it was possible. 'Colin was always complaining about the mess she made in the house with bits of stone and plaster and one day they had an almighty row and she moved out. She is eighteen, after all. She's got a one-bedroom flat at the top of Regency Terrace.' She paused and looked closely at her friend. 'What about you?'

'We're all fine. Just fine.'

That was palpably untrue, but Rita did not challenge it. Instead, she said, 'Let's have coffee in Sadlers on Wednesday morning. We haven't had a chat for ages.'

'Good idea. I'll meet you there.'

Rita left to join Colin who was becoming noisily tipsy. Somehow she had to drag him away before the booze loosened his tongue. She didn't want him telling all and sundry what he knew about Virginia Bosgrove's past love life, mainly because it would upset Barbara.

'Damn farce, if you ask me,' he said, as she joined him

to see the newly-weds off with old shoes and empty tin cans tied to the back of their car. 'I wouldn't be surprised if Kennett hadn't put him up to it.'

'Whatever for?'

'Smokescreen. To stop the gossip. Councillor Kennett is putting himself up to be a magistrate. Has to be whiter than white for that.'

'Where d'you hear that?'

He tapped his nose and grinned. 'A little bird told me.'

Slowly, as one year and then another passed, the economy began to pick up. Most of the properties in Melsham's industrial site were let to small companies which were producing consumer goods like bicycles, wireless sets and vacuum cleaners. And those in good jobs were looking for houses. On the more affluent side of town, two streets of new dwellings were being put up for four or five hundred pounds freehold or ten shillings a week, all with bathrooms and small gardens, and it went without saying that George was building them.

Nick disappointed Barbara by not passing the entrance exam to go to the grammar school with Alison, but George said it didn't matter because he would be working in the business with him. 'It will be Kennett and Son,' he told her.

'Don't you mean sons?' Barbara queried. 'Don't forget Jay-Jay.'

'I hadn't forgotten him, but he has only just started school, it will be a long time before he can join the firm, won't it? And to be honest I'm not sure he's got what it takes. He's more like you, artistic, not practical.'

He did have a point and, besides, she really didn't want either of her sons being taught George's idea of good business practice. Reminded that her younger son ought to be in bed, she rose and went upstairs to his room.

He was sitting at the desk George had bought him the year before, his red-gold head bent over a sheet of paper. When her shadow fell over him he quickly covered the paper with his arm. She smiled. 'What are you drawing? Can I see?'

Slowly he slid his arm out of the way to reveal a surprisingly good caricature of George, with beetling black brows and an oversize mouth. On his barrel-like chest was a huge blue rosette. He grinned sheepishly. 'You won't tell Dad, will you?'

She laughed in delighted surprise. 'No, I don't think he'd appreciate it. Now, it's time you were in bed.'

She told herself she didn't have favourites, that she loved all her children equally, but she was especially close to Jay-Jay and, as he grew, she imagined she could see something of Simon in him, the cheerful countenance, the desire to please, the affectionate nature. She hoped he would grow up with Simon's sensitivity and not be like George. Nowadays she rarely thought of Jay-Jay as anything but George's child, but if the truth came out, what would she do? Deny it with her last breath, she supposed, though how convincing she would be under pressure she had no idea and prayed she would never be put to the test. She kissed him goodnight and went back to the sitting room. George had gone out again, Nick was building something with his Meccano and Alison was doing her homework.

Barbara sat up in bed, wondering what had woken her. She lay listening to the wind howling round the house, rattling the windows and making a door bang. She heard something crash outside and went to open the window. As soon as she loosened the catch, the casement was whipped out of her hand. She wrestled with it a moment before forcing it shut, then stood and watched the trees at the end of the garden, swaying to and fro in a kind of frenzied dance against a sky where the clouds scudded like huge black galleons on a storm-lashed sea. One of the trees must have come down because she could see the chimneys of the manor, never visible before. It was that which had woken her.

'George, wake up.' She went back to the bed and shook him. 'George, there's a tree down in the garden.'

He groaned and stirred. 'What's the matter?'

'There's a tree down. I heard it go. Just listen to the wind. Your mother will be terrified.'

He got up and padded in his pyjamas to look out of the window, just as another tree creaked ominously and then thudded to the ground, flattening the fence they had built between The Chestnuts and the manor grounds.

He grabbed his trousers and pulled them on over his pyjamas. By the time he was halfway down the stairs, the children were awake and crowding at the landing window which gave them a good view of the garden. Sheet lightning illuminated a scene of destruction: trees down, branches broken, fences flattened. The sound of breaking glass told them the greenhouse had gone. As they watched they saw their father crouching against the wind as he battled his way to his mother's bungalow.

278

'I'll put the kettle on,' Barbara said.

By the time she had made cocoa for them all, George was back with his mother.

'I'm perfectly all right,' she said, as Barbara came forward to help her. And then jumped out of her skin as they heard another crash and all the lights went out.

'Has a tree fallen on the house?' Jay-Jay asked, grabbing hold of his mother in the dark.

'No, you don't suppose I'd be daft enough to build a house that close to trees, do you?' George fumbled in the kitchen drawer for candles and matches. 'I expect a tree has brought the lines down somewhere. Back to bed with you.'

The devastation became obvious with daylight. Trees had been uprooted, blocking roads and doing untold damage, roofs had been lifted off buildings and carried hundreds of yards. Power lines were down and heavy rain had flooded low-lying fields. Rescue teams and council workmen were up as soon as it was light enough to see, to begin on clearing up. Before he went to work, George went down the garden to inspect the damage. One of the trees inside their own boundary had come down across the fence; the copse in the manor grounds was a copse no longer and looked like a logging camp. He was thankful there had been no buildings in the vicinity.

'It could be worse,' he told Barbara when he returned to the house. 'A gang with saws will soon clear it, but it's certainly changed the view.' He put his jacket on and picked up his briefcase. 'It's an ill-wind as they say. I've a feeling I'm going to be very busy today dealing with

279

requests for repairs. And Donald had better make sure he's well stocked.'

It was typical of him to think of profit, Barbara thought, watching from the window as he fetched the Daimler out of the garage and drove off. She sent the children to school and set off for the manor.

Isobel was clearing up the hearth in the drawing room where the heavy rain had dislodged an accumulation of soot. 'The chimney is old and there are crevices a brush can't reach,' Isobel said, wiping the back of her hand across her forehead and leaving a smudge of soot to join others already there.

Barbara smiled at Isobel's appearance. She was wearing an old, grey wool skirt and a jumper which she must have found in the ragbag, it was so out of shape. Over it she had tied a huge white apron such as her cook might have worn. Her hair was crammed under a scarf commemorating the old queen's jubilee. 'You look a bit like a chimney sweep.'

Isobel peered into the mirror and laughed. 'I do, don't I? I'll clean myself up and we'll have some coffee. Luckily I can make it on the range, I don't need electricity.' She whipped off the apron and scarf as she spoke. 'Are you all OK?'

'Yes.' She followed Isobel into the kitchen. 'A tree brought the fence down and the greenhouse is gone, nothing that can't be put right. Do you want George to come and see if there's anything needs doing here?'

'No thanks, if I find any problems, I'll call him.' She tried not to sound offhand, but she didn't want George Kennett poking round again. She didn't like the man, had a fair notion that he had cheated her over the roof repairs, so she had been wary when he had arrived a few weeks before, offering to buy the manor. 'It must be a headache to you,' he had said. 'Why not be rid of it? With twenty thousand pounds you could buy a small modern house. No damp rot, no leaking roof, no blocked gutters, no draughty windows. And heating which would cost a tiny fraction of what it costs to heat this place.' She had told him she did not want to sell her home, but the dreadful part of it was that he was probably right.

They spent a few minutes drinking coffee and chatting about the storm and how lucky they were. There must have been injuries, perhaps fatalities, and some people would have lost everything. It would have far-reaching consequences. Just how far-reaching Barbara was not to know until she returned home and found George pacing the drawing room.

'Barbara, where've you been?' His voice was ragged and husky.

'I went up to see if Isobel was OK. She was busy clearing up soot, but there doesn't seem to be much damage. She said she'd call you if—'

'Barbara, listen, will you?' he interrupted.

His voice, bordering on panic, warned her something was wrong. 'I'm listening.'

'It's Virginia... She's...' He was finding it difficult to speak. 'She's dead...killed by a tree falling on her car.'

'Oh, my God.' She paused. ' What about Donald?'

'She was alone, driving home from Cambridge along the bypass beside the old copse. She was killed instantly...'

'Oh, George, I'm sorry.' What else could she say?

'Will you go and see if Donald needs anything? I can't go.' It wasn't that he was too busy, she understood that, it was simply that he wouldn't know what to say. Virginia and Donald had been married over two years but George's hurt was still too raw to comfort anyone else.

'Of course. I'll go now.'

The congregation at the funeral mirrored that of the wedding. Donald, grey-faced, followed the coffin down the aisle on leaden feet, a lonely figure with head bowed. Barbara felt sorry for him and stepped out of her pew to walk beside him. A moment later she became aware that George had followed her and regretted her impulsive action, because her husband's grief was plain for all to see and she had drawn attention to it.

Maggie Doughty had been sent by the *Melsham Gazette*. It was, so her editor told her, the town's bereavement and she was to write it up sympathetically. She would do that but she was also interested in George Kennett. He had been heard to remind people that he had advocated taking down the trees when the bypass was built, and if his advice had been taken, no one would have died – not there at any rate. It was a comment her editor had seen fit to publish, but now she was seeing something else: two men in mourning, two men weeping for the same woman, two men who could not even look at each other, let alone speak.

Maggie hated George Kennett. Her father had died because of him. They said he had taken his own life while the balance of his mind was disturbed, but who had disturbed it in the first place? George Kennett with his massive new store and its cut-throat prices; her father's rather old-fashioned hardware shop hadn't stood a chance. Even that wouldn't have been so bad except that, bowing to the inevitable and closing down the shop, he had approached George Kennett for a job. The bastard had turned him down, said you couldn't teach an old dog new tricks. Too old at fifty-five! Dad had tried to pretend he had chosen early retirement, but no one had been fooled. One day, a year later, he had hanged himself.

Looking at Kennett standing beside the grave, black suit, black tie, hair ruffling in the breeze, she saw his grief and smiled grimly. He would grieve more than that before she had done with him.

Barbara didn't know what to say to George. He hardly spoke, turning his misery in on himself, embracing it. Did he suppose she was glad about it? Of course she wasn't glad, but neither could she tell him she was sorry. It wasn't that she expected him to fall in love with her all over again — it was too late for that, far too late — but with no Virginia in the background, they might just pull themselves back on an even keel. After all, they were not in the first flush of youth, and they had three children who were fast growing into adulthood, children who needed them both. And she hadn't been blameless. If they could achieve some measure of ease with each other, that was all she could hope for, all she deserved.

She fell back on her usual palliative and began a new painting, standing before the canvas, slashing colour on it, hardly stopping to think what she was doing. The result was a windswept tree, dark against a blood-red fen sky. In the branches appeared the shadowy heads of George and Virginia, her father, Simon and the children, their faces distorted with some unseen vision of terror. It was horrible, frightening, much too revealing to leave for anyone else to see. She took it down the garden and put it on the bonfire their gardener had made with the branches of the fallen tree. Its therapeutic work done, she went back indoors and began another.

Barbara dipped her brush in black paint and wrote *The Market of Old Melsham* along the bottom of the picture and signed the corner. It had taken over six months to complete, mainly because she was so busy with other things, and it had been such a monumental task, which was what she had intended it to be. It was full of detail: the old buildings on which she had spent painstaking hours of research, the market traders, the church and the old pump where the fountain and dirty pool now stood, people chatting beside it. Looking at the figures on the canvas, some of whom had the faces of people she knew, she allowed her mind to drift.

George seemed to have got over Virginia's death and so had Donald and they continued to work together. If anything it seemed to bring the two men closer, leaving Barbara on the periphery of her husband's life which was, she supposed, where she had always been. Business, politics and golf were all he thought about. She was heartily sick of all three, but especially politics. It was politics which had ruined George as a husband. That and his craving for power. As her mother had often advised her, she had counted her blessings. She had a nice home, a husband who, whatever his faults, was a good provider, and three children who were a credit to them. She had friends and charitable work which often reminded her that there were a great many people worse off than she was, and whenever counting blessings did not seem to work, she had her painting. She spent hours in this room, absorbed in composition and colour and effect, cut off from reality, almost content.

Alison, in a printed cotton dress, her dark hair worn in two plaits, put her head round the door. 'Mum, Aunt Penny's here. Didn't you hear the doorbell?'

'Penny?' she queried in surprise. 'Why ever didn't she say she was coming?'

She cleaned her brush and hurried from the room, leaving Alison looking at the picture with her head on one side. It was huge, every inch of it covered with figures. She recognised Lady Isobel sitting upright in a carriage drawn by four horses and driven by James. There was Mrs Younger, carroty hair spilling out beneath a black straw hat and her shoulders draped in a fringed shawl, with a basket of flowers on her arm. There was Dad, sitting arrogantly on a fine hunter, and Jay-Jay, a barefoot urchin, dodging among the stalls with an orange in his hand. Gran was there, shopping basket on her arm, and Nick sitting on the back of a cart, and she was there, dressed in a crinoline of blue taffeta, a straw bonnet on her dark hair, carrying a frilled parasol. A young boy was working the old pump, and the water sparkled as it gushed into a bucket, and there was an old-time policeman in shiny-buttoned uniform and top hat, standing on the kerb. There was so much to explore, she was reluctant to leave it, but she had arranged to go to the Saturday matinee with one of her friends and she didn't want to miss the beginning. She'd come back to it later, persuade Mum to hang it somewhere where it would be seen.

Penny was like a breath of fresh air, her red-gold hair framing a face that didn't seem to have aged one iota since Barbara had first met her. She was bright, cheerful and glamorous in a dress of flower-patterned silk with puffed sleeves and a skirt gathered at the natural waist. Her hat, worn tilted to one side, had a huge brim. It was an elegantly simple outfit which had obviously cost a great deal.

'It's been a long time,' Barbara said, kissing her cheek. 'I don't need to ask how you are. How do you manage to stay looking so young?'

Penny laughed. 'With difficulty. I hope I haven't interrupted anything. Alison said you were painting.'

'Yes.'

'I'm glad to hear it. May I see it?'

'Yes, if you like. Come up and I'll show you.' She led the way. 'You'll stay for lunch? There's some ham and a salad, is that OK?'

'Lovely.'

'Are you filming in the area?'

'Not exactly. I'm going into production in partnership with Hal Erikson. He's the man who produced *Dragon Castle*. We've got a story lined up, but we need a location. I'm looking round East Anglia for something that fits...'

She stopped when she caught sight of the painting. 'Is that it?'

'Yes.'

She walked over to inspect it more closely. 'It's terrific. All those people. However long did it take?'

'Months. I started it last October.' Barbara moved over and pointed to a figure wearing a riding habit and a tall hat with a sweeping peacock feather, standing beside a slender-limbed horse. Beside her a man in the red coat and white breeches of a soldier was bent cupping his hand ready to help her to mount. 'That's you. And that's Simon.'

'So it is! How clever of you! And the ambience of the time is just right. Very Victorian. Are the buildings still like that?'

'Basically yes, though some have modern facias and windows now.'

'They could be altered,' she mused aloud. 'I'll have to go and look.'

'For your film?'

'Yes, but I need a house as well. A stately home without too many modern touches.'

Barbara laughed. 'I know the very place. I'll take you there after lunch.'

Isobel had persuaded James to teach her to drive. She was practising up and down the long drive from the gates to the house, but she couldn't get the hang of the gears and the clutch. James wasn't a good teacher, and though he didn't for a minute raise his voice or lose his natural deference when speaking to her, she could feel the tension in him, knew how hard he was trying not to lose his temper. She was unprepared for any other traffic and was completely thrown when Barbara's little Austin turned in at the gates. She stamped her foot on the brake and yanked on the steering wheel and the car slewed into a flowerbed.

Barbara stopped and ran over to her. 'Isobel, are you all right?'

She was helpless with laughter. 'Perfectly, my dear. It was entirely my fault. I'm sorry if I gave you a scare.'

James, who had left the passenger seat, was standing looking at the car with an expression of such pain on his face, Barbara began to wonder if he had been hurt. 'Excuse me, My Lady,' he said stiffly. 'Shall I put the car away?'

'Yes, do. I'll go up to the house with Mrs Kennett.'

Isobel clambered out and the two women stood and watched as he backed the Bentley onto the drive and drove it down to the road where he was able to turn it. He passed them on his way back at a steady five miles an hour, sitting very upright and looking straight ahead. 'Oh, dear, he's miffed,' Isobel said. 'He loves that old car.'

'It's hardly an easy car to drive,' Barbara said, leading the way to her own. 'Why don't you try a small one like mine? I'm sure you could manage that.'

Isobel smiled. 'I can just imagine what James would say if I suggested changing the Bentley for a Baby Austin, can't you?'

'I suppose he would think it a bit of a comedown.'

'The trouble is, he shouldn't be driving the Bentley

either: he's getting very old and he drives so slowly we have everyone hooting at us. That's why I suggested the lessons.' For the first time she noticed Penny in the passenger seat. 'Oh, I didn't realise...'

'This is Penny Barcliffe, Isobel.' Barbara opened the back door for her. 'She's a film star and a very good friend. So I've brought her to meet you.'

'If you're a friend of Barbara's, you're very welcome.' She smiled and held out her hand across the back of the seat. 'Let's go up to the house, shall we?'

After the car stopped, Penny stood on the gravel looking at the facade for several seconds before following Lady Quarenton and Barbara indoors. Isobel showed them into the drawing room then disappeared in the direction of the kitchen.

'Barbara, it's just what we want,' Penny said, looking about her.

Isobel reappeared with a loaded tea tray and set it on the coffee table. 'James hasn't come back from putting the car away.' She sat down and poured tea from a silver teapot into delicate bone china cups, added milk and offered the sugar bowl, but both shook their heads. 'He won't retire while he thinks I need him. The alternative is to sell up and move somewhere smaller and more convenient.'

'But it's such a lovely house,' Penny put in. 'I don't know how you could bear to part with it.'

'The prospect appals me,' Isobel admitted. 'I was born in this house, a disappointment to my Papa because he had wanted a son and heir, an even greater one when he realised my mother could have no more children.' She sighed. 'Sometimes I think it would be lovely not to have the worry of it.' She laughed suddenly. 'Your husband was right, Barbara, but the thought of walking out on all that history...'

'My husband?' Barbara queried.

'Didn't he tell you he'd made me an offer? I think he wants to pull it down to build houses. He could get a lot of those little boxes on this land. I should hate that.'

Barbara had not known of the offer but, then, George never told her anything. 'There is an alternative,' she said. 'A temporary one, at least. That's why I brought Penny to see you.' She turned to Penny, who had been standing with her cup and saucer in her hand, looking out of the window onto the terrace with its steps down to the lawn. 'Pen, do tell Lady Isobel about your project.'

Penny sat down opposite Isobel and explained what she had in mind. 'We won't be tramping all over the house, I promise you,' she ended. 'It's the exterior, and perhaps one or two downstairs rooms, we would like to use, especially this one because of its view of the terrace and gardens. We'd pay you very handsomely for the privilege, and believe me, it will be a privilege.'

'How long would it take?'

'Two or three weeks, after that you have your house back and a nice fat cheque in the bank.'

'Then I'll give it some thought.' She turned to Barbara. 'Does your husband know about this?'

'Not a thing.' It was said with a chuckle. 'It's nothing to do with him.'

290

They spent a little time going into more detail and then Penny and Barbara left. Hal Erikson would have to come down and have a look, but Penny's recommendation that the house was ideal for their purpose meant his agreement was almost a foregone conclusion.

Chapter Eleven

M ELSHAM WAS INVADED by strange people in strange garb, talking earnestly in little groups and calling each other 'darling'. That is when they weren't in the caravans parked in the grounds of Melsham Manor, where the actors were dressed and made-up and where they rehearsed their lines. There were cameras and miles of cable and a great deal of shouting, followed by minutes of intense silence while everyone waited for the girl with the clapperboard to announce the next take.

The manor had received an external facelift: the gardens and gravel drive had been weeded and raked, the lawns cut, the windows cleaned so that they sparkled with new life. To Penny and Hal's delight, they had even found the old Quarenton carriage under a pile of dust sheets in the coach house. It had been dragged out, cleaned up and repaired and was now being used behind two beautiful bay horses to bring the heroine to her new home. It astonished Barbara, who had gone at Penny's invitation, that her friend was able to act with all the hubbub, and she was impressed by how much patience she had, doing the same scene over and over again until both she and the director were satisfied.

'It's one way to have the gardening done,' Isobel said, coming to stand beside Barbara, while cameras, lighting and sound were adjusted for the next shot. 'The trouble is that it's a reprieve, not a final solution.'

'Then we shall have to think of something else.'

'We?' Isobel took a sideways glance at Barbara who wore a pleated skirt and a matching jacket over a plain blouse. She didn't know how old Barbara was, but judging by the ages of the children she must be about thirty-three or -four, some twenty years younger than she was. But a good friend. She found herself smiling. 'What do you suggest?'

'Why not a hydro? I saw an advert for one in the hairdresser's the other day. That was a converted stately home.'

'What on earth's a hydro?'

'A kind of clinic where wealthy women come to lose weight and be cosseted. There's an awful lot of money in it.'

'But that would mean expensive alterations and equipment, wouldn't it? And trained staff. Where would I go for that kind of money, bearing in mind all the collateral I've got is this crumbling ruin?'

'It isn't crumbling, that's just George talking. You could ask Penny. I bet she'd know how to go about it.'

'You mean it, don't you?'

'Why not?'

294

'Pie in the sky,' Isobel said, laughing. 'But fun to think about. Now, I must go and find James. He's probably sulking somewhere.'

Barbara watched her go, a tall upright figure in purple silk. She couldn't be all that old, but she dressed and behaved like a grand dame. Until you got to know her and realised she had a wonderful sense of humour and great compassion.

'Barbara.' The voice behind her was low, pleasant and vividly remembered.

She turned towards him and tried desperately not to let her confusion show. He was as youthful and good-looking as ever and she wanted to fling herself at him and be hugged and kissed, to feel his arms about her, his lips on hers, to know he still cared, still wanted her. But she couldn't even reach out and touch him, not with everyone watching. 'Simon!'

'How are you?'

She pulled herself together and smiled. 'I'm well. What about you? Are you fully recovered?'

'Yes, fit and well and back to the grind, but every now and again, I peep out to see how the world is faring, which is why I decided to come and see what Penny's up to today.'

'She's good isn't she?'

'Stupendous.' He put a hand on her arm. The effect was electric, she almost jumped from her skin. 'And how is life treating you?'

'Very well.'

'Truly?' He was looking closely at her, making her squirm.

'Yes. George is going to be mayor next year.'

'And you'll be lady mayoress. Congratulations.'

'Thanks, but I've done nothing.'

He smiled at her with his head on one side. 'Stood by him, I expect.' He watched the colour suffuse her face and decided not to pursue that line. 'How are the children?'

'Growing up fast. Alison is at Melsham Grammar School and determined to be a doctor. George wants Nick to go into the business when he leaves school, but I don't know if he will. It's early days yet.'

'And Jay-Jay? You see, I remember his name.'

'He's seven now and very artistic.'

'Seven, was it as long ago as that?'

What did he mean by that? Had he worked it out? Penny hadn't told him, she would never break a promise, but if he knew...

The tension between them was like a tightly coiled spring which was held in check by nothing more than willpower. His blue eyes were searching, probing, winkling out her inner thoughts. Until now she had not realised her feelings for him had not died but were simply lying dormant, until he reawakened them. She wanted to cry, grab hold of him, tell him how much she loved him and missed him, that he had a son, but she couldn't. Daren't.

'It's all right, you know,' he said softly. 'You did the right thing.'

'Right thing?'

'Not coming back to the hospital to see me. I shouldn't have said what I did. I was just feeling sorry for myself.'

'Please, Simon, don't say that. You were my saviour.'

'Does that mean everything is all right now?'

'Yes.' It was a monumental lie and she thought he guessed it.

The scene was finished and the film-makers broke off for lunch. Penny, her face clean of make-up but still looking incredibly beautiful in a pair of tailored trousers with a print blouse worn over them, was walking towards them with Hal, tall, blonde and very Scandinavian.

'We're off to lunch,' she told Barbara. 'Would you like to join us?'

'Sorry. I must be going, I'm on duty in the clothing store this afternoon.'

She made her escape, her senses reeling. It was as if fate, or whoever was judge of these things, was reminding her that her punishment was not something to endure for a short time, it was for ever. Why had she introduced Penny to Isobel? Why tempt fate? If Simon should come face to face with Jay-Jay... But what if he did? Simon had his own life and it was nothing to do with her.

Jay-Jay and two friends climbed over the back fence and through what remained of the woods, coming out onto the manor drive, just as a coach and horses came rattling round the bend.

'Cut!' someone yelled. 'Get those kids out of there.'

Several angry men advanced towards them, the carriage came to a stop and Penny's head emerged from it. 'What's wrong?'

'Blasted kids, got in the shot,' one of the advancing men said. 'Don't know how they got past the cordon.'

Penny laughed. 'I do. Hallo, Jay-Jay.'

Jay-Jay's face went bright pink, though he was aware

that his friends were standing with their mouths open. They hadn't believed him when he said he knew Penny Barcliffe and could get them an introduction. 'Hallo, Aunt Penny. We only wanted to see you...'

'I know, but you got in the shot, you see, and shorts and jumpers are not at all Victorian, are they? Now, I shall have to turn round and do it all again. Go and stand over there, behind the cameras, and keep very still and very quiet.' She saw her brother among the crew and beckoned him over. 'Simon, take care of them. This one's Barbara's youngest.' She pointed at Jay-Jay.

The boys allowed themselves to be ushered to one side until the scene was finished. 'I'm Jay-Jay,' he told Simon, unable to resist bragging. 'Short for Jeremy John. Penny Barcliffe is my mother's friend.'

'And Penny is my sister.'

Jay-Jay looked up at him and decided he liked his blue eyes, which had a decided twinkle. 'Why haven't I seen you before? Aunt Penny comes down all the time. Mum and her have been friends for ever.'

'I know, but I don't live with Penny, you know. We don't see much of each other. I just thought I'd like to visit Melsham again.'

'You've been here before?'

'Yes, for your mother's wedding and your grandfather's funeral.'

'I don't remember that,' he said seriously. 'Why haven't you been lately? Did you and Mum quarrel?'

'No, we didn't quarrel.' He looked down at the boy and felt an unaccountable urge to ruffle his hair, to tell him it hadn't been his wish, that some partings were even worse to bear when there were no quarrels, that if he had had his way, he would have been a father to him. 'We had nothing to quarrel about.'

For him it was a bittersweet memory, made the more poignant because of this boy who stood so sturdily beside him. If he had had the sense to grab Barbara when she was single, if she had left George... If... So many ifs. 'Grown-ups get pretty busy, you know,' he said. 'Things happen, you get on with your lives and before you know it, years have gone by.'

Jay-Jay studied him for some minutes. 'You know, I think you're in Mum's painting of Melsham. It's got hundreds of people in it. Alison and Nick and Gran and Aunt Penny. I think it's you standing beside her. You ought to see it. Why don't you come? Say hallo to Mum?'

Simon was intrigued, but not enough to invade Barbara's home, nor make small talk with the man she had married. 'I've already seen her,' he said. 'Earlier today. And I have to get back to London tonight. Another time perhaps.'

Jay-Jay couldn't wait to get home and tell everyone about it over the dinner table. 'Aunt Penny was super,' he said. 'She gave everyone an autograph and showed us how the cameras and lights worked, and the clapperboard and the rushes. I saw her brother. He was nice. I liked him.'

Barbara's hand, on its way to her mouth with a forkful of chicken, stopped halfway. She lowered it and put the fork back on her plate, being careful not to let it clatter. Then she took a deep breath. 'What did he have to say?' Her voice was high and brittle and she became aware that George had also stopped eating and was looking at her.

299

Why, today of all days, did he have to come home for dinner?

'He said he'd been to your wedding and Grandad's funeral. He came to see if Melsham had changed.'

'Which it hasn't,' George said sharply. He was still seething over Barbara introducing Penny Barcliffe to Lady Quarenton: it had ruined his plans to buy the manor, though he could not complain to her about it without having to explain why he wanted it. Simon Barcliffe could not have timed his reappearance any better if he had deliberately set out to provoke him. Which he probably had.

'I told him about Mum's picture of the market,' Jay-Jay went on, and to Barbara, ultra sensitive, it seemed that Simon's blue eyes shone from his face. 'I told him he ought to come and see it.'

'Why should he want to see that? Why did you even mention it?' George demanded.

'Because he's in it, like everyone else.'

'Whatever gave you that idea?' Barbara put in quickly.

Jay-Jay got up from the table and went to the picture, which Alison had persuaded her to hang in the dining room. 'It will be a topic for conversation,' she had said. Until now Barbara had not minded and George, who had never had any time to look at it properly, had made no comment except to say he thought it was good.

'There,' Jay-Jay said, pointing. 'Next to Aunt Penny.'

Barbara picked up her fork and made a pretence of eating, but she couldn't swallow because her heart seemed to be in her throat, blocking it. Why must a little indiscretion live with you and haunt you for the rest of your life? Guilt and love, so inextricably entwined, they could not be separated.

Frustrated by Lady Isobel's refusal to sell, George turned his attention to other ways of making money, and the proposed refurbishment of Melsham market was just the thing. It was still the thriving centre of the town, but the buildings were grimy, the tarmac worn so that the old cobbles were showing through in places, the facia boards on the shops a higgledy-piggledy mess of hieroglyphics and ill-matched colours. There were no seats, the fountain was often turned off and the water in the pool was full of debris. A place needed to look bright and prosperous to attract investment. And that would be his argument for spending money on it and, if he was canny, a good proportion of the work would come his way.

The idea had come to him when he saw what the film-makers had done, putting up temporary Victorian facades over the shops and buildings round the market, which had changed the whole character of the place. Everyone had said how quaint and charming it looked. Unfortunately most of it was only boarding and had been removed when the film was finished and the town had gone back to its mishmash of old and new. George wanted to restore the Victorian ambience on a permanent basis.

'The present proposal doesn't go nearly far enough,' he told Tony Bartram, chairman of General Purposes, when they met at The Crown and ordered a beer each. 'The whole area needs paving, York stone, red brick, something classy. What's there now is an insult, and the fountain is a disgrace. The traders could have uniform striped awnings.'

'They'll be against it if it means they pay more for their pitches.' Bartram, rotund and balding, took a swig from his glass. 'All they're concerned with is having the surface tidied up, so there are no puddles when it rains. And the ratepayers will say there are other priorities for their money.'

'We could get private funding for some of it. I have already approached Landers and they have agreed to provide a percentage, and I reckon some of the town's other businesses could be persuaded to contribute. They stand to gain and they won't want to be upstaged by Landers. It's all down to good publicity.' He smiled as a new idea struck him. 'We could hold a competition for the design of a new fountain, something befitting. We don't have to accept any of the designs, but it will give the public an interest, keep them off our backs...'

'That's a bit cynical, isn't it?'

He laughed. 'Realistic. You and I know we'd never get anything done if we had to have universal approbation first. I have only the interests of the town and population of Melsham at heart, Tony, you know that.'

'Oh, that goes without saying.'

The man's sarcasm was not lost on George but he decided not to comment. 'I want Melsham put on the map, made a place to be proud of. All I want you to do is back an amendment.'

'OK, I'll sound everyone out and see if we can get it on the agenda.'

George walked back to his office with a jaunty step, smiling to himself. He rang his solicitor and made an appointment to see him, then he summoned Donald Browning to his office.

His attitude towards Donald was ambivalent. On the surface he treated him like a friend and trusted employee, but that trust had been severely dented over Virginia, though it had never been spoken of aloud. Since her death they had rubbed along because each needed the other. Donald was his general factotum, held the fort when he was out making deals or on council business and generally kept his suppliers off his back.

'Sit down, Donald.' George had been standing by the window with his back to the room, staring out at the leaden sky, but now he turned and, going to a cupboard behind his desk, fetched out a bottle and a couple of glasses. 'Whisky?'

'Thanks. It's bitterly cold out.'

George poured two generous tots and handed one to Donald who had seated himself in the chair facing the desk and was chewing his moustache, a sure sign he was nervous. Usually he was left to get on with his work and only met George on a strictly business basis when there was a management meeting or some strategy to be worked out, involving the whole group. But drinking together became a thing of the past when he married Virginia. Her death had devastated him, as it had George, but neither was such a fool as to let that impinge on their working relationship. He sipped his drink and waited.

'You know about the market refurbishment?' George asked.

'I've been reading about it in the Gazette, but it's only

repaving and new lighting, not anything Kennett's would be interested in.'

'Oh, I don't know,' George said. 'I think it's a good idea to have two strings to one's bow, don't you? Besides, I don't think the current plans go nearly far enough. I'm lobbying for more – brick paving and the shop fronts restored, a new fountain. The contract to do all that would be worth having.'

'But you're on the council; you'd have to declare an interest, and if Kennett's did get it there'd be a public outcry about favouritism, if not corruption.'

'Exactly. Which is why I'm thinking of setting up a new company. I want you to be its managing director.'

'Why me? Why now? We're hardly out of the recession.'

'It's the optimum time. We'd get the best deals over supplies, plenty of labour, premises at rock bottom, what more do you want? Besides, we've done well in recessions before and this will be a wonderful opportunity.'

'Just what are you getting at?'

George refilled their glasses. 'It's simple. You set up the company. Let's call it Melsham Construction. There's a suitable site going on the Norwich Road. It's Gosport's old place. I don't know why he hung onto it, obstinacy I suppose, but now he's gone his son has put it up for sale. It's almost derelict so it'll be cheap, but it's got plenty of store room, so I suggest you clean it up and start putting orders in for materials, bricks, paving, things with long delivery dates, and take on some skilled men. Take Colin Younger. Get him off my back...'

'But I don't see how that will help: you'll be on the

board of the new company and you'll have to declare it.'

'It won't be anything to do with me, a rival company.'

'But what about the finance? I haven't got that kind of money, you know that.'

George laughed. The loan he had negotiated with his bank manager for the purchase of the manor would be put to good use after all. 'The money will come from a finance company. It will be my money, my investment and I'm expecting a good return, but nothing on paper, of course, not between you and me, all done through a holding company.'

Donald suddenly realised what George was driving at. 'Isn't it a bit risky?'

'It'll be worth it. When it's all up and running, you can put in a bid for the market contract. I'll make sure you get it.'

'What happens when the market job is finished?'

'Go after other contracts, the company will still be operational so long as it's something Kennett's wouldn't be interested in, roads, paving, lighting. We'll talk about it when the time comes.'

Donald was tempted. If George wasn't on the board, he couldn't complain about what he did. The idea excited him, and for the first time since the interview started, he smiled. 'And you think you can trust me?'

'Donald, I know I can trust you.' He paused, watching the other man's face. The moustache was looking very bedraggled. 'So, are you in?'

'When do you want me to start?'

'As soon as you like. I want everything completed by

May next year, a memorial to my year as mayor, although officially it's being done for the jubilee.'

'Tight.'

'But not impossible.' He refilled their glasses. 'Here's to Melsham Construction. And the future.'

The glasses clinked. 'The future.'

He'd have to break his rule never to tell Barbara anything to do with business, George decided as he drove home. If she didn't know what was going on, she might just say the wrong thing in the wrong place to the wrong person and he couldn't risk that.

Barbara sat on the edge of the bed watching George dressing to go out. He didn't often come home between finishing work and going to a council meeting, preferring to eat at The Crown. Tonight he had rushed home, swallowed a quick meal and asked her to find him a clean shirt. He seemed keyed up, almost bursting, and she wondered what was coming.

'I'm going to set up a new company,' he said, finishing the knot in his tie and turning away from the mirror to face her.

The casual way he had introduced the subject did not deceive her. 'Whatever for? I thought business was slow.'

'It is. All the more reason to diversify. I want that market refurbishment contract and the new company will make the bid.'

'What exactly will it be bidding for?'

'More than just a bit of tarmac and a few new lamps. I want the scheme enlarged, brick paving and a new fountain.'

'You'll have to declare an interest.'

'Kennett's will, but not the new company because I won't be on the board.'

'Then how will you control it?'

'Through Donald. Who else could I trust to look after my interests and keep his mouth shut?'

'But how—?'

'It's simple, my dear. Donald is about to repay my generosity and years of friendship by being an ungrateful wretch and setting up in opposition. I shall make my disappointment known, while voicing the opinion that every man has a right to better himself. I shall be disappointed when Kennett's loses the market contract, but I'll take it with a good grace and settle for whatever piecemeal jobs they award me in compensation.' He laughed a little wildly, almost as if he were drunk. 'They aren't to know I've already picked the plum.'

'Surely it's illegal?'

'I can form a new company if I want to, nothing illegal in that.'

'But deceiving the council is. George, is it worth the risk?'

'Barbara, you must know the recession hit builders as much as anyone, and Kennett's hasn't escaped. This way, everyone will benefit: town, workers and family. Trust me.'

'Oh, I do,' she said. She trusted him to twist and turn, to bully and coerce, to flatter and bribe to get his own way and there was nothing she could do about it, short of exposing him, and that she could not do: there were too many other people depending on him – his family and his employees who relied on him for jobs.

307

'They'll want a local firm for preference because it means local jobs, and as I'll have declared my interest as far as Kennett's is concerned, I shall be allowed to speak in favour of the new company, even vote for it.' He was grinning like a schoolboy and that worried her more than ever.

'What's it called, this new company?'

'Melsham Construction Limited. It has a nice ring to it, doesn't it?'

'Supposing the press find out. You'll be crucified.'

'How are they going to find out? No one knows the truth except Donald and you. Donald is utterly trustworthy and he knows what he has to lose if he blabs. And you are my wife. I expect your support. I want you to make it known, discreetly, of course, just how hurt and upset I am, that we both are, by Donald's behaviour.'

'Me?'

'Yes, you, my ever loving wife.' It was said with such venom, she cringed.

She knew – who better? – that George's actions were not always honourable, but this was downright dishonest. And he wanted to drag her into it, wanted her to be as unscrupulous as he was. 'Donald's agreed?'

'Yes.'

'Then he's a fool. I think you should resign from the council and give your full attention to the business.'

'Resign! I'd be mad to do that. It's not only the market refurbishment we are talking about. There are plans to build a new shopping precinct around Sadlers development and a new cinema, all designed to uplift the profile of this town, provide employment and encourage our young people to stay here to live and work, and keep them off the streets. And it will encourage investment.'

'But you don't have to be on the council to do that. In fact, it's better if you're not, then no one can accuse you of malpractice.'

He flinched at her outspokenness. 'But I need to know what's in the wind, what the planners are up to and who's doing what. I need my finger on the pulse and for that I need to be on the inside. There's nothing wrong in that.'

Did he really believe what he was saying? Or did he still think he could pull the wool over her eyes? 'It's all part of the way you operate, George. It goes right back to our first house. I still go hot when I think of how you did that. And then there's this house. You cheated Isobel over the land, didn't you?'

'It was a perfectly honest arrangement. She couldn't afford the repairs to her roof and I took land in payment. She had every opportunity to get another quote or ask for independent advice. No one forced her to accept my offer.'

'No, but that's just an example of the way you manipulate people.'

'Only an example?' he sneered. 'There's more?'

'You know there is. And I am not going to do your dirty work for you.' She left him and went to her studio, the only place where she felt she could be herself. She hadn't intended to have a row with him, hadn't meant to batter him with accusations, but they'd all come tumbling out, all the things she had been bottling up for years. She was so stirred up inside she thought she would pop, fizz over, like a bottle of champagne when the cork is drawn. Change was in the air, nothing would ever be the same, not the town and its shops, not the old marketplace she had painted so faithfully, not the people. For the first time she had turned on her husband, though how long she could keep it up, she did not know.

George went to see his mother on his way out. She was sitting listening to the wireless with a cup of cocoa in her hand. She looked up as he entered. 'I didn't expect you tonight. I thought you had one of your meetings.'

'I'm just off. Are you tired? I'd like to talk.'

She switched off the wireless and turned towards him. 'Talk away.'

He sat down in the chair opposite her with his hands dangling between his knees, wondering where to begin. Just when all his plans seemed to be coming to fruition, being made mayor, the market project and Melsham Construction getting up and running, his wife had to go and turn on him. 'It's Barbara. All the years we've been married and now she's questioning my business methods.'

Elizabeth laughed. 'So? They are questionable, aren't they?'

'I know what I'm doing, but she refuses to back me. She's more concerned with her charities and her strange friends.'

'Strange friends?'

'Lady Isobel, Penny Barcliffe and Rita Younger. What a combination!'

'Rita Younger is bad news, George. Always was. Always will be. Tell Barbara to stay away from her.'

'It's no good telling Barbara anything,' he said, too immersed in his own troubles to wonder why she was so adamant. 'That's what I've been trying to explain. We had the most awful row. I feel as though I'm losing control, as if everything is slipping away from me...'

'Then you'd better do something about it. If you take my advice, you'll make a real effort to soothe Barbara and get her back on your side.'

She let him see himself out. Why did he have to come and jolt her out of her serenity, dragging up bitter memories, forcing her to live it all again, the hurt and anger which had smouldered inside her for forty-odd years, with no outlet, no way of release? Surely, after all this time, it wasn't going to explode in her face? And it wasn't just that, it was a feeling – premonition was perhaps too strong a word – that there was a catastrophe pending.

The council meeting was a stormy one, with everyone getting hot under the collar. 'I can't see that this fanciful idea is the best way of celebrating the jubilee,' someone said. 'Better have a civic dinner and a tea party for the children.'

'We can do that as well,' George said. 'But we also need something permanent. At one time, when Melsham was hardly more than a village, the market square was the village green and it had a communal pump. Long gone now, of course, and replaced by that dilapidated fountain, which doesn't work half the time. A new, properly constructed fountain will set the whole area off to advantage. And a competition to design it will involve the whole community.'

Mrs Greaves, in a shapeless grey dress which did nothing for her portly figure, spoke against George's amendment, saying that the original proposal to resurface the market should be given the go-ahead, but the new fountain and other improvements should be deferred until funding was more secure. A newspaper survey had shown the project would be unpopular.

'A decision should be based on facts, not popularity,' he said. 'And the facts are that a new fountain is not only desirable, but necessary, because of the state of the existing structure. You can't leave it as it is and it can't be cleaned out and set going again because it leaks. We'd have to do something about that anyway.'

'Will anyone second Councillor Kennett's amendment?' the chairman asked after several minutes' more heated argument.

Tony Bartram put his hand up and it was carried by two votes. George was jubilant.

Barbara picked up the *Melsham Gazette* from the mat and took it to the kitchen where she poured herself a cup of coffee and sat at the table to read it.

'The refurbishment of the marketplace, originally expected to cost ten thousand pounds, has been hit by unplanned additional costs, it was revealed at last night's meeting of the town council. The estimate approved last year is woefully short of the mark and more work needs to be done than was at first anticipated. Councillor George Kennett, who has been campaigning vigorously on behalf of the new scheme, told our reporter that overspending was not uncommon on projects of this size and complexity and the benefits would outweigh the additional costs. Various ways had been put forward to raise the extra cash from the private businesses and he had no doubt it would be forthcoming.

'Mr Kennett, who is mayor elect and a well-known local businessman, denied he had anything to gain personally. "My company will be submitting a tender along with several others," he stated. "I have no influence on those who award the contract, nor would I wish to have." Councillor Kennett went on to announce a competition to design a new fountain as the focal point for the refurbished marketplace. It will be open to anyone. Entry forms will be available at the town hall and the designs should be submitted by the first of September.'

Barbara put the paper down and stared out of the window. The morning sun was dappling through the branches of an apple tree, casting shimmering light and shade over the back lawn where a couple of starlings pecked. She had been hoping George would come to his senses and realise what he was proposing to do was too risky, but it was obvious that hadn't happened. Already she sensed the paper looking for something to get their teeth into; she could feel the undercurrents, the veiled hints that all was not above board. It needed only a word in the wrong place for it all to come out and the edifice George had built around himself would come tumbling down around him. And it would bring the family down with it. Alison, Nick, Jay-Jay and his mother. Why could he not see that?

How could she go on supporting him when everything he did was despicable? Could she leave him? But that would cause the most dreadful scandal and they would all suffer, not only George who deserved it, but the children who did not. And where could she go? To Simon? Pretend there was another sighting of the old Barbara Bosgrove? But what would he say if she turned up on his doorstep, with her bags at her feet, her easel under her arm and a box of paints in her hand? That wasn't a sighting, it was a migration.

'Mum, I'm hungry.'

Jay-Jay stood before her in his pyjamas. He couldn't understand why his mother suddenly pulled him onto her lap and hugged the breath out of him.

'Sorry, George, you know how it is,' Tony Bartram said, coming out of the council chamber with a thick folder under his arm. 'We're duty-bound to take the lowest bid, unless there's something dodgy about the company, and we've no reason to think Melsham Construction is anything but a bona fide concern.'

'Oh, it's not your fault, old man,' George said, putting a big hand on the other man's shoulder. 'You did your best.'

He had withdrawn from the meeting when the contract for the work was due to be debated and had been sitting in an outside office reading the *Illustrated London News* to pass the time. He could quite easily have stayed at home or gone for a drink, but he wanted to appear as if he hoped Kennett's might be given the contract and disappointed when it was not, so he had hung around.

'I must say you're taking it very well. I'd have been flaming myself.'

'No point in that,' George said, pretending indifference.

'Besides, competition never did anyone any harm. I thrive on it.'

'What are you going to do?'

'Same as always, get on with work in hand. I'd be a fool to let everything ride on one contract, wouldn't I?'

'Of course.' Tony was relieved. 'I know you're too canny not to cover all eventualities. If there's anything else I can help you with, let me know.'

George stayed a few minutes after he'd gone, then went home himself. Tony would make sure he didn't lose out; there were other building jobs in the pipeline: the new cinema and an extension to the infants school, which was bursting at the seams because Melsham was a fast-developing town and its population was growing. And there was that yard behind Landers, with its old blacksmith's and wheelwright's that hardly anyone used nowadays, and a tumbledown cottage not fit to live in. It was ripe for development. He was smiling as he let himself into the house.

Barbara had gone to bed. He crept up to the bedroom and undressed without putting the light on. He wouldn't tell her his plans were coming to fruition: it would only start another argument and he wanted to keep her sweet at least until after his inauguration.

The mayor-making ceremony was over and everyone was crowding into the town hall for a reception: councillors, civic dignitaries, the vicar of St Andrews, who had conducted a short service in the church, representatives of the town's businesses and charities. George, the heavy chain glinting on his chest, mingled with them, full of

315

bonhomie. Barbara, looking cool and elegant, with a lighter chain about her neck, stood a little back to allow her husband to take the limelight. Her suit of cream linen was beautifully tailored and the pencil-slim skirt and the long fitted jacket flattered her figure. With it she was wearing a tan silk blouse and a slouch hat with a curved brim turned up at the back and decorated with a sweeping feather. Penny, who had gone with her to buy it, wouldn't let her buy the tiny pillbox she thought would be more suitable.

'That's a nothing hat,' she said in derisory tones. 'You are the lady mayoress, you are entitled to show off a bit.' The big hat looked good and it should have made her feel good, but how could she with George's latest scheme hanging over them like a big, dark cloud? The prospect of a year of standing beside him at public functions, being his shadow, smiling at everyone, knowing what he had done, condoning it, filled her with dread.

George was talking to a young woman with a pad and pencil busily writing down what he said. 'I trust we can count on your support,' he was saying.

'Mr Kennett, the Gazette prides itself on its independence. We report the truth as we see it.'

'Of course, but you and I know we'd never get anything done if we had to have universal public approval first. I am sure when the scheme is complete—'

'Is it true that one of your longest-serving managers has left Kennett's to go into business as a competitor, Mr Kennett?'

'Yes, I believe it is.'

'How do you feel about that?'

'I have no axe to grind, he is entitled to better himself if he can. My main concern is that Melsham should thrive.'

The reporter scribbled away and beckoned a cameraman to come and take pictures. George, seeing his wife standing close by, pulled her towards him. 'My lady mayoress,' he said.

Barbara was reluctantly included in the picture and, apparently satisfied, the reporter and cameraman left.

Barbara watched them go. She had gone through the event in a dream, talked to people, accepted their congratulations, listened politely to some of them lobbying on behalf of this or that group, and smiled. Oh, how she had smiled! Only it wasn't a dream, it was a nightmare. She was exhausted by the time it was all over.

Chapter Twelve

ZITA WAS CROSSING the road by the town hall a week later when George nearly ran her over. She had just been to collect her entry form for the fountain competition and was so deep in a fantasy about winning the five hundred pounds prize money and becoming famous, she hadn't noticed the car pull out of the side road onto Market Street. It was only a tiny bump, but the hem of her dress caught in the bumper, almost ripping it off her. He stopped to make sure she had not been hurt. 'Just look what you've done,' she said, angrily displaying a handful of torn skirt. 'You've ruined it and I can't afford a new dress...'

'I gather from your concern over your dress that you aren't hurt.' She had long, slender legs, he noticed as he bent down to extricate a piece of the gaudy orange and brown cotton from his bumper. The ripped skirt revealed a supple thigh and a glimpse of light underwear. It gave him a sexual buzz. It was crazy. He had been as good as gold ever since Virginia died, so why…? He stood up.

She straightened up, sweeping her dark hair off her face with a movement of her hand and suddenly recognised him. George Kennett, councillor and mayor and member of the Fountain Committee! 'OK, so it was my fault.' She grinned at him. 'But you can run me home, if you like. I don't fancy walking through the streets half naked. Asking for trouble, that'd be.'

'My pleasure.' He opened the passenger door and she settled herself in, noting the leather upholstery and polished-wood dashboard, then turned to look at him as he got in the other side. He had a strong face, with thick, dark brows and a touch of grey in the hair at his temples, a mature man but sexy with it. The vibes he was giving off were decidedly sensual.

'Where to?' he asked.

She gave him her address. It was only five minutes away. He drew up outside the large, old house which he had converted into flats just after the war when the housing shortage was at its worst. It was only meant to be a temporary measure, but they were still in use. 'Coffee?' she queried, when he switched off the engine. You didn't do that if you meant to drive straight off again.

He didn't answer but got out and waited for her before locking the car and walking with her to the entrance. By the time they reached the top floor he was breathless. She unlocked the door and led the way into the flat, laughing at him. 'You're out of condition.'

'I must be.'

'Don't mind the mess,' she said, taking off her short suede jacket and flinging it over a chair. 'I have to work here as well as live. No room to swing a cat. Find a seat.'

He looked about him while she put the kettle on. The room was so cluttered there was no room to sit down, except on the rumpled bed. Every chair was loaded with books or magazines, the table was covered with drawings. There was a huge half-finished sculpture of a naked man in the middle of the room, standing with his head thrown back and his arms held heavenwards. And everything was covered in a film of white dust. He pulled the bedcovers straight and perched himself on the edge of the bed.

'How did you get that up here?' he asked, nodding towards the sculpture.

'A gang of friends hauled it up on ropes through the middle of the stairwell. They nearly let it go a couple of times.' She had a deep vibrating laugh, he noticed, which made him want to laugh with her. 'Goodness knows what it would've done to the hall floor.'

'Made a big hole, I imagine.'

'Now, I'm trying to design a fountain.' She came towards him with two mugs of coffee, one of which she held out to him.

'The one for the market?' His mind wasn't really on what she was saying because she was making no attempt to hide the slit in her skirt and her firm young thighs, on a level with his eyes, were turning him on. He took the mug in both hands and gulped the hot coffee to stop himself reaching out to touch her.

'Yes.' For lack of anywhere else, she sat down next to him on the bed. 'I thought I'd use that as a basis' She jerked her head towards the sculpture. 'What do you think?'

'It's very good, but you haven't left anything to the imagination, have you?'

'Oh, I don't know...' She laughed and leant back against the headboard, curling her legs up under her, revealing even more of her anatomy. Was she being deliberately provocative? He was almost beside himself with lustful desire. Virginia had been so long ago, and until now, he hadn't realised how much he had missed the buzz of a clandestine relationship. But this girl was young...

'How old are you?' he asked suddenly, twisting himself round so that he was facing her.

'Old enough.' She put her mug down on the bedside table and stretched out her legs so that the torn skirt fell away and her cream satin knickers were on display. They covered little: he could see dark pubic hair. He looked up at her face. She was smiling and her eyes were inviting.

He put his mug down beside hers. He ought to get up and go. He ought to nip it in the bud right now. 'It's getting late,' he said lamely.

'Later than you think.'

'Yes.'

'Time is precious, you know,' she said. 'And so many people waste it, doing nothing at all or doing something they don't want to do. Now, you don't strike me as a man who wastes time.'

'No, I don't. And I am prepared to swear that you don't either. In fact, you might be called an opportunist.'

She laughed and leant forward so that her face was only inches from his. 'So, what's wrong with that? You are too, aren't you?' She began undoing his tie. 'Being in the right place at the right time, that's what it's all about, isn't it?'

He took his jacket off and flung it behind him. 'Yes. But who was in the right place at the right time tonight?'

'We both were. Fate, that's what it was. Fate.'

He laughed. 'Is this your usual tactic? It's very direct, if it is. It might put some men off.'

'But not you.' One by one she was undoing his shirt buttons. He was as stiff as a poker and she knew it. She kept glancing down at his trousers and smiling.

He picked up a handful of her skirt. 'Well, since this is already ruined, we might as well finish it off.' He ripped it off her.

It was too late to stop, much too late. He fell on her, kissing her neck, her breasts, running his hands all over her body, pulling aside the leg of her knickers to get at her. She fumbled in the drawer of the bedside table and brought out a sheath. 'Try this for size.' She unbuttoned his flies and pushed his trousers and underpants down, waiting for him to slip it on before opening her thighs to let him in. If he was shocked that she had such a thing, he did not show it. In fact he was grateful.

It was not until they lay side by side panting for breath, that he asked himself why. Who was she? If he looked at the design which lay on the table, her name might be on it. But he was too exhausted to move.

'George Kennett,' she said and laughed. 'Who'd have thought it?'

It was then he began to worry about what he'd done. There was no doubt in his mind that she had deliberately seduced him. And he had fallen for it. Now came the pay out. 'What do you want from me?'

She laughed. 'More of the same, George. Anytime you like.'

'So that you can take your story to the papers, is that it?'

'Certainly not. I wouldn't risk my reputation for a cheap trick like that.' She turned to the drawer in the bedside table and took out a packet of cigarettes and a box of matches. 'I've no more wish for publicity than you have, not that kind anyway. This is our secret.' She offered him a cigarette, and though he hadn't smoked anything but cigars for years, he took one and she lit it for him.

'What then?'

'Nothing. Don't look so worried. Unless you want to buy me a new dress.'

'Of course.' He reached for his jacket and took his wallet out of the inner pocket. 'How much?'

'My dear man, I don't have a scale of charges. I'm not a whore. I'll leave it to your generosity.'

He handed her all the notes he had, just over fifty pounds. 'Thanks.' She put them in the drawer beside the condom packet and the cigarettes, then she got up and padded over to put the kettle on. 'Want a bath while I make more coffee? It's over there.' She nodded towards a door. He picked up his trousers and shirt and went into the bathroom, shutting and locking the door behind him.

When he came out again, fully dressed except for his jacket and tie, she had put on a flowing dress of some thin cotton material and was sitting over the drawing at the table, pencil in hand. He went to stand beside her and looked down at what she was doing. 'Zita Younger,' he read aloud.

'That's me.' She looked up from what she was doing to smile at him, her dark eyes glowing.

He was horrified. What in heaven's name had he done? What was she after? He began to feel very worried. 'I'd better be going.'

She saw his consternation and laughed. 'Don't worry, George, I don't have any more time for my father than you have. I dislike him intensely. I left home as soon as I could.'

'And your mother?'

'My mother's all right. She always did her best for me. But there are some things I wouldn't tell her, know what I mean?' Her mother had adopted some of her grandmother's easy-going approach to life but on her it didn't seem to fit. Underneath, Mum longed for respectability, to be someone people looked up to, not the bastard daughter of the town whore. But because she loved her mother, Rita would never admit it. Zita recognised herself in some of her grandmother's character, the back-to-front pride, the independence, the barriers she put up which prevented personal relationships from flourishing but allowed casual ones free rein. It was an uncomfortable feeling.

He relaxed a little. 'Saves hurt, doesn't it?'

'Yes. Now drink your coffee.'

He sat and drank and they talked about the fountain project and her ideas for it, and her ambition to make a name for herself as a sculptress. Ambition was something he understood and could admire. It had been the driving force in his life. It was another hour before he stood up to go.

'Come again, won't you?' she said, helping him on with his jacket. 'You'll want to see what I've bought with the money you gave me. I'll give you a little fashion show. And George,' she added, as he reached the door. 'When you come to look at the fountain designs, remember my name, won't you?'

As he left the flat he peered over the banisters. It was a long way down; several hundredweight of stone would do an immense amount of damage dropped from that height. 'What would happen if your friends dropped your finished sculpture getting it down?' he asked.

'I'd have their guts for garters.'

'You've got your father's temper?'

'Not so's you'd notice.'

'Someone might get hurt. Wouldn't you be better working on the ground floor?'

'Can't find anywhere I can afford,' she said. 'But if you should hear of anything, think of me.'

'I'll see what I can do.' He went down the winding stairs, got in his car and drove home, in a state bordering on hypnotic.

In the next few weeks the entries for the fountain design began to flood into the town hall, hundreds of them, some conventional, some boring: there was a fish spewing water from its mouth; a mermaid with a spear that gushed water; two naked bodies entwined in what could only be described as a suggestive pose, with the water rippling over them; a kind of bell tower with water cascading over the bell; a watermill complete with wheel; a golf ball on a tee peg, someone's idea of a joke; and a pile of twisted metal that looked like nothing so much as a conglomeration of old bicycle parts. Some were well drawn, showing a lot of thought had gone into them, others were scribbled on any piece of paper that came to hand. George and the selection committee spent hours poring over them, but finally whittled them down to a shortlist of eight, whose designers would be asked to make scale models. One of them was Zita Younger.

He hadn't had to push hard for Zita to be included: her design was professionally done and the presentation was good. She had passed the first stage on merit. He'd go and tell her so; she needn't have gone to the lengths she had to be on the shortlist, but he was glad she had. She had given his life a new zest.

She laughed when he told her. 'Of course I didn't,' she said, giving him a mug of half-cold tea which tasted vile, but he hardly noticed. 'I knew it was good enough.'

'Then why?'

She knew what he meant. 'I don't know. Why do people do things? I fancied you and I could see the feeling was mutual.' She laughed, watching his face. 'Does it have to be more than that?'

'No.'

'I'll show you the dress I bought, shall I?'

He sat on the bed and watched as she stripped off the multicoloured cotton skirt and white peasant blouse she was wearing and stood in front of him in knickers and brassiere. She was slim, almost thin, with small pointed breasts and long legs. Her face was alive, her dark eyes

327

glowing and she was laughing. It made him smile, made him feel young again, as young as he had been when he first went to bed with Virginia. Zita wasn't Virginia because Virginia had been the passion of his life, but she had youth and vibrancy and she excited him. He reached out to grab her wrist before she could put the dress over her head. 'Come here.'

She went dutifully. He never did see her in the new dress.

The market scheme was causing a great deal of controversy in the town; the letters page in the *Melsham Gazette* was full of it. 'It is a gross misuse of public money,' one wrote. 'Why do we need a fountain at all? The pool is nothing but a receptacle for refuse.'

'It's no use taking notice of adverse publicity,' George pointed out at the next council meeting. 'Only those against the scheme bother to write to the papers, those who like the idea do nothing. It is precisely because the existing fountain is in disrepair that something new is needed. We must make Melsham not only a good place to live, but an interesting place to visit. Tourists bring money with them. And Miss Younger's design is far and away the best.'

'It's disgusting,' Mrs Greaves said. 'Nudity has no place in Melsham's public places. There'll be a public outcry if we use that design.'

'Then I suggest we ask her to modify it and resubmit it,' he said.

Maggie Doughty, in one of the seats reserved for the press, leant forward to study George Kennett's face.

What had he got up his sleeve? Why was he so keen on giving work to Zita Younger? Who was she? She abandoned the meeting and went down to the foyer, where the designs were on display. Beside each was a short biography of the designer. So, Zita Younger was a local woman, educated at the local school and had a qualification in horticulture which she had obtained while working for Melsham Nurseries. Supposing she had some connection with George Kennett...oh, wouldn't that put the fat in the fire? She abandoned the council meeting in favour of digging around in the back numbers of the *Gazette*.

'Modify it!' Zita cried, eyes blazing. 'No, I can't. It would spoil it completely.'

George had come straight from the council meeting and was sitting at her dining table. In front of him was a plate on which were the remains of a pork chop. There was a bowl containing what was left of a lettuce, condiments, an empty wine bottle, two glasses half full of red wine and, spread over the remainder of the space, her fountain design. He had been pointing out the source of the council's unease. 'Oh, come on, Zita. They're too big, dominant almost.'

'That's the whole idea, the male ego centred in his sexual organs.'

'Oh, is that what it means?' He was faintly amused: she took full advantage of his sexuality and he wondered if that was how she saw him. He wasn't sure whether he was flattered or not. 'You'll win the competition hands down, if you get rid of them.'

She laughed. 'An emasculated man, wouldn't that cause more comment?'

'OK, make them small and less significant. I went out on a limb for you, you know.'

'So? I'm worth it, aren't I?' She was wearing a long, flowing, cotton robe in a swirling design of orange, brown, red and black, which was almost transparent. She wore no underwear except flimsy knickers.

He smiled. 'Of course you are. Don't you want to go down in history as the designer of Melsham's famous fountain? It would be a great boost to your career. There'd be plenty of publicity...'

He hadn't lost his knack of manipulating people; she was almost won over. 'I know, but it seems like prostituting my art...'

He laughed. 'Is that worse than prostituting your body?'

'I don't do that!' she flared. 'And if you can't think of anything better to do than hurl insults...'

'Oh, but I can, something infinitely better.' He stood up and reached for her hand. 'Come on.'

She allowed him to lead her to the bed.

'Mmm,' she said later, nuzzling up to his bare chest. 'You know how to get me going, don't you?'

'Yes.' He grinned to himself over her head. 'It's a pity I have to go home.'

'Are you like this with your wife? Do you...you know...'

He chuckled. 'You can set your mind at rest. We don't do that anymore. The spark has gone.'

'Your spark hasn't gone. In fact, it's well alight.' She

lifted her head to look at his face. He had small lines around the nose and mouth and a slight thickening of the jowls which betrayed his age, but the rest of him was strong and muscular; he didn't sag anywhere. She stroked her hand across his chest, past his navel and down his inner thigh. 'Shall we do it again?'

'When?'

'Right now.'

'No, I told you, I've got to go. Council meetings go on and on, but not all night.'

'I wish they did. I wish you could stay all night. It would be fun, really wild...'

'No doubt it would, but not tonight.' She was rousing him again, but he hadn't got the energy or the time. He scrambled off the bed and dived for his underpants.

'OK. But when?' She was smiling up at him in her nakedness, revelling in it.

He sat down again, bewitched. 'I'm going to France on council business next month. Would you like to come? We'll be staying in Paris.'

'Paris?' Her dark eyes sparkled. 'You mean it?'

'Yes, but we'd have to travel separately. I have to be seen as part of the official party, but we could be together once we got there, most evenings. All night. That's what you want, isn't it?'

'Oh, yes, but don't wives go on these trips?'

'Sometimes, but Barbara never wants to come. In any case, she's got some charity meeting or other that week and, as far as she's concerned, that takes precedence.' She noticed the bitterness and smiled to herself. She had him just where she wanted him.

'You'll have to pay. I'm broke.'

'Of course I'll pay. But there's one condition. You redo that design, cut out the you-know-what. I've backed you publicly and I don't want to be made to look a fool.'

'OK. It's a deal.' She twined her arms about his neck and kissed his cheek. 'That's one on account.'

He laughed and kissed her back, full on the mouth. It went on some time before he broke away. 'Now can I go?'

'I'm not stopping you.'

He put on his shirt and trousers and stuffed his tie in his pocket before slinging his jacket over one shoulder. Then he bent to kiss the top of her head. 'Goodnight, witch.'

It was a warm night and he didn't bother to put his jacket on to go to his car, parked discreetly out of sight. The stars were out and a full moon cast a silvery light which was easily clear enough for Maggie, going home after an abortive search of the archives in the Gazette office, to recognise him. She almost laughed aloud. There was only one explanation for a man coming out of a block of flats in the early hours of the morning with his tie off, his shirt unbuttoned at the collar and his jacket over one shoulder, especially as he was walking with a swagger. The bastard! The conniving bastard!

Barbara had set up her easel to make a start on a picture she was going to call 'Autumn in the Garden' and was sketching in the outline of the summer house and the trees when Isobel arrived.

'I'm not interrupting anything, am I?' she asked,

looking at Barbara's paint-stained shirt.

'Nothing I can't leave. Do come in. The children are at school and George is away for the rest of the week so I thought I'd make a start on a new picture, to pass the time, you know...' It wasn't so much passing the time, as blocking out the knowledge that she was sure George had started another affair. Oh, she had no proof and no idea whom it could be, but she knew the signs. Bursts of insincere compliments, a pretended reluctance when he had to go out for meetings in the evenings; a woman's perfume clinging to him; telephone calls which he stopped abruptly when she came into the hall; vagueness about where he was going in the evenings; his tetchiness when she questioned him. Of course, that could easily be the fact that he was sailing very close to the wind over the market contract, but she didn't think so.

She'd spent the morning at the clothing store and worked until it had never been more organised, with everything labelled and on the right shelf and the books completely up to date, but her intense activity had been noted and she didn't want people thinking she couldn't function without her husband and so she'd come home. Rather than get under Kate's feet, she had gone upstairs and set up her easel, but even here there was no escape from her tumbling thoughts. George was in Paris and she was fairly sure he was not alone. It was Virginia all over again.

She surprised herself by not caring very much. What did bother her was that it would become public knowledge, that it would hurt Alison and Nick, both growing up and old enough to understand, that the charities she served would consider her a liability rather than an asset, but most of all, that George's sleazy business deals would all come out in the open. How could he take such risks?

She suddenly realised that Isobel was still standing uncertainly in the hall. She smiled at her. 'Shall we go into the drawing room? I'll ask Kate to make us some coffee.'

'Is that where you were working?' She noticed the heavy eyes, the puffy cheeks and the liquidity in the voice, but decided not to comment.

'No. I've got a studio where I can make as much mess as I like.'

'Then why not go there? I'd like to see it.'

Barbara went to the kitchen to speak to Kate, then led the way upstairs. 'You'll have to excuse the mess.'

Isobel stood looking round the studio in delighted surprise. Messy it might be but it was a kind of organised mess, and there were paintings everywhere, on the walls, stacked against them, piled on a table. 'May I look at the pictures?'

'Of course.'

She wandered slowly round the room, picking one or two up to examine them more closely, turning her head sideways to look at those left on their sides against the wall. 'They're very good. I've seen the one of Melsham in your dining room, and the one of Alison, so I ought not to be surprised, but you really are very talented.'

'It was what I was hoping to do after I left college. It fell by the wayside when I married George and we started a family.' She laughed suddenly. 'And please don't say, what a waste. I'd never have made a proper living at it and I certainly don't regret my children.'

334

Kate brought in the tray and put it on a table already cluttered with pots and tubes of paint, pencils and tubs of brushes, and left them.

'Now, what can I do for you?' Barbara asked. 'I'm always pleased to see you, but you didn't come to look at my paintings, did you?'

Isobel smiled. 'You remember when the film people came and we started talking about a hydro?'

'Yes.' It wasn't the only thing she remembered about that day, but it was something she had pushed to the back of her mind. Seeing Simon and then Jay-Jay inviting him to view the painting of Melsham marketplace had so nearly been disastrous. If Simon had taken him up on that... She stopped her errant thoughts to pay attention. 'Pie in the sky, you called it.'

'So I did, but you made me think. And when James had a slight stroke...'

'Oh, I'm sorry, I didn't know. When did it happen?'

'A couple of weeks ago. He isn't badly incapacitated, but he's more doddery than ever. I suggested he should find himself a nice residential home where he can be looked after, but he won't go while he thinks I need him.' She smiled. 'I can't put off a decision any longer. I spoke to Miss Barcliffe, as you suggested. I suppose I should call her Mrs Erikson.'

Barbara smiled. 'I can't get used to the idea she's married either, but I'm sure she'd rather you called her Penny. What did she say?'

'She said she would put the word around her contacts, see who might be interested. And she has a friend who's been working for a large international company and

335

would welcome the chance to manage a small privately run concern. She has all the right qualifications.'

'Sounds good.' She paused. 'I know it's none of my business, but I thought finance was a stumbling block.'

'There's someone who's interested in backing the scheme.'

'Not George?' she asked in alarm.

'No, definitely not Mr Kennett.' She spoke firmly. 'Mr Barcliffe.'

'Penny's father?'

'No, her brother. So, what do you think?'

Simon. He had not married again. According to Penny, he had said he was waiting for that special woman, the one and only, to put in an appearance and until she did he would stay the carefree divorcee. She made an effort to still her wayward heart and speak levelly. 'Isobel, it isn't what I think that matters. If you like the idea and think it will work, then go ahead.'

'I want you to be part of it.'

'But I haven't got anything to offer,' Barbara said, taken by surprise. 'No experience, no money...'

'With Mr Barcliffe providing the finance, lack of money doesn't matter. You're a great organiser, Barbara, and you get on well with everyone. And it was your idea. Say you will, please.'

'That's very flattering, but I'm not really sure I'm cut out to be a businesswoman.'

'I've asked Mrs Erikson too. She said it might be fun, an enterprise of women, except Mr Barcliffe, but he won't be taking an active part in running it. So will you think about it?'

Simon. How often would she have to meet him? She thought of refusing but realised how foolish that would be. It was a wonderful opportunity and the beauty of it was that it had nothing to do with George. 'I'll think about it, but I make no promises. It's a big step...'

'And one you'd take in your stride. Now, I must be off.'

Barbara accompanied her to the door. 'Thanks for coming, and thanks for asking me. I'll let you know. Soon.'

'Talk to Penny about it.'

Barbara watched as Isobel set off down the drive to walk back to the manor. She knew what Penny would say. 'Go for it. Show George what you're made of.' Could she? Dare she?

The coming and going of the builder's lorries, the dumping of materials and the arrival of men and equipment caused major traffic hold-ups. The shops fronting the marketplace were up in arms over loss of trade and demanding compensation and no one could find anywhere to leave their bicycles, prams and cars. 'Before this shambles it was never difficult to park in Melsham,' someone wrote to the Gazette. 'Now it is becoming like every other big town, jammed with cars and nowhere to walk because the pavements are being dug up.' There were others writing in favour, that the disruption would be worth it in the end, but tempers were running high and there had been more than one scuffle between a frustrated motorist and the workers who operated the stop-go boards to halt the traffic and allow lorries onto the site.

Colin, whose temper had never been less than volatile, lost it completely when a large truck containing hard core, which he had been directing, became wedged in a tight turn and a long queue of cars built up, stretching right round the market and out onto the Norwich Road. The town came to a standstill. One of the motorists kept his hand on his horn and yelled at him, 'Get that damned monster off the road and let people get on.'

It was more than Colin could stomach. He strode over to the car, yanked open the door and dragged the driver from his seat. 'You smarmy bastard!' he yelled. 'Sitting there doing bugger all while the rest of us work. You think honking that horn will make me jump, do you?' He had the man by his shirt collar and was forcing him back against his car. 'I don't jump for no one.'

'Get off, you great lout!' the man shouted, trying to struggle out of his grasp. Other people came to his aid and tried to pull Colin off. That was too much for Colin's workmates who waded in to help. There was a full-blown skirmish going on by the time the police arrived, simultaneously with Maggie Doughty. Order was restored, the lorry driver got his vehicle off the road and onto the market and the traffic jam was cleared.

Maggie Doughty didn't think the fracas on the market would merit more than a couple of inches on the inside pages, until she discovered the name of one of the protagonists was Colin Younger. Could she make anything of that? She stood, tapping her pencil against her pad, watching Colin go back to his work. Did he know George Kennett was screwing his daughter?

'Mr Younger?'

Colin turned to see who had spoken. He didn't know the woman. She had short boyish hair, dark eyes with a lot of depth and a ready smile with no depth at all. She was wearing a shirt with a man's tie, an ankle-length black skirt and a bucket hat pulled right down to her eyebrows.

'I'm Maggie Doughty. *Melsham Gazette*. Can I have a word with you?'

'What sort of word?' he asked warily.

'Not here. Later, after you finish. I'm doing a piece on the market. History of it, how things have changed over the years. I'm going to talk to all sorts of people, your boss and the mayor, the people who live and work on the market. So, how about an interview?'

'OK. I usually stop off at the Fen Tiger for a pint on the way home. That do?'

The pub was a small one tucked away on a back street. It was dismal and grubby. She bought him a beer and watched him as he drank half of it straight down. Then he put the glass on the stained table and smiled. 'Fire away.'

She began by asking him several innocuous questions. How old was he? How long had he lived in Melsham? Had he always been in the building trade? How long had he been working for Melsham Construction?

'A few months,' he said in answer to that. 'But if you want to know about the firm, you'll have to ask Mr Browning.'

She smiled and bought him a second pint. 'I will. He used to work for Kennett's, before he left to start up on his own, didn't he?'

339

'Yes.'

'What did Mr Kennett say about that?'

'Not a lot. What could he say?'

'They didn't fall out over it, then? His one-time employee going off and getting the market contract? I should have expected him to be spitting feathers.'

'Not so you'd notice. Fact is, they're still as thick as thieves.'

'And it takes one to know one,' she said softly.

'Hey, that's below the belt. I'm not staying here to be insulted.' He stood up, angry that he had been duped.

'Sit down, Mr Younger. I'm not interested in that. I won't mention it, I promise. I think we can help each other. I'd make it worth your while.'

He noticed her sly smile and resumed his seat. 'You want to dig the dirt on Kennett, that it?'

'Something like that.'

'Why?'

'Let's just say it's my civic duty.'

He laughed. 'Pull the other one.'

She ignored the jibe. 'Who's financing Melsham Construction? I wouldn't have thought Mr Browning would have saved enough from a manager's pay.'

He shrugged. 'Don't know, do I? But I did see Mr Browning and Mr Kennett together at Newmarket races the other day.' He'd sneaked a day off work and gone to the races, only to see Browning there, talking to Kennett. 'I thought it was funny, considering I'd heard Kennett was none too pleased with Mr Browning for doing the dirty on him.'

'That doesn't prove anything. Can you find out more?'

'What's in it for me? I could lose my job.'

'Not if you use your head. Ask your daughter. Her name's Zita, isn't it? She must know what's going on.'

'Zita?' He looked puzzled.

'Yes. She won the fountain competition, didn't she?'

'So what?'

'Wasn't it Mr Kennett got her the prize?'

'It was a committee decision.'

'Committees are made up of individuals, Mr Younger, and each has his or her own hidden agenda. It's all about persuasion and power. I think your daughter knows that.'

'What are you accusing her of?'

'Nothing, Mr Younger. But you've heard the old saying: it isn't what you know but who you know...'

He chuckled. 'Clever old Zita! But I can't ask her, not this week, she's in France on holiday. She won't be back until the weekend.'

'No hurry, Mr Younger. Next week will do. I'll give you a hundred pounds for the name of Mr Browning's backer.'

'You think it's George Kennett, don't you?'

'Maybe.'

'If you're right, it's worth more than a hundred pounds.'

'I'll have to get my editor's agreement. But it's possible. Depends what you come up with.'

'If this is true,' Toby Greenbank said after reading her notes in his office, 'it's dynamite.'

'So, what do you think?'

Toby Greenbank was a cautious man: the paper

couldn't afford thousands in libel payments. 'I dunno. Kennett's done a lot for the town. He'd be chucked off the council, and in his mayoral year too. There'd be one helluva rumpus. It could ruin him.'

'Good.'

'Are you quite sure this isn't a personal vendetta, Maggie?'

'No, it's in the public interest. We're talking corruption and taxpayers' money.'

'If George Kennett is involved with Melsham Construction, he should have declared an interest. Have you checked if he did?'

'He didn't.'

'What about Companies House?'

'Kennett isn't listed as a director.'

'So, you've only got Younger's word for it and he's an ex-con. You'd need to prove Kennett benefited financially and that he deliberately concealed this from the council.'

'Younger said Kennett and Browning were still as thick as thieves.'

He smiled. 'Maggie, it's all very well to have suspicions, quite another to prove them.'

'Supposing I get proof?'

'Then we publish, but we get the lawyers to double-check. Without their say-so we don't print a word, otherwise Kennett will take us to the cleaners. He's no fool, he'll have covered his tracks pretty thoroughly.'

'He must have made a mistake somewhere.' She was adamant. 'He must have.'

She rang Donald Browning and made an appointment to interview him. She told him she wanted his comments on the fracas in the market that morning and what he thought should be done to ease the congestion while the work was going on. She rang Kennett's too, but George wasn't available. He was in France on council business. When she put the phone down she was jubilant. He was in France and so was Zita Younger. It would make the nationals. They would make sure it ran and ran and she would make her name as a journalist. But more importantly, Dad would be avenged.

'What time do you think Dad's train is coming in?' Nick asked Alison. He had heard his father tell his mother he'd be home on Saturday, and that being a day when he did not have to go to school, he'd decided to cycle to the station to meet him.

'Well, it won't be in the morning because he's coming back on the boat train and then he has to catch a train to Melsham. What d'you want to know for?'

'No reason. Wondered what time he'd be home, that's all.'

'If he comes on the five thirty and takes a cab, he'll be here in time for tea, won't he?'

Nick wandered off, but at half past four he fetched out his bicycle and rode to Melsham station. He had a long wait, but he didn't mind that, he loved to watch the trains, the porters wheeling barrows of luggage, the guards with the flags and whistles, the crates of chickens and bags of potatoes bound for the London markets. And he liked the posters of the seaside. They'd gone to the seaside one year for a holiday, but they hadn't done that lately. He didn't know why. He supposed because Dad was always so busy, too busy sometimes to talk to him. That's why he wanted to meet him, so they could have a few minutes together without the whole family being in on it.

The train came steaming in. He'd hide and jump out on his dad as he was going through the barrier, watch his surprise and then his smile of pleasure. Peeping from behind a pile of crates, he saw his father leave a carriage and watched as he turned to someone behind him, offering his hand. A young woman jumped out and stood beside his father, laughing up into his face. And Dad was laughing down at her as if he knew her very well and liked her a lot, which was a great surprise to Nick because he knew who she was. Mrs Younger's daughter. Curious, he forgot all about his intention to surprise his father, and stayed hidden. He watched as his father picked up Zita's case and slipped his other hand under her elbow to guide her towards the exit. 'I'll leave you here,' he was saying as they passed him. 'Can't be seen together, can we?'

She laughed. 'That would put the cat among the pigeons.'

'I'll come round Monday after work.' He stopped to dig in his pocket and brought out a handful of coins. 'Get yourself a cab.'

She took it in her gloved hand and lifted her head to his. 'Thanks. And thanks for a wonderful time, George. Paris was fun.'

Nick had seen enough soppy films, heard enough talk in the playground at school, to know something was up. His father had taken Zita Younger to Paris and it was obviously meant to be a secret. And he said he'd go and see her on Monday. What would his mother say if she knew? Should he tell her? She'd want to know how he knew and that would mean admitting he had cycled all the way to the station and spied on his father. Perhaps she wouldn't believe him, and if she did, what would she do? He was suddenly afraid.

He crept out of the station, looking round for his father or Miss Younger, but neither was to be seen. He fetched his bicycle from where he had propped it against the railings and cycled home as fast as his pedalling feet could take him. By the time he arrived, he had decided to say nothing.

George had hardly got into work on Monday, when Maggie Doughty arrived and asked to see him. He was in no mood to talk to her: she was always confrontational, forcing him to justify himself over some piddling little thing she'd got her teeth into and right now he could do without it. 'Tell her I'm too busy,' he told Susan. 'Give her an appointment for later.'

'I shall miss my deadline, Mr Kennett.' Maggie had followed Susan and stood in the open doorway. 'And I'm sure you would prefer to scotch these rumours before they get out of hand.'

'Rumours?' he said, waving Susan away. 'What rumours?'

She advanced into the room and dumped her capacious handbag on his desk and removed a notebook and pencil from it before sitting down without waiting for an invitation. 'That you used your influence to get Miss Younger one of the properties on the industrial site. They're in great demand now the economy is beginning to pick up, aren't they, Mr Kennett?'

It was perfectly true, but how did she know? 'Wherever did you get that idea?'

She shrugged. 'You know better than to ask me to reveal my sources, surely?'

'Miss Younger won the fountain competition; she has to have somewhere to construct her model, nothing to do with me. There is no room at her flat—'

'Would that be ten Regency Terrace?'

He realised his mistake almost at once. 'How should I know her address?'

'Didn't she have to put it on her entry?'

'I suppose so, but that doesn't mean I know it.'

'I believe you do. You were seen leaving there a couple of weeks ago, quite late it was. Just before you went to France. Was that a successful trip, by the way?'

He was disconcerted but quickly recovered himself. He must be careful, the bitch missed very little. 'Yes, it was.'

'Good. Now, about Miss Younger.'

'No undue influence, no favouritism, no jumping the queue. I don't know who your source is, Miss Doughty, but I think you should check carefully before you rely on them again.'

'So you have never been to Miss Younger's flat?'

'Certainly not.'

'May I quote you on that?'

'I don't see why you need to quote anything at all. It's hardly newsworthy.'

'On its own, it hardly merits a couple of lines, but with all these other rumours...' She let the sentence hang in the air, daring him to ask. And, of course, he couldn't let it pass.

'What other rumours?'

'Melsham Construction, Mr Kennett.'

The hammering of his heart made his chest feel tight. What had she unearthed? Had Donald shot his mouth off? 'What about it?'

'Word is you are its real head, not Mr Browning. And that means—'

'Rubbish!'

'You deny it?'

'Categorically.'

'Mr Browning doesn't strike me as the sort of man to have ready money available to finance a large new company.'

'I assume he used his savings and borrowed from the bank.'

'So there's no truth in the rumour that Miss Younger winning the fountain competition had something to do with persuading her father not to reveal the source of Mr Browning's funding?'

He laughed aloud at the absurdity of it. 'No, of course not. What can Mr Younger possibly know about Mr Browning's financial affairs?'

'He works for him.'

'So, he may do, but I hardly think Mr Browning would confide in him, do you? Now, if you've finished this cross-examination, I have a great deal of work to catch up on.'

'Yes, of course.' She put her notebook away and stood up. 'The visit to France will have put you behind. Trade promotion, wasn't it?'

'Yes.'

'But not all business. You did manage to take some

time off. I understand you had a companion...'

She was only guessing, he told himself, she couldn't possibly know, they had been too careful, but he had to get rid of her. 'Some of the other delegates are also my friends,' he said carefully. 'So why shouldn't we socialise in our free time? There will be a press release from the council in due course. Good day to you, Miss Doughty.' His hand, somewhat unsteady, was reaching for the telephone to ring Toby Greenbank at the Gazette almost before she was out of the door.

She smiled as she clattered lightly down the iron stairs. So far, so good. He might be pompous and self-righteous, but he was wriggling like a worm on a hook; she could see it in his eyes. He had never once looked straight at her. He had something to hide. Toby might insist on having proof, but it didn't need proof. Rumours, once started, were hard to stop. He might bluster and threaten, but the public, his voters, would say there was no smoke without fire and he'd lose all credibility.

Chapter Thirteen

GEORGE COLLECTED THE papers from the doormat on his way to the breakfast table next morning. Barbara poured his coffee and set the toast rack in front of him, but he ignored it and disappeared behind *The Times*.

Idly she picked up the *Melsham Gazette*. The headline on the front page almost jumped out at her. 'Mayor denies financial involvement in Melsham Construction.' She skimmed through it with a sinking feeling in her stomach. It was happening, the avalanche she had been expecting. Now it would rush on and on until all their lives lay in ruins. For herself she hardly cared, but it would affect so many people: the family first and foremost, the Youngers, Donald, George's employees, the credibility of local government, because she was sure there had been coercion, bribes, favours done and received. Maggie Doughty wouldn't rest until every bit of dirt had been dug out and splashed all over the front page, and then there'd be an outcry and the council would be forced to hold an enquiry. And supposing she was questioned? Could she lie? Did she want to lie?

'George, have you seen this?'

He put down his paper and glanced across at her. She was holding the folded Gazette out to him, tapping it with her other hand. He grabbed it and scanned it quickly. 'The bitch. God knows why, but she's got it in for me. How did she manage to persuade Toby Greenbank to publish it? He told me the story wasn't worth risking his advertising revenue. The hardware shop alone spends thousands, taking whole pages at a time.'

'Is it true? Did you award Zita Younger the prize for the fountain to silence Colin?'

'Of course not. The idea is ridiculous. It was a committee decision. Oh, she's clever saying I'm denying a rumour, a rumour she started, I shouldn't wonder. God in heaven, what are they trying to prove?'

'That you're dishonest, perhaps?' she asked sweetly.

Rita picked her way over the debris to the door of her mother's poky little hovel in Farrier's Court. The workmen had already begun to demolish the old premises ready for the new shopping mall, though as yet Dora's house remained untouched. The ground about it was littered with broken bricks, lumps of plaster, strange pieces of iron, broken chairs, even an anvil. The constant coming and going had churned it up into rutted mud, but Mum would be enjoying it all, laughing and joking with the workmen, making them cups of tea and showing more of her ample bosom than was decent for a woman nearing sixty. She didn't act like sixty, in spite of her rheumatism.

'Comes with taking me knickers off in draughty places,' she'd said once and laughed coarsely. She loved shocking people. 'Give a dog a bad name and he'll live up to it,' was another of her sayings.

The council, having purchased the land, had promised Dora, the only occupier left in Farrier's Court, that she would be rehoused, though it would inevitably mean a higher rent. Dora, who had a philosophical attitude to almost everything, was unconcerned. 'They can't get blood from a stone,' she had told Rita.

When Rita let herself in, Dora was sitting at the kitchen table with a cup in front of her and a bottle of gin at her elbow, a cigarette dangling from her lips and the Gazette in her hand. A pair of wire-framed spectacles were perched on the end of her nose. She looked up as Rita came in, dumping a bag of groceries on the table. 'So, it's you.'

Rita laughed. 'Who d'you think it was, Rudolph Valentino?' She went to see her mother every week, just to make sure she was all right. She did a bit of cleaning and washing and fetched in the groceries and then they would sit over a cup of tea or a glass of gin, sometimes both, and exchange whatever gossip was going.

'Who's this Maggie Doughty?' Dora asked. 'She's certainly stirring it up for George Kennett. This is the second article I've seen lately. What's she got ag'in him?'

'Dunno, but Colin always swore to get even with Mr Kennett, so he might just have cooked up something, but dragging Zita's name into it i'n't right. She won that competition fair and square.'

'But there's no smoke without fire.' Dora reached out

351

for a bottle of gin and poured them each a glass. 'You've got to find out what's goin' on. Nip it in the bud...'

'Ma, Zita's twenty-one, she isn't going to take any notice of me. And Colin certainly won't listen.'

'They've got to be made to...' There was a long pause before she spoke again and then it was accompanied by a deep sigh. 'There are things you should know, things I've never told a soul.'

Rita wondered how long her mother had been drinking. She was certainly not herself. She had a wistful, faraway look in her eye which Rita had never seen there before. 'What things?'

'He was Melsham, born and bred.'

'Are you talking about George Kennett?'

'No, your father.'

'You never told me that before,' Rita said. 'You always clammed up if I asked.'

'No point. Water under the bridge.' She looked into the depths of her glass. 'Gin always makes me maudlin. I don't know why I drink the stuff. Make us another cup of tea, love, and I'll tell you the tale.'

Rita rose to move the kettle from the hob onto the range, the only means of heating and cooking in the house, fetched out the teapot, cups and saucers and a bottle of milk. Did that mean her mother was going to tell her what she had studiously kept to herself all these years? Why now?

'I was coming up to eighteen and good-looking, though I say it as shouldn't,' Dora went on, though it sounded more as if she were talking to herself than her daughter. 'I met him in the Dog and Duck. Oh, I know I shouldn't have been in there, me Pa would have flayed me alive if he'd known, but that was part of the fun, doin' suff'n I shouldn't. I'd known him since school, but never took much notice of him until then. He'd grown from a pimply schoolboy into the handsomest man I'd ever seen. He was tall, and though he had dark-red hair, his eyes were hazel.'

'Is that where I get my red hair from?'

'Stop interrupting and let me get it out.'

'OK. Not another word.'

Dora took another swig from her glass. 'We got chatting and he offered to buy me a drink and it went on from there. My friends disappeared and at closing time we left together, very tipsy. I took him to the farm where I worked and we spent the night in the hayloft. Oh, it sounds sordid, but it wasn't, it was beautiful. He was so handsome and sexy and he loved me...'

'Isn't that what they all say?'

'I believed him. He was in the navy and we saw each other every day while he was on shore leave. He said we'd be married next time he came home. It wasn't until after he'd gone back to sea I found I was pregnant.'

'With me?'

'Yes. I daren't tell my parents. I tried going to a woman I'd heard about, but I chickened out. It didn't seem right somehow, so I turned round and went home again. I thought he'd stand by me.'

'But he didn't?'

'He was married. I didn't find that out until I went round to his house. I thought he lived with his mother, but it was his wife who answered the door and she were pregnant too. It was a shock, I can tell you.'

'Then what did you do?'

'Nothing I could do. I went back home and told Ma and Pa. Pa was all for chucking me out, but Ma persuaded him it weren't the baby's fault and she wasn't going to have it said she was punishing the little 'un for my sins, so he let me stay until you were born.'

'What happened then?'

'I came to live here.' She stopped suddenly. 'I'n't that tea brewed yet? I'm parched with all this talking.'

Rita poured the tea and handed her a cup. She had never heard her mother so articulate, or so serious, and wondered what had set her off, but it had been an eye-opener. So much going on, so much grief she had known nothing about. She had always blamed her mother for her lifestyle, but now she was beginning to understand. 'Did you see him again when he came back from the sea?'

'No. He went straight off again. Maybe his wife turned him out, I don't know. I heard he'd gone to Canada. He died out there.'

'You still haven't told me his name.'

'I never thought I'd have to.'

'So? Why now?'

'Because it was Kennett. Fred Kennett.'

'Kennett?' Rita shrieked.

'Yes, George's father.'

Rita found it almost impossible to comprehend. Her thoughts whirled and then settled onto one salient point. 'George Kennett is my half-brother?'

'Yes. He's six months older than you.'

'My God! Does he know that?'

'I shouldn't think so. D'you think he'd let his wife

354

anywhere near you, if he knew? And he certainly wouldn't have got involved with Colin.'

'Does his mother know?'

'Elizabeth? Yes, she knows. When I went round to her house, she wanted to know why I was looking for Fred, so I told her.'

'Straight out?'

'Yes. She wouldn't believe me, so I gave her chapter and verse. You should have seen her face.' She chuckled at the memory. 'But she had the last laugh. I was stuck. I had a baby out of wedlock, I couldn't get a job, people shut their doors in my face. So I thought, what the hell, I might as well be hanged for a sheep as a lamb and enjoy myself.'

Rita knew her mother's reputation, few in Melsham didn't, but was it to be wondered at? What before had been an affectionate tolerance, because she was her mother who was funny and loving and generous, turned to respect. If being common and easy-going allowed you to keep your sanity and pride, then who had any right to blame her? 'So, I'm a Kennett,' she murmured. 'How should I feel about that?'

'I dunno. How do you feel?'

She considered the question for a minute. 'Nothing at all. I don't like George Kennett. Is he like his father?'

'To look at, yes, but whether he's like him in other ways, I've no idea. I've always steered clear of him.'

'And you've kept quiet about it all these years?'

'Didn't see any point in broadcasting it. There was nothing to be gained except a lot of upset. I was protecting you as much as anyone. But if that reporter unearths the truth, heaven knows what she'll make of it. I wish there was some way we could stop her.'

'I'll have to talk to Colin.'

She got up from the table and busied herself clearing the table and washing up in the yellow stone sink. Her mother seemed to have talked herself out, because she leant back in her chair and dropped off to sleep. She had had her say and now the burden of her troubles had landed squarely on her daughter's shoulders, and Rita's mind was in a whirl. One thing she was determined on and that was to protect her mother and Zita. And Barbara, if she could.

Colin was sprawled in an armchair listening to jazz on the radio when she arrived home after work that evening. He had a tankard of beer in his hand. Beside him on a low table was a knife and fork on a dirty plate. Without thinking, she picked them up and took them out to the kitchen where she added them to the pile in the sink, then went back to him. 'Turn that racket off. I can't talk above it. Unless you want me to shout. The neighbours might find what I've got to say very interesting.'

Reluctantly he switched off. 'So? Spit it out.'

'It's about this.' She tapped the newspaper she had brought with her. 'I suppose you've read it?'

'Course.' He grinned. 'I bet it's made Kennett squirm.'

She sank into a chair and stared at him. 'It was you...'

'Yup.'

'But why? What on earth did you have to gain?'

'Why should I take the rap for everything that bugger does? I served time for him and he pulled the rug from under me. And the reporter's promised two hundred

356

pounds if I find out more. We could make a new start with that.'

'Two hundred?' she queried, shocked.

'I thought that would make you sit up and take notice. She wants the low-down on Melsham Construction. Seems our friend George has been a naughty boy. Donald Browning is being used, just like I was. Melsham Construction belongs to George Kennett, Donald's only the front man. The paper is prepared to pay big money for proof.'

'You're not going to give it to them, are you?'

'If I can get it. Zita could help.'

'Our Zita?'

'Yes.' He laughed. 'Did you know Kennett is screwing her?'

'What?' she shrieked. 'George Kennett and Zita?'

'Yes.'

'Who told you?'

'The reporter, but Zita confirmed it, when I asked her. She was laughing about it, said she was only in it for what she could get out of it.'

'Oh, my God! Colin, we've got to put a stop to it. Tell the reporter you made it up.'

'Why should I? What do you want to save that bastard's skin for?'

'It's not his skin I'm thinking of, it's Mum's and Zita's. Us, Colin.' She took a deep breath. 'George Kennett is my half-brother. My father was Fred Kennett. Ma only told me today.'

He laughed. 'You're having me on.'

'I wish to God I were. Shut up while I tell you.'

For once in his life he listened while she told him Dora's story. Two days later Maggie had a break-in, and among the things taken were the notes of her conversation with Colin Younger. She was annoyed, even a little frightened at her own vulnerability, but she didn't think it was anything more than a straightforward burglary until she asked Colin to repeat his allegations and he refused, categorically denying he had ever said anything against George Kennett and she must have misunderstood him. Far from discouraging her, it made her all the more determined.

Barbara stood at her studio window looking out onto the garden. The golden hues of autumn had gone; now it looked bleak and bereft waiting for spring to bring it back to life. The trees that were left on the other side of the fence had lost their leaves and she could see the manor roof through their bare branches. She had accepted a part in the hydro project and the alterations were being done to the main house and the coach house, which was to be converted into a home for Isobel, marketing strategies were being worked out, equipment and soft furnishings being discussed. Simon hadn't come; she supposed he had stayed away for her sake. He probably supposed her marriage still meant everything to her and didn't want to upset her.

She would need to call on her courage later, not only to face Simon and treat him as a friend and fellow director, but to tell George what she was doing. He wouldn't be pleased, he'd tell her she didn't know the first thing about business; he might even want to take over. She would have to deal with that. But what worried her most was that people might say it was just another scam of George Kennett's and there was bound to be something dodgy about it.

She was worried sick by the rumours. She could see every little twist and turn of George's business deals, the bribes, their first house, the arson, the deals over the industrial site, being splashed all over the pages of the *Melsham Gazette* and probably the nationals too. It would devastate the children. And Elizabeth, too. And what would happen to her own life? Some of the dirt would be bound to rub off on the hydro project. She'd tried talking to George and been told it was nothing to get steamed up about, she was making a mountain out of a molehill. He'd got very angry and shouted at her, which just proved he was worried too; he hardly ever raised his voice. And because there was nothing else on her mind, probably on his either, if he were honest, they stopped talking about anything at all. They dealt coolly and politely with each other, but now even the pretence they had a happy marriage had been dropped in private, though they maintained it in public. They were two people living under the same roof and that was all they had in common.

A few flakes of snow drifted down from a slate-grey sky as she turned from the window and picked up the box of Christmas tree decorations, which was the reason she had come up here, and took it downstairs where she put the box on the drawing room table and began taking out the shiny, fragile baubles, the lights, the silver tinsel and attaching them to the tree. When the children were young they had all done it together, laughing and trying to guess, from the shape and size of the wrapped parcels they put beneath it, who had been given what, looking forward to the day, to the year ahead. Now all she could do was get through one day at a time: looking ahead terrified her. But whatever was happening around them, Christmas could not be postponed. She had done the shopping, made the pudding, iced the cake, pretended they were going to have a lovely time, all the family together.

She wasn't so sure of herself when Christmas Day came. George had been absent until after midnight the night before, and whatever he said, she was sure no one did business that late on Christmas Eve. He had been with her, whoever 'her' was, preferring the company of his mistress to that of his family, no matter that three of them were children. From loving him, she had almost come to hating, except that she was not the kind to hate anyone. And not half a mile away, the man she really loved was enjoying Christmas with Penny and Hal and Lady Quarenton. Penny had told her they would be there. 'A sort of try-out of the hydro,' Isobel had said. 'You'll come and share a Christmas drink with us, won't you?' She might have gone if Isobel had been on her own, but she couldn't face Simon. He had always been able to read her moods and he would know without being told that she had never been so miserable in all her life. 'I'll see if I can get away for a few minutes,' she had said, knowing perfectly well she would not. Could not.

She picked up her glass and returned to the drawing room where Jay-Jay, because he was the youngest, played postman and distributed the parcels from around the tree. He was a handsome child, good-natured and every year became a little more like Simon. How long before someone commented that he was nothing like the other two, Barbara wondered, and then what would she say?

Her children were happy with their gifts. There were books and clothes for Alison, skates and a toboggan for Nick, extra Meccano and a box of paints and brushes for Jay-Jay. George had bought pearls for her and a gold brooch for his mother. Barbara wasn't at all sure she was quite ready for pearls. No doubt they were costly, George always equated cost with value, and she thanked him and gave him a gold pen and pencil set. Soon the whole floor was littered with wrapping paper, ribbon and cardboard boxes.

They left it to go into the dining room for dinner. Everyone said it was delicious, though the adults, including Barbara, basked in the glow of too much wine and after-dinner port. 'I'll help wash up, Mum,' Alison said, getting up and gathering together a pile of plates. Barbara smiled at her, pleased by the offer, and mother and daughter spent half an hour in the kitchen companionably together, and when everything had been neatly put away, joined the others in the drawing room.

Elizabeth had dropped off to sleep in her chair. Barbara smiled indulgently and began clearing away the rubbish, folding the paper and putting it into the biggest of the boxes.

'Let's go and try out the toboggan,' Nick said. It had been snowing steadily all morning and he was tired of staying in the house. 'We could go up Long Hill.'

'Why don't we all go?' George said.

'Yes, let's.' The others were enthusiastic.

'Barbara?' George asked.

'I'll stay here and clear up the rubbish,' she said. 'If Granny wakes up and finds we've all disappeared she'll wonder what's happened. You go and have fun. I'll have the kettle on for tea when you get back.'

They wrapped themselves up in coats, scarves and gloves and set off down the drive with Nick pulling the toboggan. Barbara watched them disappear then gathered up the rubbish and took it out to the dustbin. When she returned Elizabeth was awake.

'Where is everyone?'

'They've taken the toboggan up to Long Hill. They'll be back for tea. Can I get you anything, a drink, perhaps?'

'No, I think I'll go home and have a nap.'

'You could nap here.'

'No, the sofa isn't good for my bad hip. I'll be better under the eiderdown on my own bed.'

'Then I'll take you over, the ground might be slippery.'

Having made her mother-in-law comfortable, she was letting herself back into the kitchen when someone came in behind her and put his hands over her eyes. 'Guess who?'

'Simon!' She pulled his hands down and swung round to face him. 'You made me jump.'

He was smiling down at her, his blue eyes raking her face, questioning her without words, making her breathless and afraid. 'You look stupendous.'

She was shaking, unable to believe he had been so foolish as to seek her out in her own home, when, for all he knew, her family were all round her. On the other hand, his coming had lifted the gloom which had been engulfing her for days, months, even years, and set her heart beating, making her want to smile, to laugh, to be happy. 'Simon, what are you doing here?'

'Spending Christmas at the manor with Penny. Didn't she tell you?'

'Yes, but I meant here, in my kitchen.'

'You wouldn't have come up to see us, would you?'

'I couldn't get away. Simon, I really think you should go. The family—'

'They've gone out, I saw them go. You've got time to say hallo to me, surely?'

'Hallo.'

'Oh, Barbara, unbend a little, please. I see the coffee pot is on the stove, will you offer me a cup?'

Like an automaton, she poured it for him. When he took it from her, their hands touched briefly. She became aware of nerves twitching in the middle of her belly, that somewhere, deep inside, she was opening out. Oh, no, she mustn't, she mustn't want this lovely golden man, with his wide smile and alluring eyes which seemed to be able to see right through the thin fabric of the beige crêpe dress she was wearing, through flesh and bone, to a longing laid bare.

'Why did you come?'

'Because I wanted to see you and because I was once invited to view a painting...'

'By Jay-Jay.'

'Yes, bright lad, isn't he? I could really take to him. I don't know about the others, I've never met them.'

'Simon, stop it.'

'Stop what?'

'Teasing. That's what you're doing, isn't it?'

He sighed heavily. 'If you say so. But how about showing me that painting?'

'It's in the dining room.'

He put his cup on the draining board. 'Lead on, then.'

He followed her and stood looking at the picture of old Melsham market, from a distance and then closer. 'Jay-Jay was right, everyone's in it, including me. I'm flattered.' He moved on to the portrait of Alison. 'And that's Alison.'

'Yes.'

'She's a pretty girl.'

'Yes, but she's an easy subject. The boys were more difficult.'

He looked round the room. 'Where are those?'

'Up in my studio. They weren't good enough to bring down.'

'Who said so?'

'I did. I know when something is substandard. And I hate people telling me something is good because they're too polite to tell me any different.'

'Show me. I'll give you an honest opinion, no holds barred.'

She wondered about the wisdom of taking him upstairs, but it was so wonderful to have him there, to know that someone was interested in her and her talent and not simply because she was Mrs Kennett, wife of Mayor Kennett, largest employer in Melsham. She could pretend it was only an artistic interest, couldn't she? If she kept a tight rein on her emotions and didn't let him get too near, she could talk art on an impersonal level. Just who was she trying to fool? He knew and she knew what it was

364

all about. But she couldn't bring herself to turn him away. 'OK, I'll hold you to that.'

She led the way. 'Here we are, the inner sanctum.' She gave a little embarrassed laugh. 'You don't know how privileged you are, I don't show many people up here.'

He stood looking about him. There was an uncompleted landscape on an easel near the window, framed pictures hanging on the walls and canvases stacked up on the floor below them. She watched him wandering about the room, admiring the pictures while she admired him, his lean torso, fair hair, expressive hands. Mentally shaking herself, she crossed the room and turned two canvases round. These are the boys. This one is Nick and this is Jay-Jay. I painted them a couple of years ago.'

He looked at them with his head on one side. 'They are good.'

'You promised to be honest.'

'I am. Nick is like you, isn't he? Fair and slim. I imagine he's an open-hearted, affectionate boy.'

'He is, but you can't tell that from the picture, surely?'

'Oh, yes, you've captured the essence of him, just as you've caught the essential Alison in the painting downstairs.' He turned to the one of Jay-Jay. 'This is good too...' He stopped.

She laughed shakily. 'Go on, you were going to say "but"...'

'I sense a kind of restraint, a stiffness which is different from the other two, it's as if you suddenly lost your confidence. The easy-flowing lines have gone...'

He did not have to tell her, she knew that already. It was why she had not hung the pictures. The one of Nick she wouldn't have minded hanging beside that of Alison, but not Jay-Jay, not her love child. Every line, every stroke of her brush seemed to emphasise his likeness to Simon and the red-gold hair was so like Penny's she didn't see how anyone could fail to notice. And she couldn't have hung one without the other: it would have invited comment. 'It shows? I had trouble with the colour of his hair. It's not red and it's not blonde, but a bit of both and it's difficult to get exactly right.'

'A bit like Penny's.'

She took a deep breath. 'Yes, I suppose it is, but I believe my father-in-law had auburn hair, though of course, I never met him.' She was beginning to wish she hadn't brought him up here: he was far too perceptive for comfort. She replaced the pictures against the wall and pulled out others: fenland scenes, water and skyscapes, a kingfisher diving, a village fete, an old pleasure boat sinking at its moorings, colourfully clad golfers on the fairway. He commented on them all, not eulogistically, but fairly, until he came to a miniature she had done of Jay-Jay before starting on the large one. He picked it up and ran his hands gently over the child's face. 'Can I keep this one?'

'Why?'

'To remind me of Barbara Bosgrove, who has never, in fifteen years, left my thoughts for long and never been absent from my heart.'

He knew the truth, but he would not speak of it openly. She knew, without his saying so, that if she wanted to talk to him about Jay-Jay, then he would listen, but until she did his lips were sealed. 'Simon, please don't,' she said.

'May I have it?'

She nodded and he popped it into his pocket and strolled across the room to the gramophone. 'You like to listen to music while you work?'

'It helps my mood sometimes.'

He slipped a record onto the turntable and wound it up. The soft strains of 'Smoke Gets in Your Eyes' filled the room. It had been playing the night of Penny's party, the night she ran away from him, too afraid to confront the truth. She had been running ever since. She shook herself, realising he had spoken. 'Do you remember that?'

'Yes.'

He turned to face her, putting his right arm round her waist, taking her right hand in his left and holding it against his heart. Slowly he began to move to the music. Mesmerised, she allowed it to happen, did nothing to stop what she knew must follow. She shut her eyes and held her breath, and when his mouth came down on hers, she was not surprised. Sweet and gentle, the kiss went on for a long time, while the music continued to play and they swayed together to its beat. He stopped and held her close against him, murmuring in her ear, 'Oh, Barbara, my love, my dearest love—'

'Simon, don't.' She tried to sound firm, but it was only an unconvincing whisper.

He pulled her towards him and bent his head to kiss her again. She clung to him, mouth on mouth, body against body, felt the heat of him permeating her whole body. In another minute they would be ripping the clothes off each other. It must not happen again, not even knowing that George had a new love. She laughed shakily and slipped sideways away from him and started back down the stairs before she could disgrace herself. 'I think it's time for you to go.'

He trailed after her. 'I am dismissed?'

'Afraid so.' She said it lightly, but it took all her strength to say it.

'I love you.'

'Don't, Simon, please don't.'

'Why not? It's the truth. You fill all my thoughts, every waking moment, even when we don't see each other for years.' He smiled and reached for her hand. 'You come to me in my dreams and even when I'm not asleep. I know you feel the same. Why deny it?'

'Because I must.'

'OK, I'll go. But think about this: I read the newspapers and there's no smoke without fire and I can guess what it's doing to you. When it all blows up and you need a shoulder to cry on, I'll be waiting.'

'Oh, Simon.' She blinked back tears but they refused to be contained and began to tumble down her cheeks. He pulled her towards him and bent his head to kiss her again. It was meant to be a gentle kiss, a comforting kiss, something to take away with him, but he found himself putting all his pent-up emotion and frustration into it.

'Mum, we're all gasping for a cuppa—' Alison stopped abruptly and stood gaping at them.

They sprang apart but the guilt on their faces was enough to confirm the nature of the kiss she had witnessed. 'Mum, how could you? How could you be so... so...'

'Alison, darling, it was nothing...' Barbara began, but

her daughter had fled past them and out of the room, too angry even for tears.

'Alison, what's the matter?' George appeared in the kitchen doorway, knocking snow off his boots.

'Ask Mum,' she shouted back. 'Ask her what she and that man were up to.' A reverberating bang told them she had reached her own room.

'Oh, God!' Barbara said. 'That's the last thing I wanted.'

'What's Alison on about?' He caught sight of Simon standing by the kitchen sink. 'Barcliffe! What are you doing here?'

Barbara was too upset to answer, but Simon gathered himself. Though there was nothing he would have liked more than to have it all out in the open, he knew he had to calm things down for Barbara's sake. 'I'm staying up at the manor with my sister,' he explained coolly. 'She asked me to come and deliver her good wishes for a happy Christmas.'

'And does that include kissing my wife?' George was icily calm. 'That is what you were doing, wasn't it? Or was there something more to it than that?'

'No, of course not,' Barbara said, collecting her scattered wits. 'Alison misunderstood.'

'Mr Kennett—' Simon began.

'And you can get out. You're not wanted here, not by any of us. Is that clear?'

Simon looked at Barbara. 'Please go,' she said. She remembered how she had felt when she found her father and Virginia in similar circumstances and all she wanted to do now was go to her daughter, to comfort and reassure her, make her see that her happy, secure life was not in jeopardy.

Simon, reading her mind as he always could, gave her a wry smile and left. Barbara pushed past George and went up to her daughter's room and knocked on the door. 'Alison, let me in, please. I want to explain—'

'There's no need to explain.' The voice was muffled. 'I saw for myself.'

'It wasn't like that. Let me in, please, we can't talk through a closed door.'

George had come up behind her. He banged on the door. 'Alison, it's Daddy. Let me in.' He looked daggers at Barbara. 'If you've done anything to make her unhappy, or any of the children unhappy, I'll kill you, I really will.'

'Go away both of you,' Alison shouted through the door.

They stood there for a moment longer, then turned silently and went back downstairs. Nick and Jay-Jay were in the hall looking upwards. Elizabeth, who had come back from her nap and passed Simon on the way, was standing in the doorway between the kitchen and the hall, looking puzzled.

'What was all that about?' Nick asked.

'Nothing,' Barbara said. 'Alison is a bit upset—'

'Too true she's upset,' George said, feeling so angry and betrayed, he couldn't keep quiet. 'Wouldn't you be if you found your mother kissing someone...?'

'It was nothing,' she said, stung into defending herself. 'Only a bit of Christmas fun.'

'Alison didn't seem to think so.'

'She was mistaken.'

'Nicholas,' Elizabeth said. 'I think you should escort me back home. I don't want to hear any more of this.'

'But I do,' he said. 'Dad shouldn't get onto Mum like that. Mum wouldn't do anything wrong. I know she wouldn't.'

'Do as Gran asks you,' Barbara said, her whole mind concentrated on preventing more home truths from surfacing. Jay-Jay was the most vulnerable of them all.

'No, Mum, he started it. I'm going to have my say.' He turned to his father. 'You've no room to talk after what you've been up to—'

'Nick, don't...' Barbara began, wondering what on earth her son knew. He was growing up fast, at an age to begin to know things if not to understand...

He ignored her and continued addressing his father. 'You look down your nose at Mr Younger, make fun of Mrs Younger, but you don't mind going to bed with Zita, do you?' This was only a guess, but he was pretty sure that's what they had been doing in Paris and it was much worse than Mum kissing Mr Barcliffe.

'Zita?' Barbara put in. 'You mean Rita's daughter?'

'Yes. He took her to Paris. I saw them coming off the train together and I heard what they said. "Paris was fun," she said.'

There was a dreadful silence. Nick's words hung in the air, unanswered, unanswerable. Barbara was so shocked she couldn't speak. Zita Younger. What had they done to their children, she and George? She looked at him. He looked like thunder, dark brows drawn down across his eyes, eyes full of anger and something akin to fear, cheeks tinged red.

'Nick, you don't know what you're saying,' she said, but she knew it was the truth.

'I feel faint,' Elizabeth said. 'George, take me home. I want to lie down.'

'Nick will go with you,' George said, without looking at her: he dare not.

'Jay-Jay, you go too,' Barbara said, anxious to put him out of harm's way.

Elizabeth put her hand on Jay-Jay's shoulder. She suddenly looked old and frail. 'George, come and see me before you go to bed. I want to talk to you. There is something I should have told you years ago. As for you, Barbara, I thought you'd have more sense. Two wrongs don't make a right, you know.'

'I know,' she said, as Nick angrily slammed out of the house ahead of them. 'Will you be all right?'

'Yes, I'm not in my dotage yet. Come, Jay-Jay.'

He sighed. 'And it was such a lovely Christmas until now. Why do people behave badly to each other?'

'I don't know, son, I just don't know,' Elizabeth said.

Barbara was left facing George. She opened her mouth to speak but thought better of it. What could she say? What could he say that wouldn't make matters a hundred times worse?' She turned and went back to the kitchen to wash up the coffee cups, her feet and heart both like lead. They had gone past the point of no return, she and George. She heard the front door slam as George took himself off. To his new love, perhaps? What on earth had he been thinking of? What was she going to say to Rita? She felt as if her whole life was breaking up. The family structure she had worked so hard to maintain was crumbling all round her. The scandal would spread and spread, Maggie Doughty would see to that. She looked out of the kitchen window towards the manor; was that project going to be ruined too?

'Oh, please God,' she prayed. 'Please let it all die down. Let Nick be mistaken. Help Alison. Punish me, if you must, but let me keep my secret.'

George didn't go to Zita; he walked for miles. Why had he allowed himself to become entangled with her? She was not Virginia, never could be, not in a million years; she was certainly not worth losing his children over. It was Barbara's fault. Had she invited Simon Barcliffe to the house? He had accused her once before of having an affair with him which she had vehemently denied. She'd been lying all along. He grimaced as he strode along the footpath beside the common. She had stuck by him over Virginia, but then she'd had a guilty conscience herself over Simon Barcliffe.

Damage limitation, that's what he must concentrate on. Keep away from Zita; keep away from Donald. Let him get on with the market job on his own. He'd better ring him and then get hold of Colin, find out what he'd take to keep his mouth shut, keep a low profile on the council, except for doing his job as mayor in exemplary fashion. Barbara must fall into line. She must see that. He turned on his heel and made for home.

It was gone midnight and Barbara had gone to bed when he let himself in the front door. He picked up a glass and a bottle of brandy from the lounge and crept up to the spare room, where he pulled off his jacket and trousers, loosened his tie and flung himself down to drink himself into oblivion.

Chapter Fourteen

'GEORGE! WAKE UP!' Barbara shook him, but all he did was turn over and mumble something incoherent. 'George, if you don't stir yourself, I'll throw a bucket of cold water over you. Your mother's ill.'

He sat bolt upright. 'Mum? Why didn't you say so? What's wrong with her?'

'A stroke, heart attack, I can't be sure. I've rung for an ambulance.'

'What happened?' he asked as he scrambled into his trousers. He was halfway down the stairs as he pulled his braces over his shoulders. Stopping in the kitchen to slip his feet into his shoes he raced out to the bungalow with Barbara behind him.

'I knew she was upset last night, so I went over as soon as I got up. I found her unconscious.'

George was struck by guilt. She had asked him to go and see her before he went to bed and he had forgotten, got drunk instead. He tore into his mother's bedroom and flung himself down beside her bed. 'Mum.' He grabbed her hand; it was unresponsive.

'Oh, God, no,' he muttered. This was a direct result of the upheaval the day before. It was Barbara's fault. And Barcliffe's. 'You'll be all right,' he said, addressing the unconscious form. 'The ambulance is on its way.'

They heard the bells almost as soon as he spoke. Barbara ran to let the men in. Their calm efficiency abated some of George's panic and he stood by helplessly as they took charge. He went with his mother in the ambulance, leaving Barbara to tell the children what had happened and wait for news.

It was some time before George was allowed into the ward to see his mother. 'She's rallied a little,' the doctor told him. 'But the next ten days are critical. Try not to upset her.'

He crept into the room, aware that he had not shaved, nor even washed and his clothes were rumpled. 'Mum.' He pulled up a chair close to the bed and took her hand, terrified by the pallor of her skin: it was almost transparent and her lips were blue. 'I'm sorry. I wouldn't have had this happen for all the world. But you're going to be all right.'

She did not appear to hear him. He sat and looked at her, his mind going round in circles. She was the most precious thing in his life, always had been, more than Barbara, more than the children even, and infinitely more important than Zita Younger. 'Fred,' she murmured, without opening her eyes.

'No, Mum, it's me. George.'

'Fred's gone, hasn't he? Didn't want him to go, not angry like that. He'll come back and we must make it up for the baby's sake...'

It was difficult to understand what she said, most of it was a mumble. 'Yes, Mum.'

She went on in like vein for a few minutes more, drifting in and out of sleep, muttering incoherently. He tried soothing her, and when Alison arrived to sit with her, he went home to bath and change. He was back two hours later and was relieved to see her looking stronger.

'George,' she said. 'I'm glad you came. Want to tell you something.'

'Fire away.'

'Yesterday, that dreadful row, everybody screaming at everybody else. It was yesterday, wasn't it? I've lost track.'

'I'm sorry, Mum, you shouldn't have had to witness that. Barbara shouldn't have—'

'Don't blame Barbara, you are as much to blame as she is...'

'I know.' He sighed heavily. 'I'm sorry. Don't think about it anymore.'

'Can't help thinking. Got to tell you. Didn't think I'd ever have to. Must now.'

'Please, Mum, there's no need—'

'Be quiet and listen. Mustn't go near the Younger woman again. Not ever. You see...' She stopped. 'Give me a drink of water.'

He picked up the cup and raised her head to help her to drink. She took a couple of sips and lay back exhausted. He sat and watched her for a couple of minutes and then she began talking again. 'Your father—'

'What about him?'

'He wasn't a hero, not to me, he wasn't. Oh, it was fine to begin with, but he changed, got too fond of the drink. It's terrible when two people who are supposed to love each other can't talk. I prayed he'd get over it and go back to being his old self, but—'

'He died in Canada, I know that.'

'When he came home on shore leave, he wanted to spend it all drinking in the pub with his friends. We rowed about it. He left the house and he didn't come back 'til morning. It was like that the whole week. The last night he came back in the early hours, but instead of coming to bed, he slept on the sofa. I was too angry and proud to go to him and when I went down the next morning, he'd gone back to sea. I never saw him again.'

'Mum, it wasn't your fault. You shouldn't blame yourself.'

'I don't,' she said crossly. 'He was out with that tart, Dora Symonds.'

The name didn't immediately register with him. 'Please, Mum, don't distress yourself.'

'She came to see me later,' she went on, determined to have her say, though the effort was making her very breathless. 'Wanted to know if I'd heard from your father. The cheek of it! Then she told me she was expecting his child.'

'Oh.' His mind was in a whirl. 'But it's all in the past. Don't think of it.'

'It's not in the past. It's here. Now.'

'What do you mean?'

'You know who Dora Symonds is, don't you?'

'No.'

'She's Rita Younger's mother. Rita Younger is your half-sister.'

He sat and stared at her, too dumbfounded to take it in. Then he remembered how she had reacted when Rita came to the house after Colin disappeared. He had thought it was strange because he didn't know his mother even knew her. And she was always telling him to discourage Barbara from making a friend of her, refusing to explain herself. And, too busy with his own affairs, he hadn't taken a bit of notice. 'Why didn't you tell me before?'

'I didn't ever want to. All I wanted to do was shut it out, pretend it never happened. But you can't shut out the past. It always comes back. The sins of the fathers...' She stopped suddenly too breathless to continue.

He fell silent. His revered father was not the loving husband he had always supposed him to be. His mother had lived with that for over forty years, embittered and sad. And he had made matters worse, brought it all back by employing Rita's husband. The revelation about Zita must have been the last straw. That little tart was his niece, related by blood. He was appalled and disgusted.

'There's no need to say anything to anyone,' she went on. 'Soon, it won't matter, I shan't be hurt by it anymore.' She smiled and reached out a thin veined hand to touch his cheek. She was obviously tired and, having had her say, wanted to rest. 'Go home, George, make your peace with Barbara. Talk to her. Listen to her, too. Don't let history repeat itself.'

'I'll try.' He kissed her goodbye and left. It was the last time he saw her alive. She died in the early hours of the next morning.

The whole family was united in grief. To the children she had been someone who would always listen to their woes; to Barbara she had been, after the first few months when she realised her daughter-in-law was no threat to her closeness with her son, fair and supportive; to George, she had been everything. He could not cope with his misery and spent hours pacing up and down his study, unable to sit still. He tried going to work, but found he could not concentrate and took himself out into the country and walked for miles.

The funeral was attended by almost all the older residents of the town who had grown up with Elizabeth, people from all walks of life, people he hardly knew. He followed the coffin down the aisle of the church in a daze, unable to believe what had happened. It was his fault. His and Barbara's, because he would not absolve her. But mindful of his mother's dying wish that he should make his peace with his wife, he had made no accusations. In fact he could hardly bring himself to speak to her at all.

Barbara was glad of his silence. She didn't want to talk about what had happened, she couldn't. She sat in her pew in the church, black-clad, black-veiled, feeling isolated. Her children, particularly Alison, were confused and miserable, rejecting her comfort. No one offered her solace. She didn't deserve it. Somehow she had to survive on her own. She would, too, because she and George were finished. Not yet, though, she couldn't leave him while he was at rock bottom. After the grand opening of the refurbished market the week before the jubilee celebrations, after he had ceased to be mayor, she would sit down and try to talk calmly to him about what they were going to do. It would give her time to sort out her life. She rose as the notes of the last hymn died away, and walked with George behind the coffin to the open grave, as always, the supportive wife.

Maggie, grasping at straws, consulted the register of births and deaths at St Andrew's church and found the record of Zita Younger's birth. Nothing out of the ordinary there: father Colin Younger, mother's maiden name, Rita Symonds. While she was at the record office, she decided she might as well go back a generation. And then she found it. For some reason Dora Symonds had named the father of her daughter, probably hoping to shame him or get maintenance from him. Frederick Kennett. Jeez, that would be a story and a half!

'No, Maggie,' Toby said firmly when she brought him a copy of the birth certificate. 'The mayor's a popular figure and his mother has just died. The fact that Fred Kennett strayed from the straight and narrow is neither here nor there and does not reflect on his son. If you are so determined to discredit George Kennett then you should concentrate on his business activities.'

'That reporter woman was sniffing around,' Rita told Dora. 'I don't know what she wants but she's making me nervous.'

'What did you tell her?'

'Nothing. What's to tell? She wanted to know if I was proud of Zita and I told her of course I was.'

'Let's hope she doesn't start putting two and two together. Forty years! God, after all that time, it's coming back to haunt us.'

'No, it isn't,' Rita said firmly. 'We don't have to admit anything. There's no proof.'

'You've got to tell Zita the truth, so she knows to keep mum if that woman starts asking questions. I don't trust the newspapers...'

'OK. I'll go tomorrow after I've finished work.'

Barbara showed Maggie into George's study. He looked up at her with open hostility. As if he hadn't enough on his plate, he was expected to answer this woman's stupid questions. Barbara ought never to have let her in, but she was here now and it wouldn't do to rub her up the wrong way. He motioned her to a chair. 'What can I do for you, Miss Doughty?'

'Mr Kennett, is it true you own Melsham Construction and that Mr Browning is merely fronting it?' Barbara, leaving the room, heard Maggie's question clearly before shutting the door. She stood leaning against it, her heart beating uncomfortably fast, not deliberately listening, but unable to walk away.

'Of course it isn't true,' George said. 'And if you print it, I shall sue.'

'Mr Browning worked for you for how many years?'

'I don't know exactly. Fourteen, fifteen.'

'And he was always loyal?'

'He appeared to be. But no doubt he was working

towards going it alone. I've accepted that and bear him no ill will.'

'And Mr Younger. Did the same thing apply to him? He's family, isn't he?'

'What the devil are you talking about?'

'You surely knew that his wife is your half-sister? No, probably not, or you wouldn't have been screwing her daughter. Your own niece, Mr Kennett.'

Barbara waited, hardly daring to breathe, for George's reply. It seemed a long time coming. And then he blustered. 'Where did you get that tarradiddle from?'

'From the register of births, Mr Kennett. It's there in black and white. Rita Symonds, baseborn to Dora Symonds, father Frederick Kennett. Would you like to comment?'

'No, I would not. And if you publish one word, I'll see you never work in journalism again.'

Barbara felt sick. She knew it was true. The signs had been there all along. Elizabeth's antipathy towards Rita, her insistence she meant trouble. For over forty years Elizabeth had lived with the knowledge that her husband had betrayed her and had an illegitimate daughter, now it was all bubbling to the surface again. At least Elizabeth had been spared any more pain and upset.

Barbara began to wonder about her own particular skeleton. How long would it be before that started rattling its bones and bursting out of its cupboard? It made her afraid for Jay-Jay, until now only on the periphery of events. Please God, don't let him be hurt, she begged, wondering what penance she could make to keep him from suffering. Thank goodness there was nothing on his birth certificate to arouse suspicion.

She didn't want to hear any more. She went up to her studio, put a canvas on her easel and began daubing it with paint. Anything was better than her tortured thoughts. She wasn't aware that Maggie had left, nor did she hear George go out a few minutes later.

George parked the car in the town hall car park and walked to Zita's flat. Work on the market had finished for the day and the open space, surrounded by wire fencing, was a clutter of sand, bricks, paving and diggers. He walked round it, his anger growing with every step. If he wasn't careful, he'd lose it all. He could cope with business problems but personal traumas he had never found easy. And when one led to the other and got all mixed up, he began to panic.

He looked furtively about him before entering the block of flats and climbing the stairs. Zita had rung him several times at work, demanding to know why he had not been to see her. He had tried fobbing her off, but she had threatened to go to the press with her story. He had to shut her up.

'Oh, it's you.' She opened the door in a faded dressing gown. Her hair had just been washed and hung damply round her cheeks. Without make-up her face glowed. A few weeks ago it would have turned him on, but now he was repulsed. 'About time too.' She turned her back on him to go back inside.

He followed and looked round the familiar flat. It was still as untidy as ever, although there were now no unfinished sculptures to add to the mess: they had been taken to her new workshop by some of his labourers. 'What do you want from me, Zita?' he said, refusing to take a seat. 'You must have known it had to end.'

'Course I did. I'm not complaining. It was good while it lasted, but you might have had the decency to come and tell me to my face and give me a little something to be going on with. I've had to give up my job to work on that fountain...'

'My mother died.'

'I heard. I'm sorry. But you could have come after the funeral.'

'What difference would that have made, except to prove that bitch, Doughty, right?'

'So it's the press you're afraid of, accusations of bribery and corruption. She came to see me, you know, wanted to know who paid the rent of my workshop.'

'What did you tell her?' His voice was sharp.

'I told her I did, then I threw her out.'

'Thank God. You won't talk to her again, will you?'

She laughed. 'I've got nothing to tell her. But you're here now, so we might as well make the most of it.' She turned towards him and slipped off her robe. She wore nothing underneath it.

'For God's sake, cover yourself up,' he said angrily.

'Embarrassed are you? Now, there's a surprise! You wouldn't have reacted like that a few weeks ago.'

'A few weeks ago, I didn't know your feckless mother was my sister, did I?'

She stared at him, uncomprehending. 'Say that again.'

'Your mother is my half-sister, we had the same father. Don't you understand plain English?' He laughed harshly.

'I understand English, not the rubbish you're talking.'

'You don't want to believe it? I didn't either but that doesn't stop it being true.'

She stared at him for a moment, wondering what game he was playing with her, but the anger in his eyes was all too real. She began to laugh. Her grandmother's secret was out at last. Gran and Elizabeth Kennett's husband. Oh, it was funny. She was doubled up with mirth. He strode over to her and shook her. 'Stop it! How dare you laugh!'

'Why not? It's rich.' She pulled herself free of him. 'No wonder your prim and proper ma hated my gran.'

'It killed her. Knowing what we'd done killed her.' His face was white except for two bright spots on each cheek, his eyes burning, his control on a knife-edge.

'You shouldn't have told her, then.'

'I didn't. Nick did.'

'How did he find out?'

'He saw us getting off the train when we came back from Paris.'

'You could have fobbed him off. You're good at fobbing people off.'

'You and your family ruined everything for me. Everything. My mother said you would. She predicted it years ago.'

'You didn't think so when you were fucking me, did you? You thought I was the best thing since Adam and Eve.'

'Shut up.'

'No, you shut up. You used my dad. You knew he wasn't all that bright and you took advantage of him. You used me too…'

'You've done your share of using people. You wanted to win the fountain competition so badly, you'd have jumped into bed with anyone. I wish I'd never thought of it.'

'Oh, you poor thing! My heart bleeds for you.' She had been more shaken than she was prepared to admit, and all she wanted was to be alone to think. She was sick of him, sick of herself, sick at what they'd done. She hoped her mother never found out. 'Get out!' she shouted. 'Get out and leave me in peace.'

'I'm going, but I want your word you won't speak of this to the press. And keep that father of yours away from them too, or I'll have him back inside before he can blink.'

'How dare you come here and threaten me, you rotten bastard. Get out! Get out now!' Furiously she picked up a chisel and came at him, arm raised.

He backed away, opened the door and stepped out onto the landing. She followed him out, not bothering to keep her voice down. 'You're rotten through and through, Mr High and Mighty Mayor. You're worse than my dad ever was. You might shut him up, but I'm not like him. I think I will go to the papers after all. They'd pay well for a story like this.'

He looked fearfully about him, expecting doors to open up and down the stairway. 'Shut up, Zita. Go back inside. You're making a spectacle of yourself.'

She laughed harshly. 'I don't care. You're the one who's got it all to lose, not me.'

He tried to bundle her back into the flat, but she fought him like a wild cat. 'Come on, Zita, don't be a little fool,' he said placatingly, trying to relieve her of the chisel. 'Let's go back inside and talk about it quietly.'

She stopped struggling suddenly and he let her go. She bent to pick up a large vase that stood just inside the door and threw it at him. He leant back against the banister to avoid it. He heard the sound of splintering wood a split second before the banister gave way.

Three flights down, Rita was just coming in at the front door when his body hit the ground, followed by a pot which shattered beside him. She stood and stared at him for several seconds and then looked upwards. Her naked daughter was leaning over the top, looking down. Suddenly the girl's screams filled the cavernous space.

It was Rita, brought by the police, who told Barbara what had happened. She would rather it had been Rita than anyone. Rita understood how she felt and she didn't need to pretend. It wasn't that she didn't feel grief, because she did – you couldn't live with a man for fifteen years and have his children without feeling something – but that grief was tempered by a huge surge of something akin to relief which she was reluctant to admit, even to herself. They had been living with a bomb waiting to go off, a situation so fraught something was bound to happen. She had been very afraid, and now that particular fear had been dissipated she was left with the guilt. She sat at the table in the dining room, her face chalk white with the shock of it. Not only with the fact that George was dead, but the manner of it.

'I'm sorry.' Rita, sitting facing her, was almost as stunned as Barbara. She had witnessed it, seen the body fall, heard Zita's screams which had brought everyone else out of their homes to peer down into the stairwell. Torn between rushing out again to call an ambulance and going to her daughter, she had chosen to climb the stairs to Zita, leaving others to look after George. Later, the police had come. 'It was an awful way to go.'

'Why was he there? Surely he wasn't still...' Barbara's voice faded to nothing.

'No, course not. Zita said he'd come to ask her not to speak to the press. She wouldn't anyway. What had she to gain?'

'Do you know what happened?'

'Zita was too upset to say much; it took ages to calm her down enough for the police to take her to the station.'

'They haven't arrested her? Oh, my God, will it never end? Rita, I'm so very sorry. You must be feeling dreadful.'

'Yes, but it was an accident. He leant on the banister and it gave way. They'll let her go when she's made a statement.'

'It was my fault.'

'How can you possibly say that? Barbara, no way should you blame yourself. Now, shall I make us both a cup of tea?'

She bustled out of the room and Barbara sat staring at the wall in front of her. The *Market of Old Melsham* seemed to stare back at her. A lifetime encapsulated in a picture: good and bad, happy and painful. It was George's fixation with the market that had caused all this trauma. But it was more than that and older than that: it was about how they dealt with each other, their marriage. And it must have been as bad for George as it had been for her: he couldn't cope with the disappointment any more than she could. They had both been to blame. They had been glued together by guilt. She couldn't believe it had all come to a sudden and violent end. She couldn't cry, her eyes were gritty, dry as dust.

Rita returned with the tray and handed her a cup of tea. 'Drink that, I've put a dash of something stronger in it.'

'Thank you. The children... I must fetch them home...'

'Do you want me to do it?'

'No, I must. You go back to Zita. She'll be needing you.'

'Will you be all right? I'll ring Lady Isobel, shall I? She'll come.'

'No, I'd rather be alone with the children. Perhaps later...'

Rita left and she was alone, alone with her tumbled thoughts. What to do? What to say to the children? There would be a funeral to arrange, callers to deal with, George's business affairs to sort out. How was she going to cope with it all? And the children... Oh, God, her poor, dear children.

Forcing herself to be practical she got out her car and fetched them home. They cried, they cried a lot, and who could blame them? They had loved their father and to have him suddenly snatched away had devastated them. They clung together, all four, until she broke away to get them some tea. No one ate anything. No one wanted to talk. Alison was trying to be grown-up and not cry, but every now and again a huge sob escaped her. Nick was white-faced and feeling guilty: he blamed himself for telling everybody about Zita Younger. Jay-Jay sobbed. He had loved George in the uncomplicated way of a small child. That night she heard him crying in bed and got up to go to him. She sat on the edge of the bed, stroking his beautiful red-gold hair from his face. It was then she wept too, scalding tears that would not stop.

'It was nobody's fault,' she told Alison and Nick next evening as they sat in the drawing room, nursing cups of cocoa with uneaten sandwiches beside them. The day had been taken up with practicalities, informing people who had to be told, fielding telephone calls of condolence, taking in flowers and messages, talking to the undertaker and the rector, deciding on the hymns and the order of the funeral service. Not until now, with Jay-Jay safely in bed, had they had a chance to talk. 'It was an accident. The council doesn't want a scandal any more than we do. It would sully all the work your father did for the town and ruin the jubilee celebrations. They are going to issue a statement that he was in the flats on council business. The tenants put in a complaint about the dangerous state of the banister and he had gone to see for himself.'

'Who's going to swallow that?' Nick asked.

'Everyone if we believe it ourselves. Mrs Younger will say the same.'

'Course she will,' Alison said. 'She'd want to protect her daughter.'

'Yes, just as I want to protect you and Nick and Jay-Jay.'

'You didn't think about that before.' Alison hadn't meant to bring that up, but it had just come out. 'When... You know...'

'I did, you know. You children have always been my first concern, ever since you were born. I shut my eyes to a lot of things to keep you all safe. You don't know the half of it and God forbid you ever do. But I've never been more hurt and miserable than I have since Christmas. I didn't invite Mr Barcliffe...'

'But you didn't turn him away.'

'I had no reason to. Nothing happened between us, but it was what I did, or rather what I allowed to happen, that triggered off the upset, though what your father did was—' She stopped, unwilling to hurt them any more than she had already. She put out a hand and laid it on her daughter's. 'I'm sorry, darling. I should have sent Mr Barcliffe away, but he is Aunt Penny's brother. A friend, that's all.'

'Are you...are you going to see him again? I mean...'

'He is Penny's brother, Alison, I am bound to see him, but if you mean will I seek him out, then no, I won't. My regret, and it's a profound one, is that you were hurt. Can you forgive me?'

'I s'pose so.'

It was as much as Barbara had any right to expect and she forced a smile. 'We've got a long week ahead of us and we need to stick together. No doubt, there'll be rumours, but we'll just ignore them. The public image your father set so much store by will follow him to his grave and I wouldn't have it any different.'

* * *

George's funeral service, held on a day of cold, blustery rain, was attended by everyone of importance in the town, including Gordon Sydney, the new mayor, who had taken over the mantle of office a couple of months earlier than expected. There was a eulogy from Tony Bartram, who spoke of George's selfless devotion to serving the community and how the new fountain would be a fitting memorial to him. Barbara, flanked by her children, listened with black-veiled head bowed. She could hardly take it in. The last week had been hectic, but now it was over and she was saying a final goodbye to her husband. It didn't seem real somehow. She was thirty-five years old and for fifteen of those years George – and her children – had been her life, influencing everything she did: what she wore, where she went, what she ate, even the way she thought. Now she was alone. Oh, she had the children, who were precious to her, and good friends, but they did not stop her feeling that whatever happened next was down to her.

She had gone to see Alan Fairfax, the family solicitor, and was appalled to learn just how contorted George's financial affairs were. He had apparently been robbing Peter to pay Paul for years, mortgaged the house and cashed in his pension, leaving only a small life policy for her. He was in debt to his suppliers, who had only been holding back because he was the mayor and would have been baying for blood when his term of office came to an end. To add insult to injury, she couldn't touch any of the assets of Melsham Construction because, on paper, they belonged to Donald Browning.

'I'm sorry, Mrs Kennett,' Mr Fairfax had said, looking

shamefaced. 'I only became aware of the extent of the problem when I started sorting things out for probate. He didn't always deal with me, sometimes he saw my partner and we neither of us knew the state of his bank balance. I have no idea why he lent Melsham Construction such a large amount of money without securing it.'

'Oh, I do,' she said.

'It's a good thing you were not part of the business and can't be held responsible for its debts.'

'Are there any others?'

'It's all very involved and will take some time to sort out, but I think we can secure the house for you...'

'Don't,' she had told him. 'Sell it to clear the mortgage and as many other debts as you can. I still own the farmhouse my father left me.' She had looked across his desk as a worrying thought struck her. 'They can't take that, can they?'

'No, that's yours.'

'Good. It's let to an American family and they're due to go back to the States soon. I'll move back there.' That had been one of her easier decisions. She loved the old farmhouse, it was more home to her than The Chestnuts had ever been.

She came out of her reverie to find herself on the gravel of the churchyard, following the men bearing the coffin to the open grave. The rain had stopped and a faint shaft of sunlight pierced the trees surrounding the churchyard, making swirls of rainbow colours in the puddles. She was astonished how calm, how detached she felt, as if it was happening to someone else. She was able to stand and listen to the committal service without emotion. She was numb.

Afterwards she invited everyone to the house and they all milled about, eating sandwiches and sausage rolls and drinking sherry and beer, and telling each other what a fantastic man George had been and how much they were going to miss him. Alison was white-faced and uncommunicative, but determined to be brave because she was sure that was what Daddy would have wanted. Nick, on the other hand, was red-faced and hiding his grief behind fury, and she would have to try and ease that for him, assure him his father was not a bad man. Poor Jay-Jay simply looked bewildered. She saw him slip his hand into Penny's and Penny stoop to speak to him, her red-gold head bent to his, telling him something that elicited a smile.

'I'm very sorry, Mrs Kennett,' Donald murmured, beside her.

'I know that, Donald. Don't think any more of it.'

'Yes, but Melsham Construction...' He paused. 'Do you think we could talk about it some time?'

'No, Donald, I don't think so. It's your business.' She spoke firmly and he wandered off, too embarrassed to continue the conversation.

'Barbara.'

She turned from watching him walk away, to find Simon standing beside her. He was impeccably dressed in a dark suit and a black tie, and at thirty-nine still incredibly handsome, though the years had etched fine lines about his mouth and eyes, eyes which were as blue as they had always been, as blue as Jay-Jay's. His expression of concern deepened the slight scar on his brow. 'Hallo, Simon.' Her face felt stiff with trying to smile. 'How are you?'

'I'm OK. More importantly, how are you?'

'Oh, you know. Drained. A bit bemused. I keep thinking I'll wake up tomorrow and everything will be like it was.'

'I'm truly sorry,' he said, wanting to hold her, to comfort her, and though he lifted his hand to touch her, he changed his mind and let if fall to his side. 'Please don't hate me for it.'

'Why should I do that?' she asked in surprise.

'Christmas. What happened then. If I hadn't come—'

'Nothing to do with you, Simon. It would still have happened. Please don't think about it.' She had to keep him at arm's length, to make it look to the others in the room that he was doing no more than offering his condolences and she was accepting them. She could see Alison watching them and smiled reassuringly at her.

'I'm still sorry. What are you going to do with yourself now?'

'I can't think of anything at the moment, my brain refuses to function above trivialities. I have to get over each day as it comes and look after the children.'

'Of course you do. But some time, sooner rather than later, sit down and think about what you want to do. Not what everyone else wants you to do, but what you, Barbara Bosgrove that was, want from your life.'

'There's the children—'

'They are growing up. Soon they'll leave home. Penny tells me Alison is destined for university and Nick has a career to carve out for himself.'

'That may be true, but Jay-Jay's not yet eight. It will be ages before he's old enough to leave the nest.'

'Ah, Jay-Jay.' He smiled down at her. 'I think Jay-Jay takes after you. Alison and Nick have some of George in them, but not him. He's a one-off.' He bent towards her speaking softly. 'Take care of him, Barbara. He's very special.'

She looked up at him, the tears she had been refusing to shed sitting on her lashes ready to spill down her cheeks. 'Simon, I—'

He put his finger on her lips to stop her speaking. 'I have to go now, but if you need me, you know where I am. Any time.' He kissed her gently on the cheek. 'I believe there is someone waiting to speak to you, so I'll say goodbye.'

She watched him walk away and it was as if he were taking half of her with him, the core of Barbara Bosgrove that was, leaving only Barbara Kennett behind. Had she understood what he was trying to say? Especially about Jay-Jay. Was he saying he knew? How did he know? Penny would never have broken her promise not to tell him. She took a huge breath to steady herself and turned to find Tony Bartram standing not three feet behind her. It was a moment or to before she realised he had begun speaking and she hadn't heard a word he said. She forced herself to pay attention.

'We must try and carry on as normal,' he was saying. 'It is what George would have wished. And the people of the town have been looking forward to the jubilee celebrations and the official unveiling of the new fountain.'

'Of course,' she said, wondering if Simon had really gone or was still somewhere about. Did it matter? She couldn't call him back, could she? Sleeping dogs must be left to lie.

'We should be delighted if you would consent to turn on the new fountain at the opening ceremony.'

'Oh, no, I don't think I could. I'm sorry.'

'You don't have to make a decision today. Let me know in a week or two.'

She was determined to refuse, but later, after everyone else had left, she told Penny, Isobel and Rita, who had stayed to help her clear up.

'You should do it,' Isobel said. 'I can't think of anyone more appropriate.' She was surprised at how easily the other three accepted her, a spinster from a different era, a time traveller trapped in the past, not only in the past but in a different stratum of society, one that had all but disappeared. But Barbara and her friends had brought her out of that, made her value herself.

'If George had been alive, you would certainly have been asked to do it,' Penny put in. 'He'd have made sure of that.'

'I'll think about it.'

Chapter Fifteen

SHE MOVED BACK into the farmhouse at the end of April, on a soft spring day. The fruit trees in the orchard were covered in blossom and the garden was at its best. Daffodils vied with tulips, aubrietia and polyantha. An early clematis covered the end of one wall, a cloud of white blossom. The climbing rose that stretched up the flint stone wall to her bedroom window was still there and in early summer would be a glorious trail of gold. She breathed deeply. This was a new beginning, late in life perhaps, but new. Isobel had adamantly refused to allow her to resign as a director of Melsham Manor Hydro when she broached the subject. 'Nothing has changed,' she had said. 'I need you as much as ever. And you'll need something to keep you busy, won't you?'

'Yes.' She didn't add, though she could have done, that she would also need the money. George's finances were still in a mess.

The children had gone back to school almost

immediately after the funeral; it was best that they should. If they still thought about the dreadful events of Christmas and New Year, they never referred to them and seemed to have forgiven her. Jay-Jay, though still quiet, still thinking of the man he knew as his father, was the cheerful, affectionate boy he had always been, untouched by scandal.

The market wasn't finished in time for the jubilee. Zita was so traumatised over what had happened she couldn't bring herself to finish the sculpture and it was too late to commission someone else, and the convoluted problems of Melsham Construction's finances since George's death meant that Donald had trouble paying the suppliers for the street furniture, things like lamp standards, bollards, drainpipes and paint, to finish the whole project off. And Farrier's Court, left until last, was a wide open space with nothing on it but one tumbledown house, where Dora Symonds reigned in isolation, though she had been promised one of the town's almshouses when one became vacant. The town fell back on the tried-and-tested methods of celebrating with a civic dinner, a street party for the children and jubilee mugs.

The market was finished a year late, but by then George V had died and the Prince of Wales had become Edward VIII. It was decided to leave the ceremony until his coronation, except, of course, he was never crowned. There had been rumours about him and Mrs Simpson for some time, but even so, the abdication shook everyone. The prince had been a very popular figure, but few wanted the twice-divorced Wallis Simpson for a queen. Edward's abdication speech, broadcast on the wireless, had many in tears, including Dora, who loved a good romance. His unassuming brother became George VI and together with his wife, Elizabeth, supported by their two daughters, Elizabeth and Margaret Rose, was crowned in Westminster Abbey on Wednesday the twelfth of May 1937. Although the new market had been operational for some time, it had been decided the official switching on of Melsham's new fountain would take place the following Saturday, while the town was still in celebratory mood.

Barbara sat on her bed in her underwear and stared at the dress hanging on her wardrobe door. It was made of blue silk, deceptively simple in style, with three-quarter sleeves, a sweetheart neckline, fitted waist and a skirt that fell in panels over the hips and then flared out to the hem. It had been hideously expensive, but she'd bought it because Penny had told her it would boost her morale to look good. And she needed that. Why on earth had she agreed to switch on that damned fountain? To the people of Melsham it might be something to celebrate along with the coronation, but to her it represented all that had gone wrong with her life. Anyone else would have performed the ceremony just as well. Isobel, for instance, or Penny. Penny could have done it standing on her head.

She took the dress off its hanger and slipped it over her head, then stood before the mirror and appraised her reflection. Her figure may have lost some of the litheness of youth but it was still good; her skin was still smooth and Penny had taught her how to use make-up discreetly, so that it enhanced her high cheek bones and wide greeny-blue eyes, but skilful make-up did not make her feel any less nervous. She set her wide-brimmed, feather-trimmed hat at an angle on her head, slipped into her shoes, picked up her handbag and went downstairs, just as the doorbell rang.

She opened it to see a uniformed chauffeur on the step and behind him, on the gravelled drive, the mayor's shining black Rolls-Royce. 'Mrs Kennett.' He put his hand to the brim of his cap. 'I've come to fetch you.'

'Thank you.' She took a deep breath, stepped outside and locked the door behind her, before making her way to the car. As guest of honour she was to be conveyed in style.

The big car negotiated the crowds and was waved on its way by Constable Tommy White, immaculate in his uniform. Who'd have thought that little tearaway would turn out to be a policeman, and a good one at that? Barbara remembered the day she had taken the boy to London... No, she must not think of that. It only made her feel melancholy and today she was expected to put on a cheerful face. For the most part she was cheerful. The eighteen months since George's death had softened the rawness of the emotions, the misery, the guilt, the feeling of helplessness, as the tide of their lives swept them to disaster.

The new lamp posts had been decorated with hanging baskets containing red geraniums, white petunias and blue lobelia and there was red, white and blue bunting strung from one to the next. More banners hung across the new shop fronts. Landers department store had decorated one of its windows with red, white and blue ribbon and swathes of dress material of the same colours. Another window was stacked with coronation mugs and other commemorative china and glass. She was surprised and not a little alarmed to see that the marketplace itself was so packed with flag-waving onlookers, it was impossible to see the new red-brick paving. A roped-off walkway led from the town hall to the fountain, and even that was covered with a red carpet.

The car moved at walking pace and drew to a stop outside the town hall. A huge banner hanging over the balcony proclaimed: 'Melsham's loyal greetings to King George VI and Queen Elizabeth on the occasion of their coronation, May 12 1937.' A commissionaire opened the door for her. She got out, breathed deeply to steady herself and went up the steps.

There was a crowd in the vestibule, but Tony Bartram, now mayor, spotted her and hurried forward, his heavy chain of office glinting on his jacket front. He extended his hand. 'Mrs Kennett. We are all very pleased you agreed to do this. George—' He stopped, suddenly embarrassed.

'It's my pleasure,' she said and turned to Donald who stood at his elbow. She hadn't spoken to him since George's funeral, not because she hadn't wanted to, but simply because their paths had not crossed. He was chewing on his moustache, a sure sign he was uncomfortable. She smiled and offered her hand. 'How are you, Donald?

He took her hand with a smile of relief. 'Very well. And you?'

'Very well.'

'Here is Miss Younger, the fountain's designer.' The mayor moved her on. 'You must have met?'

Barbara looked at Zita with a smile that never wavered. She remembered seeing her in Rita's house when the girl would have been about thirteen, but she hadn't seen her again until George's funeral, standing in the churchyard after the service, half hidden by gravestones. 'I believe we did meet, but it was many years ago,' she said, holding out her hand, surprised to find it wasn't trembling. 'How do you do?'

Zita touched Barbara's fingers. 'Mrs Kennett.'

'Shall we go?' Tony said.

Barbara lifted her chin, straightened her shoulders and walked beside him along the red carpet, followed by the podium party to the dais which had been erected beside the fountain and took their places.

She hardly heard the mayor's speech as she looked round at the sea of faces in front of her. She spotted Isobel sitting very upright on one of the chairs in the front row of chairs and beside her, Penny, dressed in a flame-coloured silk dress and matching turban. In the crowd at the back Rita was craning her neck to see. Her pink dress was patterned with large poppies and her bright red hair was topped by a hat whose brim was decorated with more poppies. She was laughing and waving a tiny union jack. Three friends, a most unlikely combination of characters, but she wouldn't like to be without any of them. They had kept her sane.

But it was not on her friends Barbara concentrated, but on her children who were seated on the other side of Isobel: Alison, sixteen now, raven-haired, even-featured like her father, wearing a cotton dress patterned in small flowers; Nick, two years younger, hair slicked down, looking as if butter wouldn't melt in his mouth; and nine-year-old Jay-Jay, proud and excited, his unique red-gold hair reflecting the light of the sun. He was grinning at her, his clear blue eyes sparkling with mischief. Tears sprang to her eyes but she was smiling, genuinely smiling. Life suddenly seemed worth living again.

The mayor's voice, carried by loudspeakers to the far corners of the marketplace, forced itself into her consciousness. 'It is very fitting that the man who made all this possible, though sadly he did not live to see its completion, should be honoured on this day when we are also celebrating the coronation of our new king and queen.' He paused to beam at his audience. 'I now call on Mrs Kennett to unveil the fountain and set it into motion.'

Barbara stepped down and pulled the cord which released the covering from the fountain to reveal a bronze statue of a naked man, his hands lifted skywards holding a golden globe. At his side stood the slim, almost stick-like figure of a woman and a young boy whose curly head just managed to hide the genitalia of the man. Although not lifelike, it had vision and great strength. She had been prepared not to like it, wanted not to like it, but her own sense of justice made her admit it was good.

The mayor handed her a control box and she pressed the button he indicated. Water bubbled from the globe above the man's head, ran down his arms and splashed over the woman and boy and into the pool. A burst of applause broke out from those around her. She stood facing them all, overwhelmed by the feeling of goodwill that emanated round her.

It was over and another hurdle had been overcome, another day lived towards that time, somewhere in the future, when she would no longer mourn the lost years, no longer regret the mistakes. So many mistakes. But in there, amongst the dross, were some shining days, a lifetime of happiness crammed into a few stolen hours. One day, she would be able to look back and smile and say, 'When I was young...' and not be overwhelmed by tears.

Chapter Sixteen

SIMON CAME AFTER the children had gone to school the following Monday morning. She was tidying away discarded clothes, toys, books, but it was too nice a day to stay indoors and she intended to take her easel out to the fens. She was humming to herself when she heard the doorbell. She stuffed her duster into her apron pocket and went to answer it.

In casual trousers and a roll-neck shirt, he stood on the step, smiling at her in that heart-stopping way he had. 'Hallo, Barbara.'

'Simon, what are you doing here?'

'Is that meant to be a welcome?'

'Sorry, you took me by surprise.' She held the door open for him to enter. 'I wasn't expecting you...' She stopped suddenly when she realised he was paying no attention to what she was saying: he was simply standing in front of her, his feet apart, his head on one side, raking her with his eyes. 'What's the matter?' She raised a hand to brush a wisp of hair from her face, conscious that she was wearing no make-up and that the apron she wore hid a disreputable sweater and a pair of trousers. 'I'm a mess, I know. You caught me out.'

'You're beautiful.'

'Don't be silly.' She had to be light-hearted: it was the only way she could control the beating of her heart and the shaking of her hands. She had not set eyes on him since George's funeral and that encounter had been a strange one, a sort of goodbye and yet not a goodbye. In the eighteen months since then she had often thought about him, wondered if he ever thought of her, but then she had pushed the thoughts from her as unproductive and got on with her new life, one in which, she told herself sternly, she was fulfilled and content.

Without the tensions engendered by George's double-dealing and worrying about what he would get up to next, not to mention his affairs, she had begun to be herself again, to paint again. She had been putting her pictures in the window of the craft shop, giving the owner a commission for selling them. Others were on the walls of the manor with little tickets on them so that the wealthy clients using the hydro could buy them. And the council had commissioned a copy of *The Market of Old Melsham* to hang in the town hall. She hadn't become a famous artist, but she was making a little money at it, a small step on the way to realising her original ambition. Now here was Simon looking at her in that all-seeing way of his and melting her with his smile. 'Come in and I'll make some coffee.'

He followed her into the kitchen and sat at the table to

watch her as she moved about putting the percolator on the gas stove, setting out cups and saucers, fetching milk from the fridge. The small domestic movements made his heart contract painfully. Was it still too soon? Would she turn him away, as she had done on that fateful Christmas Day? He took a deep breath, but his voice, when he spoke, was light. 'How are you?'

'I'm fine. And you?' On the surface it was an ordinary kind of exchange, but she could feel the tension, the undercurrents sweeping them along.

'Fine.'

'Then why are you here? Why now?'

'I decided it was time.'

'Time?'

'Yes. Time to find out how the land lies, to see if there's anything you want or need. I meant what I said at George's funeral about always being there for you.'

'Thank you.'

'We couldn't talk then, not properly. It was too soon. I had to wait for the right moment.'

'And you think this is it?'

'I can't be sure, but I thought it was about right and the switching on of the fountain seemed appropriate, a time to take stock, as it were.'

'For you or for me?'

'Both.' He reached out and took both her hands in his and held them to his chest. 'You escaped me once, I can't let it happen again for want of trying.'

She looked up into his eyes and then away again because the message in them was confusing her, making her realise that she still wanted him, that all her efforts to put the past behind her, and him along with it, had failed. 'Simon, I don't understand. You can't still want me—'

'Always and for ever. You remember the beginning, when you were a student and I was a lieutenant back from the war?' She nodded. 'George got there first and claimed you. I couldn't risk that happening again with someone else.'

She smiled. 'It won't. There is no one.'

'Good.'

'But, Simon, that was a long time ago. We can't go back. It just isn't possible.'

'No, but we can go forward. All I'm saying is that I still love you and that won't ever change. I loved you then, I love you now, and I always will. To eternity.'

Her heart was beating almost in her throat and her knees felt weak. The words were like a distant melody, half remembered, just out of reach, haunting her, tantalising her, filling her whole being. 'Simon, I—'

'Don't say anything, just listen to your heart.' He bent to kiss her. The old fire, the feeling of being an entity with him, the sheer power of what they felt for each other, had always felt for each other, seized her in its grip and it was useless trying to fight it. She put her arms round his neck and let her own love mingle with his, surrounding them like a benevolent cloud. 'It is the same for you too,' he murmured. 'You feel it too.'

'Oh, Simon...'

'Say you do. There's no reason why you shouldn't, no impediment at all. Say you'll marry me.'

'Simon, I don't know. I'm confused. I don't know that

I'm ready for another marriage. I don't know if I ever will be.'

Still holding her, he leant back and looked into her eyes 'Do you mind telling me why?'

She reached up and stroked the tiny scar on his face with the back of her finger. 'You know, I used to dream about what I'd say if you came back and still wanted me.' She laughed, almost tipsily. 'It was a slightly erotic dream, Simon, but now you're here, it's different. I'm different. For the first time in my life, I feel absolutely free. I don't have to consult anyone about what I do, where I go. It is a wonderful feeling of independence, of liberation. Today, for instance, I plan to drive out into the country and paint.'

'I understand, and after what you've been through, I can sympathise, but we've wasted so much time, years and years, pretending to be something we're not, trying to please all those around us we thought had a prior claim. Years we could have been together, bringing up our children...'

'Oh.' She was silent for a moment. 'Simon, about Jay-Jay...'

'What about him?'

'You know, don't you?'

'Yes.'

'How did you find out? When?'

'You remember that picture you gave Penny, the one of the children on the beach?'

'How could I forget?' That night was a memory she treasured. It had seen her through the dark days when love and affection, even respect, eluded her; it had always been there, though somehow, in the unhappiness of her

411

marriage and the trauma of George's death, it had got lost, swirled about, became indistinguishable from her need to be loved and cherished. By someone. Anyone. Even George, when he decided to turn over a new leaf. But he hadn't, had he?

'I saw the likeness then. It was there in his expression, the colour of his hair and his eyes. It was as if you wanted me to know, that you were telling me...'

'Perhaps I was. I don't know. I was very mixed up. I still am. Jay-Jay loved George. He mourned him and he trusts me, I couldn't destroy all that.'

'He's our son, Barbara. I would never do anything to hurt him. Or you. It isn't an issue. We'll do whatever you decide. But marry me, make me the happiest man in the world, let me take care of you. Please.'

'Simon, I just don't know.'

'But I don't need to stay away anymore, do I?'

'No.'

'Then I'll wear you down.' He grinned and kissed her again. 'Can I come and watch you paint? I'll be good, I promise.'

She gave a light laugh which lifted his spirits to soaring point. 'Not too good, I hope. I didn't say I wanted to be celibate.'

He picked her up and swung her round and round, before setting her down and kissing her cheeks, her lips, her throat. Then he held her away from him and looked into her eyes, smiling in a way which reminded her of Jay-Jay at his most mischievous. 'I love you, Barbara. Love you. And that means I'll do anything you want. Do you understand?'

'Yes. I love you too, I think I always have.' She laughed suddenly. 'And you're right, we've wasted too much time.' She took his hand and drew him towards the stairs.

It was stupendous, glorious. He was careful, tender, funny and loving, moving slowly, watching her, feasting his eyes on her body, waiting for her. She soared with ecstatic delight, was lifted to heights she never dreamt of, and afterwards, she lay in his arms, glowing and exhausted and profoundly moved.

'Darling, you're crying,' he said.

'I'm happy, that's why.'

'Good. We'll do it again. Often.' He sat up and reached for his clothes. 'Come on, it's a lovely day. Where are your easel and paints?'

'Already in the car.'

'Then let's go.'

He was smiling as he followed her out to the car. He'd do it her way because he loved her and she deserved his patience and respect, and if all he got to be was a lover, that was OK too, so long as she didn't send him away again. It was better than not having her at all. One day, he didn't know how far into the future it might be, she would marry him. He had waited seventeen years, he could wait a little longer.

It was Jay-Jay who made her mind up for her. Simon had been down to spend Sunday with them all and they had had a lovely time, going to Wells and taking a rowing boat out to the sands to gather cockles, and coming home to boil them up and shell them, eating them in vinegar with brown bread and butter. He had been coming down

413

most weekends to take them out somewhere, always including the children in his plans, talking to them, telling them jokes, playing games with them, until they accepted him. Even Alison had warmed towards him and the boys idolised him.

'Mum,' Jay-Jay asked, when she was tucking him into bed. The other two had gone to their room to finish their homework, always left until the last minute, especially when there were more exciting things to do. 'Are you happy now?'

'Yes, dear, very happy. We've had a lovely day, haven't we?'

'Yes, but I meant are you happy every day?'

'Yes, of course. I have you and Alison and Nick and good friends, what more can I want?'

'Will you marry again?'

'I'm happy as I am.'

'I just wanted you to know that if you did want to, I wouldn't mind.' He was embarrassed but he'd made up his mind to say something and ploughed on. 'If it made you happy, I mean.'

She hugged him. 'Oh, Jay-Jay, you know exactly the right thing to say, don't you?' Just like his father. Just like Simon.

'It isn't only me. Alison and Nick say so too. I asked them.' He snuggled down in bed, his eyes flickering with tiredness. 'I like Uncle Simon, you know.'

'So do I, darling, so do I.'

She kissed him goodnight and went down to the sitting room and told Simon what he'd said.

He got up from the settee where he had been reading

a magazine and took her in his arms. 'Then that's settled it. You'll marry me now, won't you, seeing our son approves?'

'Yes.'

He was grinning from ear to ear, as he whirled her round. 'At last! At last.'